The Alex Craft Novels

Grave Witch
Grave Dance

Grave Memory

AN ALEX CRAFT NOVEL

KALAYNA PRICE

A ROC BOOK

ROC
Published by New American Library, a division of
Penguin Group (USA) Inc., 375 Hudson Street,
New York, New York 10014, USA
Penguin Group (Canada), 90 Eglinton Avenue East, Suite 700, Toronto,
Ontario M4P 2Y3, Canada (a division of Pearson Penguin Canada Inc.)
Penguin Books Ltd., 80 Strand, London WC2R 0RL, England
Penguin Ireland, 25 St. Stephen's Green, Dublin 2,
Ireland (a division of Penguin Books Ltd.)
Penguin Group (Australia), 250 Camberwell Road, Camberwell, Victoria 3124,
Australia (a division of Pearson Australia Group Pty. Ltd.)
Penguin Books India Pvt. Ltd., 11 Community Centre, Panchsheel Park,
New Delhi - 110 017, India
Penguin Group (NZ), 67 Apollo Drive, Rosedale, Auckland 0632,
New Zealand (a division of Pearson New Zealand Ltd.)
Penguin Books (South Africa) (Pty.) Ltd., 24 Sturdee Avenue,
Rosebank, Johannesburg 2196, South Africa

Penguin Books Ltd., Registered Offices:
80 Strand, London WC2R 0RL, England

First published by Roc, an imprint of New American Library,
a division of Penguin Group (USA) Inc.

First Printing, July 2012
10 9 8 7 6 5 4 3 2 1

ALWAYS LEARNING   PEARSON

To the Modern Myth Makers:
Ladies, I wouldn't be where I am without you.

ACKNOWLEDGMENTS

Special thanks to Jessica for your endless patience. Also for encouraging me out of my comfort zone—the resulting changes took this book to the next level.

To Lucienne, for more than I can possibly list here, but especially for your guidance.

To my friends and family, for your support, your encouragement, and for dragging me out once in a while.

To my very awesome "minions," who have helped me get the word out about the Alex Craft novels.

And, of course, to you, the person reading this book. Thank you for returning for another adventure with Alex!

Chapter 1

"What do you think?" I asked, as I fumbled for the light switch. An incandescent bulb flickered on, and then continued flickering. I frowned at it, but the late-afternoon sunlight streaming through the grimy picture window prevented the gloom from devouring the room.

Rianna peered through the open doorway but made no effort to enter. Her hand fell to idly scratch behind the ear of the barghest who acted as her ever-present shadow. "What am I supposed to be looking at?"

"The official office for Tongues for the Dead," I said, waving a hand as if presenting the room.

Rianna had first suggested we open a PI firm that solved cases by questioning the dead when we were still in academy, but by the time I'd finished college, she'd vanished. Three months ago I'd found and liberated her from a power-hungry fae who'd made her a captive changeling of Faerie, and in the wake of recent chaos, we were both healing, adapting, and rebuilding. Which, in my opinion, made now the perfect time to give the dreams of two idealistic schoolgirls a second chance.

Rianna obviously didn't agree.

"Alex, I think you might need to give your eyes a little more time to recover."

"This place isn't *that* bad," I said, glancing around the room I envisioned would be a reception lobby—you know, if the firm ever became profitable enough to hire a receptionist. My gaze skidded over walls covered in graffitied runes and minor, mostly dispersed, spells before moving on to take in the balding carpet and the piles of beer cans and cigarettes tossed haphazardly around the otherwise empty room. "It just needs a little TLC."

Rianna cocked an eyebrow, and the barghest, Desmond, who was in his customary shape of an oversized black dog with red-ringed pupils, huffed, making his jowls billow.

"Okay, so it needs *a lot* of work, but the rent is affordable"—barely, and only because my landlord waived the rent on my loft as payment for the last big case I'd worked—"and it's in the Magic Quarter. A definite perk as we offer magical solutions in our investigations."

"Alex, this is a seedy back alley on the very edge of the Magic Quarter. We're about as far as we can be from the heart of the Quarter. No upscale restaurants. No spell boutiques. Not even the kitschy stores hawking overpriced, underpowered charms to norms are out this far." She glanced over her shoulder at the only other door in the admittedly less than ideal alley and lowered her voice. "And I'm pretty sure that unmarked shop is dealing black magic."

"Gray actually," I said and her eyes widened. "Hey, it's not like I went shopping. I just sensed a couple of mild compulsion spells and a lot of weak love charms when I passed by the shop. I think it's run by a matchmaker."

"And you were planning to call the OMIH when, exactly?"

The Organization for Magically Inclined Humans was originally formed as an advocate group for witches during the turmoil following the Magical Awakening. A good seventy years later they were still considered the public face of the witch population, but now their mission statement focused on education and promoting the safe and ethical use of magic. That, of course, meant they policed their own.

"Keep your voice down," I hissed. I had no desire to irritate a neighbor willing to spin gray spells—which were a short step from the really dark, soul damaging stuff. "I contacted the OMIH already. They're supposed to send an inspector out this week, and once they confirm my report, they'll alert the Magical Crimes Investigation Bureau." Which sounded like a lot of tedious bureaucratic red tape. But despite the fact I was an OMIH certified sensitive, citizens couldn't contact the MCIB directly, so we'd have to wait. The unmarked door on the other side of the alley opened, and I ducked back into the office we were actually supposed to be discussing. "Once we fix this place up, it could be nice. It has the lobby area, a bathroom, and two offices. Exactly what we need," I said, as if we'd never veered off the subject.

Rianna frowned and curled her fingers in Desmond's fur. "You can see again, so you don't need me to substitute anymore, and we both know there isn't enough business to justify the overhead of an office. Especially when you were doing fine running things through phone and e-mail."

Well, not always fine. At times I'd barely scraped by, which only highlighted her point. But I had other reasons I wanted to open an office.

When I first emancipated Rianna, she'd been reluctant to spend time in the mortal realm. But when I'd lost my sight several weeks ago after a showdown with a witch who thought the world would be better if all the planes of existence touched—yeah, no, bad idea—Rianna had stepped up and covered my cases. At first she'd left Faerie for only a couple of hours on the days rituals were scheduled. But recently she'd been spending almost all day, every day in Nekros, and while her visits hadn't completely erased the wraithlike appearance she'd had as Coleman's soul-chained captive, she now had color in her cheeks and the bruiselike circles no longer ringed her eyes. The mortal realm agreed with her. I didn't want her to disappear into Faerie again.

Besides, my ability to raise the dead was wyrd magic, and if I didn't use it, it used me. Over the last few weeks I'd had to perform a couple of off-the-books rituals, holding the shades just long enough to relieve the magical pressure on my shields. But even those limited rituals had come at a higher cost than before. If I returned to raising shades several times a week I'd be permanently blind before I hit thirty. Tongues for the Dead needed a new business model.

"I was actually thinking about expanding the firm's services. Take on some cases with billable hours not restricted to rituals and talking to shades. Cases that utilize more . . . traditional forms of investigation."

"Traditional investigation?" She cocked her head to the side. "Like what? Surveillance? Tailing spouses suspected of cheating? Maybe a stakeout?" I didn't miss the sarcasm in her tone. Rianna and I were all but night blind, to say nothing of my degrading vision. Then there was the fact that as a changeling, Rianna couldn't be in the mortal realm during sunset or sunrise without deadly consequences.

"More like locating missing persons or artifacts, tracing the origins of spells or charms. Hell, we could even do background checks if someone would pay us. Between you graduating at the top of your class in spellcasting and me being one of the top five sensitives in the city, we have skills to offer besides grave magic." I didn't mention that she'd had a couple hundred extra years' practice while in Faerie or that I had the whole planeweaving thing going on. Neither facts were something either of us wanted on a résumé. I turned back to the room, which she still hadn't entered, and waved a hand to encompass the space. "Ignore the mess and imagine what this place could look like. For instance, take that picture window. Once it's cleaned up, we can have 'Alex Craft and Rianna McBride: Tongues for the Dead Investigations' stenciled on it."

Rianna glanced at the window, which was coated in a decade's worth of dust, but the faintest hint of a smile appeared at the edge of her mouth. "You'd put my name on it too?"

"How could I not? You were the one who looked up from a mystery novel during your final year at academy and suggested the name."

The smile grew a little brighter. "I'd forgotten about that. It was so long ago." She finally stepped inside, Desmond at her heels. "Show me around?"

That task didn't take long. The doors to the two offices were on opposite sides of the room, and neither office was large—or in better shape than the front room—but each had enough space for a desk, some filing cabinets, and a couple of chairs, which would be enough for meeting with clients. There was also a small closet and a bathroom against the very far wall, but neither of us was brave enough to see what condition it might be in, at least, not yet.

"It's going to take a lot of work," she said as she surveyed the lobby.

"Then you're in?"

"Of course I am." The words were flat, void of any excitement.

I turned and studied her face. It was blank, unexpressive, and totally not the response I anticipated. "This isn't that faerie master crap again, is it?"

Sadly, it was a legitimate question. When I'd destroyed her former master, Faerie had passed all of his holdings on to me. That included an enormous castle straight out of a fairy tale and his prize changeling, Rianna. I had no interest in owning my childhood friend, but she was a changeling, bound to Faerie and its magic. If I renounced her, some other fae could take her. So I accepted the claim, and as far as Faerie was concerned, she was my property, obliged to my will.

But I considered it political bullshit, and she knew it.

"Rianna, you're free to do whatever you want, including telling me you've outgrown your interest in being a private investigator."

"Al, don't think that. It's nothing like that." She wove her fingers into Desmond's fur again, and he leaned against her leg, offering his support. "It's . . . I . . ." She shook her head. "Sometimes I forget that only a few years passed for you while I spent hundreds under Coleman's control. The freedom to want things for myself, to reach for my own dreams—

it's something I nearly forgot. Having options is a little overwhelming." She looked around the room, her gaze slow and assessing. A smile crept across her face as she peeked into one of the offices again. Then she turned toward me. "Yes, I want this. I want to be Rianna McBride, PI for Tongues for the Dead. Let's do it, boss."

"Partner," I corrected.

"Partner." The word was a whisper, but her smile spread, making her green eyes sparkle.

"It's official, then." I glanced around the room, imagining what it could be. It was going to take a lot of work.

"I guess we should start with paint," Rianna said, following my gaze. "And something for the carpet?"

"Some essential furniture too," I said, digging through my purse. "But first . . ." I pulled out a thin rectangular box. I'd wrapped it in newspaper—wrapping paper was expensive and this counted as recycling, right? Rianna gave me a quizzical look as I handed it to her.

"I didn't get you anything," she said, staring at the box in its makeshift wrapping.

"Don't be silly, just open it."

She bit her lip, as if unsure. Then a grin cut across her face and she lifted the box to her ear and gave it a good shake.

"Hey, it could be breakable," I said, and her grin grew.

"Nah, you'd have stopped me earlier." She tore into the packaging. Her perplexed look didn't change when she pulled out a small metal container engraved with her initials, but when she flipped it open, she gave out a squeal of a laugh. "Business cards," she said, pulling out the thin stack of cards. "And that's the logo I tried—and failed—to draw. You nailed it. When did you have this done?"

I shrugged, but I was grinning too. "I created the template years ago. But after you disappeared I didn't feel right using it. These I had printed yesterday. I'm just glad you said yes."

She closed the lid and clutched the gift as if it were much more valuable than a cheap case and a handful of business cards. Then she bounced on the balls of her feet before scampering over to hug me. But she didn't thank me. I don't know if that was for my sake, as I hated feeling the imbalance of debt, or simply because she'd lived among the fae so long. Either way, the hug expressed her gratitude more than sufficiently.

"So, furniture," I said as we headed back outside into the bright afternoon sun. "Unfortunately our budget is thrift, but maybe we'll luck out."

I locked our new office and we headed up the alley with Desmond following in our wake, or maybe he was taking rear guard—it was always hard to tell what the barghest was thinking. Rianna had parked my car around the corner since, legally, I couldn't drive. It was well documented that grave magic damaged the witch's eyesight, so we were required to take a vision test once a year.

Yeah, guess when mine had come due? My—suspended—driver's license currently listed me as blind. If I could avoid any serious damage to my eyes, I hoped I could retake the test and pass next week.

We were just passing the matchmaker's door, the gray magic inside pricking at my senses, when Annabella Lwin began singing the chorus of "I Want Candy" in my purse. My phone. I dug it out but didn't bother glancing at the display. When I'd replaced my phone yet again—the latest cellular casualty had been lost in Faerie—Holly, my housemate and good friend, had set her own ring tone.

"Hey, Hol."

She didn't bother with a greeting. "I want chocolate so bad, I may kill the next person I see with a Snickers bar."

"I sure hope you didn't just say that in the middle of the courthouse." After all, Holly was an assistant district attorney, and I was guessing that threatening to kill people over vending machine fare wouldn't go over well.

"I just left," she said, and a car horn blared through the phone.

"So is this where I'm supposed to be the sympathetic friend to your chocolate plight or where I offer to meet you for lunch?"

"Both? My last case for the day is over, so aside from a mountain of research, I'm free for the afternoon," she said, and her horn sounded again. "God, what I wouldn't do for just one piece of rich, dark chocolate."

I winced on behalf of the cars around her. I doubted they were driving any worse than most Nekros citizens or deserved the long blasts of her horn. Tilting the phone away from my mouth, I glanced at Rianna.

"You up for a change of plans? We'll furniture shop later. Let's go celebrate the new business over lunch and drinks."

Rianna stopped, forcing me to turn on my heels and double back. "Where were you thinking?" she asked.

"The Eternal Bloom—before Holly commits vehicular homicide."

"I heard that," Holly's voice snapped in my ear.

Rianna frowned. "Doesn't sound like much of a celebration if you can't drink."

It was true, but there wasn't anywhere we could go that all of us could lift a glass together. As a changeling, Rianna was addicted to faerie food; anything else she tried to eat turned to ash on her tongue. Holly wasn't a changeling, not currently at least, but a month ago she'd been exposed to faerie food, and one bite was enough to addict a mortal. Not that she didn't miss mortal food—hence her chocolate-withdrawal inspired rage. I sympathized. Which was why, despite the fact I'd recently learned I had more fae blood than not and was apparently going through some sort of fae-mien metamorphosis, I was avoiding faerie food. If I turned out to be too mortal to resist it, I was sure I couldn't live without coffee and Faerie didn't serve it. My abstention meant that going to Nekros's local fae bar, the Eternal Bloom, excluded me from the meal. Unfortunately, since Holly was neither fae nor changeling, she couldn't get into the VIP area, so she needed an escort and today was my day.

"We're not far from the Bloom," I said, swiveling the phone back in front of my mouth. "You want to meet in about twenty—"

A booming crash and the sound of shattering glass exploded from somewhere around the corner. The blare of first one and then the honks of several car alarms sounded.

"Shit!"

"What the hell was that?" Holly asked, her voice pitched high. "Alex, is everyone okay?"

"I don't know. It sounded like a car crash." I broke into a run, Rianna at my side. Desmond raced ahead of us, a black blur as he bounded around the corner and out of the alley.

"Are you okay? Anyone hurt?" Holly asked again.

"We're fine. Hang on a second," I said, and then under my breath muttered, "That better not have been someone hitting my car." It was new, and from the sound of the impact, something had taken major damage.

As it turned out, *major damage* was an understatement. I breached the mouth of the alley and ground to a halt, my mouth falling slack at the scene in front of me.

"Holly, I think we're going to be late," I said into the phone, but if she replied before I ended the call, I didn't hear.

A crowd was gathering in the street, people pouring out of shops and cars screeching to a halt as the drivers stared with pale, shocked faces. The impact we'd heard had been a car—not mine—a little red sedan parallel parked a few spaces behind mine. Glass littered the street and sidewalk around it from where it had exploded as the roof caved. But it wasn't another vehicle that had hit the car.

It was a body.

Chapter 2

⊷═══ ◉═══⊶

I worked around the dead on a regular basis. It was one of those unavoidable consequences of being a grave witch. But I usually entered the picture after the deceased had been dead for a while—preferably after they'd been buried. I was squeamish around blood, and there was a lot of it leaking from the mangled form that had smashed into the car's ruined roof.

"Should we call the police?" Rianna asked, moving so close her shoulders brushed mine.

I glanced at the phone in my hand. I'd forgotten I was holding it. Then I shook my head. There had to be a half dozen people already on the phone. The cops didn't need yet another nine-one-one call clogging their switchboard.

"Is anyone a doctor or a healer?" one of the bystanders yelled, running toward the body.

"I'm a nurse," a man said, separating himself from the crowd, just as a woman stepped forward with "I know a little healing magic."

I shook my head. "It's too late."

I didn't think I'd said it aloud, but several gawkers turned to glare at me, and an elderly woman who vibrated with the spells she carried sniffed and said, "Well, we have to try. That building's only five stories. He might still be alive."

Rianna and I exchanged a glance, but neither of us bothered to explain that we knew, definitively, that the man was dead. As grave witches we had an affinity for the dead. I could feel the grave essence lifting from the body, its chilling touch brushing my shields.

Besides, the man's ghost was standing beside the car, staring at the broken shell he'd once inhabited. From the confused look on his face, he hadn't grasped the situation yet. Which wasn't that surprising, dying had to take a major adjustment. Of course, this guy looked like a jumper, so he shouldn't have been *that* shocked.

What was more surprising, at least to me, was that a jumper would fight hard enough against moving on to become a ghost. Souls didn't just pop out of bodies—a collector had to pull them free. The average mortal couldn't bargain for his life, but if souls struggled enough, sometimes soul collectors released them, and they became ghosts. *But why would someone so desperate to die fight the collector?*

Not that this was the first ghost of a suicide I'd seen. I wasn't sure why the collectors allowed some stubborn souls to stay and continue as ghosts in the purgatory of the land of the dead, but while ghosts were anomalies, there were enough that I doubted it was an accident they were left behind. I was familiar with the devastated landscape of the land of the dead, and I didn't think such an existence was much of a win—neither did most of the ghosts.

But speaking of collectors . . . We'd heard the impact so I must have just missed seeing the collector and soul struggle. It was possible the collector was still here. I crossed my fingers as I scanned the gathering crowd, hoping to spot a familiar face.

I wasn't disappointed.

Death, my oldest and closest friend, my confidant, and a man who, at one point, had said he loved me, stood on the far side of the street. While the people around him were a blur in my bad eyesight, it was my psyche that let me perceive him, and I had no trouble seeing that those hooded, hazel eyes were fixed on me, his dark hair hanging forward toward his chin. The sight of him drew a smile from me that spread across my face despite the terrible scene behind me. It had been nearly a month since I'd seen him, and I missed his company so much it hurt.

Then I noticed he wasn't alone. My smile faltered. Another collector, whom I'd dubbed the gray man due to his predilection for gray clothing, right down to a dried gray rose on his lapel, stood at Death's side.

Damn. If the gray man spotted me, I'd have no chance to speak to Death. It wasn't that the gray man disliked me in particular. He simply didn't approve of mortals consorting with soul collectors.

I wove my way through the crowd of people as they pushed forward to gain a closer look at the grisly disaster. I sidestepped and dodged, all the time letting my eyes drink in Death's familiar features, the way his black T-shirt showed off the contour of a muscular chest, the faded jeans he wore. He was certainly no skeleton with dark robes and a scythe as popular media still, even seventy years after the Magical Awakening, liked to portray soul collectors. Of course, there weren't that many of us who could see collectors, and to my knowledge, I was the only living person—outside of Faerie at least—who could touch them.

Not that I'd get that chance today. The gray man spotted me as I strained against the flow of the crowd. He tapped Death's arm with the silver skull atop his cane.

While my magic let me look across planes of existence and see the collectors, it didn't give me super hearing. But I recognized a heated exchange when I saw one. The gray man jabbed his cane in my direction. *Crap.*

I gave up on being polite and pushed my way through the crowd. I'm five ten barefoot, and with my boots I easily hit six feet. But while my height let me see over peoples' heads, it wasn't like I had much bulk to put behind it. As I'd recently learned, I was built like my Sleagh Maith relations—tall but skinny. Some called it lithe. I called it curveless. Either way, it certainly wasn't helping me clear a path.

I'd made it halfway across the street and nearly out of

the crowd when Death looked at me again. He pressed two fingers to his lips, his gaze burning into me, making my skin flush as I recalled the press of those lips on mine. Then both collectors vanished.

Son of a— I stopped the thought before I finished it. A month ago, a changeling grave witch and a rogue soul collector created a massacre in an attempt to be together. So many lives were lost, all in a twisted vision of love. In the aftermath, the gray man had warned me that the relationship blooming between Death and me could never happen. Since then, I'd had no direct contact with Death.

None. Zip. Zilch.

Occasionally, I'd catch sight of him from a distance. Once or twice he'd even waved. But he always vanished before I reached him.

I was sick of it.

The worst part of the whole mess? I'd lost my closest friend. Death had been my one constant since I was five years old. At times, my only friend. But now he wouldn't—or couldn't—speak to me.

It sucked. Majorly.

Of course, that pretty much summed up the state of what passed as my love life. Falin Andrews, the other man, or really, fae, I was occasionally involved with also wasn't speaking to me. Not because he didn't want to, but because he couldn't disobey the compulsion of his queen's command.

The really sad part? Even with neither man speaking to me, either one could be considered the closest I'd come to a relationship in my adult life. I'd always preferred no strings—and certainly no emotions—attached partners. Someone to warm my bed when the grave chilled me to the bone, but nothing more. This whole relationship thing? Yeah, I wished I could get over it already.

A masculine scream pierced the air behind me, dragging me out of my one person pity party—and making me realize I was still standing in the center of the street. Good thing the cars were all stopped, the drivers, at least those who were even still in their cars, were too busy trying to figure out what had drawn a crowd to do anything sensible like drive.

Another scream rang out, half panic, half ... rage? I turned and wove toward where Rianna and Desmond stood among the wary onlookers surrounding the car. Moving closer to the scene was even harder than trying to get out of the crowd had been. More than once I squeezed between people and the heat of the press of bodies sizzled against my skin. I'd never had trouble with crowds before, but my breath was suddenly coming too fast, my heart racing. I *had* to get out of the center of this crowd. I used my arms to part people, trying to make a clear path. People jerked back at my icy touch, which gave me a little more room, but it was still slow going. And the whole time, somewhere up ahead, the man yelled, calling for someone to help, for an ambulance, for someone to do something, *anything*.

I guess the ghost finally realized he's dead. No one reacted to his cries. It had taken him long enough to get with the program, but he definitely wasn't taking the situation well.

I caught snippets of conversations as I struggled through the crowd. Most were making guesses on what happened. Had he jumped? Was he pushed? Maybe he'd been leaning against the railing and fallen. I squeezed around two gentlemen, just as one asked the other who he thought would have to pay for the damage to the car. They were debating if it would be the owner's insurance or the deceased's estate as I moved too far to hear more.

Sirens sounded in the distance by the time I made it back to Rianna and Desmond. If the ghost noticed the approaching officials, he gave no indication. He'd stopped yelling, but he kept trying to grab people in the crowd, his face a mask of dismay and terror as his hands slipped through arms and shoulders.

"We should go," I whispered as the first responders arrived. Not that they could get close to the car and the broken body on top of it—there were just too many gawkers. Us included.

The crowd thinned as people retreated to move their

cars, or perhaps they'd simply seen enough and were ready to move on and go about their days. Which was what I planned to do as well, right up until Rianna pointed out that the spot she'd parallel parked my car was blocked, at least until some of the other cars moved.

Great.

As the crowd thinned, the ghost made his way toward where we stood. He grabbed for people as they passed, his hands passing unnoticed through them. "Please," he said, his voice broken. "Please, I have a wife. She's pregnant. She needs me."

I took a step back as he neared. If he tried to touch me, his hands wouldn't just pass through me.

Rianna gave me a quizzical look. "Al?"

I mouthed the word "ghost" because I didn't want him to know I could see or hear him.

Rianna's lips formed an "O." Then her green eyes blazed like candles had been lit behind her irises as she opened her shields and tapped into her grave magic.

"Hey, remember that you're our driver," I whispered when the glow of her eyes brightened, her psyche further straddling the chasm between the living and the dead so she could hear the ghost.

"It will be fine." But she shivered. At least she wasn't far enough across that the never-ending wind in the land of the dead whirled around her.

The police arrived at the same time as an ambulance — which wouldn't be necessary. And still the ghost tried to get someone, anyone's attention. My personal policy was not to get involved with ghosts. After all, most souls stubborn or desperate enough to fight off a collector either had unfinished business they wanted to drag me into, or they were so nasty in life, they feared what might happen to them in the afterlife. I was leaning toward the former for this guy as most of his pleading had to do with the fact his wife was expecting, soon, and he needed to be there.

"Crap," I muttered, and Rianna turned her glowing gaze at me. I gave her a weak smile. "I still haven't gotten rid of the last ghost I helped." But I felt for this guy. If nothing else, I could try to calm him down and explain to him he was dead, right?

I didn't get a chance. One of the officers—who looked familiar, but I worked for the police often enough that most of the local cops looked familiar—walked over carrying a small notepad.

"Did anyone see what happened?" he asked, glancing around the small cluster of people who remained.

The woman who'd sniped at me earlier was the first to speak. "He jumped. Right off the top of the roof."

The ghost whirled around. "What? I would never—"

But the man beside the woman nodded vigorously. "I saw him too. I was right over there, coming out of Brew and Brews." He pointed at a sketchy-looking bar specializing in magically laced beer. "Looked up, and there he was." The man finished the last with a hiccup.

Oh yeah, now that's a credible witness.

The ghost's hands clenched. "You drunken liar." He took a swing at the man, which, if the ghost had been corporeal, probably would have knocked the drunk on his ass. As it was, his fist passed harmlessly through the man's jaw.

"And did either of you see anyone else on the roof with the man?" the officer asked.

The woman shook her head, but the drunk apparently enjoyed the sound of his own voice because he said, "Oh no. That guy, he climbed up on the ledge, took a look around, and then took a perfect swan dive into that there car."

"I can't listen to this," the ghost said, and for a moment I thought he might try to slug the drunk again. He didn't. Instead he walked up to the officer and said, "I would never, ever, kill myself. I'm about to have a son. A son! Why would I do this, huh? Why?"

By the last "why" he was yelling into the officer's face, who never looked up from jotting notes in his notepad. With an exasperated growl, the ghost turned away. Then his gaze landed on two men bagging his body and he forgot about the drunk and the cop as he ran down the sidewalk yelling.

"Did anyone else see anything?" The officer asked. There weren't many people left on the sidewalk now, just a cluster of maybe twelve, but they all shook their heads. The officer looked at me.

I hadn't seen what happened but . . . "I don't think he jumped."

"Alex Craft," he said. He smiled. At a murder scene. "I didn't expect to see you here."

How was I supposed to respond to that? Thankfully, before I had to come up with something to say, he continued.

"Okay, Ms. Craft, did you see what happened?"

"Not exactly."

The officer's lips twitched. "That was a yes or no question."

"I was around the corner, so I only heard the impact," I said and the officer, who had been poised to write down my statement, lowered his pen. I hurried on. "But he wouldn't have killed himself. His wife is pregnant. With a son. He was very excited about it."

"You knew the jumper?"

Jumper? Oh, didn't that sound like he'd already made up his mind. Of course, I was one to talk. I'd come to the same conclusion before hearing the ghost's diatribe.

"Ms. Craft, I asked if you knew the man."

I winced. "Uh, not exactly."

His smile faded. "Either you knew the man or you didn't because if you'd raised a shade and questioned him, I'm pretty sure someone here would have mentioned that fact."

Crap. I glanced at Rianna. Her eyes no longer glowed, and I had no idea how much of the ghost's one-sided altercation with the eyewitnesses she'd seen. She tilted her head to the side and shrugged, which didn't tell me anything.

I took a deep breath and let it out again before saying, "His soul didn't transition properly. So—"

"Our dead guy left a ghost," the officer finished for me. "And the ghost swears he didn't jump."

Okay, I was impressed. Despite the OMIH's attempts to educate the public on different kinds of magic, grave magic was too rare for most people to bother learning the details. Academy trained wyrd witches knew the difference between shades and ghosts, but your average witchy witch didn't—even those trained at prestigious spellcasting schools. I gave him an appraising look. He was thirty tops and, judging by the fact he wore several charms and at least two rings holding raw Aetheric energy, was a witch. If he was wyrd, I couldn't spot any of the telltale signs of an ability burning out one of his senses.

"I'm impressed." Credit where credit's due, and all that. Him knowing the difference also saved me a lot of time trying to explain the difference.

The smile was back and he gave me a careless one shoulder shrug. "I try."

Right.

Someone in the crowd cleared his throat, and the officer snapped to attention, his gaze locking on his pad and the last note he'd taken.

"So you talked to his ghost. Did he tell you his name?"

And back to the case. *Thank goodness.* Except as I thought about it, I realized out of all the pleading and ranting the ghost did, he never once mentioned his or his widow's name.

"I can ask," I said, turning toward where I'd last seen the ghost. He wasn't there. "Uh, I think he followed his body."

The officer closed his notepad. "Well, then, guess we'll have to solve this one with good old-fashioned police work." He winked. "We should go out for a drink sometime."

"Take him up on the offer," Rianna whispered, nudging me. "He's a cute one."

Was he? I would have called him average, but then, both Death and Falin set the bar pretty high when it came to looks. Unfortunately, I had a bit of a reputation among the boys in blue—I'd taken more than a few home with me after working a case. But I wasn't interested in Officer . . . I glanced at his nameplate . . . Larid.

"I have to pass," I told him and he had the gall to look

shocked. *Geez, is my rep that bad?* I hadn't slept with *that* many of the cops. Hell, I hadn't slept with anyone in over two months.

When he turned on his regulation polished heels and walked away, Rianna turned to me. "I closed my shields as soon as the cops arrived. Did the ghost really deny jumping?"

"Vehemently." I recounted the ghost's reactions to the witness statements.

"Huh," she said, a slow smile spreading across her face. "I have an idea."

She jogged after the officer. I caught a flash of light reflecting off something she pulled out of her purse, but didn't realize it was the business cardholder I'd just given her until she passed one of the cards to him. They spoke for a moment or two more before she headed back to where I stood, gaping at her.

"Did you just ask him out?" *At a crime scene?*

"Don't be silly," she said, snapping closed the clasp on her purse. "I simply asked him to pass our card on to the widow and let her know that we know her husband's death wasn't suicide, and that Tongues for the Dead is willing to prove it."

I blinked at her. "You didn't." But I had no doubt that was exactly what she'd done.

Rianna smiled a smile so mischievous, it looked exactly like the ones she used to flash me back in academy. Those typically came right before she suggested we test out a school-banned spell, like turning soda into whisky. Without her smile slipping an inch she said, "Hey, we've expanded the business. We need to get the word out, right?"

"Right?" I said, but even I heard the uncertainty in the word. Handing out business cards at crime scenes reeked of sleazy, like a talking dead version of ambulance chasing lawyers. But she did have a point about needing the business. That didn't mean I had to agree. At least, not until I saw if it worked. "Let's get out of here. If we don't make it to the Bloom soon, Holly will probably eat the doorman."

                          *   *   *

"Caleb's going to kill me," I said as Holly pulled her car to
a stop in front of the house we shared.

Since Rianna had parked my car in an overnight garage
near the Eternal Bloom, there should have been more than
enough room for Holly to pull into the driveway, but tonight the drive was full. Three sleek black vehicles surrounded the car that belonged to Caleb, our third housemate
and landlord.

I'd seen those cars before. They belonged to the Fae Investigation Bureau. Which meant the house was being
raided.

Again.

"We could keep driving," Holly suggested, letting the car
idle instead of putting it in park.

A tempting idea. Except if Caleb found out he'd be livid.
Actually make that more livid than he likely already was.
Besides, if the FIB were here . . . *Falin probably is too*.

I shook my head and pushed open my door before Holly
had time to cut the ignition. Climbing out of the car was a
relief, the balmy September air soothing my exposed skin,
which tingled from the amount of metal in the vehicle. It
wasn't a fae friendly car.

I started toward the side of the house, where a staircase
led to a private entrance to my one room loft above the garage. I'd made it only halfway across the lawn when the front
door opened.

"Alex," Caleb yelled, his voice echoing off the houses on
the quiet suburban street.

I cringed but turned dutifully toward my friend and
landlord. "Another raid?"

He marched down the front steps, thrusting a tri-folded
bundle of pages at me. His normally tanned-looking skin
had a slightly green tinge to it, his glamour slipping under
his anger. "They're looking for the Sword of Frozen Silence
this time. That artifact has been missing for half a millen-
nia." He took a deep breath. "This is harassment."

I plucked the search warrant from his fist and passed it to Holly—she was the lawyer after all. She studied it, scanning the small printed text. All I needed to see was the signet stamp. It had been endorsed by the Winter Queen herself. Even if the warrant wasn't legit, there wasn't a higher authority in Nekros's fae population. And the fae policed themselves.

"Is she trying to irritate us into submission?"

"Not us. You." Caleb's eyes bled to black as he glanced over his shoulder at his defiled sanctuary of a house. "What did you turn down this time?"

"A feast held in my honor." I studied the scuff on the toe of my boot. "It would have been tonight. Caleb, I'm—"

His head snapped around, his sharp look stopping me from apologizing—we both knew better. That didn't make me feel any less guilty.

"You need to pick a court or declare yourself independent, or this is never going to stop," he said, and I looked away. "There is a revelry on the equinox. Go to it. See Faerie at the height of its magic. Choose and make this stop."

It wasn't that easy and we both knew it. If I picked any court other than Winter, I'd have to leave Nekros as this was currently the Winter Queen's territory. If I declared myself independent, there was nothing to prevent her from continuing to harass me. Still, he was right about one thing, I couldn't put off choosing forever.

I was saved from the overworn argument by the front door of the house opening and a man stepping into the doorway. The near dusk hid his features from my bad eyes, but the light from the house poured out from behind him, outlining a very familiar sleek but muscular body that his tailored suit accented perfectly and making his loose blond hair glimmer. My heart stalled, my breath catching.

Falin.

As if trying to make up for that lost beat, my pulse sped up, my heart fluttering in an attempt to escape my chest. I took a step forward, toward the house, before catching myself—and Caleb's dark glare.

"I can't stay here and watch them tear apart my house, again." Caleb's teeth were green now too, his fae-mien almost completely revealed. He glanced at his car. His blocked car.

"I'll give you a ride," Holly said, holding up her keys.

Caleb had as much trouble with Holly's car as I did, more if he couldn't get his glamour back up to protect him from the iron and steel, so it said a lot when he nodded and marched toward her vehicle.

"You coming?" Holly asked.

I glanced from Caleb to the figure in the doorway. "I, uh . . . I should probably walk PC."

"Yeah, you're thinking about your dog right now," Holly said, shaking her head. "I don't know if this is tragically romantic or just pathetic, but it's your heartbreak."

She was right. I knew she was, but I couldn't help walking toward that open doorway. I'm not sure my legs would have listened had I tried to stop them from climbing the steps.

Falin didn't move, not even a muscle twitch, as I approached. I wanted to see him smile. Hell, after the kiss he'd said good-bye with a month ago, a kiss so full of promise, of need, I wanted those lips to do a lot more than just smile. Not like that could happen. His face was hard, impassive. But his eyes betrayed him. Ice blue, but oh so warm as they swept over me.

"Hi." My voice was breathless and not from the three squat steps I'd climbed to reach the door.

"Ms. Craft. I trust you saw the warrant." The words were crisp, professional, and cold enough to make me flinch. Only the lingering warmth in his eyes gave me hope.

"I saw enough to know it's bullshit." I leaned back against the doorjamb crossing my arms over my chest. "She's not going to stop until I accept one of her invitations, is she?"

He looked away. Neither of us had to clarify who "she" was. Falin was the Winter Queen's bloody hands, her assassin, her knight, and was completely bound to her will. Her current compulsion prevented him from having any contact with me outside of a professional capacity. Even our discussions were limited to FIB business. But then she sent him here, to my home, on these damn raids. Why? To remind me that if I wanted Falin I had to come to her first, had to join her court? Or was she simply torturing both of us, making him the instrument of her harassment because she was a possessive bitch and he *belonged* to her, not me?

I didn't know, but I should have gone with Caleb and Holly. Seeing him, being so near, but with the queen's icy barrier between us, hurt. My staying had been cruel to both of us. I pushed away from the doorjamb and started into the living room and the inner stair that led to my apartment, but paused as I took in the havoc the FIB agents had rendered on Caleb's normally orderly house. They weren't breaking anything, just ransacking the place so it looked like a mini whirlwind had hit the room.

Damn, no wonder Caleb had been so pissed. The previous raids hadn't been this bad.

"Alex."

I stopped at Falin's voice. It was still distant, but not quite as cold as it had been a moment before. I turned, hoping when I made the full one eighty I'd find his chilliness would have as well.

No such luck. His expression was just as hard as when I'd turned away.

"If you have a case you think involves fae, or have any trouble that might call for FIB involvement . . ." He pressed a card into my palm, his gloved fingers tracing the back of my hand as he drew back again.

My stomach did an inappropriately excited somersault for such a small gesture. I swallowed, but the wall was still there between us, as if the movement hadn't been intentional. *But it was.* He couldn't break his queen's commands, but he'd bend them as far as they'd go. And man, was I ever tempted to go find a case involving fae. Except that would mean looking for trouble, and enough found me without me actively seeking it.

Someone farther inside the house called Falin's name as I glanced at the card he'd given me. It was his business card, but he'd scrawled his cell number on the back.

"Actually," I said, slowly. "I am having fae troubles. I'm being harassed. Think the FIB could put a stop to that?"

For a moment, his hard facade broke, a small lopsided grin breaking through as he shook his head not in a "no" but in sad amusement. The change lasted only a moment. By the time I blinked, his expression was set and cold once more. That invisible distance was even worse for the contrast to the small slivers of emotion that escaped.

I hated this.

I hated that Falin could be so close and yet so far away. I hated that Death disappeared whenever I saw him.

I was so through with emotions. If only I could find an OFF switch.

An agent called for Falin again and he closed his eyes, squeezing the bridge of his nose between thumb and forefinger. "I have to go. Don't interfere with the raid, Ms. Craft."

"Wasn't planning on it," I said, heading for my apartment and the Chinese crested awaiting a walk and food. I might know the raid was bullshit, but I also knew better than to interfere. If you crossed the FIB, not only did you not pass go or collect two hundred dollars; you also didn't go to jail. You went straight to Faerie.

Chapter 3

It took us the better part of a week to get the new Tongues for the Dead offices something akin to presentable and ready to open, but it took me only three days to discover the major flaw in having an office: someone had to be present during posted business hours. Since Rianna was at a gravesite, right now that someone was me.

Not that any clients had visited the office yet. At least, not any new clients. A woman who'd contacted me before we opened had, under protest, stopped by to sign paperwork and drop off a retainer fee, grumbling about the drive the entire time she was here. The office? Yeah, not so much a success thus far.

I sighed and tapped the touch pad on my laptop to wake the screen.

"You look bored."

I jolted at the unexpected voice and my thrift-store chair screeched in protest as my heart jumped to my throat. Not that I didn't recognize the voice, or the approaching shimmery form dressed in baggy jeans, loose T-shirt, and open flannel shirt so threadbare it would have been nearly transparent even if it hadn't been worn by a ghost.

"Hey, a little jumpy there, Alex?" Roy, my self-appointed ghostly sidekick asked, shoving his hands in his pockets.

Then he squinted, staring a little too hard. "Your magic is overflowing again, isn't it?"

I gave an inward cringe. It had been almost a week since I raised a shade, and my magic was battering my mental shields in an attempt to escape. "That obvious?"

Roy shrugged. "You're sort of . . . flickering."

That wasn't good. Roy, being a ghost, existed in the land of the dead, which was separated from the reality and the living by a chasm. All grave witches could bridge that chasm—that was how we raised shades—but as a plane-weaver, part of my psyche *always* touched the land of the dead. Despite that, Roy had once told me that I was usually as shadowy and uninteresting looking as any of the living, at least, until I actively drew in grave essence. Then I apparently lit up like a roman candle. If I was flickering, my power was clearly slipping.

I should have taken the ritual in the cemetery today—I'd just wanted to give my eyes as much time as possible to recover.

"So whatcha working on? Do we have a case yet?" Roy asked, leaning forward to stare at my screen. He made a face. "Apparently not."

I blushed and closed the laptop, hiding the two windows I'd had open. One of which was the Dead Club Forums, which was the unofficial digital gathering place for the small population of the world's grave witches. The other window was the reason for my embarrassment. It held a game that's sole premise involved slingshotting birds at strangely colored pigs. I wasn't sure how the creators had done it, but I'd swear they worked a spell into the code. That was the only way to explain why the game was so unnaturally addictive.

"What do you need, Roy?" The question came out snippier than I meant—the pressure of holding my shields was wearing on my nerves—and the ghost jerked back. He took a step to the side and hunched his shoulders, all but broadcasting his hurt feelings.

Well, crap. I squeezed my eyes shut and buried my face

in my hands. I really had to loose my magic soon. If I didn't use it, my shields would crumple with my will. Considering those shields were the only things keeping the different planes of reality from trying to converge through me, I needed to make sure I—and not my magic—was in control when I lowered them.

I was too fae to apologize, so instead I said, "I didn't mean that the way it sounded."

"I know." But his tone carried a sulking note.

I dropped my hands from my face and glanced back at him. As soon as my eyes fell on the ghost, the barrage of magic attacking my shields found a crack. I mentally grabbed at the slipping power, trying to draw it back.

Too late.

That part of me with an affinity for the dead, that power that let me reach across the chasm, spiraled out of me. What it wanted was grave essence, which every corpse contained, but the office was warded, and no grave essence could make it through. So it reached for the next best thing—a ghost.

Roy straightened with a jolt as my power hit him, his eyes flying wide. Then color bled into his clothes and hair as my magic pulled him closer to the land of the living.

I clamped down on the power, tightening my shields. I imagined the living vines that kept the dead out—and my magic in—slithering closed. A cold sweat dripped down my neck, but I stopped hemorrhaging magic.

Roy gasped—typically an unnecessary action for a ghost—and then doubled forward. "Geez, Alex, warn me next time," he said between ragged breaths. "I mean, you know I'm more than willing to let you siphon however much power into me that you want, but what the hell was that?"

"An accident." I frowned at him. With my shields this locked down, I should have been as disconnected from the other planes as possible. Instead my peripheral was filled with the chaotic mix of several planes. And Roy, well, I wasn't sure if enough power had spilled out of me to make him manifest in reality, but his color was wrong, and in more than him being too vivid for a ghost. Or maybe it wasn't his color. Maybe it was the way my psyche perceived him. Something was definitely off. "Are you okay?"

"Yeah, just . . ." He straightened and rolled his shoulders. "It's never hurt before."

He winced, and my frown deepened. Ghosts are dead. As such, they can't be killed. They can fade out of existence, but they can't die, and before this moment, I'd have sworn nothing could hurt Roy. Or at least, nothing had before, even when I'd siphoned enough power into him that he fully manifested in reality.

Roy looked around the room as if seeing it for the first time, and maybe he was. The land of the dead overlaid the living world perfectly, except that everything on the other side of the chasm was ruined and decayed. The farther from the chasm the ghost went, the worse the destruction. Even with my planeweaving and grave magic, I'd seen only the first couple of layers, but Roy had told me that in the heart of it there was nothing but dust and wasteland. Depending on how far into reality my magic had pulled Roy, he might be seeing the room almost as intact as it truly existed.

"So am I here?" he asked, curiosity peeking through the wince claiming his features.

"Not sure. Why don't you try walking through that wall." Now I was the one with labored breathing. I couldn't keep my shields locked this tight much longer.

The ghost frowned at me. "You know I can't walk through walls. Not unless they aren't there in my plane."

"I know." Pain built behind my eyes, between my ears, and clawed down my spine. "Roy, I have to loosen my shields. If you don't want a repeat performance from a minute ago, you might want to get out of here."

His gaze moved toward the door, but he shoved his hands in his pockets and didn't move. "I'm ready this time."

I almost made him leave anyway. After all, he'd been a factor in the magic overwhelming me. But if a ghost in the room set me off, how the hell was I going to step foot beyond the wards? As soon as the first tendril of grave essence reached for me, my magic would pummel through my shields. My grave magic preferred humans, but if I lost control, it would settle for any mammal or avian corpse in the vicinity. Wouldn't that be something to loose in the Quarter? It would definitely get Tongues for the Dead noticed, but not in a good way. I shouldn't have waited so long between rituals. Case or no case, as soon as Rianna returned, I needed to head to the nearest cemetery.

But first I had to see if my magic would flare out of control again if I let my shields return to a maintainable level.

"Okay, fair warning," I told Roy. Then I loosened my mental hold, letting the vines in my mind relax—not open, they still maintained a solid wall, but no longer in a vice-like knot. The pain in my head lessened as I stopped working so hard, and I waited for the assault from my own magic.

It didn't come. The magic didn't even rise to test the weakened shields. I blinked in surprise. I could still feel it inside me, like I was a cup filled to the brim and close to boiling over, but for now the magic wasn't overflowing. I let out a sigh, relaxing back into my chair.

"So it's done?" Roy asked, his expression torn between disappointment and relief. At my nod, his shoulders rolled forward a bit and he said, "Oh, okay."

He looked around my sparsely decorated office and then reached for one of the only things on my desk besides my laptop—a framed photo of my dog. I leapt from my chair and grabbed it before he could.

"Hands off," I warned.

"Ah, come on, Alex, I just want to see what that little jolt did," he said, shoving his thick-rimmed glasses farther up his nose.

The first time I'd pumped magic into Roy, he'd gone from an average haunt not able to interact with reality at all, to a passable poltergeist capable of moving small objects when he concentrated. I'd siphoned power into him a few times since then, but it had always been small, controlled amounts. Even with that, he was getting better at picking up, and sometimes throwing, real objects—and I had the broken dishes to prove it. Of course, if he was fully manifested currently, he'd be able to interact with anything he wanted until the energy dissipated.

"Go play with that chair," I said, nodding at one of the two client chairs at the other side of my desk—not that any clients had actually sat in them yet.

Roy glanced at the chairs and his shoulders sank as if he were deflating into himself. "You know, I've been thinking . . ." he said.

Uh-oh. Did I even want to know?

Not that I had a choice. After shuffling his feet for a moment, Roy looked up, but his gaze was somewhere over my shoulder as he spoke. "I was . . . Well, since I'm here all the time anyway . . . I just thought . . ." He trailed off again and I was beginning to think he'd never get around to whatever he wanted to say when his gaze snapped to meet mine, he straightened, and said, "I think I should have my own office."

"You're a ghost."

"Yeah, but you're not using the room next door."

"Roy, that's a broom closet."

The ghost frowned at me, but he didn't back down. "You don't have a broom."

True. But we'd eventually have to get a vacuum cleaner as the office was carpeted. I almost said as much, but Roy was still standing up straight, watching my expression, and I knew that he must have been building up to asking me about an office for days.

"Why would you want an office that exists in the living world? I mean really, what's the point?"

"Because it would be mine," he said, his gaze going distant for a moment. Then his eyes snapped to me again and he clearly didn't like what he saw in my expression. "Oh come on, Alex. It's not like I haven't been helpful before. Remember when I helped you sneak into the State House? Or when I trailed those Spells for the Rest of Us guys? I can help on your cases. I just want my own office."

The last was more whine than statement, and his bottom lip protruded slightly as he shoved his balled fists into his pockets. Geez, I hated when he pouted.

"Okay, fine. The broom closet is all yours," I said, and Roy immediately perked up, a smile breaking across his face. "But you'll have to share it with a vacuum when we finally get one. And you have to get along with Rianna."

That smile darkened and fell as quickly as it had appeared. I couldn't exactly fault the response, after all, Rianna *had* played a major role in his death. Not an easy thing to forgive and forget, even if she had been under someone else's control at the time.

"Just stay out of each other's way," I said as the ghost slouched into a sulk. Avoiding each other shouldn't be hard, she couldn't see him unless she tapped the grave, so as long as he ignored her, everything should be fine. A small smile crept along the edge of Roy's mouth and I added, "And no hurling objects at her."

The smile slipped and he gave me a *"Who me?"* look, which I didn't buy in the least.

"If I hear about her getting assaulted by office supplies, you lose all rights to the office," I warned and his shoulders curled farther forward as he huffed out a breath.

"Fine. Can you bring my blocks to my office?"

I nodded. I'd bought him the blocks to save what was left of my dishware.

"And the Scrabble game?"

Again I nodded.

"And can I have my name added to the door?"

"Don't push it."

"Ah, but—" Whatever argument he might have concocted to try to convince me that putting a dead norm's name on the sign was a brilliant plan stopped abruptly as the chime on the door rang through the front room.

I expected to feel the familiar tingle of Rianna's magic, but I could sense only the smallest bit of magic, and it wasn't familiar.

I jumped to my feet. A client? *Finally*. I rushed around

my desk, but Roy stepped into my path, his eyes wide behind his thick-framed glasses.

"Am I . . . ?" The whispered question trailed off as Roy
gave an exaggerated wave of his hand and I knew he was
asking if he would be visible to whomever had entered.

I honestly had no idea. The ghost looked pretty solid to
me, but he always did so I wasn't a great judge. Then there
was the fact I still had other planes filling my peripheral
vision, giving me glimpses of the world decayed, of colorful
wisps of magic, of the emotional shadow of those who'd
passed through the room before, and occasionally flashes of
planes I couldn't identify. Recently, determining if what I
saw was what everyone else in the world saw was a lot more
complicated than it should have been.

"Just go with it," I whispered back. "If the client sees
you, we'll deal with it."

Then I stepped around him and rushed into the lobby to
greet what I hoped was our first walk-in client.

Chapter 4

The woman standing in the center of the lobby was a complete stranger, but I immediately guessed who she was. Or, at least, I knew who she was related to—the ghost standing behind her was the jumper Rianna and I had encountered last week.

"Welcome to Tongues for the Dead Investigations," I said, stepping forward and extending my hand. "I'm Alex Craft."

The woman, who looked to be in her late forties and very, very pregnant, tore her less than impressed gaze from studying the lobby and turned those critical eyes on me. I got the distinct impression she disapproved of my appearance even more than that of the ramshackle office. Of course, despite her swollen belly, she wore what had to be a tailor-made dress suit, complete with pearls and fat-heeled pumps that her water-bloated ankles pudged over. I, on the other hand, owned only two pairs of dress slacks and I'd already worn those this week. Today I had on a pair of hip-huggers. They were black and I'd paired them with a flattering blouse, so I thought I'd pulled off something close to business casual.

My prospective client clearly didn't agree.

She frowned at me before releasing the death grip on

her designer purse and reaching out to give my hand a limp squeeze. Pain shot through my fingers and up my arm. If I hadn't spent the last two months perfecting not flinching whenever I came into skin contact with someone, I would have winced. But I had practiced, and I kept my smile locked tight on my face. Still, I was thankful when she dropped my hand, even though she pulled back as if I had some disease that might be contagious.

Several months ago my body temperature had dropped significantly, so much so that the touch of someone running your typical 98.6 was uncomfortably hot against my skin. But I was accustomed to that. The pain from her touch had been deeper, sharper. I glanced at her well-manicured hand and noticed a thick ring of dull metal.

Iron.

So Tongues for the Dead's first walk-in client was firmly anti-fae. *Great.* And wasn't that just my luck? Of course, judging by her disapproving expression aimed at, well, *everything*, she might turn around and waddle right back out of our office. And I wasn't sure I'd be disappointed by her doing just that. Of course, we needed the money if we were going to really fix this place up, and I definitely needed to raise a shade.

"Would you like to have a seat in my office?" I asked, taking a step to the side and gesturing toward my open door.

The woman continued to study me and Roy stepped forward, extending his own hand. "I'm Roy Pearson."

She didn't even glance at him, though the other ghost looked up, and on seeing Roy, shrank back a step behind his wife.

Well, that answers that question. Whatever I'd done to Roy, I hadn't forced him to manifest.

When the woman ignored Roy, he frowned, gave me a nod, and then stepped back, his eyes on the other ghost. Neither spoke. They watched each other warily, and I realized this was the first time I'd seen two ghosts in the same place outside of a cemetery. Ghosts were so rare, I'd never considered that they might avoid each other intentionally or what would happen if they crossed paths—judging by the hostile glances between these two, nothing good.

"You're very cold," my potential client said.

I'd been so busy watching the ghosts' interactions that I'd missed the fact she'd finished her assessment. Her expression wasn't pleased, but apparently I'd passed, at least enough for her to finally deign to speak to me.

I shrugged off the comment but kept my face in what I hoped was a politely professional smile. "Hazard of the job."

"Then you're the grave witch? The one who talks to ghosts?"

My gaze flickered to the shimmering form behind her. Oh, I could talk to ghosts. But that wasn't why people hired me. Ghosts were rare anomalies—which wasn't properly represented at the moment as I had two in my office. But as a general rule, ghosts occurred only when something went wrong. Grave witches raised shades, which were the collective memories stored in every cell of the body given shape by magic. I didn't bother correcting her. Instead I nodded and said, "I'm one of two investigators with the firm."

Roy cleared his throat, clearly miffed at being left out. I ignored him as he disappeared through the door of the broom closet.

"Would you like to step into my office and discuss your case, Ms . . . ?"

"Mrs. Kingly," she said, but this time she walked to my office, her movements slow as she waddled with one hand supporting her belly and the other clutching her purse. The ghost followed, shiny ephemeral tear tracks evident on his cheeks. The woman tottered when her heel caught in a hole in the carpet that Rianna had used magic to disguise. The ghost threw out his arms, trying to support his wife. His hands passed through her with her none the wiser of his presence. I jumped forward, but the woman straightened before I reached her, which was probably for the best. I had the distinct impression she wouldn't have appreciated me touching her. She waddled the last five feet to my office, her husband haunting her wake.

If Mrs. Kingly had been less than impressed with the front room, my office didn't do much to improve her opinion. A salvaged, battered desk took up most of the small area. It left just enough space for my chair and the two almost matching client chairs. The room wasn't exactly cramped, but if I closed the door it would get claustrophobic fast. At least she didn't stand there assessing the room with disapproval this time, but lowered herself awkwardly into one of the chairs. I spent half a moment wondering if I should offer some sort of help, but I didn't know what she might need so instead I scooted around my desk and sat in my own chair.

"I assume you're here about your husband?" I asked once we were both settled.

My client startled, her eyes flying wide before the expression turned into something that looked a lot like suspicion. Of course, she'd just walked in off the street and had no idea her dead husband was following her around. I probably should have approached the topic less directly, but I wasn't used to dealing with clients face-to-face until after all the details of a case were worked out.

She studied me with narrowed eyes for a long moment before finally saying, "I suppose it doesn't matter how you guessed that, but yes, I'm here about my husband, James Anderson Kingly." She touched her belly and added, "Senior." She paused, looking away from me. "Do you have a tissue?"

Crap, tissue. That was definitely something I should have in the office. I added it to my mental shopping list because if we had grieving family members walking in to hire us, this was unlikely to be the only time someone asked for a tissue. I shook my head to let her know I didn't have any and noticed for the first time that under Mrs. Kingly's perfectly applied makeup, her eyes were red from crying.

"There's a bathroom on the other side of the lobby. I can show you to it."

She sat there, silent, unmoving, her gaze focused on the window on the far side of the room. Then she shook her head, but she still said nothing. I didn't push her. Her husband had just died, which didn't excuse the chilly demeanor she'd treated me with, but it factored into the equation. Appearances were clearly important to her, and she was too proud to break down in front of a stranger, so I gave her time to collect herself, even if that meant she'd wrap herself back in that disdainful armor she'd walked in wearing. Finally she turned to me, and while her eyes were shiny as if tears could fall at any moment, the glare she speared me with was cold. Hard. *No big surprise there.*

"An officer gave me your card and said that you'd told him that James didn't kill himself," she said, opening her purse and producing the card, which wasn't mine, but Rianna's. Of course, as the card had been torn into several pieces before being taped back together, the only thing legible was the name of the firm. "Can you prove that claim?" she asked. "Can you prove it wasn't suicide?"

My gaze slid to the ghost, who'd sunk to his knees beside her and was carrying on a rambling monologue about how he loved her and their baby and how he would never have killed himself. She couldn't hear a word of it, but I could. Not that he knew that. I looked back at his widow.

"Your husband has been quite insistent about the fact he had too much to live for and wouldn't leave you and the baby."

Her lips pursed and the muscles around her jaw twitched as she clenched her teeth. "Ms. Craft, I have no interest in what platitudes you think I might want to hear. I suppose next you'll tell me you can feel my husband's presence and he's close by, watching over me. I shouldn't have come here. You're nothing more than a charlatan profiting off the grief of the weak-minded."

It took every ounce of self-control in me not to reach out and make her husband's ghost visible just to prove how very real my magic was. But as tightly wound as she was, I wasn't sure what that kind of shock would do to her. She looked about to pop, and I didn't want to send her into premature labor because I sure as hell didn't know how to deliver a baby. Instead I settled for saying, "I assure you that I am fully OMIH certified in grave magic."

She gave a huff under her breath.

"What exactly is it you want me to do for you, Mrs. Kingly?" Because surely she hadn't come to the office simply to insult me.

"The police have written off my husband's death as a suicide. Whether you are a fraud or not, it seems the two of us are the only ones convinced he didn't jump off that building, regardless of what witnesses saw or what evidence the police think they found. If you can truly prove that his death was . . ." She stopped and this time the tears that had been threatening trailed over. She flicked them away without a word and I dutifully ignored the tears.

To fill the silence while she regained her composure I said, "I can raise his shade and find out what really happened on that rooftop." Or I could just talk to his ghost, but if she needed proof for her insurance company, only a shade's recounting of the event would be legally sufficient. While the court system was still working out the validity of allowing shades to testify in their own murder cases, insurance companies had acknowledged the validity of shades' claims for nearly fifteen years. A ghost could swear and promise as much as they wanted, but just like when they were living, ghosts could lie. Shades couldn't. They were just recordings of a person's life. If I raised James Kingly's shade and he said he jumped, that would be the end of it. If he said he tripped, the insurance company would have to rule it an accidental death and pay out.

"Normally I would encourage you to join me at the gravesite, but I imagine your husband's funeral was closed casket and you don't need to remember him as he died." Because the shade would look exactly as it had the moment the soul left it—which would have been after Kingly hit the roof of the car. I hadn't taken a close look, but I'd seen enough to know that no one needed to see her loved one in that condition. "You can send your lawyers and insurance reps to the graveyard to meet me—"

"This has nothing to do with insurance." Mrs. Kingly's words were all but a shout and if she could have shoved herself out of the chair and stomped out, she may have done so in that moment.

"I . . ." I caught the apology before it left my lips. I had too much fae in me to offer false regret and there was no reason to incur a debt over something like this. But I couldn't leave the sentence at just "I" so I finished by saying, "I didn't know."

She could have frozen a lake with her glare. Again I wondered if she'd walk out, but after a moment she said, "And James isn't buried. He's still at the morgue."

I blinked and counted backward to figure out how many days he'd been there. Medical examiners usually tried to get bodies back to their families as quickly as possible, but James had been there over a week. If the police were so certain he'd committed suicide, why wouldn't they have released the body by now? I repeated as much aloud but Mrs. Kingly gave me only a grim shake of her head.

"I've called in every favor and used every bit of influence my family has to encourage the police to investigate James's death, but despite everything—even my threat to not donate to the annual police ball this year—they are still releasing his body to Sweet Rest Funeral Home tomorrow. His body can't be allowed to leave the morgue. If it does, they'll never prove he was murdered."

"Murdered?" I was assuming there had been an accident. I'd certainly seen no sign the man had been murdered. Granted, I hadn't arrived until after he hit the car, but the police had looked into the matter. If there were indications someone had pushed him over the edge of that building, they'd have continued looking into the case. "You're convinced it was murder?"

"There is no other explanation."

I disagreed but kept my mouth closed.

"James shouldn't have been on that roof, and he

shouldn't have been anywhere near the Magic Quarter. We're Humans First Party. We don't support magic or its practitioners." She lifted her chin, as if daring me to say anything about that last bit of information.

I almost groaned, but I should have guessed she supported the Humans First Party, an anti-fae/anti-witch political group. The ring, the attitude—it all made sense. Except that she was here. And one other thing.

"Do you know what a sensitive is, Mrs. Kingly?"

She gave a sharp shake of her head, but the fact she didn't meet my eyes betrayed the lie. Not that it mattered.

"A sensitive is someone who can feel magic," I said, and not only did she continue to avoid my eyes but a flush of color filled her cheeks. I continued: "As well as being a grave witch, I'm a sensitive, which means I can feel the charm you're wearing. It's a good one. A medicinal grade charm to help with your pregnancy, if I'm not mistaken."

She didn't try to deny it, nor did she lift her gaze.

"You look very young, Ms. Craft." She wrapped her arms under her belly as if cradling the child within. "James and I were so focused on our careers when we were younger, we didn't even think about starting a family until I was in my late thirties. We were established then. It seemed like the perfect time. But we had trouble conceiving, and once we did . . ." She paused as the words caught in her throat. "I miscarried. Twice. When we got pregnant a third time, we decided to give this baby the best chance we could. That's the only reason we turned to magic."

I sighed. I couldn't help it. The Humans First Party members tended to be extremists, but from what I'd seen, her attitude was typical: magic and its users were dangerous and needed more regulations and restrictions, unless, of course, a party member wanted to secretly utilize that magic. Unfortunately, they were extremists who were gaining seats in Congress. Even Nekros had a Human First party governor, but then, he was actually a fae in deep hiding—and my father—so that was a different and entirely screwed up situation.

I didn't know what to say to Mrs. Kingly. I wasn't going to turn her down as a client simply because she was a hypocrite—I'd worked for worse. The real problem was that I doubted I could get the results she wanted. I might be able to prove her husband's death was an accident, maybe, depending on what the shade said. But murder?

I glanced at the ghost of James Kingly. He cooed sympathetic reassurances to his wife—which she couldn't hear and were no help to me in figuring out what had happened to him. I wished I could get him alone for a moment and ask him some questions, but I didn't see how without alerting Mrs. Kingly to his presence, which would have probably made his day but was likely to push her over the edge of what she could accept.

"He wouldn't have killed himself, Ms. Craft," she said in a small voice. One that lacked the edge she'd brandished since walking through my door. "And he wouldn't have run off. He wanted this baby."

"Coming to the Quarter isn't an indication he was running off. Maybe he was looking for another charm for the baby?"

She shook her head. The tears had finally won, cutting paths through her makeup and making her mascara run. Oh yeah, I definitely need to get some tissues for my desk. The ghost pushing to his feet drew my attention from my living client.

"I didn't. I swear to you I didn't," he said, his shimmery hands curling into fists and then flexing again. He paced behind her. "Why would you say I ran off? I never left."

Okay. Now that was odd.

I looked at my client, whose bravado had completely crumpled under her grief. "When you say he ran off, what exactly do you mean?"

She scrubbed the tears from her eyes with the base of her palm, further smearing her makeup. "He . . ." She broke off to sniffle. "He called me after work, about four days before . . . before it happened. He said he had to take some clients to dinner, which wasn't unusual except that he hadn't told me about it beforehand. That was the last time I heard from him. I reported him missing the next day. When the police showed up at the door"—she sniffled again—"I knew it was bad news. I couldn't think of any reason he wouldn't have come home if he were okay. I just didn't expect . . . I didn't expect them to tell me it had just happened. Or that they suspected he'd jumped." Another sniffle. "You said you have a bathroom?"

I showed her to it, but grabbed the ghost's arm before he could follow her inside.

"Hey," he yelled, staring at my hand on his arm. "You, you can see me?"

No, I randomly grabbed at air and happened to catch the arm of a ghost. Of course, I really didn't expect any other response. The question was practically obligatory. Grave witches were the only people who could see ghosts, and we weren't exactly plentiful. As far as I knew, I was the only grave witch who could also touch ghosts. Still, I wanted to avoid a scene directly outside the bathroom door. The wood wasn't thick and me having a one-sided conversation wasn't likely to instill much confidence in my client. So I pressed my finger over my lips and dragged the ghost back to my office.

"What really happened on that roof?"

The ghost stared at me wide-eyed for a moment before saying, "You really can see me? And hear me? You have to tell my wife I love her and that I didn't jump."

"Right, I got that already. Now, the roof. What happened?"

The ghost frowned. "I'm not sure."

Seriously? "How can you not be sure?"

"I . . . I don't remember going up to that roof. One minute I was in Delaney's, a little Irish pub between work and my house, and then I hit a car and some guy was pulling me out of my body."

That "guy" would have been the collector, though since both Death and the gray man had been there, I wasn't sure which one, but that wasn't the important part of the story.

"Let's go back to the beginning. You were with some clients at the pub and then what?"

"And then nothing. Just pain and the feeling of my head caving in and my bones snapping." The ghost shivered with the memory of his quick but gruesome death.

That would mean he was missing a little more than three days—which could happen, I'd lost hours and days in Faerie before—but he hadn't said he'd gone to the Eternal Bloom, Nekros's only fae bar. "Okay, so you were at the Irish pub. Who are the clients you were with?"

The ghost swallowed. "Uh . . ." I could almost see the thoughts circling around in his head, trying to decide how to answer, how much to admit to. He'd never taken clients to the little Irish pub. I could see it all over his face. But he was still trying to decide if he should tell me as much.

And that was the problem with ghosts. They could lie.

Chapter 5

By the time Mrs. Kingly emerged from the bathroom, her makeup was once again perfect—as was the cold chip on her shoulder. Aside from the fact he'd lied to his widow during their last conversation, I hadn't learned anything useful from James, and of course, I went back to ignoring him as soon as the door opened and Mrs. Kingly reappeared. James didn't want to talk about whatever had happened during those unaccounted for days. I'd have to wait until I questioned the shade to get any real answers.

"You can do the ritual tonight, right?" Mrs. Kingly asked, and I hesitated, my hand halfway across the desk with the blank contract for hire that Rianna and I had drawn up as well as several OMIH regulated forms.

Tonight? "I don't do nighttime rituals."

"You don't need darkness and moonlight and all that?"

I didn't groan at the stereotypical—and completely incorrect—assumption but my "no" was perhaps overly terse. I ended up blind enough in broad daylight, doing rituals at night would be downright stupid.

"But you can do it today? His body will be picked up tomorrow and you need to prove it was murder before he leaves the morgue."

Her insistence was on the side of frantic and I had the

feeling that she was one breath away from either yelling or a repeat of the earlier waterworks. Neither appealed to me, so I aimed for a placating smile and tried to keep my voice calm as I said, "I can raise the shade this afternoon, but I can't give you any guarantees that his death will be decreed a murder. It all depends on what the shade says."

"It's murder." The words were matter of fact without any room for question as she signed and dated a consent form to grant me access to her husband's body while in the morgue.

I wished I could be half as sure.

"And find out where he was those three days he was missing. I'm assuming kidnapped by whomever killed him, but I need to know." The smallest tinge of doubt crawled into her voice with the last, as if some small part of her believed what everyone kept telling her—that her husband's death was a suicide.

Well, I'll know soon enough.

I went over the contract with her but she stopped me when I reached the portion about paying a retainer fee upfront.

"How will I know you've really performed the ritual? What if something goes wrong? Am I just out that money?"

"You're more than welcome to accompany me," I said and the color drained from her face.

"You could maybe, record it? In audio I mean. I don't want to see . . ."

I nodded, not making her finish the sentence. Since I'd be performing the ritual at the morgue, making a recording wouldn't be an issue. Hell, when I consulted for the police, the ritual was always recorded. The fact that all the equipment needed was already set up for autopsies helped. I'd just record the ritual and then detach the audio file for Mrs. Kingly.

We were finishing the last of the paperwork when the chime on the door sounded. This time I did recognize the tingle of magic—Rianna. She popped into my office, Desmond at her side, but backed out again when she saw the client at my desk. She smiled, but curiosity peeked through her expression. I wasn't surprised when her eyes flashed with an inner light as she opened her shields. Her gaze landed on the ghost of James Kingly and that smile widened as her eyebrows raised in an expression I recognized well from our academy days. I could almost hear the unsaid *"I told you so."* I wanted to roll my eyes—just like I would have when we were younger, but I didn't think Mrs. Kingly would find that half as amusing as Rianna. I waved my hand, the movement more shooing motion than greeting.

Once Mrs. Kingly left, I grabbed my purse and headed across the lobby. "I'm off to the morgue."

Rianna looked up from a paperback—a mystery novel, no doubt. "You'll be back in time for dinner?"

She needed to be inside Faerie during sunset and sunrise as those were the times *between*, when day and night changed and Faerie's magic was at its weakest. If she strayed in the mortal realm without Faerie's magic supporting her, all her years would catch up with her. I'd seen it happen to another changeling and it wasn't a pretty way to die.

"If it looks like I'm running late, go on without me. Holly and I can meet you there." After all, Rianna didn't need me to get into Faerie, and with signs of fall all around, the sunset was earlier each evening. Holly, on the other hand, needed an escort who was on the VIP list.

Rianna nodded, but her expression dropped slightly before her eyes returned to her book. I waved at Desmond as I passed him. The barghest ignored me, which was pretty typical.

I'd just reached the front door when I paused.

"Oh yeah, by the way," I said, my hand hovering over the door handle. "I forgot to tell you. Roy moved into the broom closet." And with that, I left.

"She's roped you into this wild-goose chase too, huh?" Tamara, the lead medical examiner and one of my best friends, said as she wheeled a sheet-covered gurney out of the morgue's cold room. "I mean, it's a terrible, tragic thing, and I pity her having to deal with it in her condition, but she needs to come to terms with the fact her husband jumped."

"So you don't think there's a chance this is anything other than suicide?" I asked, but I was only half paying attention. Grave essence was wafting out of the now shut door of the cold room, and despite the fact I once again had my shields locked as tightly as I could possibly maintain, I could feel its cold but seductive touch. I could also feel the fact she had nine bodies in the room, and the gender and approximate age of each—way too much was getting through my shields.

Tamara didn't notice my distraction, that or she was accustomed to me acting a little odd in the morgue. "Not a chance. This guy didn't just jump, he dove off that building, and judging by the injures I found—and almost as important, those I didn't find—he didn't attempt to brace himself or break the fall."

Then why is the ghost so insistent? I glanced at the gurney. The lumpy form the sheet covered was too flat, the outline wrong for an adult man's body. But it was a body, and from my interaction with his ghost, I could tell without a doubt it was Kingly's body. I was glad that sheet wouldn't have to be removed, but I wasn't looking forward to seeing the condition of his shade.

"You staying for this or are you going to send in one of your interns?" Because chain of evidence demanded someone official stay with the body while I performed my ritual, but I knew Tamara had just acquired a couple of new interns and she enjoyed breaking them in by letting me freak them out.

"Oh, I'm staying," she said, crossing her arms over her chest. "After everything that woman put my office through, I want to hear this selfish prick admit he jumped. Besides, I've barely seen you in a month. Holly is suddenly too busy to go to lunch, ever. And you've stood me up for dinner twice. I'm seriously having a case of third wheel syndrome here. Too old to hang, maybe?"

She made it sound like a joke, but I could hear something else, something hurt, in her voice. I cringed and tried to hide the reaction by focusing on digging through my purse.

I found the tube of waxy chalk I used for drawing circles for indoor rituals and started working my way around the gurney.

"You know that's not it. The timing just hasn't worked. Besides, you're not that old."

Tamara huffed. "I'm a bride in my late thirties trying to plan a wedding without the help of my two closest friends."

I nearly dropped the chalk. "You and Ethan finally set a date?" She'd been wearing a huge diamond for at least four months now, but while Ethan had proposed, he wouldn't commit to a date.

"Yeah." A dreamy smile spread across Tamara's face, her eyes going distant and a slightly dopey expression claiming her face. Then her gaze snapped back to me and the softness faded. "And you'd know that, and that I want you and Holly to be my bridesmaids, if you weren't avoiding me."

"I'm not avoiding you." And it wasn't a lie, or I wouldn't have been able to say it—I was too fae to lie. And that was part of the problem. Holly and I were both dealing with issues tied in with Faerie, and well, we hadn't told Tamara any of it. The less she knew, the safer she was. Even though the fae had come out of the mushroom ring seventy years ago, they were still a secretive bunch. But I was feeling guilty enough that if she pressed me, I might just spill more than I should. How had I missed that they'd finally set a date?

I rushed the last quarter of my circle—which in my haste was more oblong than circular, but it would work—and flicked on the camera.

"I'm going to start the ritual now," I said, knowing that I was only stalling the conversation, not stopping it.

The look Tamara gave me confirmed that fact, and I closed my eyes so she couldn't see the guilt there. Not much I could do about that right now.

Concentrating, I focused on clearing my mind and centering myself—not an easy task with Tamara's news rambling around my brain on top of the grave magic fighting to break out of my shields while grave essence struggled to force its way in. I took a long breath. Let it out. I couldn't cast a circle with grave magic, and I wasn't working without one, especially when my magic was behaving erratically. I breathed in again, focusing on my lungs, my body, as I struggled for some semblance of calmness.

It took me longer than I liked to block out the distractions enough to concentrate on the obsidian ring on my finger. The ring carried raw energy drawn down from the Aetheric plane, and unlike my grave magic, which was a wyrd ability and had only one true purpose, this raw Aetheric energy was limited only by the caster welding it. I channeled a thin stream of the stored magic into the circle I'd drawn and a shimmering blue barrier sprang up around me.

The assault of grave essence immediately lessened. It didn't vanish—after all, I had James's corpse in the circle with me, which emanated the power of the grave. But the circle did block out the other corpses in the morgue, making the grave essence clawing at me in an attempt to crawl under my skin manageable, if not exactly comfortable.

Of course, letting it in was exactly what I had to do.

I removed the silver charm bracelet that carried my extra shields, and as soon as I unlatched the clasp, my pent-up magic roared to the surface, testing the now weakened resistance between it and the grave essence that raked across my mind. I still had my personal shields, but my psyche had already crossed the chasm separating the living and the dead enough for a howling wind to swirl around my circle, blowing curls in my face. If I'd opened my eyes, I knew I'd see the room in the ruined devastation that existed on the closest layers of the land of the dead. But I wasn't ready to open my eyes yet.

I still had the most important part of the ritual to complete.

I cracked my mental shields slowly, trying to control the outpour of magic. It almost worked. My magic latched on to the corpse as grave essence flooded my body, filling my blood, my very bones, with the chill of the grave. The invasion hurt. I was alive. The essence looking for a home in my body wasn't. I might have been cold to the touch for most people, but I still had my own living heat, and it warred with the chill of the grave.

So I released that heat, giving away a part of myself and sending it into the corpse already filled with my power.

Then I opened my eyes. The room had decayed around me, at least in appearance. Though if I wasn't careful, the seemingly threadbare sheet covering a gurney so rusted a bump might turn it into a mound of red rust could blend with mortal reality, becoming the true state of the objects. That was what it meant to be a planeweaver. I could tie different planes of existence together. And the land of the dead wasn't the only reality now filling my vision. The Aetheric, the plane of magic, was also visible as it filled the room with swirls of colorful raw energy. If I wanted, I could have reached out and drawn on that magic. A dangerous temptation, very dangerous, as witches were meant to touch the Aetheric only with their projected psyche. Beyond those planes were others, but I tried not to focus on them because I had very little control over my planeweaving ability, and no one to teach me.

Instead I focused on the body under the rotted sheet. With so much of my magic filling the corpse, it took only a twitch of my will to form the man's memories into a shade. It sat up through the sheet, seemingly unaware of its crushed and misshapen head and broken body. I averted my eyes from the mangled mess. Unlike ghosts, which tended to look like how the person had perceived themselves during life, shades always appeared as the body existed the moment before the soul was collected.

With the shade raised, I focused on a new mental shield I'd spent the last month constructing. It sprang up in my mind's eye like an opaque bubble around my psyche. Immediately the layers of different realities dimmed. They didn't disappear, and the shield didn't stop the grave essence, but in theory it helped prevent my powers from reaching across those planes of reality. Also, from previous rituals, I'd noticed that my eyesight took considerably less damage when my psyche only *looked* across the planes through the shield, as opposed to having an open channel.

Shield in place, I turned back to the shade I'd raised, though I couldn't bring myself to look directly at its misshapen form.

"What is your name?" I asked. I knew his name, of course, but usually when I raised a shade in the morgue, it was for an official police case, and the shade had to identify itself for the record. It had become habit.

"James Kingly."

"James, do you remember how you died?"

The shade sat perfectly still, not answering. Shades always answered immediately, unless the question was outside the scope of what the body remembered. His death shouldn't have been hard to recall.

A bubble of panic built in my chest, pressing against my lungs so it was hard to breathe. Shades were nothing more than memories held together by grave magic and the witch's will, but my magic had become erratic recently and I'd filled the corpse with a hell of a lot of it.

Then the shade spoke, the delay, which had felt like forever, only a few seconds. "There was blood and pain. Things were broken. I was on my back and then . . ." He trailed off, which meant that was the moment a collector had freed his soul and the RECORD button on his life had stopped.

Okay, so he'd described the moment of his death. I'd asked that same question to hundreds of shades and most described the events leading up to their deaths, not just the last moment. *Did my grave magic go wrong?* It was the one magic I'd always been able to rely on behaving. My spellcasting sucked, and the whole planeweaving thing was new and a mess, but I'd always been able to raise shades, and I was damn good at it. So what the hell was going on?

"Before the blood and pain, what were you doing?"

No hesitation this time. "Sitting in Delaney's draining my second beer."

I stared at the shade, speechless. *That isn't possible.*

From outside my circle Tamara said, "How can he not remember jumping? His blood alcohol level wasn't near high enough for him to have stumbled over the edge of that building in a drunken stupor. And where the heck is Delaney's— I've never heard of it. I thought shades couldn't lie."

"They can't." Or at least they weren't supposed to be able to. They were just memories. All will, ego, and emotion had left with the soul when it was ripped from the body.

"Rest now," I told the shade, pushing it back into the body. I drew part of my magic out of the corpse, and then called the shade again. It returned, slightly more translucent than before. I asked the shade the same question, and got the exact same answer.

"That's not possible," I said, seriously wishing I had a chair inside the circle because collapsing into a seat sounded like a plan. But that wasn't an option. "James, do you remember being on the roof of Motel Styx?"

"No."

"Have you ever been to Motel Styx?"

"No." No hesitation. No emotion. It was the type of response I expected. Except it wasn't true. I knew, without a doubt, that he'd been at that building.

What the hell?

"I think the OMIH might have to reevaluate the honesty of shades," Tamara said, pacing the edge of my circle.

Maybe, but . . . "James, did you jump off the roof of Motel Styx?"

"No."

"Have you had suicidal thoughts in the last six months?"

"No."

"Did you lie to your wife about meeting clients and instead go to an Irish pub?"

"Yes."

"Why?" I hadn't had a chance to ask James's ghost that question before his wife returned, but then he'd been dodgy about admitting he'd been at the pub for any reason other than what he'd told his wife. I much preferred the shade's direct, unemotional answers.

"When Nina got pregnant, we both agreed that since she couldn't drink, I wouldn't either. But I needed a beer."

Or two, apparently. "What time did you leave the pub?"

The shade didn't answer.

Tamara stopped pacing and frowned at the shade through the blue haze of my circle. "What is wrong with him, Alex? Doesn't he have to answer you?"

He did. *Unless he doesn't know the answer.* I no longer feared my magic had gone awry. Everything the shade said confirmed what the ghost had told me in my office. But that meant that James Kingly had lost three days of his life, including the moment he'd decided to die.

Chapter 6

I put the shade back in its body because there was nothing more it could tell me, and then I reclaimed my heat and wrapped up the ritual. Tamara wheeled James Kingly's body back to the cold room as I stood there blinking at the thick gray film coating my vision.

"How are the eyes?" Tamara asked, and I turned toward the sound of her voice. As she crossed the room, I could track her movement, but as soon as she stopped, she blended into the bleakness. Either my expression or my silence was answer enough because she said, "That bad, huh?"

I shrugged, hating the pity in her voice nearly as much as I hated the blindness. Times like this were when it was tempting to open my psyche and see across planes. It could be confusing, seeing multiple layers of reality stacked on top of each other, but at least I could see. Of course, that would only exacerbate the problem when I finally locked my shields again. Currently the shadows were gray, not black, and I could make out the outline of the shelves and tables in the room, so hopefully my vision would soon clear enough that I could safely navigate to the elevator. Until then . . .

"You want some coffee?" Tamara asked, as if reading my need for a distraction.

"That would be great." And warm. I shivered. *I should have brought a jacket.* Except I hadn't planned on raising a shade when I'd left the house, and September in Nekros was not what you'd describe as cold. Sometimes the nights were chilly, but after the blistering heat of July and August, September was downright comfortable. Of course, that meant I sometimes forgot to carry a jacket.

Reaching a slightly trembling hand toward what looked like the outline of one of the autopsy tables, I started in the direction of Tamara's office.

"You need help?" she asked, and if I'd had any heat left, it would have rushed to my cheeks.

I hated being treated like an invalid, more so because sometimes it truly was necessary. But not right now. "Just lead the way," I told her, because as long as she was moving, I could see her.

I followed her gray shadowlike form, managing to graze only one counter . . . and slam my shoulder against the doorframe of her office. The small "mmph" that escaped me on impact made her stop, but, thankfully, she didn't mention the misstep. All and all, not my most successful pathfinding.

If my eyesight continued to degenerate this rapidly, I might need to look into some alternatives. Maybe I could train PC as a Seeing Eye dog. Of course, I couldn't even get the six pound Chinese crested to walk on a leash without pulling. Who knew where we'd end up if I relied on his guidance.

I shuffled around Tamara's office, searching for a place to sit. As I sank gratefully into Tamara's spare chair, I heard the coffeemaker turn on. Central Precinct was infamous for the burnt sludge most of the cops choked down, but here in the morgue, Tamara kept her own machine and a stash of good dark roasted coffee beans.

"So did anything strange stand out in Kingly's autopsy?"

I asked as the smell of rich coffee wafted through the small office.

"Let me glance over my notes," she said, and I could almost hear the frown on her face, even if I couldn't see it. I knew her well enough to guess she was kicking herself, sure she'd missed something.

"He likely jumped, even if he can't remember," I said as I heard the sound of her file cabinet opening. "You weren't wrong about that."

Paper crinkled as she riffled through a file. "All the physical evidence pointed that way. But there had to be a spell involved, right?" She paused. "Or could brain damage have caused the memory loss?"

I considered the idea. Memories were stored in every cell of the body, but they were limited to what the soul experienced and remembered. Dementia, brain damage, brainwashing, or spells affecting memory—if powerful enough—could change what the body recorded and what the shade reported. But I didn't think brain damage was the issue in this case. "Kingly died too soon after impact for the damage to have changed his memory."

"Alex, he died *on* impact."

I didn't bother arguing if life ceased when the body died or when the soul left the body. Remove the soul, and the body dies. Even if it takes a couple minutes for the person to be considered medically dead, the shade would have no memory of that time. On the other hand, a body could be medically dead but the soul still in it, and the shade would know everything that happened to the body after death until the soul was finally freed. Which equalled true death? It was a topic on which a medical professional and a grave witch were unlikely to ever agree.

Tamara was silent as I heard her turning pages. My vision was finally recovering, and I could clearly make out the outline of her leaning over the file on her desk. I let her review it in silence. The pot of coffee finished brewing before she finished reading, so I stood and made a fumbling attempt to locate the Styrofoam cups that were always on the shelf above the coffeemaker. Except, nothing I touched felt like a cup, and as I was still seeing mostly gray outlines, the one thing that looked like it might be cup shaped turned out to be a container of powdered creamer.

"You're out of cups."

"Oh, sorry. I meant to tell you. I'm using mugs now," she said, and slid open her bottom drawer, retrieving two ceramic mugs.

I'd cringed at her use of the word "sorry" though it had been more expression than true apology so the incursion of possible debt that hung between us was small. If it had a monetary value, it would have been worth no more than a penny or two, but I still hated the feeling of imbalance. Of course, it was an apology, not an expression of appreciation, so at least I had the option of not accepting.

"Mugs. Really?" Yeah, my sarcasm sounded mean, but it was the only way not to forgive her. I was going to have to tell her I was fae—or, at least, fae enough to count—soon or we'd eventually run into unavoidable and weighty debt. But if I started telling people, it became more real. Not that the fact I spent time in a pocket of Faerie almost every single day didn't highlight it nice and bright.

"—and Ethan's always going on about how bad Styrofoam is for the environment," Tamara was saying. I'd been so caught up in my own thoughts that I hadn't been listening, but it sounded like she was still talking about the mugs and I hadn't missed anything important.

"So you didn't tell me the date you two picked," I said, picking up the steaming coffeepot.

Tamara took the pot away from me, which was probably a good plan. Color was returning, but the world was still blurry. After she filled both mugs, she handed me one and then added a heaping spoonful of creamer to the other. She didn't ask if I wanted any, we'd been friends long enough for her to know I took my coffee black.

I clutched the hot mug and inhaled the heady aroma, but a pang of sorrow washed through me at the scent. Death loved coffee. It was something we shared, literally. Even before I'd realized I was a planeweaver, Death and I discovered if we were in physical contact, he could interact with whatever else I was touching. Both of us holding one mug, while he watched me with those deep hazel eyes over the rim as he took a sip? I swallowed. It wasn't one memory, it was dozens. Every time I drank coffee—and I drank a lot of coffee—I half expected him to show up, that easy smile on his face. But he didn't, or at least, he hadn't in over a month.

"I'd offer you a penny for you're thoughts, but they look more valuable than that," Tamara said, and I startled, sloshing hot coffee on my fingers.

I didn't yelp, or curse, but it was a near thing.

"Napkin?" Tamara held out something I could barely make out, and I accepted the napkin. As I dabbed at the spilt coffee, Tamara said, "So you were pretty deep in thought."

I shrugged. "It was—" I waved a hand, not finishing because I didn't want to talk about Death and I couldn't lie and say it was nothing. "But you were going to tell me the date you and Ethan picked."

For a moment I didn't think she was going to let me get away with changing the subject, but then she said, "Well, after much debate, we've settled on October fifteenth."

I nodded, my lips pressing together as I considered the date. "That gives us a little over a year to plan the wedding. This should be fun."

Tamara was so silent the very air in the room stilled. I squinted, trying to see her expression. I couldn't.

"What is it?" I asked. Silence. "Tam?"

"Not October of next year," she said, her voice quiet. Too quiet. "This October."

"That's less than a month away."

"Well, you would have known sooner if you and Holly hadn't stood me up for dinner last week." Her voice was most certainly not quiet anymore.

I cringed. "It wasn't intentional. Something—"

She cut me off. "Came up. I know. I heard the excuse already."

A lump of guilt settled in my stomach, and the coffee that had smelled tempting a moment before no longer held any appeal. Everything was so complicated these days. I opened my mouth to tell her about the trips to the Eternal Bloom, of how time sometimes got a little screwy—she already knew the VIP room was a pocket of Faerie. I'd told her that much after losing three days there a few months back. But the reasons we were going was Holly's secret, not mine, and it wasn't my place to share. I snapped my mouth shut so hard my jaw clicked, and Tamara turned back to the file on her desk.

I changed the subject. "So after five months of being engaged, why the sudden rush?"

Tamara's chair creaked, the sound loud in the suddenly thick silence.

"You're not—" I started, but she cut me off.

"I see only one abnormality in this autopsy."

I wasn't going to let her get away with that. "You are. You're pregnant."

Again her chair squeaked, and even if I couldn't see her features, I could feel her glare. "Do you want to hear about Kingly's autopsy results or not?"

"Yes, but . . ." I suddenly didn't know what to say. It seemed we were all keeping secrets, and I'd just blundered into Tamara's. She and Ethan had been living together since they got engaged, but once he'd popped the question—and claimed half her closet—he'd proven reluctant to agree on a date. But how could Tamara be pregnant? I could feel the charm that protected against both STDs and pregnancy near her left foot, where it must have been attached to an ankle bracelet. It was easy to pick out because I wore the exact same charm on my bracelet.

Tamara sighed, and as if sensing my thoughts said, "No charm works perfectly all the time. Now do you want to get back to Kingly?"

I gave her a minute nod, and she pulled the file in front of her, running her finger down the page. "The only odd finding in autopsy was that James Kingly's glycogen stores were low, as were his red blood cell count. If he hadn't killed himself, he might have eventually died of inanition."

I cupped my mug of coffee and frowned. "So in English, what does that mean?"

"Basically, he appeared to be starving to death. Which is odd, because his stomach contents included veal, haricot vert, escargot, and a really expensive cabernet sauvignon—not any beer, by the way, no matter what his shade claimed. Kingly also had digested food in his intestines, so he was definitely eating. I'd guess he had some sort of wasting disease, though I didn't find any mention of it in his medical records. He had to know though. When he went in for a physical two months ago he was pushing the top of his ideal weight range for a man of his age. He'd lost nearly seventy-five pounds since then."

"That's odd. His widow didn't mention anything about the rapid weight loss." Or about a disease. And the ghost certainly didn't look like a man wasting away, though that didn't mean anything as he may not have accepted the illness as part of his identity. "Did you send blood work off to find out what was killing him?"

I could almost feel Tamara frown. "Those tests are expensive and the lab is constantly backlogged. The man jumped off a building. Why? Maybe he realized he was dying anyway. Maybe being a father late in life terrified him. I don't know. But regardless of his reason, his cause of death wasn't a mystery. It still isn't. He died from massive blunt force trauma when he slammed into that car."

She had a point. I considered questioning the shade again, but it was getting late and my eyes were only just recovering. Another ritual so soon would compound the damage. I could ask Mrs. Kingly, or James himself as I was sure he was still following his wife around. Of course, none of them may know if the anomalies weren't from a disease but from a spell. I ran the idea past Tamara and she sighed.

"I guess I'll have to send a sample to the lab now because I take it that you're going to tell Mrs. Kingly all of this."

I gave her a sympathetic smile that verged on a wince. "That's what she hired me to do. But even if the near inanition thing was caused by a spell, it wasn't what made him jump off that building." The darkest of magics could kill, and compulsion spells could make people do terrible things, but no compulsion spell could overcome the will to survive and make someone jump off a building. "Did any spells show up during the autopsy?"

I still couldn't see clear enough to make out Tamara's features, but I could tell by the way the brown of her hair filled the space where her face had been that she'd looked away. "I had several bodies from major cases when Mr. Kingly arrived. The detective in charge was already convinced Kingly was a jumper, and I sort of deprioritized him. If there had been any spells, they were gone by the time I examined him." She paused. "Is it possible this is some kind of elaborate scam? Could his memories have been erased after he died?"

I chewed at my bottom lip. "I'm not going to say it's impossible, but it would take some major magic. If dark magic was used to erase a living person's memory, it would be a spell aimed at the core of the person. But once the soul is gone and the STOP button is hit on a body, the magic would have to change every single cell in the body. I was at the scene within a minute or two of Kingly's death. If someone had worked a spell like that, I'd have felt it. I saw them take the body away, theoretically directly to here, so if a spell was cast on Kingly, it would had to have been during transport. But, the ghost's story matches the shade, which pretty much guarantees the shade wasn't tampered with postmortem."

"James Kingly could be in on the scheme," Tamara said, and while I had to agree it was possible, it didn't seem likely. "Or the memory wipe could have been activated while Kingly was falling from the building. That would explain the shade and ghost both having the same memory, right?"

It did. But memory wipes were nasty spells, and I surely would have felt it while at the scene. Of course, I might be a sensitive, but I was far from infallible. I'd also been distracted by Death's presence.

Still, whatever had happened, this case was definitely more complicated than a simple suicide. And I was starting to agree with Nina Kingly—it looked a hell of a lot like murder.

Chapter 7

M y eyesight had improved to a passable level by the
end of my second cup of coffee, and, after promising
that I'd help Tamara shop for wedding dresses later in the
week, we said our good-byes. Then I took the elevator up
one floor to Central Precinct proper, went through security
again, and made my way to the office of my favorite homicide detective.

"John, you busy?" I asked as I knocked on his slightly
ajar door. Then I peeked my head inside.

John Matthews, a bear-sized man with a spreading bald
spot and a mustache that up until recently had been red,
looked up from his desk. "Alex, girl, what are you doing
here?" he asked as he hastily shoved the papers on his desk
into a large file folder.

I took that as an invitation and stepped inside. "Mrs.
Kingly hired me to—"

John made a rude sound before I could finish the sentence. "That woman. She just can't accept her husband
bailed, in the final sense."

Wow, my client had certainly made an impression around
here. Not that I liked her any better, but the fact she was an
overly opinionated bigot didn't mean she was wrong.

"Actually, I think she's right, John."

He harrumphed under his breath. "Yeah, Jenson said you'd given a report to the first responding officer at the scene. Said you'd claimed to have spoken to the man's ghost and he said that he hadn't jumped. Alex, as much as that woman might not want to face the facts, the case for suicide is rock solid."

"Unless magic was involved," I said, sliding down into one of the chairs in front of his desk.

John shook his head and opened his desk drawer. He drew out a folder and passed it to me. "The day James Kingly jumped, the OMIH was surveilling a business that had been reported for gray magic. When the investigator saw Kingly climb over the railing, he snapped some photos. Kingly was alone. No one made him jump, and even I know compulsion spells can't overcome the will to survive."

The "even him" was because John wasn't just a norm, he was a null—completely devoid of any magical ability.

Perfect. I had a pretty good idea what business had been under surveillance. The damn matchmaker I'd reported. *Well, as they say, no good deed goes unpunished.*

I opened the thin file. It included little more than the responding officer's notes, a brief of the autopsy report, and two pictures, each showing a skeletally thin man. In one he was halfway over the railing. The next he was in the air and definitely not pushed because he'd jumped upward. I returned the photos and handed the file back to John. I had to admit that they were rather damning. And yet, I still had my doubts. Not just because of the shade's missing memories. The weight loss, and the fact the Kingly's hadn't mentioned he was ill, bothered me.

"I don't know how it was done yet, but the pieces don't add up," I said, and told him about the shade and the ghost missing three days of their memories, about the abnormality Tamara had found in the autopsy, and about the theories Tamara and I had batted around. None of which had a satisfactory answer. "It's worth looking into at least, isn't it?"

John ran a hand over his haggard-looking face. "Alex, I'm running a joint task force with narcotics on a triple murder. I don't have time to look into a suicide just because a shade has memory loss."

"But I don't think it was suicide."

"You have no evidence that it wasn't either."

I frowned but was forced to shake my head. If the shade had said he'd been murdered, a case would have been opened, but the shade not knowing what happened just muddied the water. With physical and eyewitness evidence pointing to suicide, I didn't have anything that could definitively prove James Kingly hadn't simply freaked out about being a father, gone out on the town for a couple days, then in a fit of guilt had someone erase his memory of the time. *But when would the spell have been cast? And how?* It could have been a potion he drank as he fell, or maybe something time-released? John was right, while it was suspicious, I couldn't prove anything.

I pursed my lips and glanced at the large folder on John's desk. "If I look into your triple—no charge—will you at least reopen the Kingly case?"

John looked away, his eyes fixed on the mostly empty pen holder on his desk. "Alex, it's not like I don't want to help, or that I don't appreciate everything you've done for the department in the past—God knows we've closed some cases we'd have never done without you, but I can't let you in on my current case."

I blinked at him for a moment. I'd met John by chance during my first year of college. He'd seen me in a cemetery chatting with a shade and asked if I could talk to murder victims as well. He'd cut some red tape to get me on the books as a consultant, and in all the years since, he'd never once refused my offer to help, especially if I waived my fee. And a triple homicide? That was big. Why would he possibly . . . ?

His eyes cut to me for a moment before darting away, and he leaned forward to straighten his stapler. "It's not personal, Alex," he said, his mustache, now nearly white, tugged down as he frowned. "It's not that you're exactly a persona non grata in the department, and you know I care for you like you're my own daughter, but you've been neck deep in two of the largest murder cases any of us have seen in as long as I've been on the force. Hell, they were my cases and I'm not even privy to all the details, I've just been told they're closed and to stop investigating. A gag order from the governor himself. All anyone here knows is that you were found in the center of two very nasty-looking ritual scenes. It hasn't exactly engendered you with the brass."

"So what you're saying is that I'm no longer on retainer for the NCPD?"

He straightened the pile of folders, pushing them up beside the stapler, and I noticed that he was, either consciously or subconsciously, building a wall of office supplies between us. "It's more that we've been told to consult you only as a last resort. We have a witness to the triple—if he ever comes down off whatever drug cocktail he's on. And there's still physical evidence to process." He added a coffee mug to the growing line of supplies. "And to complicate your position, the first round of appeals just went before the court for the Holliday trial. If they throw out the testimony of the shade, it could bring any evidence found or warrants issued from evidence shades have provided into question."

I forced my back straighter, lifting my chin, because the only other option was to slump into a miserable pile in John's chair. I was still cold from my contact with the grave, but that didn't stop burning heat from building behind my eyes, threatening to turn into tears. Two months ago I'd raised the shade of Amanda Holliday. The five-year-old's shade was the first to ever be used as a witness in the victim's own murder trial. We'd gotten a guilty verdict, and I'd known it would go through appeals, but I thought it would get me more business, not less. As for the sealed cases, I sure as hell hadn't meant to get involved in them, and wasn't I already paying a price for that involvement?

It had been several weeks since John called me in on a case, but that happened sometimes. I wasn't a shortcut for good police work, especially since the department's already overtaxed budget had to pay my fee. Sometimes a month or two passed before a case hit a wall and John called me. I'd also considered that maybe he'd heard I was recovering and was giving me time to recuperate.

It had never occurred to me that my position with the police had turned precarious.

Giving John a curt nod, I pushed out of the chair and said, "Well, I guess that's that. I'll get out of your way." Then I turned on my heels and marched toward the door.

The heavy office door was swinging shut behind me when John called my name. I stopped, trying to keep my face neutral as I turned and stuck my head back inside. "Yeah?"

John slumped in his chair, looking like what he needed most in the world was at least one good night's sleep—which it didn't look like he'd had in a long time. When he heard my voice he glanced up, finally meeting my eyes. "It's been a long time since you came by for Tuesday dinner—hell, I've missed quite a few myself, but I promised Maria I'd make it this week. Why don't you join us? You can bring what you've dug up on your suicide case. Maria will kill us if we discuss cases at the dinner table, but I've a nice bottle of Scotch. We can break it open and look over what you've got."

I stood there a minute, studying the weary lines in his face, and I was struck once again by how much he'd aged in the last few months. After a long moment I nodded, accepting the verbal olive branch he'd offered. "I'd like that."

John smiled, making his mustache twitch. "Good. It's set then. But, Alex," he said, his smile slipping. "Call first. Regardless what I promised my wife, if a new development occurs, I might not be able to break away from my case."

I nodded and waved good-bye. Then I left Central Precinct feeling only slightly less dejected by my dismissal.

I called Holly as soon as I reached the sidewalk. Central Precinct was a multipurpose building. As well as the morgue in the basement and the central police station on the lobby floor, the building housed the crime lab on the second floor, and several floors of offices, including a suite devoted to the district attorney and his staff. As an ADA, Holly would either be here or a few blocks away at the courthouse. I'd lost track of time while waiting for my vision to clear and then talking to John, and now taking the bus was no longer an option if I was going to make it back to Tongues for the Dead by six. Which meant catching a cab—not a cheap trip from the middle of downtown to the Quarter—or catching a ride with Holly if she was still around. She rarely broke away from work on time, so I gambled that there was a good chance I could skip the cab.

The phone rang. And rang.

This would be the day Holly made it to dinner on time.

I'd accepted I was going to get her voice mail when Holly finally answered. "I'm not late. It's not even dusk yet. And sunset isn't until six forty—I looked it up."

Or not.

"No worries, you're not late." *Yet.* But I kept that last bit to myself as I forced false cheerfulness into my voice. That was something I'd been doing a lot recently. Holly had always been intense, but since her misfortunate trip to Faerie and subsequent addiction to their food, she'd become down right volatile, her moods unpredictable. As she'd been kidnapped to be used as a bargaining chip against me, I felt responsible.

She hadn't admitted it, but I think sometimes part of her blamed me too.

So I weathered her bad days, both in guilt and in hopes of saving a seven-year friendship. I didn't make friends easily, though I'd clearly been doing a bang-up job of trying to lose them.

I smiled because I'd always heard people could hear a smile through the phone. "I'm actually glad you're still at work. I'm at Central Precinct and I was sort of hoping I could catch a ride with you."

"Oh," she said, the sharpness fading from her tone. "Alex, I didn't mean—"

"I know," I said, cutting her off in case she apologized. She'd been renting from Caleb even longer than I had, and as he was fae and one of the house rules was no apologies, she usually remembered. But me being fae—or enough so that I suffered their weakness of iron and could call in debts—was new to all of us. "So, can I bum that ride?"

"Yeah, of course." Papers rustled in the background. "Just let me finish what I'm working on and pack up. I'll be down in"—she paused—"fifteen minutes?"

That worked for me. We said our good-byes and hung up.

Since I had some time to kill, I dug Mrs. Kingly's contact information out of my purse. This call did go to voice mail, which was a relief. I wanted more time to consider the case before she grilled me for details. I left a message with an abbreviated breakdown of what I'd learned, without extrapolating any theories—she already hated magic. This case presented an interesting puzzle, and it was exactly the kind of investigation that the new Tongues for the Dead should be able to handle. Now I'd just have to convince Mrs. Kingly to keep me on retainer and investigate the suspicious circumstances and anomalies in her husband's alleged suicide.

I reported that the police still refused to open a homicide case, but that the medical examiner planned to look over the body again before Kingly was picked up in the morning—or at least, Tamara had said she would. She was as curious as I was. I wrapped up the message by suggesting Mrs. Kingly make an appointment to discuss the details of my findings in person. What I didn't tell her was that who I really wanted to speak with was her husband—whom I assumed still tailed her. I also didn't mention the recording of the ritual. Tamara e-mailed me a copy before I'd left, and as promised, I planned to strip the audio for Mrs. Kingly, but only if she insisted on hearing it. There was nothing she could learn from that recording except that one of the last things her husband did was lie to her. I might not particularly like the woman, but I'd spare her that pain if I could.

With my call complete, and still no sign of Holly, I

claimed one of the benches in the bit of green space surrounding Central Precinct. Closing my eyes, I tried to focus on perfecting the mental shield I'd spent the last month building. But constructing new mental shields took concentration, and mine was fractured, my thoughts circling back to my case.

The shade having absolutely no memory of the time he was missing bothered me. I'd raised a shade or two of people who had been victim to memory altering spells before, and there were always fragments of the original memory left behind. But not in this case. It was like the soul had hit pause for three days.

But how is that possible?

I knew one person who might know. Death. But even if he weren't avoiding me, there was a good chance he couldn't tell me. The collectors had a fairly rigid code of secrecy. But I still would have liked to discuss it with him, see if he could at least point me in the right direction.

"Are you out there?" I whispered. The light breeze picked up the words, carrying them away, but no jean-clad collector appeared. Not that I expected him to.

I sighed. Unless I wanted to go troll some high-risk area—like an intensive care unit—hoping someone died and that Death happened to be the collector to respond, I had no idea how to find him. He'd always found me, popping in from places unknown and leaving the same way.

I'd have to puzzle this out on my own.

So how did the memory wipe tie into the suicide? They had to be connected—the timing was too convenient otherwise. But why? And how? And most important of all, if James was an innocent victim, what kind of magic was I dealing with?

Chapter 8

❊

"What is all that?" Rianna asked, as Holly dropped a stack of books and journals on the table.

Holly's lips twisted as her nose scrunched in distaste. "Research for a case."

Rianna eyed the stack as she lifted a bowl to her lips and sipped what looked like barley soup. Holly's "fifteen minutes" had turned into an hour. I'd told Rianna to head on without us, and I was glad I had. The sun had been dipping below the horizon line as Holly and I walked into Nekros's one and only fae bar, the Eternal Bloom.

I always insisted on sitting in the back of the bar, and Rianna had secured our normal table. As I moved to take the chair against the wall, Desmond looked up from where he'd been lapping up his own bowl of soup on the floor. He gave a huff that sounded a lot like a laugh and regarded me with red eyes that betrayed his amusement that even after a month of nearly daily visits, I still chose the chair that let me watch the room.

"Hey, if you want to make fun of me, stand up straight and say it," I told the barghest.

The amusement in his doglike features bled into hostility, and he curled a lip, exposing yellow canines. Once I might have shied back, but he didn't make a sound, which meant he didn't want Rianna to know. As such, it wasn't likely he'd attack me. I shook my head at the barghest. He had a humanoid form. I knew that for a fact as I'd seen it when I'd gotten caught in the Realm of Nightmares. But whenever I saw him with Rianna—and I never saw Rianna without Desmond—he was in the form of an oversized black dog. A few weeks ago I'd started to ask why he always remained in one form, but the shaggy black dog had knocked me on my ass. I hadn't tried to ask again—though that didn't stop me from picking at him when he picked at me.

I scanned the room from my seat in the corner, fully aware that the barghest's amusement wasn't exactly inappropriate. At this point, I surveyed the room more out of habit than paranoia. The Bloom would never be my favorite place, or somewhere I felt particularly safe, but familiarity breeds acceptance. While my first couple of visits ranked right up there on my panic scale with running blindfolded through a minefield, I'd now rate our time in the Bloom more in the range of walking through a bad neighborhood at night. Caution was smart, but there was no reason to be terrified. I knew what to avoid: the fiddler playing the endless dance, the enormous tree growing through the floorboards that hid the door to the winter court—which wasn't actually a hazard unless you were avoiding the Winter Queen, which I was—and the tree's amaranthine blooms that gave the bar its name and had an enthralling effect if studied too closely.

As for the rest? Well, I barely noticed the seemingly random movement of the sun or moon above the branches of the enormous tree, and even the trolls, dryads, goblins, fauns, and all the other unglamoured fae of every size and color were becoming familiar. I hadn't spoken to many, but most were local independents who frequented the bar regularly so as I glanced around the room I recognized many of the fae. Occasionally I'd spot a changeling or a fae still wrapped in glamour, but in truth, Rianna, Holly, and I were the odd ones in this crowd.

And the other patrons treated us as such.

It had taken me a couple of weeks to realize, but the resonance of the bar changed slightly whenever strangers or court fae entered the room. And if a Fae Investigation Bureau agent arrived? The change wasn't just slight. Of course, while humans thought the FIB were a nationalized organization in charge of policing and maintaining order in the fae population, in truth each branch worked for whatever court ruled that area. That made the local division of the FIB the Winter Queen's enforcers. And I knew firsthand that the independents in Nekros had every reason to distrust her.

My quick scan of the room showed that aside from the slight disturbance from Holly's and my entrance, the atmosphere of the bar was relaxed and jovial. *Good.* I turned back to the table as Holly pulled papers out of the satchel she carried. She didn't look any more pleased by them than she had the stack of books.

"I thought you enjoyed prepping for cases," I said. She certainly used to attack the task with gusto.

She collapsed into her chair and slumped forward. "Yeah, I do. When it's *my* case. I'm sitting second chair, again, and to a junior prosecutor." She pressed the palms of her hands against her eyes, her fingers sliding into her straight red hair and making it fall forward around her face. "I *have* to get on the DA's good side again."

I didn't know what to say. Holly might not look intimidating with her heart-shaped face and pixie features, but she could dominate a courtroom and move a jury. She was in her element in trial and her talent hadn't gone unnoticed. Her career had been on the fast track. For the past year the DA had been batting her good, career-making cases. He'd even made her second chair to him in the Holliday trial, and whatever the higher court's ruling, that case was going down in history, and Holly's name was attached to it.

Then she'd gotten tied up with Faerie, and the last month had been disastrous for her career. It wasn't just the food either.

It was the damn doors.

The first time I'd visited the VIP section of the Bloom, I hadn't realized the significance of signing the ledger—on both sides of the door—and signing out again. That was a mistake. One I paid for by losing three days in the mortal realm while only an hour or two passed in the Bloom.

Now we meticulously signed the ledgers every visit, but the doors were still unpredictable. Usually we'd emerge only moments after entering, regardless of how much time we spent inside. Sometimes the amount of time that passed in the Bloom corresponded relatively equally to the time in the mortal realm—knowing precisely how close they lined up was impossible as watches weren't feasible when time rarely lined up properly. Gaining extra hours was great, and equal time was fair, but on a couple of occasions, time in the mortal realm had accelerated and passed much faster than that in the Bloom.

That was the real reason we'd missed dinner with Tamara last week. We walked in the Bloom at six, spent roughly forty-five minutes inside, and walked out to find it midnight. At least it was the same day. That wasn't the first time either. A week earlier Holly had missed a morning court date—which was why she was on the DA's shit list. It was also why she skipped breakfast now when she had morning trial.

I thought at first that we'd done something wrong, but no, the damn door was just finicky and there was nothing anyone could do about it. The fact we weren't allowed to talk about the Bloom hiding the door to Faerie didn't help, as that meant Holly was left scrambling for excuses. I wished I could offer her some solution, or even a suggestion, but I had nothing. Hell, I was barely dealing with my own issues with Faerie.

A light click-clack of approaching hooves sounded as a faun carried a tray laden with food to our table. He first placed a platter in the center of the table. The aroma of roasted lamb, spices, and rosemary wafted up from it, making my mouth water. The faun then set down steamed asparagus stalks, followed by a stack of sticky buns. When he started passing out plates, it took all my willpower to lift one gloved hand and wave mine away. Rianna claimed it with a quick "for Desmond" and a gesture to the barghest. The server only shrugged, like he didn't care one way or the other. He set down several tall, waxed leather flagons and placed a pitcher on the table. Then, without a single word, he turned and clip-clopped away.

"So what's tonight's lie?" Holly asked, dropping her hands to look at the small feast laid out across the table. Whereas I had to resist sneaking a bite, Holly picked up a thick slice of lamb and dangled it between two fingers at arm's length as if the oh-so-tender-looking meat were a sweaty sock or dead rat.

I sighed. After we'd lost half the morning two weeks ago—and Holly had lost the respect of her boss—she'd decided, illegal or not, she'd sneak Faerie food out of the Bloom. Not a lot, of course, just enough so that she'd have some options, be able to snack in the middle of the night, and maybe eat lunch at work once in while. Sneaking out food was an idea we'd discussed on multiple occasions, but Caleb had vehemently vetoed even the suggestion.

But Caleb wasn't there the night Holly had gotten the equivalent of a demotion. She was devastated and desperate, so I'd helped her smuggle out the food.

The thing no one ever told either of us about Faerie food? The reason that, more than being illegal, it was taboo to take it into the mortal realm? That's because Faerie food is real only *inside* Faerie.

The second we stepped foot into the mortal realm the roasted chicken and the half dozen sweet rolls turned into toadstools. And as if that wasn't bad enough, they almost instantly browned and shriveled into squishy, foul smelling fungus.

After that Holly had sworn off Faerie food. Completely. She'd claimed she would rather starve to death than eat glamoured toadstools. And she gave it a damn good try. She made it four days on nothing but water before Caleb finally

convinced her that she had to eat. Now she did so with re-
luctance, as if she saw those toadstools regardless what
delicious-looking dish the server set in front of her.

Holly glanced at me. "Will you at least look at it?"

And by "look" she meant See, as in through glamour. I
pressed a gloved finger against my lips. The fact I could see
through—and even break—almost any glamour wasn't a
well-known fact. Folklore was full of stories about the fae
putting out the eyes of those who could pierce glamour. I
assumed it was less of an issue now that I *was* fae, but I
didn't like taking chances.

Not that I wasn't going to look. I'd just appreciate a little
more discretion. I cracked my shield of vines, simultaneously raising the new opaque bubble I'd been forging. As
best as Caleb was able to explain it, the Bloom was a pocket
of Faerie, but not truly a part of Faerie. It was more of a
bleed-over zone for the doors between the two realms. That
said, it was still more Faerie than not, but small amounts of
planes that existed only on the mortal realm bled into the
pocket, like a thin layer of the land of the dead and a few
wisps from the Aetheric plane—neither of which existed in
Faerie proper. So when I looked at the room on a psyche
level only the smallest patina of gray filled my vision, and
the fae constructed tables and chairs remained whole, un-
damaged.

But as interesting as I always found that, it wasn't the
reason I was peering at the world through my psyche. I
wasn't sure if it was my planeweaving ability or the natural
growth of my sensitivity to magic as the fae in me emerged,
but when I opened my mind I could see magic and spells
as well as see through glamour to the truth underneath.
What I couldn't see through was glamour that reality had
accepted as real and so became not just believable, but
true.

I had no doubt that the food had started as glamour, but
Faerie had fully embraced it, and the feast spread across the
table was real—even if it hadn't always been.

"It's exactly what it looks like," I said, snapping my shields closed.

Holly nodded but stared at her plate another moment before taking a deep breath and picking up one of the sticky buns. She nibbled on the edge, as if testing to make sure it really was what it appeared to be.

I'd been so busy trying to convince Holly to eat that I hadn't noticed the drop of noise in the room as the patrons leaned close, keeping their heads down and murmuring instead of joking boisterously with goblets and flagons raised. That is, I didn't notice until Desmond pawed my leg, a quiet but menacing growl escaping his throat.

Then I noticed. Big time. The ambiance of the room hadn't turned frightened, which meant it wasn't a FIB agent causing the change, but it was definitely cautious.

Not that I had trouble spotting the man who'd caused the disturbance. His hair shimmered like crystal in the ethereal glow that emanated from somewhere under his pale skin as he strolled through the bar. He moved with the air of someone who thought all those he passed were beneath him, or perhaps, were there for his amusement. While the patrons didn't meet his eyes, many looked up after he passed and stared at the Sleagh Maith, who was enchantingly beautiful without his glamour. But he knew exactly how good he looked, which in my opinion, made him far less attractive. As did the fact I knew who he was.

Ryese. The Winter Queen's nephew.

I ducked my head, hoping he wouldn't spot me, but it was too late. He walked straight toward our table.

"Good morrow to you, Lexi," he said, using the obnoxious nickname the Winter Queen had given me after deciding, in her words, that Alex was too dreadfully masculine.

"It's evening, Reeses." Yeah, okay, intentionally mispronouncing his name just because he used a nickname I hated was childish. Sue me.

Ryese glanced up at the canopy of branches where the roof of the bar should have been. Enough light filtered through the glossy leaves to show that despite the fact dusk had fallen in the mortal realm as we entered the bar, in the Bloom the sun was in the eastern part of the sky. I didn't bother explaining myself.

"May I join you?" Ryese asked, moving Holly's stack of research.

"No," I said at the same time both Holly and Rianna said, "Yes."

Ryese smiled, taking the seat opposite me. "Quite a feast they've laid out for you. And yet, once again, you are not eating."

It wasn't a question, and I couldn't lie and say I wasn't hungry, so I simply ignored him. I was much more concerned with the fact that both Holly and Rianna were staring at Ryese like he was the last source of oxygen in the world and they needed to be near him to live.

Crap, they're bespelled.

The sad part? I doubted he'd done it intentionally. As a race, the Sleagh Maith were a lot like the ever-blooming amaranthine flowers: so pretty you couldn't help looking at them, but the more you looked, the more caught up you became. I clearly hadn't inherited that particular trait, but Ryese possessed it in spades.

At my side, Desmond nudged Rianna's knee. When she didn't react, he nudged her stomach, first gently, but when that didn't work, hard enough to knock the air out of her. She blinked, gasping for breath, and then looked around, as if she'd forgotten where she was. Desmond gave a soft whine and she blinked again.

She swore under her breath. I caught only bits of it, but what I could make out was very unflattering toward Sleagh Maith in general and Ryese in particular. I didn't take it personally. Rianna lowered her gaze, locking it on the food in front of her and as far from the glimmering fae as possible. She curled her fingers in the hair on Desmond's nape as if the barghest could keep her grounded. Then she very pointedly ignored Ryese.

Not that he noticed. This wasn't the first time he'd

crashed my dinner, and more than once he'd made it clear he regarded changelings as little more than ornamental furniture.

Was it obvious I didn't like the guy? The fact he'd carelessly bespelled two of my best friends didn't improve my opinion of him.

Unfortunately, Holly didn't have a fae guardian to bring her around. I called her name, once, twice, a third time. She didn't notice. Of course, she was closer to Ryese. Him sitting across from me put him directly beside Holly.

I shot a glare at the fae. "Can't you tone down the . . ." I waved my hand.

"You just gestured to all of me, dearest."

I gritted my teeth at the term of endearment because I wasn't his "dearest." Hell, I wasn't his *anything*. Nor did I have the least bit of interest in becoming such. I was ninety percent sure he was here because the Winter Queen sent him. She was determined to add me to her court by any means necessary, and I wouldn't put it past her to send her nephew to seduce me. Hell, she'd offered him to me once before. The fact I'd passed was why I reserved the other ten percent when it came to his motives. Ryese didn't take rejection well. When I'd turned him down, it was just possible I became a conquest to be won for his pride's sake.

Whatever his motive, he was doomed to fail. He was as trustworthy as a viper, and had an ego larger than could fit at our table. Besides, he sucked at the whole seduction thing. I just wished he'd figure that out and stop showing up uninvited.

"Glamour yourself, would you?" I said, having to force the words through my still gritted teeth.

"Afraid you can't resist me much longer?"

I laughed, I couldn't help it. "Trust me. That's never going to be a problem. But you are disturbing our meal."

Ryese's pretty face darkened with rage. His eyes, which were so pale I'd have thought he lacked irises if not for a thin ring of blue on the outer edges, narrowed, and he turned, looking at the bespelled and besotted Holly at his side. When he reached out to stroke her cheek, she moved into his hand, sighing with pleasure at his attention.

"Do. Not. Touch. Her."

Ryese didn't drop his hand, but he did turn toward me. "Dear heart, she's not the one I want to be touching."

I think he meant for the words to be suggestive, but the darkness I'd seen flash across his face when I'd laughed at him was still evident in his voice, so it sounded like the touch he wanted involved strangling me.

"You're in my seat," a deep voice said behind Ryese, and the fae whirled around.

Caleb put his hands on the back of the chair and stared at the fairer fae. Caleb wore the familiar glamour he favored. One that made him look like your average boy next door with sandy-colored hair and a friendly face. Well, typically friendly—right now his expression was as hard as the marble blocks he spent most of his time carving into decorative but powerful wards.

"I was invited," Ryese said, his tone haughty petulance. "And besides, I was here first, green man." He made the last sound like a slur, pointing out how much farther down the food chain Caleb was than the conceited son of a bitch.

"Actually, you weren't invited. I told you that you couldn't sit there," I said. "And Caleb has a standing reservation at my table, so that is, in fact, his chair."

Ryese frowned at me.

I'd been receiving a crash course in all things fae recently. Rules, laws, customs—whatever Rianna and Caleb could cram in my head. I was trying to learn and retain it. After all, knowing how to play the game was the only way I was likely to keep my freedom. Maybe the only way I'd survive. From what I understood, all Sleagh Maith were considered royals in the courts. From there each court had their own way of determining the standing of the courtiers, which mostly just made my head hurt when Rianna had explained it. One thing all courts agreed on though, was that the independent fae were at the very bottom, their rank not much higher than changelings—who were property—so that said something about how low court fae considered the independents.

My rank in Faerie's hierarchy was unclear. I was neither independent nor court fae. There was no precedent for a completely unaligned fae. In fact, the words "impossible" had come up more than once. Of course, I didn't quite fit in any of the fae boxes. In all appearance, I was born human but either became fae or the fae in me woke under the Blood Moon—I still wasn't clear on that detail. Since then, other fae sensed me as Sleagh Maith, and yet, how much of me was fae and how much human no one knew. The fact I hadn't been born tied to a court or grandfathered into the independent's vows further muddled the situation. It also lent credence to those who considered me more human than fae.

So where did that put me in Faerie's hierarchy? Caleb and Rianna had been debating that for weeks. It was pretty clear Ryese outranked me, so he could sit anywhere the hell he wanted. But he had asked, and I'd said no. Rianna and Holly had said yes, but even if I were only feykin—a mortal with fae blood—I still outranked a changeling and a human.

I could almost see Ryese weighing these facts in his mind. After whatever conclusion he came to, he rose, slow and casual-like, as if it were his own idea.

"Until next time, dearest Lexi," he said, reaching for my hand, most likely to kiss my knuckles, but he faltered when his fingers touched the stiff material of my gloves.

He'd seen them before; it wasn't like I'd been hiding my hands. There were only three reasons fae wore gloves: fashion—which for the winter court appeared to be stuck in the Tudor period, but my gloves were clearly not a part of my ensemble; the second reason was for fae in the mortal realm, as gloves protected their hands from iron, but we were in Faerie, not the mortal realm, which left the final reason a fae wore gloves and that was because Faerie took the phrase "his blood is on your hands" very seriously. I'd killed another fae, and I'd had a damn good reason to do it, but now I wore his blood.

Ryese's palms were spotless.

As he'd already taken my hand, he didn't change mid-gesture, but gave me a stiff bow, not touching more than my gloved fingers with his hand. Then he straightened, and without another word or a glance at Caleb, he turned and strolled back toward the giant tree and the door to the winter court.

Once the fae had vanished behind the trunk of the tree I turned to Caleb. "I don't think I've ever been happier to see you in my life."

The stony glare he gave me as he sank into the chair told me he didn't agree. Not at all. Then all his attention turned to Holly. She had a vague, unfocused look on her face now that Ryese was gone.

Caleb reached out and squeezed her shoulder, shaking her gently. "Holly, can you hear me?" She blinked, but her eyes didn't focus. Caleb rounded on me. "How could you let this happen?"

"I . . . What?" I stared at him. Not knowing what to say. It wasn't like I'd called Ryese over and said, *"Hey, why don't you mesmerize my friend?"* I realized my jaw had dropped, my mouth slightly open, and I snapped it closed, my teeth hitting with enough force to resonate up my jawbone. I crossed my arms over my chest and met Caleb's accusatory glare. "What was I supposed to do? Ryese just showed up."

"You're supposed to protect her while she's here." Caleb's glamour was slipping, making the angry slit of his mouth cut farther across than humanly possible, and blackness bled into his eyes as a greenish tint showed through his tan.

I gulped. I'd seen Caleb this pissed before, but never had his anger been aimed at me. Some primal part of my brain told me I needed to back away, to get away from the monster transforming in front of me.

Beside me, the legs of Rianna's chair screeched as she pushed away from the table. "I'm going to . . ." She pointed to the door to Faerie. "See you at the office tomorrow," she called over her shoulder as she and Desmond all but ran from the table.

I didn't blame her.

Unfortunately, regardless of what that primitive fight or flight part of my brain told me, running wasn't an option. I swallowed again and focused on making my voice flat, emotionless—or at the very least, not riddled with fear. I didn't quite succeed as I said, "What should I have done, Caleb? Jump across the table and stab him? Or maybe you think I should have let him take me to the winter court so he wouldn't be a threat to Holly?"

"You—"

But whatever he was going to say was cut short when Holly mumbled something, the words so quiet I couldn't hear them. Apparently Caleb couldn't either.

"What was that?" he asked, his voice gentle as he squeezed her shoulder.

She still wasn't focusing on anything.

"He's so pretty," she said, her tone distant and wistful. Then she turned *toward* me, but didn't exactly focus *on* me. "He wants you, Alex. It would make him happy. You should definitely go for it."

The last sentence sounded like the Holly I knew and used to barhop with. The middle bit? Not so much.

I moved to the seat Rianna had vacated so that I'd be directly across from her. "Hey, Hol, you in there? Snap out of it."

Caleb frowned at me again, but Holly blinked. Then blinked again. Her eyes narrowed. "Wasn't someone else here?" She blinked rapidly and then gulped hard enough I could see her throat working. "Al, I feel kind of strange."

"Need a bucket strange or need a drink strange?" Oddly enough, that wasn't the first time in our friendship I'd asked that question.

"Drink. Definitely a drink." She shook her head as if the movement would help clear it. Then she seemed to notice Caleb for the first time, and the fact he still gripped her shoulder, worry written over his not-quite-human face. Holly's head tilted to the side, her expression still not sharp, but closer to clear. "What are you doing here?" she asked Caleb. "And what's with the freaky half glamour?"

He stared at her for several seconds before releasing her shoulder and sinking into his chair. Then he pulled the entire platter of the remaining lamb in front of him and grabbed a thick hunk of the meat.

"I'm here," he said between bites and his now fully black eyes cut over in my direction, "because a particular FIB agent mandated an inspection of my workshop 'due to reports of possible suspicious behavior.'"

I cringed. Another raid?

"This has to stop, do you understand me, Alex?"

Again he was making me responsible for someone else's actions.

"Exactly what do you want me to do, Caleb?" I asked, my voice low. Falin might be conducting the raids, but we both knew it was the Winter Queen ordering them and they weren't likely to stop unless I joined her court.

Caleb shoved the platter away. "I don't know. Figure something out. I'd hate to be forced to evict you, but this is intolerable."

Something in my chest clenched, stealing my air, preventing me from speaking.

Holly gaped at Caleb. "You can't mean that?"

He didn't answer her.

"Caleb?" I said, squeezing the word out. My voice was thin. If he kicked me out . . . I'd lived in Caleb's house for over seven years. I'd say he and Holly were like family, except I didn't like my family. I cared about my friends a lot. I didn't have any idea where I'd go if he made me leave. And I'd just put all my money into renting the office for Tongues for the Dead. I didn't even have the money for a deposit if I had to go on an emergency apartment hunt.

Caleb frowned at me for what felt like forever; then he dropped his head and rubbed a hand over his face. The green faded from his skin, his glamour solidifying. "Just go, Al."

Go? My throat closed. He really was kicking me out?

He looked up and whatever he saw in my face made his expression soften. "Home, Al. Go home."

Oh.

"And attend the revelry in a few days. You need to see more of Faerie so you can choose your damn alignment and stop this madness."

I had no idea what to say. So I nodded and then did as he asked and left.

Chapter 9

⊷⊶⊜ ⊜⊶⊷

I wasn't sure what I'd find when I returned home. The raids had been progressively worsening. Caleb was right—it was ridiculous. And yet, as I got off at the bus stop and walked toward the house, I hoped Falin would be there. That I'd see him. Or at least, part of me wished that. The smarter part knew it would only hurt if he were still at the house. But I guess it was better than hoping I'd spot Death on the way home. At this point, that would require wishing someone dead.

My car was the only vehicle in the driveway when I reached the house, and only a Chinese crested greeted me at the door. I hated how disappointed I was by that fact. Falin had the irritating tendency to enter my life like a whirlwind, stirring up emotions, and then leaving just as quickly. Right now he was out. Again. I sighed. Pining over men I couldn't have? That wasn't me.

"You're the only man I need in my life, right Prince Charming?" I said, picking up my little six-pound dog. PC licked my nose, the white plume of his tail wagging. *See, I have puppy love. I don't need prince mysterious or prince unpredictable.*

Yeah, tell that to the ache in my chest.

I glanced around my apartment. The drawers with

clothes hanging precariously out of them and open cabinets were proof the FIB had swept my room in their raid. Oh, it had looked worse than this before, but it hadn't been a mess when I left this morning. That was due entirely to the fact that when I'd inherited Coleman's castle, I'd also inherited the brownie and garden gnome who lived there, or more accurately, they'd inherited me. Faerie might say the castle was mine, but the brownie, Ms. B, ran the place and had long before Coleman owned it. Throughout history and folklore, brownies bonded to the land or to a family. Burn a brownie's home to the ground and they'd tend the ashes. A family brownie would follow the bloodline, even when they didn't wish it to.

Ms. B had always been a land-bound brownie, but for reasons I couldn't begin to understand, she seemed to like me. I rarely saw her, but for the last month my apartment had been consistently cleaner than in the last seven years I'd lived here. I sighed as I scanned the mess. *Great.* The room looked more trashed than searched, and I walked around the room pushing things back in drawers and sliding them shut, PC following at my heels.

When I passed the bed, I froze, a splash of color catching my eye. I turned. Thoughts about the mess scattered as if they'd never been there as my attention narrowed to a bloodred rose lying on top of my white pillowcase.

I sank onto the bed, staring, waiting for the rose to vanish. To prove to be a figment of my imagination.

But it didn't.

I reached out a tentative hand and touched the velvety smoothness of a petal so deep a red it verged on black. I'd never considered myself a flower girl, and with my dating habits, it wasn't like I'd received many, but I couldn't help smiling as I stared at this single, solitary rose. I picked it up gingerly, mindful of the large, curved thorns running the length of the stem right up to the rose's delicate bloom.

Appropriate.

I hoped to find a note, or message, or anything, but there was just the rose. I frowned. *If I were a note, where would I hide?* I glanced at the stack of mail on my counter—or what had been a stack of mail. Now it was scattered over the countertop and littered across the floor

Oh crap. That stack was where I'd tucked Falin's business card. I'd considered programming his cell number in my phone, but I was afraid I'd be tempted to call him and I didn't want to hear the cold tone of his voice. So I'd hidden the card from myself among piles of other papers, junk mail, and flyers. Now I dug through the scattered pages, searching.

No. No. No. It wasn't there. Did one of the agents find it? Had they seen the scrawled number on the back and reported Falin to the queen? *Crap, oh—wait.*

There, tucked between a get well card and a coupon for pizza, was the card. Relief washed over me as I picked it up. Then I just stood there, rose held carefully in one hand and Falin's card in the other.

Behind me, PC whined.

Oops. I'd gotten so distracted, I hadn't walked him yet and he likely had one very full puppy bladder.

"Sorry, little guy," I said, pocketing the card. "We'll go out as soon as I get this in water."

Not that I owned a vase. I filled a chipped drinking glass with water and set the rose inside. Then I grabbed PC's leash and took him for a much needed potty break, all the while fingering Falin's card in my pocket.

I spent the rest of the night on the Dead Club forums searching for anyone with experience with shades missing memories. Most old posts I ran across were the expected: dementia, long-term brain damage, even a couple of posts about memory spells—though none that occurred as close to death as in the case of James Kingly.

I started a new thread, detailing the more unusual points of the case without revealing enough that anyone would guess my client's identity. Not that anyone of the Dead Club was local. To the best of my knowledge, Rianna and I were the only grave witches in Nekros currently and the next closest lived more than a hundred miles to the east in Atlanta. But I still kept the finer points and the exact nature of Kingly's suicide vague to protect my client's privacy. I went ahead and added a line or two about the medical abnormalities discovered in autopsy, as well as the peculiar weight loss. With our affinity for the dead, some grave witches went into fields dealing directly with bodies. If I was lucky, I'd find another medical examiner who'd seen these same oddities paired with memory loss.

But I wasn't lucky.

The boards were crowded, so my thread received ample attention, but most of the responses were more question than answer. Unfortunately, they were all questions I'd already asked myself, so not much help. Some users offered theories, and while I appreciated their out of the box thinking, the ideas were clearly not fully thought out. Such as the user who suggested that my client had died that first night, at the time of the memory loss, but his body had been guarded from collectors for three days until his suicide was staged and the soul allowed to be collected.

At first blush, not a terrible theory. If killed inside a circle or inside a cemetery or some other place a collector couldn't traverse, a soul could get stuck inside a dead body until the body decayed so far the—usually already faded— ghost popped free without the assistance of a collector. But for the theory to work one would have to overlook the fact that Kingly had definitely jumped off the top of the building, not been a dead body tossed over the side. And the memory loss? A soul trapped inside a body still recorded what was happening. Being dead it couldn't see or hear, but it would be aware of the body decaying around it. Kingly's shade hadn't recounted anything like that. From what he'd said, he'd died from the fall. Besides, Tamara would have noticed if the body had been several days dead before hitting the roof of that car.

Sadly, that theory was the most plausible suggested. And

it was impossible. I left the thread active, just in case, but logged off for the night. Then I collapsed onto my bed, still fully dressed.

It was after two, and I was tired, but the conflicting and seemingly impossible details of the case buzzed around my mind. The fact Kingly had jumped off that building was undeniable. But was it suicide or murder? Had something happened in the three missing days that would have driven the man to kill himself? It was possible. Seemingly more possible than murder as not even the darkest blood or death magic could overpower one's sense of self-preservation. And what about the memory loss? I'd heard rumors about agents whose knowledge was so classified that each carried a spell in his or her body that would obliterate the shade in the event of death. No shade meant no way to extract secrets postmortem.

But Kingly was a norm—would he have considered the fact that whatever happened during that missing time wouldn't die with him? The timing of the missing memories was highly suspect as well. Not so much when the memory loss began, but when it ended and the shade started recording again. If Kingly had acquired some charm or potion to erase his own memory, the logical time for him to activate it would be on the roof, or after he jumped as he might not have remembered he wanted to jump if he activated the spell too early. The shade didn't remember the roof. Or the fall. No, the memories started again *after* hitting the car. According to Tamara, medical death had occurred *on* impact. So medically, Kingly was dead before his soul started recording again.

Then there was the fact I hadn't felt any magic at the scene. Granted I hadn't gotten very close and the Quarter has its own ambiance of never-ending magic that numbed my sensitivity. But Tamara hadn't felt any trace of a spell either, and a spell that could do what was done to Kingly? It had to be huge, which should have made it hard to miss.

Unless it wasn't a spell.

What was it Conan Doyle's fictional Baker Street sleuth had said: "Once you eliminate the impossible, whatever remains, no matter how improbable, must be the truth."

What if I wasn't looking for a solution in witch magic at all, but one in fae magic? Though he was dead, I knew of at least one fae who could steal bodies and walk around in their skin. Of course, when he stole a body he ejected the body's soul, taking its place. Kingly's soul had been inside his body until the end. *Unless it was removed and then reinserted?* But was that possible? And if it was, wouldn't Kingly's ghost remember the missing three days? *And wouldn't the body have started decaying as soon as the soul was removed?*

Again I wished I had a way to contact Death. He may or may not answer my questions about whether a soul could be removed and returned, but at least I'd have someone to talk to and bounce ideas off. I'd heard Caleb and Holly return hours ago, but I hadn't dared go downstairs. So now, completely alone aside from the dog snoring lightly on the pillow beside me, I reviewed everything I knew again, tried to examine it from different angles. Any way I looked at it, nothing fit.

I frowned at my ceiling. Maybe I was making this too complicated. Witch magic could explain the memory wipe but not the compulsion to jump, but maybe fae magic could overcome self-preservation? I'd never heard of anything like that, but folklore was filled with stories of fae tricking mortals to their death. Of course, they usually made things that weren't there appear through glamour, like a guiding light hanging several feet past the edge of a cliff.

I stopped. Could that be it? Could Kingly remember being at the bar and then being dead because he was experiencing a glamoured illusion of the bar? Maybe the days weren't missing. I just hadn't asked him to recount the correct events. If he'd been trapped in an illusion, he could have thought he was climbing off his barstool or walking across the room when he "jumped" off the building. Except, if that was the case, where was he during the missing days?

I had no idea. But I knew someone who might.

I dug the business card out of my pocket and flipped it over, staring at the number. *He did say to call about trouble involving fae.* I couldn't be positive my case did, but I finally had a legitimate excuse to contact Falin.

Chapter 10

I checked that I'd entered the correct number three times before I tapped the CALL button, my heart thudding hard enough I felt it in my throat. It rang once, twice.

I hit END. My breath fast for no good reason.

What are you doing, Alex? I was just calling him about business, right? It had nothing to do with the fact I wanted to hear his voice. *Yeah, even I can't convince myself of that.*

It would be smarter not to call. To avoid all contact until I forgot about him. Not like that would be easy with the weekly raids or him leaving roses on my pillow. I glanced at where the rose sat in its chipped glass on my bed stand and a shiver of excitement tingled through me. I closed my eyes, my body reacted to the memory of our last kiss, my skin tightening and my breath catching, even though I didn't want to remember.

And of course, thinking about the fact I didn't want to think about it only made everything worse. My heart raced, encouraging the giddy feeling in my chest and my palms dampened with nerves. What, was I fourteen again? This was pathetic.

There were two men I was currently interested in. And the fact of the matter was that I couldn't have either of them. *So get over it, Alex, and make the damn business call.*

At least Falin had a phone. Short of a suicide attempt, I couldn't call Death.

I hit redial before I had a chance to change my mind again. The call was answered on the first ring.

"Andrews," a deep voice, rough with sleep, said as way of greeting.

"Falin?"

There was a pause, then, without a hint of the earlier grogginess, "Alexis."

My name, my true name, was a whisper from his lips, as if he barely dared to believe I'd called, and as if the one word were so much more. I used to hate my given name, used to hear my father's disinterested or disapproving tone in each syllable. But Falin made my name sound intimate, like a caress.

I shivered, though it was warmth, not a chill, that flushed my skin. On the other side of the phone I heard him move, most likely to sit up, and I imagined the sheets falling away to pool at his hips. Okay, yeah, he was naked in my imagination. *So pathetic.* And not conducive to finding out the information I needed.

Right. Kingly. The case. Focus on that.

But when I opened my mouth, regardless of my intentions, what I blurted out was, "I got the rose."

Smooth.

And worse? The phone was silent. He'd hung up.

Damn the queen and her edict.

I hit REDIAL, too angry to bother thinking it through.

"This better have something to do with the fae," he said without a word of greeting. The warmth present in his voice when he'd first said my name was gone. Now his tone was hard, professional.

It stung. Even if I knew why. The rule was no fraternizing. Shop talk only.

So I got down to business and told him everything I knew about the events surrounding Kingly's death. Falin stopped me a few times for clarification, but mostly he just listened. When I finished, he was silent long enough that I checked to make sure he hadn't hung up again.

No, we were connected.

"Falin? Are you there? Could a fae be behind this?"

He answered my question with a question. "The police are not looking into this as anything more than a suicide?"

"Since the shade can't say he was murdered, no, they won't open an investigation."

Silence again. Thick, and heavy, even through the phone. Moments dragged, as if he were putting off what he didn't want to say. And I soon understood why—it certainly wasn't anything I wanted to hear.

"There is no reason for the FIB to get involved in the case."

"But—" I started.

He cut me off.

"If the FIB opens an investigation, even discreetly, it would imply we believed the fae or fae magic was involved. Even if an investigation proved otherwise, the humans would be suspicious of the next suicide and many more after that. Do you know how many people attempt suicide every hour in this country? It reeks of a potential political nightmare."

My free hand curled into a fist, my nails biting into my palm. "So because no one is questioning Kingly's death, it's okay to let a murderer go free so that it doesn't create bad press for your queen."

"This is not an FIB matter." Cold. Hard. Matter of fact. There would be no arguing.

And it hurt. *Sticks and stones my ass.* It wasn't even the words, it was his tone that could cut.

"Fine," I sounded defensive. I could hate it, but I couldn't help it. "Can you at least tell me if there are any fae in the city capable of the kind of magic it would take to force a mortal to commit suicide?"

"Ask your green man."

"I can't. Caleb is currently pissed and threatening to evict me because of your raids."

The silence was different this time. Sharper, with an edge of surprise. Then he sighed and I could imagine him running his fingers through his long blond hair the way he did when lost in troublesome thoughts.

"Some fae can intensify emotion, turning irritation into rage or sadness into despair," he finally said. The hardness had left his voice, in its place what could be described only as weariness, but not actually friendship. "And as you guessed, some fae can create illusions so flawless a mortal could walk into their death while seeing something benign. But force a man to jump from a building using compulsion?" He paused. "No, our magic could no more do that than a witch's could."

I wanted to thank him. I opened my mouth to do just that. Then I closed it again. It would be reckless and foolish to create a debt over a bit of information. Falin belonged to the Winter Queen. If I was indebted to Falin, she was the one who could call it in.

"Okay." The word was flat, not showing the appreciation I wanted, but I was tired. This conversation, this *game* we were playing—it was too hard.

"Anything else?" he asked.

Yes. I had so many questions. But none pertained to the case. "No."

He paused a long moment, then said, "Sleep well, Alexis," his voice once again warm, soft.

I tried to savor the kindness in that tone. To let it take away the sting and the awkwardness of our conversation, to let it remind me that he wasn't avoiding me on purpose.

It wasn't enough.

And yet, I'd call again if I could. I knew I would.

"G'night," I whispered.

Too late. He was already gone.

"That sounded tense."

I whirled toward the direction of the voice. Roy sat in the

corner of the room, slowly and deliberately picking up one block at a time.

"How much did you hear?"

The ghost shrugged and a green block with the letter B on it slid through his fingers. He let out a string of curse words that made my ears burn.

"Leave them," I said. "I'll gather your blocks and take them to your broom closet in the morning."

"You mean my *office*."

Nope, I'd meant broom closet, but I kept my mouth shut. If he wanted to call it an office, it would be an office. Stretching my arms over my head, I yawned, and my jaw popped. Clearly I'd been gritting my teeth too much lately. Though if that was Ryese's fault or the fact the case kept leading me in circles, I couldn't be sure.

"I'm going to bed," I told the ghost, which by long-standing agreement, signaled that he had to leave. "Wish me a solution to this puzzle in my sleep as opposed to good dreams, will you?"

"Case not going well?"

"Understatement." Though in truth, I didn't have a case. Not yet at least. I'd been hired only to perform a ritual, but I was invested in this mystery so I hoped Nina Kingly would hire me to continue the investigation.

"Anything I can do. I am a private investigator, after all."

I rolled my eyes. I'd given him an office and now he was a PI? "Roy, you know you have to have a license to be a PI in Nekros, right?"

"So what, I need to take a test?"

I yawned again, my eyes momentarily tearing from exhaustion "Yeah, a test. And about forty hours of classes, which, as the teacher wouldn't be able to see you, you would be hard-pressed to prove you attended."

"That's discrimination."

"Well, you could gather a bunch of ghosts and protest discrimination against the corporeally challenged. Unfortunately, no one would notice."

He frowned, but the look wasn't just unamused, it was . . . frightened?

I'd been headed to the bathroom to brush my teeth, but that look stopped me. It also made me remember how Roy had acted around James earlier in the day.

"You don't get along with other ghosts, do you?"

"You wouldn't either, if you were dead."

"You're right. Ghosts are intolerable," I said, giving him a pointed look. I was tired. It was time for bed.

His frown didn't change, if anything, it etched itself deeper in his face. "A better word would be insatiable."

Huh?

"You ever see a ghost fade?" he asked, wrapping his arms around his chest as if holding himself together.

I nodded. Most cemetery haunts were so faded they no longer remembered who they'd once been.

"Yeah, well, there's only one way to keep from fading, and that's to maintain a certain level of leftover life force. By whatever means necessary."

I had the feeling I didn't like where this was going.

"I'm guessing not too many ghosts attach themselves to planeweaving grave witches who pump them full of power?"

Roy stared at me, the unmistakable "duh" written across his face.

I swallowed, forgetting how tired I was. "So ghosts cannibalize each other for their life force?"

He nodded.

That was . . . well, I had a lot of deplorable words to describe it, but what made my skin crawl was much more personal. I saw a soul being sucked dry in my nightmares. And not my soul, because I was the cannibal. The scary part was that the nightmare wasn't just a bad dream. It was a memory. Yeah, there was a reason I had blood on my hands when I visited Faerie.

"So when you and Kingly were sizing each other up . . . ?"

"Hey, I've got you," Roy said. "I was just making sure he wasn't going to jump me. Something's obviously been sucking on him. If I didn't know better, I'd guess he'd been dead years, not a week."

Interesting. "Can you be more specific?"

"Not really. Might have been another ghost, but I'm thinking something nasty from the waste. Everything is energy in the land of the dead, and most of the really bad stuff hangs out in the wastelands."

I'd read that last bit in school years ago. It was why grave magic should be performed only in a circle.

"So what makes you think something ate part of our ghost?" I asked, leaning against the bathroom doorjamb.

"Are you kidding? He's newly dead so he should be at the strongest he'll ever be unless he starts hunting and draining other ghosts. Instead he looks like someone stuck a straw in him and sucked out a chunk of his core. Kind of weird though. It's like he's fading from that one section outward. Sort of like how rot spreads."

I stared at Roy. *Well, maybe he does deserve his own office.* I certainly hadn't noticed anything odd about Kingly's ghost. Granted, what he'd said only added one more question to my already long list, but maybe if I knew the right questions to ask, I'd hit the right answer.

Chapter 11

❧✦❧

Nina Kingly was waiting for me when I arrived at Tongues for the Dead the next morning. Clearly she'd missed the part of my message about making an appointment. In fact, there was only one portion of my message she appeared to have heard.

"What do you mean they have pictures of James alone on the roof? I want to see them," she said before I could so much as insert my key in the lock.

I waited until I'd unlocked the place and turned on the lights before answering. "I don't have the photos. They are part of the official police file."

She stared at me with too much of the whites of her eyes showing. "I need to sit down," she said, her voice wispy, breathless.

Crap, I was about to have a pregnant woman hyperventilate in my office.

Grabbing her by the elbow, I guided her to the second-hand love seat in the lobby. She collapsed onto it.

"It's true. It's all true," she said between gasps, her arms wrapped under the bulge of her stomach. "He left us."

Her husband's ghost knelt at her side. "I didn't, sweetie. I didn't. Calm down. Please calm down."

But she wasn't calming. Her breaths were fast, shallow.

The ghost twisted around, looking right at me. "Do something."

Like what?

I knelt beside him. "Mrs. Kingly?"

She didn't even look at me.

"Nina, you've got to calm down," I said, touching her arm.

No reaction. *What will happen to the baby if she passes out?* I was guessing nothing good. I had to get her calm.

Except she didn't know me. Wasn't responding to a thing I said. I briefly considered manifesting her husband, but seeing the ghost might shove her over the edge. That left me with one other option. One I wasn't sure would work but was positive she'd despise.

She can bitch at me after she's calm.

I unhooked my charm bracelet and pulled on her arm so I could clasp it around her wrist. She didn't fight me, which was probably a bad sign.

"What are you doing? Help her," the ghost yelled.

"I am."

My bracelet contained mostly shields, but I had a couple of other charms I kept on reserve. One of which was a spell I used when I couldn't calm myself enough to center and project my psyche into the Aetheric. It was like a double dose of Xanax and an hour's worth of meditation all rolled into a couple of seconds. Clamping my hand around her wrist so that I pressed the charm against her skin, I channeled a trickle of magic from my ring, activating the charm.

Nina Kingly stilled. She leaned back against the love seat, her body going limp, boneless as she took a long, slow breath. Her head rolled to the side, and she looked at me, making a sound that may have been a moan or a really elongated "Oh."

"That's nice," she said, smiling and sinking farther into the love seat—which I wouldn't have said was possible until she did it. "Did you know your eyes glow?"

She didn't sound the least bit disturbed by that fact.

"What did you do?" James asked, his hands clenched at

his sides as he looked from me to his now placid and listless wife.

"I calmed her," I said, reclaiming my charm bracelet.

As soon as the clasp closed around my wrist, Mrs. Kingly's brow scrunched together, but she didn't lift her head from where it lolled against the back of the couch.

"The lights went out," she mumbled, staring at me.

Okay. Clearly too much happy charm for her.

"Mrs. Kingly, do you remember what we were talking about earlier?" I asked, standing across from her.

She nodded, the movement so exaggerated it would have been comical if it hadn't accompanied her saying, "James killed himself."

"That's what the police believe," I said, "but there are a lot of pieces that don't add up."

"You mentioned that on the phone" she said, her words slurred.

Right. She was out of it. I wanted her to consider what I'd found and hire me to continue investigating, and right this moment she probably would have. But it would be an agreement under magical influence, which was not only unethical. It was illegal.

Which meant any business talk was going to have to wait.

"Well, when you're feeling up to it, if you would like to talk about what I found, I'm going to be in my office," I said, and when she only smiled, added, "It's right through that door." I pointed, but her expression didn't change.

Okay then.

I turned toward the ghost. "May I speak with you privately?"

James looked from his wife to me and back. For a moment I thought he'd refuse, and I'd have understood, Nina was in a rather . . . odd state of mind. But no matter how out of it she appeared, I didn't think she would miss me questioning what to her would appear as thin air. I'd already said more to the ghost in front of her than I should have, but I hoped she wouldn't remember.

After another moment of hesitation, the ghost nodded and followed me to my office. I shut the door behind us so that my voice wouldn't carry to the woman in my lobby. When she came to, I didn't want her to hear me and think I was talking to myself. Coming off as crazy isn't a good way to impress clients.

"You can have a seat," I told him as I stepped around my desk. "If the chair is there for you, that is."

The ghost looked at the two chairs. "I don't think they'd hold."

I only shrugged. Roy could sit in them, but he was pretty juiced up on my energy half the time. This ghost, on the other hand, appeared less substantial than he had the day before. I remembered what Roy had said about the ghost looking like something had sucked part of Kingly out from the inside. I didn't spot it at first, but then I saw the softball-sized area that was slightly less substantial than the rest of him.

"Your shade confirmed your story," I told him, not surprised when he gave me a dull look in return. While I might have doubted him, he'd known he wasn't lying. "The fact that your memory goes from the bar to being dead with three days missing in between makes me think you didn't kill yourself, regardless of all the evidence to the contrary. The problem is, no magic I know of could force you to throw yourself off a building. Can you think of anything, anything at all, that could have happened at the bar or directly after you left that you'd be so ashamed of that you'd be forced to erase your own memory and jump off a building?"

"Of course not! I've never been suicidal in my life."

"So you don't have any deep dark secrets that could have threatened to come to light? Gambling debts? Drug use? Mistresses? Love child?"

"No. I'm devoted to my wife and if you brought me in here just to slander my character, I'm leaving."

"Calm down, Mr. Kingly. I'm just trying to eliminate possibilities," I said, opening a new document in my computer labeled JAMES KINGLY. After adding a line about his claim to sainted behavior, I looked up again and said, "How was work? Was there any tension in the office?"

"There's tension in every office, but nothing unusual. I got along with most of my coworkers and tolerated the rest."

I added *"No work problems"* to the file. And I knew from previous conversations with Mrs. Kingly that money wasn't an issue. I frowned.

"What about your disease. Where you having trouble managing it? Or maybe you couldn't face the idea of having passed it to the baby?"

"What are you talking about? I was as healthy as an ox. I hadn't been sick since—" The chime on the door sounded and the ghost whirled around, ready to charge back into the lobby.

"It's my partner," I said, recognizing Rianna's magic. I added *"denies being sick"* to James's file.

A light tap sounded on my door, which opened a moment later, allowing Rianna to poke her head into my office. "Did you know there's a drunk pregnant lady in our lobby?"

"She's not drunk. She's . . ." I hesitated. "Calm."

Rianna lifted both eyebrows, giving me an incredulous look. "She's more than calm. What happened?"

"She was hyperventilating so I used my meditation charm on her. It seems something went a little awry."

"A little?" She shook her head. "You want me to look her over, see if I can help?"

I didn't have time to consider her offer before James raised a fist, shaking it at both of us. "No more magic." If ghosts had color, I think he'd have turned red. "Hasn't it done enough harm? This is why it should be more closely regulated and witches—"

I stopped listening to his Humans First diatribe; I'd heard it all before. To Rianna I said, "The effects can't last much longer, so just let it wear off naturally."

With a shrug that screamed "If you say so" Rianna ducked back out of the room, shutting the door behind her.

Once she was gone, I turned back to James Kingly.

"What made you decide you needed a drink on your way home from work? Was that habit? Something someone who knew your schedule would expect?"

The ghost shook his head, but he didn't elaborate.

"Well, if you have no problems at work and no problems at home, why did you lie to your wife and go out for a drink?"

I could have sworn the pale, shimmery face drained of what little color the ghost had. "I . . . saw something." He swallowed, his Adam's apple bobbing hard. "I just needed to get it out of my head."

The ghost's penchant for vagueness was becoming irritating.

"What did you see?"

"It was . . ." He shook his head and collapsed into one of the chairs. Or at least, he tried to. He'd been right about it not holding him and he slid straight through to the ground.

I stepped around my desk and helped the shaken ghost to his feet. He held on to my hand longer than what would be considered polite, long enough that I wanted to tug free, but I knew exactly why he did it and that he wasn't trying to be rude or sexual. He was just trying to understand.

"Why is it I can touch you but no one else? I mean, no one. I keep trying. No one but you even sees me," he said, his voice full of wonder laced with sorrow.

"That's a long story." One we didn't have time for because his wife would surely come around soon. I returned to my chair on the other side of the desk. "Now, what is it you saw?"

The ghost stepped backward, his face scrunching and his lips disappearing as he chewed at them.

"I need to know, Mr. Kingly. If you stumbled into a dark magic ritual or—"

"No, nothing like that. It was just a horrible, horrible tragedy." He glanced down at the chair again, as if he wished he could sit, but he didn't try again. "I was at the gas station, filling up my car, when a man carrying an empty plastic milk carton walked up to me. He asked if I could fill it for him.

Gas is so expensive right now, but this guy, he was in bad shape. All skin and bones. And the clothes he wore? They couldn't have been his. It looked like what he really needed was a hot meal, not gas, but I filled the jug for him. I even offered him a little money, and I never do that. He refused the money and thanked me for the gas. He was so polite." James paused, his eyes distant with memory.

"Then what?" I asked, because if a homeless person's appearance prompted him to drink, he was a hell of a lot less stable than he liked to let on.

"He . . . he took his jug of gas and walked out into the middle of the street. Then he dumped the entire gallon over his head, letting it run down him, soaking his clothes. He pulled a cigarette out of his coat pocket. Then a lighter." The ghost's Adam's apple quivered. "The flames moved so fast. One moment he was dripping in the middle of the street, the next he was covered in flames." He paused again, chewing at his lip. "I thought it was a prank at first. I think we all did. Because he stood there, not making a sound. I assumed it had to be magic. Maybe some sort of charm that prevented fire from burning flesh, they have those, right?"

I didn't interrupt him to tell him that no charm, no matter how powerful, would allow someone not to be burned by that sort of proximity to fire.

"People were pouring out of nearby stores and businesses to see this man standing perfectly still while covered in flames. He must have been burning for a full minute, and we were all watching him, when all of a sudden, he started screaming and running around, flailing his arms. No one knew what to do. We ran from the gas station because if the fire got near those pumps . . ." He shivered. "But he never made it that far. His screams stopped almost as suddenly as they started, and he collapsed. This flaming heap that smelled of burnt hair and charred flesh. It was . . . I needed that drink."

"How long before that second drink and your last memory did this incident occur?"

"Incident? It was a fucking nightmare. It was terrible.

The man was so nice. So polite. I had no idea he'd use the gas *I* gave him to kill himself. What was he thinking? Why would anyone want to go out that way?"

I didn't have answers for any of those questions, but it was certainly interesting that my suicide victim had witnessed a suicide.

He'd talked to the man directly before the stranger had flambéed himself. Kingly obviously felt sympathetic toward him, and guilty he'd given him the gas. Could Kingly have been suffering from some sort of shock? Sort of a posttraumatic stress that left him wandering without any memory. Maybe he did kill himself?

Though shouldn't the shade have some sort of memory of that time? Even if it were jumbled? Besides, would someone in a state of shock go out for a meal including veal and a hundred dollar bottle of wine? That didn't fit.

I tapped a pen against the desk, beating out an uneven rhythm as I thought.

I had two very public suicides. It was strange, though the real question was did the first suicide act as a catalyst for the second? Was it James's tipping point? A coincidence?

Or was it a pattern?

Chapter 12

I'd have liked to ask James more questions about the suicide he'd witnessed, but we'd run out of time. My door flew open, revealing a fuming Mrs. Kingly.

"I should sue you," she said, moving faster than I thought a person could at a waddle. "How dare you use magic on me." Then she collapsed into one of my chairs, wrapped her arms around her belly, and began weeping. Not just crying, but loud, body-shaking sobs.

I sat at my desk, my pen hanging frozen in the air, and stared at her. *What do I say now?* Hell, more than say, what was I supposed to do? I glanced at her husband, but he looked as lost as me.

Across the lobby, Rianna's door opened as she stepped out, staring at the wailing woman in my office. I jumped from behind my desk, and all but fled the room. Rianna met me halfway across the lobby.

"Now what did you do to her?"

"Nothing," I whispered, my voice a hiss.

We both looked at the sobbing woman in my office.

"So what are you going to do?"

I frowned. "Remember to buy tissue," I said, and then stepped around Rianna and headed for our small bathroom.

I pulled a few sheets off the roll of toilet paper and turned, but even three rooms away—granted small rooms with all the doors open—I could still hear her crying. I glanced at the paltry wad of single ply toilet paper in my hand. *Oh hell.* I unhooked the entire roll, taking it back to my office with me.

I set the roll on my desk and handed Mrs. Kingly the loose wad I'd already pulled free. She took it with a trembling hand and blew her nose. The loud sound seemed almost profane coming from the uptight, proper woman. Making sure the roll of toilet paper was within her reach, I placed my wastebasket beside her and then retreated behind my desk.

By the time I'd claimed my chair, she had the roll of toilet paper in her lap. She blew her nose again, a loud, honking sound. I made a point of not watching her, but woke my laptop and wrote down every detail I could remember from James's report on the suicide he'd witnessed. When I reached Kingly's description of the man I stopped. He'd called him skeletally thin. *Which is exactly how I described James in the photos John showed me.* I put an asterisk beside the words before moving on.

By the time I finished typing, Mrs. Kingly's sobs had quieted. I could still hear the rasp in her chest, as if the tears could start again any moment, but for now, she was maintaining at least a semblance of control. When she looked up, what was left of her makeup was smeared, and her eyes were glassy and red rimmed. The effect was that her eyes looked bright blue, the color highlighted in a way that all her makeup had not accomplished. Not that I was advocating crying as a fashion choice.

I closed my laptop. *Damage control time.*

"I shouldn't have used magic without your permission. I should have called an ambulance," I said. I'd apologize if I had to—a debt was better than getting sued—but I wasn't ready quite yet.

She shook her head, a stray tear falling from the corner of her eye. "You saved my baby." She cradled her belly. "He already wants to come early, but the doctor insists we try to give him at least another week. He suggested bed rest and that I keep my stress down." She laughed, a hard, ugly sound. "As if that's possible, given the circumstance. But if I had lost James's baby . . ." She pulled more paper from the roll. My wastebasket was already half full of crumpled white paper.

I'd have to put more toilet paper on the list along with tissue.

"I must look a fright," she said, scrubbing under her eyes. "And I owe you the rest of your fee. I'll write a check." Her hands shook as she pulled her checkbook from her purse. "How much do I owe you?"

I blinked at her, still reeling from her drastic swings from threatening to sue me to all but thanking me and then to calmly moving on to business.

"Ms. Craft?" She looked at me, her pen hovering over her checkbook.

"I'd like to continue investigating this case."

Her eyes narrowed. "My husband killed himself. I'm going to have to accept that."

"It is possible." Maybe even likely. "But there are still a lot of questions that don't have answers. Like the memory lapse his shade experienced."

She pushed away from the desk, crossing her arms over her chest. "Your magical failings are something you can look into on your own dime. I was a fool to go against my beliefs, but I was out of options, and I suppose, you did get me information."

Gee, now isn't that a compliment.

I worked hard to keep my smile in place. "Don't you want to know where he was for the three days he was missing?"

The stern set of her crossed arms loosened, but didn't drop. She looked away. "Of course. But you said the shade couldn't tell you. Did he"—her voice caught—"could he even tell you why?"

"No. And despite the fact he was alone on that roof, there is still some possibility he didn't intend to jump."

She went still, then, as if in slow motion, her head turned. Tear-reddened eyes, a little too wide, locked on me. "You're talking about magic."

"I haven't dismissed the possibility."

Her hands locked into fists, and her lips quivered as if she were caught between screaming and crying. But she did neither. Instead, when she spoke again, it was in a hard, low voice, so quiet it was barely above a whisper. "That explains it. He didn't leave me." Her head snapped up. "Then he *was* murdered."

I took a deep breath. Let it out. "Like I said, I haven't dismissed the possibility. But, if there had been overt magical evidence, the police would already be investigating. Magic has limitations, and forcing someone to commit suicide is out of the scope of witchcraft."

Her nostrils flared. "Then it must have been a fae."

"I'm not drawing any conclusions until I have all the facts," I said, working hard to keep my face empty. Right now, she'd grab on to any doubt she spotted. "Mrs. Kingly, do you have a photo of your husband. Something recent."

The question threw her off balance, her mouth opening and closing like a fish. Her anger didn't waver, but confusion tightened her features. Confusion and distrust. Her eyes narrowed and she searched my face as if she were studying a trap she knew would spring if she didn't disarm it. "Why?"

"I have a theory," I said, and when her expression didn't change, I asked. "Was your husband ill?"

"Ill? Heavens no. James rarely even caught a cold."

Which was what his ghost had said as well. "And how much would you say your husband weighed on the day he disappeared?"

Her glistening but stony eyes flew wide. "That is an inappropriate question."

I waited, but when it became clear she wasn't going to answer I said, "On the day he jumped from the Motel Styx he weighed only a little over a hundred pounds."

"That . . ." Mrs. Kingly shook her head and dug her

phone out of her purse. "No, that can't be. This is my James."
She opened a photo app on her phone before passing it
across the table.

I picked up the phone and studied the picture. I knew
what James Kingly looked like, of course, as his ghost had
been in my office for the last hour, but ghosts were almost
always idealized projections of a person's self-image. The
ghost James was neither fat nor thin, but an average, healthy
looking balance. He also had a full head of hair. The James
in the picture was beginning to bald, and while he wasn't
overweight exactly, he had plenty of padding—and not
from muscle. Neither image fit the disease-wasted man
who'd jumped from the top of the Motel Styx.

"When was this photo taken?" I asked, passing the
phone back to her.

"I took it a week before he . . ." She stopped, her eyes
misting, and she gazed down at the photo, a small, broken
smile touching her lips. "We wanted to see the fall colors in
the Botanical Garden. That's where it was taken. It was a
wonderful day." She pulled more toilet paper from the rapidly dwindling roll.

One week. *He had to have lost the weight in the days he
was missing.* And nothing natural could make a man drop
seventy pounds in three days.

"Mrs. Kingly, I want to continue investigating your husband's case. The police may have dismissed the case as suicide, but I think there are too many questions to be satisfied
with that answer."

"And why should I hire a witch instead of a reputable
investigator?"

I ignored the implication that the two were mutually exclusive. "You should hire me because *if* magic is involved—
and at this point, I'm inclined to believe it is—you'll need
someone not only familiar with magic, but able to detect
spells. You won't find another investigator in Nekros with as
high a sensitivity to magic. Another PI might use charms to
detect magic, but charms can be unreliable and they can't
determine what the magic does. I can." I leaned forward,

clasping my hands on the table. "I am capable of following this case wherever it leads, magical or mundane."

"How do I know you wouldn't cover for a fellow witch?"

"Would you cover for a murderer simply because he *couldn't* perform magic?" I asked, and she sniffed, but I wasn't expecting an answer. "Can you e-mail me that photo, so I can show it to people as I track his movements over the missing days?" As an afterthought I added. "And a personal item, something he used a lot or carried with him, would be good." I couldn't do a thing with it, but Rianna might be able to concoct a spell that would help.

Mrs. Kingly's lips flattened as the edges of her mouth tugged downward. "I'm not agreeing to anything yet, but answer me one question. And really answer this time." Her eyes fixed on me, hard enough to pin me to the chair. "Do you think my husband was murdered?"

I thought of the photo of a healthy man with round, smiling cheeks, of the emaciated man who'd thrown himself from a roof, of the shade with absolutely no memory of the days prior to his death. Then I lifted my gaze to the ghost who looked as eager to hear my answer as his wife because he honestly didn't know what happened.

"Yes, I do."

Mrs. Kingly nodded. "Then get me a contract. You're hired."

Once the Kinglys left I considered my next step. I had two obvious starting points: head to Delaney's, the bar where James's last memory ended, or look into the suicide case he'd witnessed. I glanced over the notes I'd taken from the ghost's account of the suicide. Besides the timing, and the fact both suicides had been public, one major detail struck me. James had described the man as being just skin and bones. Which was exactly what James looked like before he threw himself off a building to crash onto a populated street.

I chewed at the end of my pen, glancing over everything I'd written. It was still midmorning, so I doubted the bar

would be open. That left tracking down the crispy corpse.
There had to be some connection between James's vagrant
and what had happened to James himself. I just didn't know
why. Or how. James was the last one in contact with the man
before he killed himself. Had a spell spread to him like a
virus? Stranger things had happened. I'd once contracted a
soul sucking spell from contact with an infected shade.

I was still staring at my screen when Rianna walked into
the room.

"So does Tongues for the Dead have our first case of real
investigative work?"

I nodded. "Yeah, but it's kind of ironic. I'm looking at
where to start my investigation, and I'm leaning toward a
conversation with a shade."

"I thought you already raised the Kingly shade and
didn't get anything out of him."

"And that's what's so significant." Between last night's
fiasco at dinner and the fact the Kinglys had been waiting
for me when I arrived this morning, I hadn't had an opportunity to fill Rianna in on more than the most basic details
of the case. It was past time to update her. After all, she was
the mystery nut, and this puzzle was right up her alley.

"You're right, the earlier suicide is definitely worth
checking out," she said after I'd brought her up to speed.
She'd perched on the edge of my desk, and despite the fact
we were talking about not one, but two horrific deaths, she
was grinning, her eyes distant as if she were visualizing different scenarios. "And a spell spreading like a virus is an
interesting idea, though it still circles back to one major
problem."

"How or if it forced the men to kill themselves," I said,
knowing exactly what she was thinking. It was the same
stumbling block I'd been running into since I took the case.

No magic, witch or fae, could overcome self-preservation.
Not directly at least. Falin had mentioned spells and abilities
that amplified emotion. A spell couldn't compel someone to
jump off a building or douse themselves in gasoline, but
maybe it could exaggerate situations until suicide appeared

the only way out? That would sidestep the willpower di-
lemma if the victim chose death, even if a spell was why they
felt the need to die.

But then why doesn't the shade remember?

The theory didn't explain the missing memories, the
weight loss, or the chunk sucked out of the ghost. Those had
to be explained by a spell, didn't they? And yet, it couldn't
be a spell. But if it was, the suicide James had witnessed had
to be when he'd picked up the spell.

I pushed away from my desk, and Rianna jumped, startled by my sudden movement. That didn't last long. Her
gaze swept over my face, curiosity radiating around her.

"You thought of something?" she asked, sliding to her
feet.

"More like made a decision," I said. I needed to talk to
that earlier suicide victim. To find out if his experience cor-
related to Kingly's.

But first, I had to figure out Mr. Crispy's name.

Chapter 13

❦

Tamara's cell went straight to voice mail, so I called the ME's office, but reached an intern who informed me that Tamara was in the middle of an autopsy. I didn't want to get Tamara in trouble, so I left just my name and a message for her to call me ASAP.

While I waited, I pulled up the *Nekros Times* online archives. I hoped I'd luck out and find something about Kingly's overcooked mystery man. I knew the date the event had occurred, so I queued the articles from the following day's paper. The article described the event as "tragic" and "deeply saddening" but was only a couple paragraphs long. Kingly had told me more than the paper's account of events. And worse yet, the man was listed only as "an as yet unidentified male." That wouldn't help me find his family or his gravesite. I searched for follow-up articles, but found none.

The *Times* having failed me, I pulled up a search engine. It took a good fifteen minutes of playing with keywords before I found an article on a news blog. It was much more detailed—and grislier—than the article in the *Nekros Times*, but it still didn't list the man's name. I checked out the comments, and was disturbed by how many people thought becoming a human torch would be an awesome way to go. More than once commenters asked if he was testing a charm in an experiment that went terribly wrong. Answers went both ways, which tended to happen on the 'net where anyone could claim to be an expert. One commenter linked to a cell phone recording of the event. *Okay, my opinion of society just went down a notch.* At the same time, there could be something in the video that could help in my investigation. *If Kingly's crispy horror is directly involved.*

I bookmarked the location without watching it.

I'd found three more equally unhelpful news posts on the suicide by the time my phone rang. Tamara sounded tired when I answered, her voice rough and throaty.

"You okay?" I asked. "You sound sick."

She huffed a laugh. "In a manner speaking, so if you're calling to invite me to lunch, I'll pass."

Morning sickness.

Her chair squeaked and I imagined her leaning back and propping her legs up after hours of standing over an autopsy table.

"So what's up, Alex?"

"I'm looking for the name of a suicide that probably passed through your cold room a little under two weeks ago."

Tamara groaned. "Another suicide? What are you advertising these days?"

"Don't worry. I just need a name this time."

I described the manner in which the man had died. As I spoke, the other end of the line went eerily silent.

"Tam, you still there?"

"Who hired you to look into that case, Alex?" I could hear her frown through the phone. It wasn't the response I'd expected.

"No one, directly. It came up in the course of the Kingly case. Why?"

"He's a John Doe. Not that there was much left to identify him by. His hands were destroyed so no prints, and no one would ever be able to identify what was left of his face."

Nearly two weeks as a John Doe?

"He's been cremated already, hasn't he?" A suicide victim who had appeared homeless before lighting himself up? Yeah, the city wasn't going to hold on to that corpse for long. And while I was damn good at grave magic, no one could pull a shade from cremated remains—the extreme heat obliterated everything.

Well, there goes that lead.

"Actually, that case got to me. He's still in my cold room." Tamara's chair squeaked again and she made a small "mmph" sound as she stood. "Since no family or friends have come forward, how would you like to officially identify our crispy friend?"

And just like that, the red tape was cut and I had legal access to the shade. Now to hope he held the key to this mystery.

"Here he is," Tamara said, pushing the gurney out of the cold room.

I could sense the preservative charm on the corpse, and the charms in the morgue that moderated the smell were functioning, but as the gurney approached, the scent of burnt flesh wafted over me.

"This is going to be bad, isn't it?" I asked as I drew my circle.

"I've worked on worse, but yeah, he's pretty bad." She looked vaguely green, but I'd seen Tamara examine a corpse's innards without so much as a crinkle of her nose. She looked at the body clinically, not seeing a person. I guessed that her current pallor and the fact her face was all tight lines had nothing to do with the man under the sheet.

"Why haven't you made a charm, yet?" I asked.

Tamara frowned, cocking her head to the side and giving me a puzzled look.

Right, I'd totally skipped the segue. "For the morning sickness, I mean. Why not make a charm to take care of it?"

"Oh." She looked away. "If I make a charm, anyone the least bit sensitive will pick up on it. Including my mom and sister who are flying in this weekend. Theoretically, Ethan and I were the only two who were supposed to know, but I suppose you've told Holly by now."

"That's not my place." After all, we were all keeping secrets these days.

If I hadn't been looking right at her, I'd have missed the fact her shoulders relaxed ever so slightly. *She really is worried about people knowing.*

"You ready for me to turn the recorder on?" she asked, changing the subject. "I want to know who our John Doe is."

"Yeah, go ahead." I looked down at the shape under the sheet. "But first, why this one?"

"Huh?"

"You said this case got to you. Why?"

She stepped over my still inert circle, and joined me beside the gurney. "You think you can look at him in the flesh?"

I cringed back. "Can't you just tell me?"

"No, this is something you have to see." She folded back the sheet exposing no more than a foot and a half of the body beneath.

I knew it was a body only because my innate ability to sense the dead told me as much, but my eyes certainly didn't agree. My brain rejected the blackened mess mixed with areas of dark red and thick, puss-colored blotches as ever having been a living person.

"You're not going to be sick are you?" Tamara asked. I swallowed the taste of bitter bile and shook my head. She nodded in approval. "Good, then come closer and look at this."

I stepped up to the side of the gurney again, staring at the thing she'd exposed. I'd expected a charred skeleton when I heard how he'd died, but there was still a lot of flesh left. I stared, not making sense of what I was seeing until I noticed the two translucent splotches almost evenly placed in the front.

His eyes. It was a head.

I'd stopped breathing at some point, which I didn't realize until my body forced me to gasp in air—air that tasted

of char and dead flesh. My stomach twisted, and for a moment I thought I'd lied to Tamara and I would, in fact, be
revisited by the half pot of coffee I'd called breakfast. I
squeezed my eyes closed. *You can do this, Alex. Calm down.
Slow, shallow breaths.*

I could feel Tamara watching me, but thankfully, she said
nothing about my reaction. I might need dead bodies, but I
most definitely didn't *like* them.

Opening my eyes again, I made myself look at the thing
on the gurney. The ear closest to me was gone, and I could
only barely make out a blackened lump that had once been
a nose between cheeks that had split open, exposing that
yellowed, pustules substance.

"What am I supposed to—" I lost the question as my
gaze moved to where the lips had shriveled and drawn back,
exposing a mouth full of pointed teeth. They looked like
something that belonged in a shark's mouth, not a man's.

"Damn," I whispered the word, more to myself than anyone. Tamara nodded her agreement, but I couldn't look
away from those teeth. Nothing human had teeth like that.
"Is he fae?"

"No, I had an RMC test run. Not only is he a human; he
was most likely a null."

The Relative Magic Compatibility test, or RMC, was still
considered fringe science by most. The results weren't ad-
missible in any court, but they were fast, easy, and inexpen-
sive. With a DNA sample, a tech created a slide and placed
it in the RMC reader. The machine stored a minor charge
of Aetheric energy, which it attempted to infuse into the
sample. Then it measured the reaction to that energy on a
cellular level and created a pretty little chart.

Norms, as in the two-thirds of the population who were
nonmagical humans, created low level readings that looked
a lot like a rolling wave well below the first marker. Nulls,
the humans who not only lacked any magical aptitude, but
often had at least partial immunity to magic, registered on
the chart as a flatline. Witches produced charts filled with
large mountains and valleys. The more powerful the witch,

the higher the spikes. But regardless of what the Humans First Party preached, norms, nulls, and witches were all human, the difference being that some could channel magic and some couldn't. Fae, on the other hand, weren't human. Placing a fae sample into the RMC reader produced no graph. Instead it spit out a single, vertical line in the center of the chart.

I stared at the razor sharp teeth filling the man's mouth. "You're sure the machine was calibrated correctly?"

"Trust me, I double-checked."

"So it's what, cosmetic? On a homeless man?"

She tugged the sheet back over the man's head, which was a relief—I'd seen as much of John Crispy as I cared to.

"I'm not convinced about the homeless part either," Tamara said as she stepped away from the gurney. "That is, unless soup kitchens are now serving caviar and champagne."

Yeah, no. I didn't see that happening, and from Kingly's description of the man, it didn't sound like he could have sauntered into a place serving such items without drawing attention.

"And then there is this." She crossed back over my inert circle and picked up a file from a nearby equipment tray. I reached out my hand for it, but she shook her head. "Not until after the ritual. I want to hear him say his name first." When I just glanced from her to the folder she said, "Suffice to say that several witnesses to the event sat down with sketch artists. The resulting images immediately pinged a missing persons report. But the dental records didn't match."

Go figure. This guy must have had a hell of a smile. I was shocked Kingly hadn't mentioned the teeth. Neither of the Kinglys were extremely open-minded, but James spent several minutes with the man. Surely he would have noticed the jagged, razorlike teeth—a smile like that would be hard to miss—but all Kingly had said was that the guy was "so polite."

Odd.

"We should start," I said and began my ritual as soon as Tamara turned on the recorder.

The shade that sat up from the body was almost worse than the body itself. The body had continued to burn after death, making its features hard to determine. The soul had left the body a little earlier so that even without distinct color, its burnt body looked raw. For the second time in as many days I found myself looking anywhere but at the shade I'd raised.

"What is your name?"

"Richard Kirkwood," the shade said, not the least bit hindered by his burnt lips or sharklike teeth.

From outside my circle Tamara made a triumphant whoop. "I knew it. Ask him when he got his teeth changed."

This was supposed to be my interview, but Tamara was the one who'd arranged it, so I complied.

"I never altered my teeth," the shade said. "I did have a root canal two years ago."

Tamara grumbled something disparaging about shades. I ignored her.

"Do you remember having all your teeth sharpened to points?" And lengthened by the look of them.

"No."

"Have you ever had the desire to do so?"

"No."

This interview was eerily familiar.

"Mr. Kirkwood, do you remember how you died?"

"Fire. I was on fire. I could hear people screaming and then . . ." Then the collector came for him.

"Do you remember how you caught fire?"

"No."

"Do you remember asking a man to fill a milk jug with gasoline?"

"No."

I glanced at Tamara. She stood perfectly still, watching the shade with a loose jaw, her lips slightly parted. But while her mouth might indicate shock, there was dread in her eyes.

"What was the last thing you remember before the fire, Mr. Kirkwood?"

"Going to bed early. Kelly was working a double at the hospital, but I didn't feel well."

"And what day was that?"

"Friday night."

I looked at Tamara and she flipped through the missing person report. With a nod she said, "Kelly Kirkwood filed the report. She was worried when she returned from her double and her husband wasn't home. When he hadn't returned the next morning, and didn't answer his cell phone, she reported him missing."

He didn't pull his combusting trick until the following Tuesday, so like Kingly, he was missing three days.

"Is there a picture?" I asked Tamara, and she turned the file to show me a printed photo. Between the decay from the land of the dead and the blue haze of my circle, to say nothing of the random swirl of Aetheric energy, the picture was completely obscured. I shook my head. "How about weight, did she list it in the report?"

Tamara nodded. "She has approximately a hundred and sixty pounds listed. She must have been guessing. Very poorly too. I'd estimate he weighed between ninety and a hundred pounds at time of death."

Which fit the description of a scrawny man in clothes that hung off his bones that Kingly had given me. And if I was right, though I half hoped I wasn't, Richard's wife hadn't been as bad a guesser as Tamara assumed. Not if Kirkwood suffered the same transformation as Kingly. I turned back toward the shade. Then regretted it and moved my gaze slightly to his right.

"When was the last time you weighed yourself, and how much did you weigh at that time?"

"Wednesday. Kelly and I always weigh in on Wednesdays since we joined a gym. My last weigh-in was one hundred and sixty-three pounds."

"That's impossible," Tamara said. "A person can't lose sixty pounds in six days."

But he had, and so had Kingly. "Three days," I muttered.

"What?" Tamara asked leaning close to the edge of my circle.

"He lost it in three days. The same three days he was missing." Whatever spell had infected Kingly and Kirkwood, it wasted them before, well, wasting them. To the shade I asked, "Do you remember anything odd happening on Friday?"

It was a dicey question because it required the shade to evaluate the subjective notion of what could be considered odd. Shades could recite the events in their lives—often in horrific detail—but opinions left with the soul along with emotions. I wasn't surprised the shade sat mute.

I tried again. "Did you meet anyone new on Friday? Did anyone ask you for a favor?"

"No."

Damn. If Kirkwood had spread whatever made him waste away to Kingly, how did Kirkwood catch it?

"Did your routine change in any way on Friday, besides that you went to bed early."

"Yes. I normally go home at lunch and walk Missy in the park. We didn't make it to the park because a man threw himself in front of a bus."

My mouth went dry. Another suicide?

"Did you see this happen?"

"Yes. Missy and I were walking down the sidewalk and the man was standing on the curb. He watched the bus approaching and then jumped into its path. He hit the front first, before disappearing under the bus and getting drawn into the wheel well." He said all of this with a level voice.

I didn't feel half as calm. A queasy uneasiness reverberated through every cell in my body. Three bodies couldn't be a coincidence. Nekros had a serial killer. Weapon of choice: suicide.

Chapter 14

Tamara gave me the name of the man—or really, boy, as he was a freshman in college—who'd thrown himself in front of the bus: Daniel Walters. But that was all she could legally give me. Unless I had an official form signed by the family and granting me permission to access the boy's files, she couldn't release any information about the autopsy. She did pull the file though, and as I was on my way out, she told me the four most important words that her report could possibly contain: *"He fits the pattern."* Then she wouldn't say anything more about him—or his next of kin.

"Thank goodness you're back," Rianna said when I walked through the doors of Tongues for the Dead.

"Everything okay?"

She shrugged. "Aside from being bored to tears and tired of being inside the office?"

I knew all about that. Until yesterday, I'd been the one stuck. We'd been open only four days, but it was already clear we needed to find a solution to one or the other of us having to be present during business hours. *What we really need is a receptionist.* But that wasn't exactly in the budget. Yet, at least. I could dream, right?

I filled in Rianna on everything I'd learned at the morgue.

"This is a lot bigger than Kingly," she said, her voice hollow with shock.

"Yeah, and Kingly is still the focus, but tracking this thing back to its source is part of finding out who killed him." *And how.* The spell seemed to spread by witnessing suicide, or really, murder disguised as suicide.

That thought made me stop, my stomach souring. "So far, every victim saw the previous die. When Kingly jumped . . ."

I didn't have to finish the sentence. We could both guess that someone on the street that day was infected and going to die—if they hadn't already. In the cases we knew about, the cycle took only three to four days. *How many bodies does this thing have to its name?*

And why?

"It acts more like a parasite than a spell, doesn't it? Using up bodies and then jumping hosts," I said thinking not only about the emaciation but also the damage to Kingly's ghost.

"Unless everyone who witnesses the death is affected, or infected, or whatever." Rianna's hand dropped to Desmond's head, her fingers scratching behind his ear absently as she spoke.

"Wouldn't we have heard about a sudden spike in suicides?" Of course, I hadn't heard about Kirkwood, and his method of death had been extreme. What if the other suicides were less public or didn't succeed? It was definitely something to look into. "If it's a spell that spreads like a pathogen, we could have an epidemic of suicides."

We were both silent for a moment. It wasn't a pleasant thought.

Rianna broke the silence first. "But why?"

She'd moved so that her legs pressed against Desmond, the barghest's touch clearly a reassuring warmth for her.

I shook my head. "Some sort of life cycle? In nature, there are parasites that infiltrate the host's brain and force them to act suicidally stupid. Like fish flashing to attract birds or ants climbing to the tallest blade of grass so they're eaten by a cow. It's all part of the parasite's cycle of life."

Rianna's eyebrows lifted, and heat burned in my cheeks.

"Roy's been watching the nature channel a lot," I mumbled, then cleared my throat. "But whether we're talking about some sort of parasite jumping hosts or a spell crafted to spread, the cycle involves suicide. I'm going to look for more victims, and I need to track down next of kin for Daniel Walters. Or at least figure out where he's buried."

Rianna nodded, and then, surprising the hell out of me, she smiled. "That's all computer stuff, right? I mean, you'll be searching obituaries, archived articles, and stuff here in the office?"

It was my turn to cock a skeptical eyebrow, but I nodded. Her smiled brightened.

"Great, then I'll grab James Kingly's photo and head to the Irish pub he remembers being at last. Maybe he left with someone or at least told someone where he was going."

Divide and conquer—I liked it.

We said our good-byes. Then I booted up my laptop and settled into the task of locating Daniel Walters as well as any other recent suicides. I seriously hoped Daniel was the only one I found.

My senses buzzed with foreign magic as soon as the door chimed. Not that people carrying magic was unusual— especially in the Quarter. From vanity charms to shields to idiosyncratic spells, everyone except the staunchest Humans First Party members and complete nulls utilized household grade magic. Occasionally I'd sense some heavy defensive charms, and once in a blue moon I'd pick up on a weaponized spell. Though, typically only when I hung out with officers from the Anti–Black Magic Unit because carrying fully prepped offensive spells was illegal without a license.

But whoever had just stepped into the lobby was carrying an armory's worth of spells—more than any ABMU officer I'd ever met—and I had about thirty seconds to decide what to do.

As I had no offensive magic, my best bet would have been to jump into a circle and hope I could hold it against a full-on magical assault. Except I hadn't etched a permanent circle in the office yet. *Definitely need to remedy that.*

Not that I had time now.

That wave of magic was almost to my office door. I pushed back from my desk in case I needed to duck for cover. The desk might have been a thrift store find, but it was real wood and would make a decent barrier, at least for a couple of seconds. Then I drew my dagger. The fae-wrought blade pulsed in my hand, anxious to be wielded after what it considered too many weeks of disuse. It clearly didn't understand that with the kind of firepower I felt in the lobby, if I needed the dagger, I'd probably be dead before I lifted my hand. Still, I felt safer having a weapon. Though that didn't mean I needed to provoke my heavily armed visitor by brandishing a blade when they walked through the door, so I concealed the dagger in my lap and waited.

A shadow fell over my threshold. No, not over, it crossed through it.

I blinked, forcing my eyes to focus on the woman who'd entered my office. She hadn't made a sound as she moved, and she offered no greeting. Because of my eyesight, I kept every corner of the room bright, but the woman wore a cocktail of charms that not only made the eye want to move away but also gathered darkness around her. The fact she wore black-on-black leather and had her dark hair pulled back in a tight braid certainly didn't hurt the whole clinging to shadows thing. Even her eyes were such a dark brown they appeared black. If I hadn't been a sensitive and she practically leaking magic, I might not have noticed her.

My dagger throbbed, its not quite cognizant presence pressing against the edge of my mind, urging me to go on the offensive before this very potent threat made the first move. I loosened my grip on the hilt, hoping that would quiet the blade. Right now I needed all of my concentration to watch the stranger.

She sidestepped away from the door, the movement graceful and silent. She was working hard on not being seen, which made me more than a little nervous. The dagger liked it even less. It had saved my freedom and my life before, so I didn't take its urges lightly. Though when it came to the dagger, moderation was important. It had a compelling urgency in its desire to fight, to cut, to wound, and it would guide my body if I let it, which made it both a great weapon and a tempting liability. For years I hadn't carried it for just that reason, but with the way my life had been going the last few months, I never went anywhere unarmed.

The woman took another step sideways, her gaze locked on my face. I forced my eyes to stay with her, to ignore the magic trying to redirect my attention. She frowned as she watched me track her. Then she dropped the perception charms and stalked forward, her movement predatory and confident.

"Are you Alex Craft?"

"Yes?" I didn't mean to make the answer a question, but nervousness made my voice waver. *Way to keep control of the situation, Alex.*

I opened my shields, just enough that I could get a better look at who—or what—I was dealing with. The woman's soul glowed an unmarred yellow below her skin, which meant she was human and despite the exorbitant amount of offensive magic she carried, she didn't dabble in the dark. And speaking of magic, she was armed to the teeth with it. Spells were worked into her clothes, gathered in pouches around her belt, and contained in small vials lining a tactical bandolier slung across her chest. But all the spells I spotted in my quick scan, while lethal, were bright in color, so legal—assuming she was licensed.

I slammed my shields closed. Even though my peek across the planes lasted no more than five seconds, the room dimmed once I pushed the planes away. I blinked, just once, to let my sight readjust.

I opened my eyes to a crossbow leveled at my face.

I froze, my breath dying in my chest. I wasn't familiar with the liquid spell I sensed encapsulated in the crossbow bolt, but it definitely felt like it would turn incendiary on impact. Of course, at this range, I'd be dead before the spell had time to activate.

Even the ever-eager dagger didn't like our chances. I dropped it in my lap and lifted my hands, palms open in surrender.

"What do you want?" I asked, my voice ragged with fear I didn't bother hiding.

She didn't lower the crossbow. "Your eyes flashed."

I gave her a cringing smile. "The light?"

It wasn't a lie, it was a question.

Her stare cut at me, as if she could peel back the truth by studying me. I'd been holding my breath too long, and my lungs burned, competing with my heart on which would burst first. Then, as suddenly as she'd aimed the crossbow, she lowered it. With a quick bend of her arm she returned the weapon—still loaded—to wherever she concealed it behind her back.

My breath rushed out in a whoosh that tasted of stale fear. *What the hell have I gotten into?* I sank lower in my chair as the woman pulled a wallet out of the inner pocket of her jacket.

"Briar Darque," she said, flashing her MCIB badge as well as her certification and a license I'd never seen before.

Magical Crimes Investigation Bureau? I'd met one or two inspectors in the past and I'd always gotten the impression they were the magical equivalent of IRS auditors, not GI Jane.

"I think there's been some misunderstanding," I said, my voice thready. The hand locked around the hilt of my dagger shook. Working to regain my composure, I cleared my throat and sat up straighter. "I'm the one who called the

OMIH. To investigate the gray magic wafting from the shop up the alley?"

"I don't give a damn about a couple of love spells," she said, stepping forward. "The MCIB sends me when magic goes seriously wrong. You're alive, so I'm guessing you fucked up and didn't report it. I'm here to fix the problem."

A problem she clearly considered to be me.

Chapter 15

❖━━◦◦━━❖

It said something about my life when a heavily armed official accused me of causing magical havoc and I had to wonder which incident she meant. That being the case, I didn't bother to guess. If being the daughter of the most devious manipulator I'd ever met had taught me anything, it was when to keep my mouth shut. I wasn't about to volunteer information she might not already have.

I'm not sure what response Briar Darque expected, probably that I'd deny involvement before I even knew what I was being accused of, or perhaps she thought I'd throw myself at her feet and beg the OMIH and MCIB's mercy. Whatever she anticipated, silence clearly didn't fit. Or impress.

Scowling, she stalked to the edge of my desk, and putting her palms flat on the surface, loomed as she leaned into my personal space. "You have nothing to say?"

She was so close I either had to lean back or crane my neck to look at her. If I leaned back she'd see the dagger in my lap, so I didn't have much choice but to meet her challenging stare head-on. So that's what I did—besides, I hated when people loomed. I'd guess Darque was on the tall side of average and her biker boots gave her another inch or two, but if I stood up, I'd be taller. Not by much, and I had no doubt she could kick my ass from this side of the Quarter to the other, but I still hated the cheap intimidation tactic.

"Are you charging me with something, Inspector?" My tone was flat, neutral. I think even my father would have been proud.

Darque's lip curled as she straightened and reached into her jacket. She pulled free a folded manila packet and flipped through the contents before dropping a sheet of paper in front of me.

I glanced at it. A good half dozen newspaper clippings had been taped to the page, dates scrawled in a quick hand beside each. The oldest was from a little over three weeks ago and was a very short report about graves being disturbed in the graveyard south of Nekros. The writer dismissed the event as a juvenile prank. The clippings proceeded chronologically and mentioned disturbed graves in other cemeteries across Nekros. The most recent was from last week. Several bodies had gone missing from the Fairmount, a small cemetery I'd visited only once or twice as the suburban area around it—and thus most of the graveyard's tenants—were of the Humans First persuasion. A reward was being offered for information that led to the return of the bodies and the capture of those responsible.

I looked up at Darque. "Grave robbing? You think I have something to do with this?"

She cocked an eyebrow and dropped another piece of paper in front of me. It was another newspaper article, but not a back-page piece, this one was the lead article from yesterday. I was vaguely familiar with the story—I'd seen it earlier when I was looking for information on Richard Kirkwood. Now I read it more carefully.

A pair of teenagers had driven off the road just south of the city. The car had been found wrapped around a tree, but most of the couple's injuries appeared to be from an animal attack, not the accident. The girl had been DOA, but the article listed the boy as being in intensive care.

"I don't get the connection," I said, handing the pages back to Darque.

"Do you know what kind of animal causes this type of injury?" she asked, dropping several photos in front of me.

After examining Kirkwood earlier, I was already beyond my daily threshold for brutalized bodies. Hell, between Kingly and Kirkwood, I'd like to think I'd hit my cap for the month, especially since John had made it clear the NCPD wouldn't be calling anytime soon. I didn't want to look at any more bodies, even in photographs.

Not that Briar was giving me a choice.

I glanced at the array of photos, glad I hadn't stopped for lunch on the way back from the morgue. Of course, the burn of stomach acid at the back of my throat wasn't much better. The photos were of the two teens and at first, all I saw was the color red and a lot of pale flesh, then I started picking out details. When my gaze landed on a close-up of flesh torn away to expose bone, my stomach clenched tight enough to knock the air out of me. I tore my gaze away.

"I don't know what kind of animal did it."

"Look at them." She pushed the photos closer to me.

I glared at her, and she crossed her arms over her chest, tapping the folder against her elbow in an impatient rhythm. Oh, I really didn't want to study those pictures. Of course, if my stomach gave another heave, I'd add a different color to the photos. *And look like a weakling.* Which I couldn't do in front of this woman.

I picked up the nearest photo. It had been taken while the couple was still in the car. The boy had been driving, and he hung forward, limp against the restraint of his seat belt, the deflated air bag in front of him. There was so much blood it obscured the actual wounds. The girl had been in the backseat, and not wearing a seat belt. The wreak had thrown her forward, so she was caught with her lower half still in the back and her upper body wedged between the front seats at an unnatural angle.

I put the photo down.

The next two were of the car itself. The first was from the

outside, and was a close-up of the car door covered in dried smears of blood around the door handle. The next was of deep blood stains on the backseat—presumably where the girl had been before the wreck. She must have been lying down and bleeding heavily based on the size of the blood pool covering the seat. I stared at the photos, imagining the teens, injured and frightened, clawing at the door to get it open. The girl might not even have been conscious, her boyfriend laying her in the back before sliding behind the wheel. The hair on the back of my neck stood on end. I pushed the pictures to the side.

The rest of the photos were from the girl's autopsy. I couldn't decide if the cleaned and clinical close-ups of her wounds were better or worse than the bloody accident scene. I reached the picture I'd first seen where skin and muscle were stripped away to show white bone behind the flayed flesh, and I was proud that my stomach didn't heave this time, at least, not hard enough that my body betrayed me to the watching MCIB inspector.

I forced myself to make sense of the image, and decided I was looking at the femur bone in her leg. My stomach gave another painful lurch. Having identified the injury, I shuffled the photo to the bottom of the stack. The next image was of her back. Claw marks crisscrossed over her shoulders, one set ending in deep puncture marks where the creature had dug in its claws. I couldn't tell the actual depth from the photos, but judging by the location, I'd have been shocked if her lung wasn't perforated.

Was she even alive when she reached the car?

I stared at the carnage that had been her back and shivered. Then I shut my eyes and forced myself to take a deep breath. I needed to be analytical right now, not emotional. Opening my eyes, I counted the claw marks. They were in rows of five. Not a cougar then, or there would have been rows of no more than four.

"My best guess would be a bear," I said, looking up from the pictures and hoping I'd never see them again. "There are black bears in this region."

"Look at the pictures of her arm."

I gritted my teeth, but shuffled the stack of photos until I found the two Darque wanted me to look at. One was of the outside of the girl's arm and showed four deep lacerations. The other was of the inside of the same arm. I could see the tips of the gashes from the previous image, but what the photographer had been trying to capture was a single laceration on the inside of her arm that was almost perfectly centered with the outer gashes. The blood drained from my face as I looked from one photo to the other.

Apparently I'd finally given Darque a response she wanted, because she leaned forward and tapped the picture of the girl's inner arm. "Ever seen a bear with an opposable thumb?"

Crap. Definitely not an animal. Not a mundane one at least. Wild beasts of legend were occasionally spotted roaming the wilderness outside the city. And not just around Nekros, they were appearing in all the previously folded spaces that had opened after the Magical Awakening. I assumed it was only a matter of time before they started appearing in the few remaining undomesticated areas from the pre-Awakening period as well.

But if it was some unnatural or magical beast, why come to me? Or did they suspect a fae? There were any number of fae who sported talons or claws. But again, if they suspected fae, there was no reason for Briar to be here. For one thing, *I* obviously didn't have claws, and for another, if the OMIH had any inkling of my heritage, this would be a very different conversation. I was a card carrying, OMIH certified witch, but I had the feeling if Tamara put my DNA sample into the RMC reader that I wouldn't register human. Not that I was advertising that fact. So why the hell did the MCIB send a militant investigator to grill me?

I gathered the photos into a stack and pushed them across my desk toward Briar. "I don't see the connection."

She stared at me, her hard gaze searching my face. Her expression screamed that she expected to find deceit in my features. *Fat chance.*

Darque glanced at her wrist, and a flicker of surprise crossed her face. "You really don't get it," she said as if she couldn't believe it.

I followed her gaze to a small charm pressed flat against her wrist. *A lie detector charm?* I tried to focus on the one charm, but she had so much magic on her, picking such a small spell out of the mess was impossible. But I'd put money on a lie detector.

She looked up and opened her folder again. "I have your file. You're certified to work as both a grave witch and a sensitive, and are ranked exceptional in both. You opted out of attempting to certify in any division of spell-crafting." That fact earned a note of disbelief, as if she couldn't understand why any witch wouldn't certify in at least low-level spell-crafting. I wasn't about to tell her that I wouldn't have passed. Not that I needed to say anything as she'd already moved on. "Yes, I thought so. You were trained at a wyrd academy. You must have been taught this. Reports of grave robbing and grave desecration? Victims attacked during the night, and found with wounds consistent with a humanoid not two miles down the road from where some of the reports of nighttime disturbances in a graveyard occurred?"

I hadn't known they'd been anywhere near the south graveyard. The article had only said the car had been found south of the city. But now that I knew, and she presented it all together . . . "You think we have ghouls?"

"And she proves she's not a complete idiot. Yes, ghouls— in at least four different graveyards. Which means you, Ms. Craft, are being charged with murder."

Chapter 16

Murder. The word ricocheted around my head and then rattled down my spine, making my whole body shake.

"I didn't—" I wanted to say I hadn't killed anyone, but I had. The fact it was only in defense of myself and those I cared about didn't change that I'd killed. Nor did it stop the nightmares.

But I hadn't murdered anyone. And that I could say.

"Really? What do you call what happened to this girl?" Briar tossed the photos across the desk again. "You created a prime ghoul and allowed it to kill, more than once, judging by the fact at least three cemeteries are infested. That's murder by magical proxy."

"No." I'd had quite a few magical *issues* in the last few months, but creating a prime ghoul—the first that would bridge the way for more of the creatures to cross over from the land of the dead—wasn't on the list. There were only two ways to create a prime, one involved a grave witch who was actively in contact with the grave to die and her body be possessed. The other was for a grave witch to, either by accident or design, allow a creature from the land of the dead to cross through her and into a dead body, turning it into an animated cannibalistic corpse. I'd felt the dark things in the land of the dead before and I stayed the hell away from them.

"Ms. Craft, I'll be honest. While seeing you locked away for your crimes is important, what is on the top of my to-do list right now is finding and destroying the prime. Tell me where to find it and I'll let my superiors know you cooperated. You want that, trust me, because I'm in a hurry, which means I won't hesitate to dose you with a compulsion spell and then ask my questions." She fingered a vial on her belt, just in case I doubted she'd use such a spell. "A lot of paperwork goes with compulsion spells, and paperwork pisses me off. I suggest you cooperate, because you won't like me pissed."

That I believe. Unfortunately I didn't have the answers she wanted.

"You have the wrong person," I said, trying to keep my voice level and not provoke her.

"Like hell I do. Your file speaks for itself, and besides, not only are you the practicing grave witch in the area, but there is witness testimony."

"That's impossible," I sputtered, any semblance of calm evaporating. I'd never even seen a ghoul, let alone created a prime—and creating monsters was the type of thing a girl wouldn't forget. "Who's your witness?"

"I won't reveal my sources, but the story was corroborated. Or do you deny using the dead to attack a group of witches?"

I blinked at her dumbly, waiting for my brain to scale the wall of shock and give me a clue. No use. I had absolutely no idea what she was talking about. I would never do something as stupid as tangle with the creatures on the other side of the chasm. Except ghosts of course, but they hardly counted as they were souls not meant to exist in the land of the dead.

I stopped. *Ghosts.*

A month ago I'd been kidnapped by a group of magic drunk skimmers who'd wanted me to rip a hole into the

Aetheric for them. I'd manifested every haunt in the graveyard as a distraction.

"I'm assuming your sources are either in the mental
ward or jail," I said and Briar glowered.

"So you don't deny it."

"I don't deny utilizing a handful of ghosts to escape
armed kidnappers, who, by the way, had recently attacked a
unit of ABMU officers after going mad from direct contact
with the Aetheric. No, I don't deny that. But they were
ghosts. *Ghosts.* And ghosts can't become ghouls."

Briar frowned, but it had an edge of justification in it.
"So you did, in fact, use your grave magic to utilize the dead
as a weapon."

"No, I created a distraction. And I did it only so I didn't
get my head blown off."

"And I'm sure you have an excuse you find equally jus-
tifiable for why you created the ghoul. Now where is it? For
so many graveyards to have ghouls it must not be trapped
behind cemetery gates."

"I told you, I didn't—" I started to say, but paused as
Briar reached into her jacket. I braced to dive out of the
way if she followed through on her threat to hit me with a
compulsion spell. But it wasn't a potion or charm she pulled
free but another photo.

"Look at this boy," she said, dropping the photo in front
of me. "He's already transitioning. In a couple of hours he'll
pass beyond saving. Then there are only two paths for him.
One, the transition finishes, he dies and rises as a ghoul, or
two, he's terminated before he finishes changing and his
body is destroyed so he can't come back. And that would be
my job."

She tapped the photo, forcing me to look at the boy and
all the machines hooked up to his body.

"I hate terminating kids," she said, fixing me with a dark
stare. "So prove something decent exists in you and tell me
where the damn prime is because there are only two ways
to save this boy. One is to kill every ghoul that so much as
scratched him—not an easy task as they don't come out in

the day and tonight will be too late for him. Or I can cut the chain from the top. Kill the prime and all the other ghouls lose their anchor and lay still like good corpses. Which do you think I prefer?"

"I didn't create the prime. Check your lie detector. I'm telling you the truth."

Her lips curled back, revealing gritted teeth, but she lifted her wrist to check the charm. "Unbelievable," she muttered. "Either you're pathological or using a counter charm. Hand over your bracelet and any other magical items you have on your person."

This couldn't be happening.

When I didn't immediately comply, Briar fingered something in her pouch and said, "Remember, Ms. Craft, I wield the full authority of the MCIB in this investigation. If I think you are actively hindering my investigation or pose a threat to me, the OMIH, or the general population"—in one swift movement she swung the crossbow off her back and leveled it at my chest—"I can disable you by any means necessary."

I gulped hard enough that I felt the movement all the way to my pounding temples. For the second time in an hour, I was on the wrong side of a crossbow. At least it wasn't loaded with a steal-tipped incendiary round this time. I hadn't seen her make the change, but the crossbow was now loaded with a bright blue foam bolt that carried a nasty concoction that felt like an immobilizer, a sleeping spell, and a draught that could temporarily block a witch's ability to channel Aetheric energy. The last was a heavily regulated spell, and I had no idea who or what she thought she'd face that she'd need to combine all three. After all, a witch who can't move *and* is unconscious wasn't going to be casting any spells. But I guess I had to give Briar Darque one thing—she was certainly thorough with her overkill.

She twitched the crossbow, just the smallest jerk of a motion, but I got the message loud and clear. She *would* shoot me if I didn't comply, and quickly.

I needed no additional prompting.

The obsidian ring where I stored Aetheric energy went on the desk first. Then I unclasped my bracelet as directed, and tossed it on the desk. As soon as it broke skin contact, I lost the benefit of my extra shields. I almost never took off the bracelet unless I was inside a circle. Even this morning, when I'd used my meditation charm on Nina Kingly, I'd never lost skin contact with the shields. *Well, at least I'm not on the street.* Then I'd really be in trouble. Inside, the building's wards kept grave essence from assaulting me, but the wards couldn't do anything about the fact I was a living, breathing, nexus in which the planes of reality converged. My personal mental shields kept my psyche grounded in mortal reality, but there was always a little slippage, tendrils of my mind that tied parts of me to the other planes. The shield bracelet helped me ignore those other planes. Without the added barrier, my psyche's favorite two planes, the Aetheric and the land of the dead, stopped just hovering in my peripheral and swam across my vision.

To add insult to injury—not to mention my aching head—the cacophony of magic radiating off Darque intensified as my ability to sense magic heightened without the buffer the external shields provided. I winced, she wasn't carrying so much magic that it would overwhelm me, but the magic grated at my remaining shields, announcing itself and vying for attention. Unfortunately, that wasn't the worst of it. The real issue, the dangerous one, was the breeze making my loose curls flutter across my face. A breeze that shouldn't have existed in a building with no open windows.

The land of the dead. I was way too close.

Darque was saying something, but I zoned her out as I took a deep breath and concentrated on centering myself. With my eyes closed, I ran a quick check of my mental shields. My main shield of living vines was solid, but I urged the vines just a little closer, tighter. I couldn't maintain it that way indefinitely, but it wouldn't start taking conscious effort to hold it for at least an hour. I did a quick scan of my inner shields, the ones that protected my core. All were intact. I erected my new shield—the opaque bubble that let my psyche look but not touch. Though I'd been working on it the better part of a month, the shield wasn't ready for extended use because it still took conscious effort to maintain. Once I finished constructing and integrating the shield, it would be tied into the same part of the subconscious that reminded me to blink or to breathe. But I was far from that stage with the new shield. Which meant I wouldn't be able to maintain it longer than a half hour or so. I hoped like hell that Briar would return my external shields before the barrier failed.

Taking one more deep breath, I released it slowly, mentally running one more check on my shields. Then I let my focus lift back to my body and opened my eyes. The wind from the land of the dead had ceased and the magic surrounding Darque no longer threatened to throw me into sensory overload. Unfortunately, I'd missed everything the woman had said in the interim.

"What?" I asked, looking up at her.

"I said do you have any other magi—Fuck!" Darque stumbled half a step back before catching herself. "Do you want me to shoot you? What the hell are you doing? Your eyes are glowing like lanterns."

My vision was still adjusting to the overlay of the swirling colors of raw magic from the Aetheric and the patina of rot and decay from the land of the dead superimposed over mortal reality, so I wasn't sure, but I thought I saw her force herself to ease her finger from the trigger of her crossbow.

I lifted my hands in supplication. "The charm bracelet holds my extra shields. Without them the light show is unavoidable."

Her eyes narrowed and she studied me as if waiting for an indication I was prepping an assault. If I didn't have a crossbow pointed at my head, the situation might have been funny. After all, while my eyes glowing like night-lights may look unnerving—I'd been told that more than once—I wasn't remotely close to being a threat. Not even with my planeweaving. Oh, I could drag her weapon into the land of the dead and let it rot, but first I'd have to reach it and she'd plug me before I made it over the desk.

"I have one more bit of magic on me," I said without lowering my hands. "It's a dagger. If I pick it up to put it on the desk, are you going to shoot me?"

She looked like she just might, but all she said was, "Move slow."

I did. Since the dagger was already in my lap, there wasn't even much moving involved.

"That's it?" she asked and at my nod, she motioned me to stand.

Without lowering her crossbow, she used a spellchecker to sweep me for spells. As she reached my boots, I remembered that the hilt I carried the dagger in was also enchanted. *Crap, this chick might just be unstable enough to shoot me where I stand if she thinks I lied.* Who the hell would authorize her to carry, let alone make her an MCIB investigator?

But the spellchecker didn't change color or make a sound as it passed the fae-enchanted leather. I almost let out a sigh of relief—except then she'd realize she missed something. Once she'd waved the spellchecker over every inch of me, she stepped back.

"Okay, let's try this again. Tell me about the prime."

"I don't know anything about it. I didn't even realize we had ghouls until you told me."

Briar watched her wrist as I spoke. Then she let out a string of curses, some of which I'd never heard before. Once she finished, she tucked her crossbow behind her back again. "Get your charm bracelet, your eyes are freaking me out."

I was more than happy to comply. Grabbing the chain of charms, I clasped it around my wrist and immediately the pressure in my head eased. Unfortunately, while the overlay of other planes thinned, they didn't vanish, as if my psyche was reluctant to let go. I pushed them away, and the wisps of color and signs of decay retreated to my peripheral once more. The room darkened. Not a full fade to black or even a graying out, but it dimmed as if one of the lightbulbs had gone out. *Better than I expected.*

I reclaimed my obsidian ring from the desk, but when I reached for my dagger, Briar stopped me.

"Not that," she said, grabbing the dagger before I could pick it up.

As soon as her fingers closed on the hilt, her face tightened, her eyes widening as her lips thinned. Her hand spasmed open and the dagger clattered back onto the desk.

"Fuck. What the hell was that?" she said, ducking her head as she rubbed small circles in the soft spot just above where her jawbone met her ear.

I stared, dumbfounded. I'd always known the dagger had some form of awareness, and recently it had bonded with me to the point it followed me around in Faerie. Despite that, no one had ever had a problem touching it. Not that I walked around handing the dagger to people, but most of my friends had held it at one point or another. No one had ever had the reaction Briar just did.

Of course, Briar Darque isn't a friend. And the dagger hadn't liked her since she walked through the door. Still, what exactly had it done when she touched it? I'd never know if I didn't ask.

Briar's glare morphed into an uncertain frown at the question. "What do you mean what did it do? It screamed the most disharmonious wail I've ever—" She stopped, her brows creasing. "You couldn't hear it, could you?"

I shook my head and Briar gave the dagger an appraising look. For a moment I thought she'd try to pick it up again—and I think she considered it—but her hand flexed in the air above it before dropping to a pouch on her belt. She pulled out a bag with an OMIH crest stamped on it. It wasn't until she broke the seal on the bag that I realized it was a magic-dampening evidence bag.

She wasn't seriously . . . ? But she was.

"I'll have to confiscate this," she said as she flipped the bag inside out and put the inert side over her hand like a glove.

"You can't just take my dagger." Actually she probably could. Hell, for all I knew, I was still under arrest despite the fact I'd proven I hadn't created the prime.

"You'll get a reimbursement slip for the dagger's value. But I've never seen an alarm spell quite like that. The guys at the lab will want to try to reverse engineer it."

She's seriously taking my dagger because she wants the spell? That was ridiculous. No, worse than that, it was government sanctioned theft. Hell, it wasn't any better than some of the bullshit the FIB pulled. *And lucky me, I currently answer to both.*

She picked up the hilt through the charmed plastic, and her body went rigid, her shoulders hitching.

"Son of a—" She jerked back, dropping the dagger again. This time it landed pointed side down and the blade sank through the solid wood of my desk.

"Great," I muttered as Briar continued to curse. But she didn't stop me as I grabbed the hilt and pulled the blade free. It slid through the wood as easily as if the desk were room temperature butter. Sometimes having a blade that could cut through anything was less than convenient. Its slightly alien presence fluttered at the edge of my mind, urging me to attack Briar while she was still off balance.

And that was the reason carrying it was always a risk.

Propping one foot on my chair, I shoved the dagger into its enchanted sheath. I could still feel it in the back of my mind, but it was a hell of a lot easier to ignore it sheathed.

"Did you enchant that thing?" Briar asked. She'd recovered from the dagger's second mental assault and now watched me with a predatory wariness, her weight balanced, ready for a fight.

I put my foot back on the ground and turned to face her, my hands in front of me and my body open and, hopefully, nonthreatening. "It was a gift, and your lab won't be able to replicate the spell. It's fae-wrought, the magic imbued in the otherworldly metal."

She cocked an eyebrow, her expression evaluating as she studied me. Then she shifted her weight back so she didn't look like she would lunge over the desk at any moment. *About time.*

"You're full of surprises, Alex Craft, and definitely not what I was expecting." She picked up the file she'd dropped on the desk earlier.

"Since you entered my office armed to the teeth, do I want to know what you were expecting?"

Her lips curled in something that passed for a smile only if you considered a tiger baring its teeth a sign of friendship. "Your OMIH files are very interesting, more because of what is missing than what is in them. You have no known next of kin, no birth records, and yet you have all the required paperwork to be a legal citizen. Even your academy records indicate nothing about your past as your fees were paid by an anonymous benefactor." She looked up, searching my face for a response.

A response I didn't give. I'd been through this particular line of questions before. When I'd changed my name my father had buried any and all paperwork that could tie me back to him. And when he buried something, he was thorough.

"Fine, we'll ignore the mysterious past in which there are no records of your existence before you enrolled in academy at eight, and we'll move on to more recent events." Briar flipped the page. "Your file reads like a cover-up, full of redactions and missing reports. A notation mentions you being involved in an event at the governor's house in which his daughter was maimed, and yet, while a record of the police being deployed exists, there's no official report—or unofficial either. Nor is there any record of your rumored arrest on that night. More peculiar though, is that the first responders have no memory of ever reaching the governor's house."

I remained perfectly still, focusing on keeping my face blank. The event she was talking about had occurred three months ago, under the Blood Moon, and was when my life was turned upside down and inside out. And the governor's daughter? Yeah, that was my younger sister. The blood I sported on my hands when I went to Faerie I'd earned trying to keep her alive.

"Another notation suggests that you might have a connection to a series of holes into the Aetheric. But again, there are no official records that mention your name. A warrant was apparently issued for your arrest by the FIB—which is more than odd as you're a witch not a fae, but regardless, records of that warrant are also missing. Oh, and you're rumored to have been involved in both the Coleman case and the Sionan River murders. Both of which are classified as closed despite the fact no one was ever apprehended. At least a record of those cases exist, though both were sealed—"

I didn't miss the "were" in that.

"—But guess what. Once I got the order to have them unsealed, all details were vague and you weren't mentioned. Do you see where I'm going with this?"

"That you base your judgment on rumors?"

Her glare could have pinned me to my chair as easily as one of her crossbow bolts.

"No, I'm thinking you have some very powerful connections who are covering your tracks. Something is rotten here, and it surrounds you."

I couldn't deny that someone was covering the truth about what had happened—my father most likely, so I sidestepped because I had to admit words like "rumored" and "involved" coupled with missing records did make me look suspicious. "I assure you, any involvement I had in the events mentioned involved working the case, not the crime."

She glanced at her wrist, checking her lie detector spell. Her jaw clenched as she shook her head. "I don't suppose you have a suggestion of who might know more about the prime ghoul?" she asked as she gathered the photographs she'd scattered over my desktop.

I didn't, though there were a number of possibilities. While she was correct that I'd been the only local grave witch for most of the last four years, recently Nekros had been a hot seat for grave witches. Not counting Rianna—

because she'd no more create a ghoul than I would—I could think of a half dozen grave witches who'd passed through Nekros in the last three months and not all of them were what I'd consider good guys. There were two in particular who I knew for a fact were bad news. But they were both dead—okay, one had started out dead, but now he wasn't walking around anymore.

Ashen Hughes's ghost might still be in Faerie, but even if I knew how to find him, I doubted I'd get any help out of him. The fact that he worked for a slaver who'd tried to soul chain me and sell me to the highest bidder and I'd sort of separated Ashen from his already dead body pretty much put a damper on our relationship. And as for Edana? Well, she'd screwed with reality and to stop her, I'd ripped reality from around her. Not even dust was left of her now.

But even as twisted as those two grave witches had been, I couldn't think of any reason why they'd create a prime or how ghouls would have benefited either of their plans. A prime could be controlled to a certain extent, until it started killing people to create more ghouls. Then the hive mind mentality of the creatures overwhelmed the witch's will and you ended up with a nest of corpse-eating walking dead. You'd have to be an idiot to create one.

"I have no idea."

Briar snorted and turned toward the door, her dark braid whipping behind her. She hesitated at the threshold and glanced back over her shoulder.

"You might not be responsible for the prime ghoul, but there is something weird going on with you, and as soon as I deal with the immediate threat, rest assured that I intend to find out what." Then she stalked out of my office.

Chapter 17

It was hard to concentrate on searching obituary columns after Briar left. It may have been the fact my pulse was still irregular from having a crossbow thrust in my face not once, but twice, getting accused of murder, learning that Nekros had ghouls, or the fact I had attracted the attention of an MCIB agent.

I jumped at the sound of my phone, my heart leaping to my throat. *Rianna, it's just Rianna.* But despite the fact I knew it was her—she was the only person set to Rob Zombie's "Living Dead Girl"—I couldn't stop my hand from trembling as I dug the phone from my purse.

"Hey," I said, trying to sound natural. I failed. My voice came out raw, hoarse, as if I'd been screaming.

If Rianna noticed, she didn't mention it. "So get this," she said over the background sound of a crowd. "The bartender remembers James Kingly. Apparently he'd once been a regular at Delaney's, but hadn't been around much of late. The bartender said that two weeks ago, Tuesday night was slow and since Kingly was sitting at the bar, they'd had more than just a passing conversation. Well, about an hour after he arrived, Kingly stopped midsentence and without explanation—or paying—excused himself. The bartender assumed he was headed to the john, until Kingly walked out the front door. The bartender followed, intending to make Kingly pay for the beers. When he got outside, he found Kingly pointing his key fob at each car he passed, as if he had no idea which was his."

Well, that was certainly odd. "Did the bartender mention how many drinks he'd served Kingly?"

"Yeah, Kingly was in the middle of his second when this happened."

Which was exactly when his memory loss hit.

"Did the bartender say anything else?"

"Yeah, he said Kingly called the beer rat piss. He also wanted to know if I was going to pay for the drinks. We don't have an expense account, do we?"

Right now we barely had next month's rent, but I couldn't expect her to pay for case expenses out of her own pocket, and we could always bill Mrs. Kingly—though if she demanded an itemized invoice, a charge for two beers wouldn't look good.

"He already gave you the information you need, so unless you think he's holding something back, forget the drinks. If he wants to collect on Kingly's debt, he can contact Nina," I said, but the question did bring into focus the fact that building a petty cash reserve was another thing on my list of things to do for the business—it was getting to be a pretty long list.

"Agreed," Rianna said. "But now I'm not sure where to go from here. If we were super spies we'd just hack the city's traffic cameras . . ." Rianna's grin was all but audible, and I shook my head. Not that the smallest smile didn't crawl to my own lips.

"Yeah, I don't think that's on our résumé," I said as I woke my computer. What did we know that could help us? What similarities were there between Kingly and Kirkwood? The suicides, of course. And the memory and weight loss. But what else?

It hit me. Their stomach contents. They'd both eaten very expensive cuisine shortly before death.

"Look for fancy restaurants in the area," I said, and filled her in on my reasoning.

"Not a bad idea," she said. The background noise dimmed, as if she'd stepped out of the pub. "So how are things going with your searches?"

"Actually—" I was about to tell her about Briar's visit when my eyes stumbled over the very name I'd been searching for but had apparently been too preoccupied to notice.

Daniel Walters, age eighteen, was described as an all-star high school football champ who left this world too early. It mentioned the names of his parents and younger sister, and—most important for my purposes—mentioned the date and time of the graveside service to be held at Green Hill cemetery.

Pay dirt. The service had long passed, but now I knew exactly where to find the body.

"Al? Alex, you there?" Rianna called from the other side of the phone. I hadn't been paying attention.

"Yeah, I'm here. But I'm going to close the firm early today—I'll leave a note on the door with our numbers."

"You found something?"

Yeah, I'd found the next link in the chain of suicides. *Now to see if Daniel Walters started it or was another victim.*

"You don't remember jumping in front of a bus?" I asked the shade, my eyes fixed firmly on the marker where his headstone would be placed when it arrived. I'd made the mistake of looking at him when I'd first called the shade. Just thinking about the mangled body made me shiver. I'd never realized exactly how much damage being hit by a bus could do. *No wonder the family opted for a graveside service, there certainly couldn't have been a viewing.* I'd seen morticians do some amazing work, especially when they added a couple complexion charms to the mix, but more than half this boy would have had to have been rebuilt, like Humpty Dumpty.

"I remember the tire inches from my face and then—" He stopped as the memory ended.

It was the answer I expected, but I'd had to ask anyway.

"What is the last thing you remember before seeing the tire?"

"Feeling like I'd caught the flu. I called Allison to cancel our study date. Then I went to bed early."

"And what day was that?"

"Tuesday."

I nodded. Kirkwood had seen him jump in front of the bus on Friday. Three days again. That fit with both Kirkwood and Kingly's cases.

"Daniel, did you see anyone die on Tuesday?"

"No, not that day."

I frowned. "You saw someone die another day? When?"

"Monday."

That didn't fit the pattern. Both Kingly and Kirkwood had seen a suicide on the day their memories stopped. *Why did it take an extra day to affect Walters?* Unless the timeline between suicide and memory loss was shortening with each case. I hadn't thought about it before, but Kingly witnessed Kirkwood flambé himself only an hour or two before his memories stopped and he'd undergone a personality change. But Kirkwood had seen Walters play chicken with the bus during his lunch hour. It wasn't until that night, sometime after he'd gone to bed, that his memories stopped. There was another thing too, Kirkwood had also mentioned feeling ill.

"Daniel, the death you witnessed, how did it happen?"

"A man walked onto the football field. He had a shotgun and coach yelled for us to go to the locker room, but the man turned the gun on himself, put the barrel in his mouth, and pulled the trigger."

Another suicide.

I expected it, but I still cringed at the apathetic delivery from the shade. The other suicides: jumping in front of a bus, diving off a building, and even the incineration, could be suicides of opportunity, the public aspect coincidental. But a man walking onto a crowded field with a shotgun sounded like he'd gone out of his way to make sure there were witnesses.

So I had a witnessed suicide, lost time, a shade that re-gained awareness only in the last seconds, possibly after mortal death if the initial collision with the bus killed him before he was sucked into the wheel well. I'd have liked to know his stomach contents at time of death, but he wouldn't know what he'd eaten during the time he had no memory. Which left only one important question left to prove a pattern and not just a coincidental fluke in two of the victims.

"Daniel, how much did you weigh?"

"Two ten," the shade said without hesitation.

And now for the hard part—at least for my stomach, because now I had to try to guess the death weight of a kid who'd been rearranged by a bus.

The shade's left arm was fairly intact, so I focused on that. A skinny forearm led down to a knobby wrist and hands with insubstantial skin that sank in hollow valleys between thin bones. His sticklike fingers were so thin they looked too long for his body. Yeah, no way had he weighed anywhere near two hundred pounds at the time of his death.

"Hey, what are you doing?" I shrill female voice yelled.

I whirled around in time to see a pretty girl of no more than eighteen drop her backpack and dash across the cem-etery lawn.

Oh crap. I didn't know if she was the sister mentioned in the obit or just a friend, but she didn't need to see Daniel this way.

"Rest now," I told the shade, pulling back my power, and shoving the thing too crushed and broken to look human back into its grave.

But not fast enough.

The girl's scream cut through the stillness and she col-lapsed to her knees just outside my circle.

"That was . . . Was it . . . It was, wasn't it? Oh my god. I knew, but—" Her words broke off, fat tears rolling down her cheeks.

The shade was gone now, but she stared at the place he'd been as if his image was seared into that spot. I reclaimed what I could of my heat and released my hold on the grave, but I didn't push back the different planes of reality—this was the second shade I'd raised today and I was going to pay for it. Wandering around blind wasn't at the top of my priority list right now. Especially with a near hysterical girl just yards away.

"You were a friend?" I asked, kneeling down to her level. My circle still separated us, throwing a haze of blue between us that made the brilliant yellow of her soul look slightly green.

The girl nodded. "We were, I mean, I thought . . ." She scrubbed at the tears on her checks with the back of her hand. "Did you ask him why?"

I knew which "why" she wanted. She wanted to know why he'd killed himself. Suicides had always been my least favorite cases to work because whatever answer the shade gave was never enough for those who'd been left behind. This time though, this was even worse. *Do I tell her it was murder? That he didn't make the choice?* I didn't know. And I still hadn't proven to the cops that they had a killer on the loose, so I avoided the question.

"What's your name?" I asked the girl.

She scrubbed at more tears. "Allison."

"Okay, Allison, can I ask you a few questions?" I didn't wait for her to answer before going on. "When was the last time you saw Daniel?"

"Wednesday morning."

Wednesday? That was during the shade's memory loss. A twinge of excitement ran through me. This girl might know something, even if she didn't realize she did. But I couldn't let that excitement show while I squatted beside her friend's grave.

"I need you to think back to Wednesday. Did Daniel act strange? Did he do or say anything strange or out of the ordinary?"

The girl looked at the ground, but that didn't stop me from seeing the flush that lit her face. "He'd had a bad couple of days. Something happened at football practice, and then he started feeling ill. I'd talked to him the night before, when he'd canceled our study session—I was tutoring him in math. He said he had to cancel because he was coming down with the flu. He sounded awful, actually sick. Not like the times he claimed he was and then went to a party. So I picked up breakfast at the cafeteria for him and took it to his dorm room. I felt bad for him, you know? Until I got there and discovered he definitely wasn't sick. He'd blown me off. Again. Not completely surprising, I mean, he was a football player and I'm a math nerd." Her ears turned the color of strawberries and I could almost see the heat coming off her flushed face. "But then he invited me in and I, uh, missed all my morning classes. I've never skipped classes before but . . ."

By the depth of her blush, I guessed they hadn't made up the lost tutoring time. "You had sex?" I asked, and when she cringed, I inwardly cursed myself for my bluntness. Tact wasn't my strongest trait.

She pushed off the ground and ran a hand through her dark hair so that it fell into her face. "I have to go." She turned all but running for her dropped backpack.

"Wait," I yelled, after her. She didn't stop. *Damn it.* I broke my circle and rushed after the girl. The planes were still overlaying my vision and I tripped over a bouquet of flowers that had been so withered in my vision I hadn't noticed them.

I didn't catch up with Allison until the cemetery gate. "Wait," I said again, catching her arm.

She jumped, chill bumps shooting across her bared skin. "Damn, lady, you're cold."

In more ways than one. Because I was about to grill her about her dead crush. "When you were . . . with Daniel on Wednesday, did he seem odd. Different?"

"Yeah, he picked me instead of one of the coeds who would have loved to jump into his bed. That odd enough for you? Clearly sleeping with me was a sign of severe mental stress."

Her lips quivered and she made a sound that could have

been a laugh or a sob—was probably both. Angry tears made her long hair stick to her cheeks, and her shoulders trembled, even though she didn't make a sound. I guessed it wasn't just the first time she'd slept with Daniel, it was the first time she'd slept with *anyone*.

When Allison wasn't hiding behind her hair—or blotchy from crying—I bet she was a very pretty girl. A girl who deserved better than a football player that used her to keep his GPA high enough to play. I wanted to hug the girl, to tell her it would be all right. That she'd find someone better. But even though only seven or so years separated our ages, she was still more teenager than young adult, and I knew she wouldn't believe me—I wouldn't have at her age. Hell, with the state of my love life, I wasn't in any position to offer advice.

But I could give her one thing. "He really was ill Tuesday night. He said he went to bed early and shades can't lie."

She looked up, blinking at me. "Really?"

I nodded, giving her my best sympathetic smile, because I was about to push her again. "Allison, I wouldn't ask if it weren't important, but when you were with Daniel, did he seem confused?"

"I don't want to talk about this anymore." She turned down the sidewalk.

I kept pace with her. "Did he use your name?"

Her head shot up and she rounded on me. "Of course he—" She stopped. Her mouth opened slightly as her jaw went slack, and her shoulders shook as a new tear slid down her cheek. "No. Not once. And after . . . after he asked if I knew where he parked his car." Lines of frowns creased her forehead. "He didn't have a car. I thought he was hinting that he wanted to borrow mine. I gave him the keys and told him which garage it was in. That was the last time I saw him."

Her eyes were too wide as she looked up at me. "There was something wrong with him when we . . ." She trailed off. Her lips, her nose, her chin, and just about every muscle in her face quivered. She hugged herself, tucking her hands in her armpits.

I wished I could have lied. Could have told her that his shade said he'd wanted her for a long time or that it was the happiest morning in his life. But his shade didn't even know that morning existed. And I couldn't lie. So I remained silent.

She stared at me for several more seconds, and then turning on her heels, she all but ran away.

A hard knot of guilt twisted my stomach as I watched her go. I'd just taken what was probably a bittersweet memory of the last bit of time she spent with someone she cared about and torn it to shreds. But I'd needed to know if Daniel was himself, or if he was someone else entirely.

It sounded a hell of a lot like the latter.

Chapter 18

❖━━◦ ◦━━❖

I called Rianna for a ride before releasing the other planes
of reality and surrendering to the inevitable darkness.
The world was still little more than inky blackness by the
time she picked me up.

"Your instincts were right on the mark," she said as I
climbed blindly into the car—only to find a barghest in the
front passenger seat.

"It's my car, I've got shotgun," I told him, and the doglike fae huffed, but climbed into the back. After slamming
the door, I fumbled with the seat belt as Rianna pulled
away from the curb.

"So you found a restaurant where Kingly ate?" I asked
once the satisfying click of the buckle latching finally
sounded

"A restaurant? No. I found three. And get this, as I was
showing the photo around, I warned people he might have
been considerably thinner. The staff at all three restaurants
said he looked exactly like he had in the photo. Including
the five star joint he ate lunch at on Friday."

"But . . ." I blinked in the darkness, my thoughts racing.
Tamara had said he'd eaten within hours of his death. I'd
seen the pictures of the skeletal figure on the roof. Hell, I'd
seen enough of the shade to know he wasn't a husky man

when he dove off that building. "That means whatever sucked the health and vitality out of him did it in hours, not days."

That or he'd been processed by something that could use glamour to make the withering body *look* unchanged.

"Here's another interesting thing," she said and I heard her flip on the turning signal. "After striking out at the nicer-looking restaurants close to Delaney's, I did a search on my phone for five-star joints—the types of places that would serve caviar and escargot. It took me a couple of hours and way too much driving to figure out, but he hit them in alphabetical order. I mean, he started in the middle of the list, but despite the restaurants being scattered across town, he went to Maven's on Wednesday, Ophelia's on Thursday, and Pandora's Delight on Friday—which might explain why he was in the Magic Quarter though not how he ended up on the roof of a seedy place like Motel Styx."

I gave a low whistle at the named restaurants. The first two were pricey and hard to get into without making reservations weeks in advance. Or so I'd been told. I'd certainly never been to either. Hell, I didn't even own any clothes likely to meet the dress code for such places. But Pandora's Delight? Now that was a different story altogether. Oh, they still served five-star cuisine, but it was a members only establishment, largely due to a floor show that included a lot of sex appeal and even more magic. I'd been inside once, by invitation of one of the owners who'd been under the mistaken assumption that magic as showy as grave magic might both frighten and captivate his members. I'd taken advantage of the free meal before turning him down flat. I didn't disturb the dead for entertainment purposes.

"How did Kingly get in to Pandora's Delight? He was Humans First Party—no way was he a member."

"I asked the same question. He had money. And was quite generous with it, apparently. That was one reason the doorman remembered him," Rianna said, the car slowing as she stopped for a light. The darkness was finally peeking back from my vision, but not enough that I could puzzle out our location from the shadows surrounding the car.

"I wonder where he got the cash," I said, more to myself than to Rianna. She answered anyway.

"His own bank most likely. He used his name and credit cards most of the time so it wouldn't surprise me if he used his bank card to pull funds."

I frowned. "He was reported missing. You'd think the cops would notice the charges on his cards."

My vision was clear enough that I could see Rianna shrug. "I don't think he was missing long enough."

Maybe not. I chewed at my bottom lip. But if Kingly used his own card, tracking his movements would be a hell of a lot easier. *And if Kingly did, would Kirkwood and Walters have as well?*

It was definitely worth looking into. *And speaking of Daniel Walters* . . . I filled Rianna in on what I'd learned from Daniel's shade as well as Allison's comments about his actions during the time the shade couldn't remember.

"This isn't a spell, is it?"

"Doesn't seem that way." And if it wasn't a spell, the prospects that left were terrifying because possession was moving up the list. The thought about possessed bodies reminded me of the ghouls and Briar, which I hadn't told Rianna about. Considering Rianna was also a grave witch, Briar was likely to jump her next. She could use a heads-up about the militant inspector. I was just finishing recounting the conversation as the familiar tingle of magic from the Quarter filled the air.

"Ghouls, seriously?" Rianna shook her head. "I always assumed they were the boogeymen of grave witches. You know, horror stories the teachers told us to ensure we always worked within a circle."

"Apparently not," I said as she pulled to a stop in front of our office. We were officially closed for the evening by this point, but I needed my laptop and, with dusk approaching, Rianna needed to return to Faerie.

As soon as I climbed out of the car, Desmond crawled to

the seat I'd abandoned. I frowned at the barghest, who was little more than a large black blob to my bad eyes. Color was seeping back into the world, but the late evening sun didn't help. My thoughts had circled back to Kingly and Walters's strange behavior, and before shutting the car door, I turned back toward Rianna. "When Coleman—"

She cut me off. "Whatever we're dealing with, it couldn't be like him. It took elaborate rituals for Coleman to switch bodies."

And the body thief hadn't burned through and discarded bodies anywhere near as fast as whatever we were dealing with. There was also the fact the shades were still in the body at death. It didn't add up. The more we learned, the less everything fit together.

"You're sure you don't want me to take you home?" Rianna asked as I slung my purse over my shoulder.

"Make you drive out to the Glen only to have to return to the Quarter so you can get to the Bloom before sunset?" I shook my head, which throbbed with my tangled thoughts. "It's not worth the risk. What if you hit a traffic jam? I'll be fine, but it would be nice if you could ask Holly or Caleb"— if he was speaking to me yet—"to pick me up after dinner."

"Sure," she said, and I noted the relief in her voice. Shutting the door, I stepped back so she could get to the Bloom. She wasn't exactly cutting it close, but it was closer than she liked.

I waved at the blur that was my car before letting myself into the offices of Tongues for the Dead. Only the smallest amount of the evening sunlight filtered through the front window, which pretty much left the lobby pitch-black to me. I sighed, feeling along the wall for the light switch when a crash sounded from farther inside the office and a shimmery head popped through the door of the broom closet.

"Hey, Alex," Roy said, stepping though the door once he saw it was me. "Where have you been? Someone stopped by the office while you were gone."

Just my luck. "Do you know who it was?"

"She left a note. I put it on your desk." The accomplishment in his voice at moving a piece of paper from one room to another was so thick that I couldn't help smiling.

"Good work," I told him and the ghost beamed.

"So are we on the same case? What can I do?"

"Yes, to the first and as to the second, I'm not even sure what I can do," I said, my smile falling away as weariness from a day filled with two rituals, a visit from a militant official, and too many questions without any answers settled on me once again.

The ghost's glowing happiness evaporated. "Oh, well, I guess if you need me I'll be in my office." He floated back through his door without another word.

If I could have thought of a single thing I needed that he could accomplish, I'd have gone after him, but I had nothing, so I retreated to my own office. As Roy had promised, a folded note sat in the center of my desk. I picked it up and found it contained a name, Kelly Kirkwood, followed by a phone number and the words *please call me* in all capital letters.

I woke my computer and squinted to make out the time on the screen—it was quarter till seven. After business hours for sure, but not actually late. *But am I up to talking to the widow of a man I identified this morning?*

Not really, but it wasn't like I had much else to do while I waited for Caleb and Holly.

I dialed the number provided. It was answered on the first ring.

"Hello?" the female voice was hoarse, and the single word had the slightest hitch in it, as if the speaker would break into tears at any moment.

"Hi, this is Alex Craft, I'm calling for—"

"Oh, thank goodness. I'm Kelly," the woman said, cutting me off. "You identified my husband, Richard, today."

I couldn't tell from her tone if that was a good thing or a bad one. I mean, sad, obviously, but some people got rather pissy when grave witches raised their loved ones without permission. As I didn't know which way Kelly Kirkwood would swing, all I said was, "Yes, ma'am."

"Why did Rick do it? Did he tell you? The medical examiner wouldn't say, but I have to know. Please."

I cringed at her please as much as the plea to know why, which I couldn't answer. Or could I? Didn't she deserve to know that her husband hadn't killed himself?

My hesitation wasn't long, but I also wasn't the one anxiously waiting an answer. She was.

"I'll pay you," she said, "even if the police already paid you, I'll pay you your normal rate for the ritual you already performed. Just tell me what he said."

"Mrs. Kirkwood—"

"Kelly."

Okay. "Kelly, when I raised your husband's shade today, it was for more reason than to identify a John Doe. He came to my attention in connection to another case I'm working."

"Are you saying Rick did something illegal? Is that why he thought the only option was . . ." She trailed off, and though she didn't make a sound, I was sure she was crying on the other end of the line.

"No, it's nothing like that." I paused, uncertain. But if it were me and someone I cared about, I'd want to know. "I'm investigating a chain of murders. Your husband—he was one of the victims."

"Murder? The police said it was suicide. Are you certain?"

I couldn't give her all the facts because I didn't have them. Actually, I had almost no facts. Just a lot of questions and a couple of guesses. "There are certain similarities in several supposed suicides."

"And? What similarities? If Rick was killed, who did it? And how? When the police first thought that they had found him, I read up on the burn victim. I couldn't believe it. Couldn't believe that Rick would kill himself, especially not like that. It was too horrible. Then when the dental records didn't match . . ." She trailed off. "They never told me why the dentals didn't match. The officer I spoke to said it might have had something to do with the fire. Do you know?"

"I don't know why they didn't match," I said, not lying because they *should* have matched. I had no idea what had happened in the missing days that changed his teeth so drastically. "As to your other questions, I can't really discuss the case."

"What if I hire you to investigate Rick's death?"

I frowned, which she, being on the phone, couldn't see. "As your husband's death is almost certainly connected to the other cases, once I find the who and the how for my other client, your husband's case will be solved as well."

"Yes, but if I hire you, you'll keep me informed."

A good point, but she seemed too anxious, too eager. "Mrs. Kirkwood, while I hate the idea of turning down clients, you called to find out why your husband killed himself. I tell you that I believe it is murder, and you offer to hire me to investigate—"

"And you want to know why I believe you," she said.

"Exactly."

"Are you married, Ms. Craft?"

"No."

"A boyfriend, then?" she asked.

That was a loaded question. Thankfully she didn't wait for me to answer.

"If he vanished one night, and then you were told he'd killed himself in a horrific way, who would you believe: the person telling you the man you know and love killed himself without any warning or the person who told you he was murdered?"

Both the men in my life had a tendency to vanish, and I wasn't going to touch the love part, but in my gut I knew she was right—I'd never believe Falin or Death would take their own lives.

"Okay. Come by in the morning to sign paperwork. Also, it would be good to have a recent picture of Richard, so bring that with you tomorrow," I said, and then I told her about the shade's missing three days and the rapid weight loss. I didn't mention the contents of his last meal or the change to his teeth, nor did I tell her who the other victims were or my suspicions on how the victims had become infected.

"What could do this?" she asked, and this time the tears were obvious in her voice. "I have a little talent for magic, but Rick was completely null. Half the time the charms I made malfunctioned if he tried to use them. So if it was magic . . ." She broke off.

So he really was a null. Well, at least we knew Tamara's Relative Magic Compatibility machine was functioning.

"I'm not ready to speculate yet on the cause, but I'll keep you updated." I paused. "There is one other thing you can bring that will help us track Rick's movements while he was missing. Could you bring a record of his bank and credit card purchases for the first three days he was gone?"

"I haven't received the statements yet, but I can print them online," she said, and I heard the unmistakable click-clack of her typing. She gasped, the inhalation sharp even over the phone. "This can't be. His cards must have been stolen."

"Do the charges stop on the Tuesday he died?"

"Yes, but—"

"And the charges include five-star restaurants?"

"How did you—? Your other case. Did that case also have the hotels and the . . . the . . ." Her voice broke, her pain audibly raw as she said, "It's printing. I'll see you in the morning."

A moment before she disconnected I heard a single, aching sob. Then the line went silent. I stared at my phone for several heartbeats wondering what her trail of "the's" had led to that she couldn't bring herself to say. *I guess I'll find out in the morning.*

But I wouldn't know if the other victims had the same charges, not unless I saw their statements as well. *Or if it is something I can track another way.* I'd have to wait and see because I seriously doubted I could convince Nina Kingly to share information about her husband's financial transactions. She already treated me like a charlatan half the time.

I woke my computer and glanced at the time. It was

nearing eight. Either Holly and Caleb had abandoned me, or it was one of the days the doors to Faerie had decided not to give us extra time. I just hoped the time in the Bloom wasn't moving at a fourth the time as mortal reality—I really didn't want to be stuck at the office until midnight. I couldn't call, not while they were inside the Bloom; since I'd already asked for a ride, I couldn't take a cab home and not be there when they arrived. Which meant I was stuck for the duration.

I opened my browser. I hated the idea, but now that Kirkwood was officially my client, I needed to watch the video I'd seen linked to one of the articles about his death. It was saved in my bookmarks, so finding it was no problem. Convincing myself to click the button, now that took a minute. Was it just this morning I'd seen the end result? It seemed like days ago, but thinking about him brought back the grotesque image of the blackened and split skin. And the smell, suddenly my entire office stank with the remembered smell of burnt hair and charred flesh.

Okay, Alex, you're not doing yourself any favors here. Just get it over with.

Easy to think. Hard to do.

Taking a deep breath, I let it out slow and loaded the video.

It had obviously been shot with a cell phone, the person holding it moving so the frame shook. But as a whole, the footage didn't start out too terrifying. Kirkwood was already engulfed in flames, but he just stood there, like a statue. People I couldn't see gasped, cursed, and even cheered.

"Dude, are you getting this?" someone off camera asked. *"This is so hard-core. What kind of charm do you think he's using?"*

"Hey, you smell that?" another voice asked.

"Ulgch, yeah." The first voice again, and then yelling. *"Hey, mister, I think something's going wrong."*

Other people had realized it too. The cheering had stopped and people were yelling. Some at the burning man, who still stood perfectly still, others to people outside the video's frame.

In the poor quality of the recording, I couldn't see much more than the darkening of Kirkwood's skin beneath the lapping flames. No, it wasn't his skin. I stared as something dark poured out of Kirkwood, like a miasma of black that reflected the orange flames back in a prism of color. Whatever the darkness was, it wasn't quite a figure, at least, not a humanoid one. The last bit flowed out of the burning man.

Then Kirkwood screamed.

His arms flapped at his sides as if the movement would help extinguish the flames that were consuming him. He made it three steps before collapsing in a burning heap. A man appeared in the space behind Kirkwood and my breath caught at the sight of the familiar form. *Death.* In the back of my mind I'd known the video might catch an image of the collector, even if the boys shooting it couldn't see him. But Death's sudden appearance caught me off guard, and for a moment all I could see was the grainy image of the man who'd always been the one constant in my ever-mutable and chaotic life—until he'd vanished. A fresh wave of loss washed over me.

Then the black T-shirt pulled tight across his chest as he reached into the burning heap in front of him, and the full horror of Kirkwood's murder crashed into me again. In the background the boys making the video were speaking, and somewhere someone retched, the sound ugly and raw. I sympathized but I didn't dare look away from the computer. Death pulled back a clenched hand. Without opening my shields, I couldn't see souls, at least, not unless they transitioned from pure light to the land of the dead as a ghost. So Death's hand looked empty, but I knew he clutched Kirkwood's soul. He flicked his wrist, sending Kirkwood on to wherever souls went. Then Death stood, staring at the dark miasmic form on the edge of the screen. The video quality wasn't good enough for me to read his expression, but his stance radiated anger. Despite that, he didn't move, didn't go after the figure.

"What is that thing?" I asked the grainy image of Death.

He didn't answer. Not that I expected him to.

The boy holding the phone ran toward Kirkwood, and the screen bobbed in jolty, vertigo-inducing motions. I tried to focus on Death and the other figure, but as the amateur cameraman couldn't see either, he aimed the phone only at Kirkwood. Death and the dark cloudlike figure were shuffled toward opposite edges of the screen as the boy moved closer. Then the miasmic creature shot off screen in a blur. *To Kingly?*

I wanted the boy holding the camera phone to turn, to follow it. He didn't.

Death vanished a moment later.

Other people rushed into the frame, carrying coats, drink bottles, blankets—anything to try to help extinguish the burning corpse. They were too late, but they couldn't know his soul was already gone. Somewhere a witch created a glob of water, and it jetted like a fountain from off the screen.

I glanced at the progress bar. The video went on another fifty seconds but I'd seen everything I needed. I turned off the sound and backed the video up to where the thing poured out of Kirkwood. *It's like it was riding his body, directing it.* Kirkwood didn't regain control until that rider left. And Death could see it. I was sure he could. So why didn't he do anything about it? It wasn't natural, that was certain. I wanted the video to end differently this time. But, of course, the rider rushed off the frame in one direction and Death vanished to wherever soul collectors went.

I needed to talk to Death. He'd seen it. He had to know what it was, maybe even how to deal with it. Except even if he were speaking to me, in all likelihood—since the rider suppressed its host's soul—it would fall into the enormous category of things the collectors couldn't discuss.

I sighed and backed up the video again. I magnified it, trying to get a better look at the rider. Enlarging the image didn't help; it just caused it to pixilate.

How likely is it that what I saw was a spell vacating and

jumping bodies? I shook my head, dismissing the possibility. I hadn't seen a face in that darkness, but I was positive that when Death stared at it, the thing stared back at him. That made it cognizant, a being.

A fae?

Not one I'd ever seen before, but that didn't mean much. I grabbed my phone and scrolled through my recent contacts. I had no trouble finding the number I wanted—in truth, I didn't even need to scroll, I'd memorized it long before I ever dialed it.

I clicked the video back on again as the phone rang.

"Andrews."

Falin really needed to learn the word "hello." Not that I bothered with it either.

"This is business," I said before he could ask. "I'm looking for a fae who can jump from body to body without a ritual. It basically overrides the soul, taking control of the host until it sucks them dry. Outside of the body it's just a formless mass. Dark, but also iridescent."

Falin was quiet for so long, I feared he wouldn't answer. Then he said, "There are certain fae who can feed on human energy, eventually draining them with extended exposure—night hags and anything in the incubi family come to mind—but they all have solid forms. Does it look like the wraiths the shadow court uses as guards?"

I considered the shadows given form that I'd seen when I visited Faerie last month. "Those were more substantial than this thing. This was more like—" I froze, a sick realization hitting me. This thing riding mortal bodies. It wasn't like a fae.

It was like a ghost.

"I have to go," I said, hanging up.

On my screen, Death was staring at the malevolent thing that had poured out of Kirkwood.

"I wish you were here," I whispered at his image.

"I do hope you're talking about me," a deep and wonderfully familiar voice said.

I tore my gaze from the screen. There, in my doorway,

stood Death, his thumbs tucked casually into the loops of his faded jeans and an easy smile on his face.

I jumped to my feet and then froze because my heart felt like it might leap across the room before me. And I did want to run to him, to touch him and make sure he was real. But if he vanished on me, the crush of disappointment might break every bone in my body.

"Are you really here, or am I finally having a good dream?"

His face turned serious, those intense dark eyes searching me as if looking for a wound he could bind. "Still having nightmares?"

"This is not a social call," another voice said, and the gray man popped into existence in the room, his cane twirling like a baton.

"Which is why he shouldn't have come," a female voice said as a third soul collector, one I'd dubbed the raver because of her white PVC pants, orange tube top, and neon dreadlocks, appeared in the room.

I sank back into my chair, my insides too heavy for my legs to support. "If I'd known there'd be a party tonight, I'd have brought drinks," I said to none of the collectors in particular.

"Trust me, this is no party," the raver said, her long nails tapping against the plastic of her pants. "This is an intervention."

An intervention? She *had* to be kidding. But when I glanced at Death, his face was serious and he gave me a single, solemn nod. Damn. An intervention of what? They'd already inserted themselves into my relationship with Death to the point this was the first time I'd been in the same room with him in a month.

"You need to drop this case, Alex," Death said, and I gawked at him.

I couldn't drop the case. The police didn't believe the victims were murdered. If I didn't gather enough proof to convince them of the truth, who would? And then there was the firm's budding reputation to consider. I couldn't drop my

first case. Though I had to admit, when someone whose pri-
mary occupation involved collecting the souls of the dead
told me to drop something, I couldn't ignore the warning.
The case wasn't worth dying for, but then, they hadn't said it
would come to that.

"Don't warn me off—prepare me. What is that thing?
How do I stop it from jumping bodies?"

The three collectors exchanged a look I wasn't invited to
participate in. Then the raver turned toward me. "You see
far too much, girl."

"Walk away." The gray man pointed his cane so the silver
skull grinned at me a foot from my face. "Walk away and let
someone else deal with it."

"Who? Who can deal with it? You guys can see it and
have made no effort to stop it."

The three collectors went as still as statues. Then they
turned toward one another, as if in silent conversation. I
could read enough of their expressions to know that Death
wanted to tell me whatever they silently debated. I guessed
the gray man would vote no, which left the raver, who was
the swing vote and tended to waver more than the other
two. I hoped she was feeling charitable toward me today.

She raked a hand through the air in a dismissive gesture.
"She'll figure it out anyway," she said.

The gray man, with his youthful features disguised under
the blandness of his appearance, snapped his cane against
his thigh, but gave a sharp "Fine" before turning toward me
again.

"It does not exist on a plane we can touch, so we cannot
do anything about its actions. But that doesn't mean *you*
need to get involved. Walk away."

His message delivered, he vanished. The raver lifted a
brightly dyed eyebrow, as if daring me to disagree; then she
also vanished.

Which left Death, his handsome face torn, a mix of want
and pain in his eyes as he stepped closer.

"I know you have to go," I said.

"I don't want to."

I knew that too—it was written in every movement of his body—but I didn't say it. There were laws against a mortal and a collector having a relationship. A month ago I'd even seen a horrific example of why. But I missed Death. I wanted him in my life.

I had a circle of people I considered my best friends, but Death was more than just a good friend or potential lover. He'd been there for the worst moments of my life, knew the secrets I told no one else, knew me. And despite everything he couldn't tell me, I knew him. Oh, I didn't know his name or understand his magic, but I knew his easy laugh, his kindness, his compassion, and yes, his flirtatious streak. I might *want* him as a man, but I *needed* my friend.

"If we went back to the way things were before . . . ?"

Death stepped around my desk and brushed a curl behind my ear. The simple, familiar gesture sent a shiver of excitement through me. *Okay, maybe going back would be hard.*

"That wouldn't be enough anymore," he whispered, as his fingers tilted my face toward his.

I dropped my gaze, avoiding the emotions in his eyes. His nearness woke a giddy excitement in my stomach, something much more than friendly, which carried on its heels the itch of guilt because he wasn't the only man who affected me this way.

I changed the subject. "I have the artifact the witch and her reaper used in their ritual. Shouldn't you take it?" After all, it allowed mortals to interact across planes—including the collectors' plane.

I hated that damned artifact. It contributed to Death's absence this last month. Though, to be fair, the actions of the twisted couple couldn't be blamed on a magical relic. Still, in the aftermath of that horrible night, something inside me warned me not to turn the artifact over to the police.

"Is it secure?" Death asked, his expression turning serious.

I nodded. "It's in a magical dampening box in my apartment."

"You're probably the only mortal with no use for the artifact, so that will be enough for now. I'll find out what should be done with it." His thumb ran along my jaw, sending shivers down my body. "That will give me an excuse to return."

He leaned forward and his breath tumbled over my lips, smelling of dew and clean, fresh turned earth. I froze, uncertain if I wanted to pull away or accept the kiss.

It turned out I didn't have to make the decision.

A hand with bright orange nails appeared, grabbed my shoulders, and jerked me back, making my chair tilt as it rolled over the uneven carpet.

I yelped, more in surprise than anything, and the raver stepped between Death and me.

"You two seriously need a babysitter," she said, crossing her arms over her chest and glaring first at me and then him. "Time to go."

Death said nothing, he just glanced over her head, meeting my gaze, and then vanished. She followed suit.

I sat there, alone in my office, still seeing the look in Death's eyes before he left. Those eyes that could smile even when he wasn't; those eyes that could tease. But tonight, in that last look, what I saw in those eyes reminded me of words I only half remembered from when I'd been dying under the Blood Moon. And that terrified me, because that night Death had said he loved me.

Chapter 19

I stopped in the doorway of the Tongues for the Dead office, the morning sunlight streaming in behind me and reflecting off the burnished wood of a large executive desk. A desk that hadn't been there when Caleb and Holly had picked me up at midnight.

Okay, either I'm dreaming or the desk fairy came overnight.

I blinked, waiting to wake up. I didn't and the desk was still there. *Desk fairy it is.*

And the desk wasn't the only new item. A large leather chair sat primly behind it, a blotter, a phone—which was even more a mystery as we didn't have a landline—and a computer were placed neatly on the desk's surface. Against the other wall, the threadbare seat had been replaced with a leather and wood love seat and two matching chairs. And on the wall opposite the main door? A grandfather clock taller than me.

I stepped back out the threshold, closed the door, and stared at the words Tongues for the Dead stenciled on the window, Rianna's and my name under it. Yes, this was our office.

I opened the door again, expecting the ragtag collection of furnishings we'd had since opening a week ago to have reappeared. No, the expensive lobby decor still filled the lobby.

"Hello?" I said, not expecting an answer. If Rianna had been here—and she never beat me because of the erratic nature of the Bloom's door—she would have left the door unlocked. Which meant I was alone with an office suite worth more than half a year's rent.

Or at least I thought I was alone, until the door to my personal office swung open.

I dropped to a crouch, my hand moving to the hilt of my dagger. It was silly really. What did I expect? Burglars? Their MO was to take stuff, not replace junk with better stuff. Or maybe the office was the prop of a serial killer with an executive fetish.

From where I was squatting, the large desk blocked the bottom half of my door, but I expected to see the torso of whoever had opened it. I didn't. The chair squealed, twisting slightly, and then a thud sounded as small bare feet landed on the top of the desk.

I straightened at the sight of the brownie, who stood maybe two and a half feet tall and nearly as wide. Her long, quill-like green hair trailed behind her, hanging over the back side of the large desk. Her small fists rounded and she pressed them against her hips.

"Ms. B?"

"You're late," she said, coal-colored eyes hard as she pointed to the large grandfather clock. The larger hand currently pointed at the three. "I expect you here on time tomorrow."

"On time?" I repeated like a parrot. It was my business. How could I be late? Of course, I did have the hours posted on the door, and according to them I was, in fact, fifteen minutes late.

I almost asked her how she'd gotten into the locked and warded office, but I knew better. She bypassed the locks and wards on the house just as easily. I took another look around the room. There were even paintings on the walls.

"Is all of this glamour?"

"Of course not. That would never do," she said, and the way she cocked her head implied she was questioning my general intelligence. She looked about to say more when the phone—the one that shouldn't have had a live connection—rang. "Tongues for the Dead," Ms. B said in her gruff voice. She'd never be a phone sex operator, but she did sound surprisingly professional. "Yes, bring them in, we're ready." She set the phone back on the receiver and turned to me. "You planning on catching pixies in that trap?"

I blinked, then realized my jaw was hanging loose. I snapped my mouth shut.

The chime on the door sounded and Rianna said, "Oh hello." But she didn't step inside and she wasn't talking to me. Two large trolls ducked under the doorway, not that they could stop ducking after they were inside—the ceiling had only an eight-foot clearance. The first carried four chairs, two with blue velvet seats and silver accents and the other two with green and brass.

"Blue this way," Ms. B said, and turning jumped from the desk. Her hair rustled as she padded across the floor, which I noticed with more than a little shock was now a deep cherry hardwood instead of the ratty carpet. The small brownie headed into my office, and the troll with the chairs, Rianna and I followed.

My office's transformation wasn't quite as drastic as the lobby's, but then there wasn't much room to be drastic. My mismatched client chairs were gone, but were quickly replaced by the blue ones the troll was carrying. My chair, which had already been fairly nice, was still there, but I had to do a double take to realize the desk was the same as it had been stripped and refinished.

"I managed to salvage it," Ms. B said, a note of pride in her voice.

The troll set the chairs down haphazardly. As Ms. B positioned them to her satisfaction, I looked at the other changes. I now owned a filing cabinet stained the same color as the desk and chairs, the broken blinds on my window had been replaced and blue curtains hung around them, and best yet, a mini fridge with a microwave and coffeepot on top sat in the farthest corner.

"Okay, I'm impressed."

Ms. B clucked appreciatively and then turned toward Rianna. "Your turn, girl."

She scampered out of my office and across the lobby to Rianna's. Both trolls followed this time, one setting a new desk in the center of the room and the other placing the final two chairs. Rianna's room was decorated with the same dark wood as mine, but where my accents were blue and silver, all of hers were green and brass. Desmond even had an oversized green velvet dog bed, which he immediately investigated.

Rianna and I looked at each other, sharing an approving nod.

"The small one goes in the little room," Ms. B told the troll who still carried one desk, the size a pupil might use in school.

She got a desk for Roy? If he weren't already dead, I guessed the ghost would keel over from joy. I couldn't wait until he saw it. But one nagging worry scratched at the edge of my mind.

"Ms. B, how did you pay for all this?"

"From your treasury of course."

My treasury? I made a mental whimper that I managed not to allow to escape any farther than my thoughts. "So, Faerie money?" I gave a despairing glance at all the beautiful things—which we were going to have to return. Faerie money didn't remain money long; it turned back into leaves or rocks or whatever it was made from after a few hours, which meant everything was technically stolen.

"Not Faerie money," the brownie said. Her expression was hard to read because of her very inhuman, coal-colored eyes and lack of a real nose, but she sounded offended.

Rianna elbowed me in the side and whispered. "Coleman made good money as governor. Of course, he also knew how to spend it, but he left quite a bit when he died."

"I have a vault of money?" My voice sounded far away as I imagined what I could do with an entire vault of money.

"Not anymore." Ms. B walked back into the lobby.

My shoulders sagged, just a little. "Oh." *Well, at least the office looks presentable, I guess.* Though a bit of savings to invest back into the business wouldn't have been amiss. *I bet even Nina Kingly can't find fault in this setup.*

As if my thoughts summoned a client, the door chimed. I turned.

A mousy-looking woman with short cropped brown hair stood just inside the door, her eyes wide as she took in the now lavish lobby.

Ms. B hopped onto her desk. "Welcome to Tongues for the Dead, where not even death can keep secrets."

That *so* wasn't our tagline. Besides, Death was more than capable of keeping secrets. I should know.

The woman looked toward the desk, and her shoulders jumped as her gaze landed on the brownie. "Oh, uh. Hello?"

I stepped forward. "Hi, I'm Alex Craft," I said, holding out my hand.

The woman gave me a relieved smile. "Kelly." She took my hand and pumped it a little too vigorously. "Kelly Kirkwood."

Crap. With everything that had happened with the collectors and then the surprise of Ms. B's redecorating, I'd forgotten Kirkwood's widow was supposed to stop by this morning. The collectors' vague warning unnerved me, but I'd told Kelly that I'd work her case and I would stand by my word. After all, I had a business to get off the ground and dropping my first two cases wouldn't be the best start.

My hand tingled both from Kelly's warmth and her grip by the time I reclaimed it. Rianna hovered in her doorway and I motioned her over. "Mrs. Kirkwood, this is my associate, Rianna McBride. We'll be working your husband's case together." That got an eyebrow lift from Rianna, but if Kelly noticed Rianna's reaction, it didn't stop her from giving Rianna as enthusiastic a handshake as she'd given me.

Introductions complete, I moved on to the more important matter. "Did you bring the items we discussed?"

"Right here." She held up a thin manila folder.

"Perfect. Let's have a seat in my office."

With any luck, we'd find a pattern we could use to track the rider.

An hour and a half later, Kelly had signed the required paperwork, paid our retainer fee, and then, after I'd promised to keep her up-to-date, she'd left to plan her husband's funeral. Since then Rianna and I had poured over Kirkwood's purchases for the three days he'd been possessed. We'd expected the five-star restaurant charges, and as Rianna had noted with Kingly's cuisine choices, they were in alphabetical order—this time Jeniveve, La Belle, and Le Rouge, which, on a list of Nekros's five-star restaurants, were directly before the ones he'd eaten at while in Kingly's body.

"It's been what, thirteen days since Kingly died? What restaurant is thirteen spaces below Pandora's Delight—that was the last place Kingly ate, right?" I asked. We were hours from lunchtime, but if we knew where the rider was going, finding him would be a hell of a lot easier.

But do I want to find him? I couldn't help thinking about the collectors' visit last night and their warning to let someone else handle the case. But I'd called John after Death had left, and he'd insisted I lacked enough physical evidence to open a homicide case.

Which leaves us to find the rider. That didn't mean we had to engage him, just find him and then call in the big guns. I glanced at Rianna, waiting for her to check on the restaurant.

She pulled out her phone and in a few clicks, had the search results she'd used the day before. "Problem," she said, frowning. "There are only nine more five-star restaurants listed."

Damn. That meant he could be anywhere. Would he start

back at the beginning? Or return to favorites? I had no way
of knowing.

The rest of Kirkwood's charges weren't terribly enlight-
ening. The hotel he'd stayed at was also a five-star establishment, but he'd stayed there both of the nights before he'd
doused himself with gas and we didn't know where Kingly
had stayed. The rider had also hired escorts, which I hadn't
even realized Nekros had until I looked up what the—
rather outrageous—charges on the card were.

"Why did he go to a ballet?" Rianna asked, pointing to
one of the final charges on the card.

I shook my head. "He also attended four movies and
went to an art gallery." I stared at the charges. "What is it
doing? I mean, it's pretty obvious that it's eating good food,
staying in luxurious places, indulging its libido, and all
around living the highlife on its victim's dime before sucking the body dry and jumping to a new one, but why?
What's its point?"

Rianna shrugged. "Does it have to have one? Maybe
that's the extent of it."

Supernatural identity theft? Yes, but this ended in death,
not a battle with creditors.

"There has to be some sort of plan though, right? You
don't just kill people to—" I didn't finish the sentence because at that moment an excited ghost popped through the
door.

"I have a desk! A real desk," Roy said, his opaque glasses
sliding down his nose as he bounced on his toes like a child
who'd been promised all the ice cream he could eat.

"I wish I could take credit, but it was all Ms. B."

"Ms. B? You mean the . . . ?" He pointed toward the
lobby.

"Brownie. And yes. She apparently decided we needed
new office furniture." And hadn't consulted anyone first,
which I wasn't exactly complaining about, we looked a hell
of a lot more professional, but she'd appointed herself office
manager and I wasn't sure how I felt about that.

Rianna gave me a quizzical look. "The ghost?"

I nodded. "He's excited about his desk," I said and a moment later lights lit behind Rianna's eyes as she tapped the grave so she could see and hear Roy. He ignored her, though I knew from what Roy had told me in the past that she'd just lit up like a torch in the land of the dead.

Well, ignoring is better than fighting.

I glanced at the paper in front of me. We needed something to compare Kirkwood's experiences to. I knew the rider had slept with Allison in Daniel's body and that while riding both Kirkwood and Kingly it had dined well, but what about the rest? Did the host's personality have any influence?

"Roy, you up for your first assignment?"

The ghost beamed at me. "Just say the word."

"I need you to convince James Kingly to come to the office."

Roy's expression fell. "The ghost?"

"No, his dead body. Yes, of course the ghost," I said, but he looked so crestfallen that I added, "I know you don't like dealing with other ghosts, but if you run into any trouble of the energy stealing sort, I'll give you a full recharge when you get back, okay?"

He nodded, but he looked far from thrilled. He didn't object though, so that was a plus. I got Kingly's address from the paperwork Nina had signed and read it off to him. Roy's wave was anything but enthusiastic as he retreated farther into the land of the dead where he could travel faster.

Once he was gone, I looked at Rianna who was watching me with an amused expression, her eyes once again back to normal. "They're always real to you, aren't they?"

"Ghosts?"

She nodded.

I shrugged. "Sometimes I'm afraid that one day I won't be able to tell the difference between who and what is real versus what is slipping through from another plane." I pushed away from my desk and stretched. I'd been sitting still too long.

Walking over to the coffeepot, I discovered Ms. B had stocked a very nice dark roast bean. I started to prepare enough coffee for two before I remembered that Rianna couldn't actually drink it and paused, scoop hovering over the filter.

"Do you mind if I?" I nodded at the coffeepot. Rianna just shrugged and a lump of guilt tugged at me. When we'd been at the academy she'd needed her morning cup of coffee just as much as I had. It was downright rude to make it in front of her.

"Oh don't look like that, Al. And don't give me that startled face either. I've known you too long not to know how you think. Drink your coffee. I listen to your stomach rumble while you watch me eat at the Bloom all the time. I can brave the scent of coffee." She winked at me and said, "I'll enjoy it vicariously through you. Though I will take some water if you have it."

Did I have water? I had no idea. Yesterday I hadn't even had a fridge. I opened the mini fridge and discovered that not only did I have water, but it was artesian spring water in glass bottles. I laughed at the absurdity of it. At home I lived on cheap takeout and frozen dinners. Here I had water that probably cost a dollar an ounce.

"So you didn't find anything in the obituaries?" Rianna asked after I handed her one of the bottles. When I shook my head, she pressed her lips together. "You won't feel bad if I double-check?"

"Go for it. Maybe you'll catch something I missed." I'd searched for hours, but hadn't run across a thing and Tamara hadn't mentioned any new bodies arriving at the morgue fitting our pattern. It had been thirteen days since Kingly died, which, if the rider stuck to its schedule of keeping a body for only three days, meant we should have had four more bodies. But I'd found nothing that fit.

Rianna pointed to my laptop with a "may I?" gesture and I nodded. Once my coffee finished brewing, I walked back to my desk and pulled out the scrap of paper where I'd jotted Daniel Walters's parents' number. When I'd tracked down their phone number last night, it had been far too late to call. I wasn't sure now was a better time, after all, it was midmorning on a Thursday, but it was worth a shot. I didn't have much else to do while waiting for Roy to return with Kingly.

Daniel's father answered on the second ring.

"Hi, I'm Alex Craft, a private investigator with Tongues for the Dead."

"Yes?" I'd never realized so much skepticism could fit in one short syllable.

"Well, sir, during the course of one of my investigations your son's death came to my attention and—"

"We're not interested."

"Wait," I yelled into the phone, trying to catch him before he hung up. The expected click didn't sound. "Mr. Walters?"

"I follow the news, Ms. Craft. I know who you are and what you do. I respect your right to do magic, but please leave my son and my family at peace. We've been through enough."

"I respect that, sir, and I'm not trying to cause you any more grief, but the case I'm working involves identity theft followed by the apparent suicide of the victim. Did your son have any unusual activity on his bank or credit cards in the three days prior to his death?"

"My son was eighteen, Ms. Craft. He didn't have a credit card," the man said, the words harsh and cutting. Then he sighed. "But he did have a card in case of emergencies. The bill arrived yesterday. I haven't opened it yet." I heard the floor creak as he walked, then the sound of ripping paper. "Let's see—" He gasped, and then released a string of curses, his voice thickening with each one.

"Mr. Walters? Mr. Walters." I wasn't yelling into the phone, not quite, but Rianna looked up from my laptop and lifted an eyebrow. It took me calling his name twice more before he quieted, and by that point his words were so heavy with emotion, I think it was the threat of breaking down more than me calling his name that made him stop.

"Mr. Walters, I'm assuming by your reaction that there are unexpected charges. Are any to five-star restaurants probably"—I racked my brain for which restaurants in town would qualify and alphabetically fall just before Jeniveve—"Isabella's and two others."

The other side of the line was silent so long I thought he might not answer. Then he said, "Yes, there's a charge for over two hundred dollars at a restaurant called Isabella's. You said you are investigating identity theft and *apparent* suicides. You believe my son was murdered?"

"We have compelling evidence to point to that conclusion."

Again silence. "Then why aren't the police the ones calling me?"

That gave me pause. "I don't have an answer for that, sir," I said, which was a nonanswer, but the only one I could provide. "Sir, can you tell me what the other uncharacteristic charges on the card are for? I'm assuming two more restaurants and a hotel?"

He listed them off for me, including more movie tickets, an enormous bar tab at a strip joint—which led to more cursing—and tickets to a show at a community theater. "My son hated musical theater," he said and I could almost hear his head shaking through the phone. "Have the police opened a murder case? Or a fraud case?"

"I don't know. I'm working for private clients."

Silence. Then he said, "Thank you for bringing this to my attention, Ms. Craft. I will see that my son gets justice." The phone clicked as he disconnected.

I felt the chasm of debt open between me and this stranger I'd never met, and it wasn't a small one, which meant however terse his words, he truly was thankful.

I sighed and set down my phone.

"Well, you're doing better than me," Rianna said, turning my computer back around. "You're right, nothing suspicious or matching the rider's MO in the obits, and no articles on public suicides. Do you think he took the victim out of state?"

I hoped not. The likelihood we'd be able to track him went down considerably if he did, and we couldn't strike out on our first two official cases as a newly incorporated PI firm. I started to say as much when Roy popped back into the room.

"One ghost, as requested," he said, motioning to the middle-aged ghost who appeared behind him.

"Gold star, Roy," I said, since I couldn't thank him.

"Yeah, whatever. I'm going to go sit at my desk and wait for a *real* task in the case." He sulked his entire way out of the room.

"Why am I here?" Kingly asked, his hands twisting in front of him as he looked around the room.

"You want to know where you were those three days you can't remember, right?" I said and the ghost nodded. I told him about the restaurants, which currently was the extent of what we knew. His eyes didn't bug out at the mention of Pandora's Delight, so I assumed he had no idea what it was. Once I listed off the restaurants I said, "We assume you also stayed at a hotel, but we don't know which one, nor do we know what else you did."

"But how can I help? I don't remember any of it."

Okay, this was the dodgy bit. "We want to check your credit activity."

The ghost's hands clenched at his side. He not only dismissed the idea completely; he adamantly objected. It took twenty minutes of arguing, Rianna and me pointing out that since he was dead his accounts were frozen, and pushing that this could help us solve his murder before the ghost finally relented.

We found much of the same as we had with Kirkwood and Walters: first-class food, escorts, movies, shows, a gallery opening gala, first-rate hotel. Kingly fixated on only one of those.

"I hired whores?" The ghost paced, his hands clenching and unclenching at his sides. "How could I do that? Nina, oh poor Nina, she'll never understand."

"One, your body hired them. From what I can gather,

you weren't in control or conscious at the time. And two, I see no reason to share that detail."

The ghost paused midpace. "You won't tell her?"

"Not that kind of detail." I didn't point out that she'd receive the bill from the credit card company. The ghost was upset enough.

"Alex," Rianna said, her voice lifting with excitement. "The hotel is the same." She pointed at the name on the screen and then at the one Kelly Kirkwood had brought us. She was right. Walters had stayed elsewhere, but Kirkwood and Kingly stayed at the same hotel.

So did that mean he'd found a favorite, or had it just been convenient? *Could his current body be there now?* I had no idea, but now we had a clear pattern of action.

I was comparing our three lists for any other overlaps, from theaters to escort services, when my phone buzzed, dancing across the surface of my desk. I picked it up absently, letting it ring twice more before I glanced at the display.

Then my heart skipped a beat. I knew that number.
Falin.

"Hello?" I said, my voice sounding thin, thready.

"I need you at the morgue," Falin said, his voice cool and commanding. "I have an emaciated corpse who allegedly committed suicide. He's fae."

Chapter 20

"I should perform the ritual," Rianna said as we passed through security at Central Precinct. "Based on the times the credit cards were typically charged, we only have an hour before the rider indulges in a five-star lunch. That's not a lot of time, and my eyes recover faster."

She had me there. I nodded agreement as I submitted to being scanned by a spellchecker wand. The security guard motioned me past, but when he turned toward Rianna he frowned.

"No dogs in the building, ma'am."

Desmond curled his lips, showing massive canines and as his eyes narrowed, I swear the red ring around his pupil glinted.

Rianna threaded her fingers through his raised hackles. "He's not a dog, he's a barghest."

The security guard blinked at her, and I could almost see the thought "bar guest" crossing his face.

"He's fae," I said, before the man actually said the thought out loud.

"A fae dog is still a dog, and we don't allow pets."

"But you allow working dogs, right?" I said, which made Desmond turn that glare on me. I ignored him. At the guard's nod I said, "You saw our credentials and you know we're headed to the morgue to raise a shade, but did you know that I've been blind for up to a week after using my magic?"

"Are you claiming he's a Seeing Eye dog?"

"Folklore often portrays barghests as guardians who lead lost travelers home," I said, not answering his question in the least, or mentioning that more often barghests were considered portents of death.

The guard frowned but after a moment's hesitation, nodded. "Fine, but you need to get him a vest or something."

"Right," I said, only I was suddenly imagining the shaggy fae in a paisley sweater vest and it was all I could do to keep a straight face.

Once the guard waved the spellchecker over Rianna, he motioned us through the metal detectors, which didn't make a peep. The fact we were both carrying enchanted daggers that neither the spellchecker nor the metal detector caught was both a relief—because I was armed—and worrisome, as that meant other people could be as well. Once we checked in and clipped on our visitor passes, we headed to the basement.

Falin met us outside the double doors of the morgue. He didn't smile as we approached, or even say hello. He just nodded with a sort of grunt.

It reminded me of when we first met.

"So, are you going to tell us anything about the body?" I asked as he held open the door.

"I believe you're the one who is supposed to tell me what happened."

"Well, first we have some paperwork," Rianna said, pulling a folder out of her bag.

Falin frowned at her before turning to me and cocking an eyebrow.

"I think this one is pro bono," I whispered, relieving her of the folder. At her incredulous look, I whispered, "We raise the shade, and if it proves to be connected to our case, we get help from the FIB."

"Yeah, because the FIB are known for working well with others."

I glanced over my shoulder at Falin, but his hard expression gave away nothing. I assumed he'd called because now that a fae might be involved, he could legitimately offer assistance on the case while remaining within the bounds of the queen's edict. But Rianna was right. If we raised this victim's shade and it traced back to the rider, the FIB might very well try to crowd us out of the case. While I wanted to hand it over to the officials, the FIB wasn't the group I'd pick. I needed to be able to report results to my clients, and fae involvement could tie my hands—and tongue. Which meant we needed rules before the ritual. Fae loved their damn rules.

I turned and walked over to Falin. "We're willing to trade our services."

"And what are you asking in exchange for the ritual?" he asked, not a note of caution in his voice, and an amused glint in his eye as if I was doing exactly what he hoped. Unfortunately that glint could have meant he wanted me to circumvent the queen's compulsion or that I was playing into a plan far less beneficial to me.

I wanted to believe he held my best interests in mind, so I charged ahead. "That the agent in charge personally assist us in the case we're currently working." I added no stipulation that the ritual had to grant him the information he wanted or that it prove to be connected to the case. He should have added those conditions to the agreement, it was standard protocol for fae to try to secure the better deal in any trade, but his lips just twitched to flash a lopsided grin.

"Deal." And then the grin was gone, the cold, chilly wall erected by the queen's edict between us again.

Without a word he stepped around me, and headed toward the cold room. I sighed, overly aware of his silence. I might be working with him, but this wasn't much better than our awkward encounters during those damned raids. I'd hoped that if we shared a case we'd at least manage a civil conversation, but clearly that wasn't going to happen.

The disappointment hit the bottom of my stomach, making me feel hollow. Not that I could do anything about it. Though I wished he'd try a little harder. Surely he could find more wiggle room in the queen's command?

With a second sigh, I glanced around. Rianna, Falin, and I were the only ones in the morgue. That never happened.

"Where's Tamara?"

"On break," he said as the seal on the cold room door broke with a slurping sound. "This is fae business."

He vanished into the room and then returned a moment later pushing a gurney. The figure covered under the white sheet was small, no more than four feet.

"He's not a child is he?" I could normally get a sense of age off corpses, but I'd encountered very few fae corpses and while I could feel that he was definitely male, his age felt undefinable.

"No, he's a duergar. They're a small people. Nasty temperaments, but they are one of the best metalsmiths. I'd gamble the dagger you carry was made by a duergar."

I had no response to that, so I said nothing as Rianna drew her circle. Falin frowned as she dragged her tube of waxed calk around the gurney.

"You're not performing the ritual?"

"We have other leads to follow today and I need my eyes."

The frown didn't change, if anything, it etched itself deeper. "Can she raise a fae shade?"

Rianna, who had finished her circle and moved to the center, sent a cutting glance in Falin's direction.

"She's a very capable grave witch," I said, but in truth, I had no idea. I could feel grave essence lifting from the duergar, but it felt different from the grave essence that leaked from human corpses.

"I'm going to start now," Rianna said, and I nodded.

Her circle, a thick purple barrier, sprang into being faster than I could have summoned one, but when she turned toward the small body, nothing happened. I held my breath, willing her the ability to raise the shade. I should have gone in the circle with her. She was by far the better witchy witch, but my grave magic was stronger.

Wind whipped around her, making her red hair fly in all directions. Desmond paced the outskirts of her circle, each step broadcasting his apprehension.

Come on, you can do this.

All at once, the circle stilled, the wind dying down to a light breeze. An almost transparent shade sat up through the sheet. It was a weak shade, but it was a shade.

Rianna sagged as she let out a breath, and the already thin shade wavered, but it didn't fade.

"Okay," she said, her voice a strained whisper. "You can question him now."

Falin glanced at me and I almost told him that his face was going to get stuck in that frown if he didn't stop soon, but the seriousness in his eyes didn't leave room for jokes. In fact, it didn't leave room for me, which hurt even though I knew the queen's compulsion was behind his frosty demeanor.

"Duergar," he said, stepping closer to the edge of the circle. "Why did you take your own life?"

The shade didn't answer.

Falin shook his head. "It didn't work. She's not strong enough."

Now it was my turn to frown. "She is, you're asking the wrong questions." I joined him at the edge of the circle. "What is your name?"

"Gromel." The shade's voice was far away, like hearing an echo that bounced off several walls before it reached us, but it was audible.

"Gromel, do you remember how you died?"

"To the burn of iron and my innards in my hands."

I grimaced. The shade was so faint that I hadn't realized what I was seeing in its lap was its own guts. I looked at Falin. "He disemboweled himself?"

"With an iron sword and then finished it off by slitting his throat."

I shivered and turned back to the shade. "What is the

last thing you remember before . . . holding your own guts."
Ick.

"I heard a strange sound and I went out of my cave to investigate. I found a man lying on the rocks. He must have jumped from the bridge, but the fall didn't kill him, not quite. His body held a breath or two of fading life. I decided to give him to the kelpie, so I picked him up. Then I was somewhere else, the burn of iron and my insides outside."

That sure sounds like the work of our rider. "What day did you find the man on the rocks?"

"Ten days before the equinox."

That wasn't possible. The equinox was when the revelry Caleb and Rianna wanted me to attend occurred, and it was rapidly approaching. I glanced at Falin.

He must have misread my confusion because he said, "The equinox begins at dawn tomorrow."

I nodded. "And Gromel killed himself this morning?"

"Yesterday, right at sunset when his power was weakest and he was least likely to heal from the wounds."

So the rider knew something about killing fae—or Gromel had survived the rider's initial attempt. Still, even if he'd failed once, ten days before the equinox meant that the rider had inhabited Gromel for eight days. He'd only ever kept a body three days before now.

While that meant we were looking for fewer bodies, I really hated when the bad guys changed the rules.

Chapter 21

Half an hour later the duergar was back in the cold room awaiting an agent from the FIB to pick up his remains and we were on the road, heading toward the closest five-star restaurant. The original plan was to split up and cover more ground, but Rianna had pushed too hard in the ritual—wobbling out of her circle to collapse into a chair—and as weak as she was, I couldn't send her off on her own. So she was in the backseat with Desmond, I had shotgun, and Falin was driving.

I seriously needed to requalify for my driver's license.

The only upside? Falin had acquired a tablet with all the reported missing persons from the last two weeks and the case file from the duergar's suicide scene, which had been a museum of all places. Of course, that was where he'd acquired the sword, so it made sense.

We knew the rider jumped to a witness of his previous host's suicide, so with luck, someone mentioned in the case file would also be in the missing persons database.

I tapped the screen, flicking through the older photos. The victim I was looking for wouldn't have come home last night—I only hoped he'd been reported missing already. As I scrolled, a familiar face popped up on the screen.

"That can't be," I whispered, staring at the face of the

man who'd been in Brew and Brews, the one Kingly's ghost had taken a swing at on the day the rider made him jump from Motel Styx. The drunk had been missing since that day, which meant he wasn't the host we were looking for, but I'd bet he'd been the host following Kingly. *Was the rider that close and I couldn't tell?*

I should have noticed a huge, miasmic blur rising out of a body and jumping into another, how could I not? Of course, I hadn't been there at the exact moment Kingly had died.

If I had just opened my shields . . . What, exactly? Even if I'd seen the darkness inside the drunk, I wouldn't have known what it meant.

Besides, it was too late to sit here and bemoan what I did or didn't do. If the drunk had been a host, he was dead now. Either he was the man on the rocks or he was the one who'd passed the rider to that man.

"Did you find the host?" Falin asked, glancing away from the road long enough to make me want to grab the wheel.

"Not the current one. Now you drive and I'll look."

Once he would have smiled, would have teased me. Now all the sharp angles of his face remained hard, untouched, as he turned back toward the road without a word. Something inside me twinged, a small, invisible wound. I forced my focus back on the tablet.

Scrolling through the files, I located the people reported missing today. It wasn't a long list: two men and one woman. My first instinct was to dismiss the woman out of hand, but just because the rider hadn't possessed a female yet didn't mean he *couldn't*.

I opened the case file from the duergar's suicide, scanning names of the witnesses. "And we have a match."

"You found him?" Rianna asked, holding on to the back of my seat as she peered over my shoulder.

"Michael Hancock," I said, double tapping the picture of a man in his mid-thirties. The image filled the screen of the tablet. "The rider has always used the victim's real name and cards before, let's hope he still is."

Rianna and I pulled out our phones, which earned another glance from Falin.

"We looked up the number to the two hotels we know the rider has frequented as well as a few other five-star resorts before we left the office," I said as way of explanation.

The phone rang several times before the desk clerk answered. I forced a smile into my voice. "Hi, I was wondering if you can connect me to Michael Hancock's room."

"I could, but it would just ring. Mr. Hancock isn't currently in his room."

Jackpot. And a chatty clerk, or a bored one. Whichever, maybe I could use it to my advantage.

"So he went to lunch already? I was planning to meet him"—not that the rider knew that—"but I don't know the name of the restaurant. You wouldn't know, would you?"

"Actually, he asked me what my favorite restaurant is. I sent him to Pollyanna's Porch. Have you ever been there?"

I'd never even heard of it, but my super helpful desk boy offered me directions. I was so never staying at that hotel if I wanted discretion—not that I could afford to stay there in the first place.

As soon as I hung up, I relayed the directions to Falin and twenty minutes later we were pulling into Pollyanna's Porch. It was one of those places that reminded me that despite the fact we were a large city in an unfolded space that hadn't existed a hundred years ago—at least as far as humans were concerned—this was still the South and people enjoyed old Southern charm. Which was clearly what Pollyanna's was aiming for with its country bed-and-breakfast design and huge wraparound porch complete with painted wooden swings. I half expected to be greeted at the door by a gray-haired woman wearing an apron covered in flour. But no, it was a restaurant, and while it tried to maintain its quaint charm inside, the bustle of servers in the midst of the lunch rush broke the spell.

We bypassed the hostess and PLEASE WAIT TO BE SEATED sign. When the hostess objected, Rianna assured the woman that our party was already here and ignored her when she objected to our "dog."

"What if he took one look at this place and turned around?" I asked. After all, while Pollyanna's might make it into a cultural magazine, it was a far cry from the five-star restaurants he'd been patronizing.

"And what if he didn't?" was Falin's response.

Point. We might as well check. It was the only lead we had.

The dining area consisted of two floors and had been divided into several themed rooms. We split up to search, Falin heading upstairs, Rianna going right as I took the left. I walked into a crowded room that instantly made me think of apple pie—which could have been the red and cream wallpaper or the pictures of apples hanging on every conceivable surface, but I was betting on the charm that filled the room with the scent of baked apples. I'd just turned the corner when a pair of arms grabbed hold of my shoulders.

A scream built in my chest but melted in my throat as a pair of very familiar hazel eyes met mine. Death pressed his finger over my lips, and then led me behind a fake potted tree.

"What are you doing here?" I whispered as I moved into the corner, as hidden from the room as possible. "You avoid me for a month, then you show up last night with a cryptic warning, and now you're here? Your timing is rather suspect." Because his presence could mean we were on the right track in hunting the rider or could simply be because for the first time in a month, I was working with Falin. Death was not the fae's biggest fan. *Not that Falin is being anything but coldly professional.* I looked at Death. "You know, I don't know if I want to hug you or hit you."

He chuckled, the sound bridging the space between us. Then he leaned his forehead against mine and gazed down at me. My world filled with him, with the familiar shape of his jaw, with the dark hair that fell forward to brush against my skin, with the hazel eyes that held every color and gleamed with an inner smile. A smile I felt myself returning because it was Death.

"Hello to you too," he said, amusement lacing his voice.

We'd flirted for years, but it had always been harmless, our body temperatures too drastically different for anything more than a little teasing.

Until recently.

He lifted a hand and stroked my cheek with the edge of one finger. His eyes betrayed his continuing amazement that we could touch, and a thrill surged through me. Of course, it wasn't like I'd been completely unaffected even when he'd been so cold his touch burned. Now warmth flushed my skin at the light caress, and I took a deep breath, trying to calm my body's reaction.

The part of my brain still functioning reminded me that this was Death. That pursuing anything would change everything. Hell, it had already changed everything. There could never be anything between us. It was just hard to remember that sometimes—like when he was close enough that I could feel the tickle of his breath against my skin and smell the sweet scent of dew that I always associated with him. He watched me, watched my reaction to his nearness, his touch, and those eyes with their kaleidoscope of color held so much emotion that I had to look away.

Death's finger reached the corner of my mouth, and he traced my bottom lip. My breath caught, and my gaze snapped back to his eyes.

His pupils dilated, his gaze fixed on my lips. Something inside me tightened as my pulse quickened. I wanted him to kiss me. Wanted to feel his lips crushed against mine, to know what it would be like to open to him, to explore his mouth.

No, bad idea, Alex. A very bad idea. Not to mention Falin was around here somewhere. I swallowed, a twinge of guilt curling in my stomach.

Our flirting was close to blurring the lines. To becoming too serious. Dangerously so.

With the exception of his "intervention," Death had been

acutely absent from my life, and that, coupled with Falin's icy cold shoulder, meant my emotions for both men were still a tangled mess. The idea of a relationship with either man scared the crap out of me, and yet the last month had been emotional torture. Not that a relationship with either was an option.

Oh, Death might be tantalizingly close right now, but he'd leave again. A relationship between a mortal and a collector wasn't tolerated. We'd flirted and teased, but never taken it to that next level.

We were so close, a deep breath would bring us in contact. I wanted that so bad it terrified me. His hand moved to the back of my neck, wove into my loose curls. We were both breathing a little too fast, and yet neither of us closed those last few inches.

"We're running out of time," he whispered, his voice low and hoarse.

Time? "If you vanish and start avoiding me again I'll—" What? Never talk to him again? That was the exact opposite of what I wanted. "I'll . . . I'll root you to reality."

I might even be able to fulfill that threat.

He smiled, and then leaned toward me. It took every ounce of self-control I possessed to step back. But I did step back.

"Don't. If you're just going to leave again, don't." Because it would hurt worse, and his extended absence had already hurt enough.

Death squeezed his eyes closed. When he opened them again, some of the light had left them, and something inside me mourned the loss. But the distance was necessary, for both of us. His face turned serious and he glanced over his shoulder before saying, "You need to leave this restaurant."

"I'm guessing that means the rider is here."

He tilted his head. "Rider?"

"Yeah, you know, the weird miasmic creature that seeps into mortals, rides them around for a while, and then discards them like yesterday's dirty underwear?"

He stared at me. Then a smile broke across his face and

he shook his head in silent amusement. "I've missed you so much."

"So stop vanishing," I said and the amusement melted from his face. I changed the subject. "So how did this creature get here?"

"We believe it was pulled through one of the rifts in reality a month ago."

Pulled? I groaned. "By the skimmers?" I asked and he nodded. Those fools were like a pox that wouldn't go away. I remembered them standing around the rift by the river, drawing anything and everything they could pull. The raw magic burnt at least one from the inside out and drove most of the rest insane. They hadn't differentiated what kind of magic they drew, but the rift had connected to more than just the Aetheric plane, and it wouldn't surprise me if one grabbed the rider and took it into his body. *Those fools.*

"Alex?" A whispered voice called.

Death glanced over his shoulder. "There's no more time. You have to leave. Now."

I swallowed, and a lump of fear slid down my throat to hit my stomach hard, a sick feeling oozing over me. I might flirt with Death, but his job was collecting souls. "If I stay, am I going to die?"

He frowned and I swore the colors in his eyes spun. Then he stepped forward and I was engulfed in his arms, his warmth, his scent.

"No," he whispered the word into my hair. "No. You will not die." It sounded more promise than prophecy and something about the way he said it made me tremble.

"Alex," the loud whisper called again.

The tension in Death's body was palpable and he squeezed me tighter. Then he stepped back until he was an arm's length away, his hands on my shoulders. "Promise me, Alex. Promise me you'll walk out of here and stop looking for that creature."

I couldn't promise that. I didn't.

His face clouded, and he closed his eyes, his head hanging downward. The voice called for me again, and Death glanced toward it. I couldn't see anything beyond the tree and I doubted he could either. When he turned back, he didn't say a thing. He simply leaned forward, his lips touching mine in the lightest of kisses. He was gone a fluttering heartbeat later.

My fingers moved to my lips. That fleeting, ghostlike kiss? It tasted of sorrow.

Chapter 22

"Alex." The caller had stopped using that loud whisper and I could clearly make out Rianna's familiar voice.

I was still behind the potted tree, reeling from Death's ambush appearance, and now more unsure than ever about, well, everything. But I couldn't hide forever.

Rolling my shoulders and straightening my back, I marched out from behind the fake tree. Rianna stood in the center of the room I was supposed to be searching. Which I was doing a bang-up job on considering I'd been totally oblivious to the fact there were other people in the room for the last however many minutes. When Rianna saw me, she hurried forward but stopped short still several feet away.

"I'd ask where you've been, but I think asking what the heck were you doing is a lot more appropriate," she said, her gaze sweeping over me.

I frowned, glancing down at myself. From what I could tell, I looked presentable. Death and I had hardly touched, so my clothes weren't in disarray. I glanced back at her in confusion.

"You're flushed, but your eyes, Alex. If you were anyone else, I'd say you look like you'd seen a ghost—but that wouldn't be unusual for you. What happened?"

I shook my head. Rianna was one of the few people who knew about Death, but only because we'd been roommates for so many years and she was a fellow grave witch so could see him if she tried. But I wasn't about to talk about what had—or what hadn't—happened, or about his warning.

"So you found Michael?" I asked, changing the subject.

"Yeah, but before we accost a random person who might have just decided to take a break from his wife, it would be good if we could confirm he really is being ridden. Do you think you'll be able to tell?"

Without opening my shields? Obviously not or I'd have noticed the rider on the street when Kingly died. But if I gazed across planes, I'd probably be able to see *something*. "It's worth a shot. Lead the way."

We headed upstairs and walked through two dining rooms to where Falin waited in a small recess. He gave me a once-over as I approached and a nerve over his temple twitched. I froze. *Can he tell I was with Death?* Falin and I weren't together. He couldn't even *talk* to me in a casual conversation. But I still didn't want to hurt him. *How did things get so complicated?*

I stepped around Falin and glanced into a bright dining room filled with large picture windows, sun-brewed iced tea in tall pitchers on the sills, and paintings of lemons in brilliant shades of yellow on the walls. Every table was filled, but it took only a moment for me to spot our quarry. He sat alone, a tinted glass in front of him but no food. *Good, maybe that means he hasn't eaten yet.* Which if this was our guy, would give us plenty of time to get the Anti–Black Magic Unit down here to contain him.

But first to confirm he was being ridden.

I cracked my shields, simultaneously erecting the protective bubble around my psyche. The confusing array of planes flooded my vision. The wooden tables decayed, the chairs so dilapidated I had to work hard to believe the patrons could sit in them. Aetheric energy whirled in wispy spirals in the air, making the witches in the crowd obvious not only because of the magic I could see on their persons, but because the Aetheric hugged close to them, as if it wanted to be used. I blinked, forcing my eyes to focus past that to the people themselves. Most glowed a crisp yellow, the color I associated with humans. One was blue, which I didn't see often and had recently learned indicated a feykin—a human with fae blood. Beside me, Falin's soul was brilliant silver—fae.

Michael, though, his soul was different. I saw a hint of human yellow, but mostly it was dark as if it had been dunked in tar, only the smallest halo of dull light escaping that shiny, slick blackness. Even from across the room, staring at it made my skin crawl.

I slammed my shields shut and blinked as I waited for my eyes to readjust. Between the extra shield and the short exposure, the damage was minimal, the room only slightly dimmer than before.

"It's him," I whispered. "Let's call the ABMU." *And hope they take us seriously.*

"I don't know if we have time." Rianna pointed to where a waitress plopped a black billfold in front of the rider, a credit card sticking out the top—which meant not only had he already eaten, but he'd paid.

Crap.

"Can you arrest him?" I asked, looking at Falin.

"Technically, yes, but as he appears to be human, it would be unadvisable for the FIB to take him into custody."

Which was a long way to say no.

The rider pulled Michael's wallet out of his back pocket and put the credit card away. Damn it, he was about to leave.

"It looks like we're moving on to plan B."

Rianna cocked her head to the side. "We have a plan B?"

"Nope, we're winging it. I'll try to keep him here as long as possible, you contact the ABMU."

Falin clenched his jaw, but I shot him a glare that said if he was going to object he better be ready to take action himself. He didn't say a thing. *Fine.*

I glanced at Michael, who was finishing off the last of his

drink. He'd leave any second. How long would it take the officers to arrive? Hopefully I'd need to distract him for only a little while. I started toward the dining room, but paused. Death's urgent request for me to leave nagged at me. I knelt, retrieving my dagger. Then, balancing the pommel and hilt in my palm, I let the flat of the blade rest along the underside of my forearm. It wasn't the safest way to hold a dagger, especially one that liked to sink into flesh, but as long as I kept my arm turned, all but the decorative scrolling on the cross guard, which showed on either side of my wrist, was hidden from the rider and the rest of the patrons, whom I didn't want to panic by stalking through the room armed. Falin frowned, his eyes betraying more than a little anxiety, but he didn't say a thing or try to stop me as I walked into the dining room.

And by walked I meant sashayed.

I might be tall to the point of lanky, but I had killer boots and a great outfit and I knew how to draw an eye or two. Hell, I'd made an art out of meeting guys at bars. I could distract one joyriding body snatcher. After all, he'd hired sex workers while in previous bodies, so he couldn't be that hard to pick up.

"This seat taken?" I asked, letting my voice go husky as I gave Michael my best come-hither smile.

The rider looked up through Michael's eyes. Well, *up* to a certain extent, at least. His gaze made it as far as my chest and then sort of got stuck, like I'd applied superglue to my cleavage.

"Now it is," he said, motioning me to sit.

And this would be the winging it part.

"I haven't seen you here before," I said, dropping my gaze and drawing a small circle on the table with my index finger. "Sitting here all alone, it looked like you needed company."

"Did it now?"

I looked up through my lashes, aiming for coy. The smile he wore showed a lot of teeth and reminded me of a predator who'd just spotted dinner. *Except I'm the one hunting.*

At least I hoped so.

I wanted to shrink away from the hungry look in his eyes, but I couldn't afford to back down. I had to buy us time. I forced a demure smile to my lips and my finger stopped moving in random swirls as I traced the rune for luck on the table—not that I put any power behind it. Beneath the table, I clutched the hilt of my dagger tighter, but I ignored the buzz of excitement it sang at the edge of my consciousness. The dagger was a last resort. Michael was a victim and I had no intention of hurting his body if I could help it.

"Perhaps we should go somewhere more private?" the rider asked, reaching across the table.

He doesn't waste any time, does he? I couldn't let him walk out of here and risk losing him, but I sure as hell couldn't leave with him, so what was I supposed to do? While I sat there undecided, his hand slid over mine, stopping the half finished rune for focus.

It had to be my imagination, but I swore that under the blistering heat of human skin I could feel something cold, hateful. I jerked my hand away before thought caught up with action.

"Buy a girl a drink first?" I said, but my voice shook, my smile wobbling.

And he wasn't buying it.

His eyes narrowed, a dark film sliding across his iris, glimmering darkly like oil on water before disappearing again. I shivered, I couldn't help it.

"Who are you?" he asked, the words precise and cold with none of the hunger from earlier. Oh, but the predator was still there, he was just looking at a different kind of prey now. "I've seen you before. You're the witch from outside Motel Styx."

"And you're the one who was wearing James Kingly's body when he went over the edge."

The rider stared at me through Michael Hancock's eyes. The shock showed first, and then he threw his head back and laughed.

That scared me worse than anything else he might have

done. My muscles clenched, my legs bracing to jump from the chair, to run for cover. But we were in a crowded room. He wouldn't do anything stupid. Would he?

When he looked at me again his eyes glittered with amusement and that slick, oily darkness once again filled his irises.

"It's almost a shame," he said. "I wasn't done with this body yet, but you. You are interesting, and I can't let you spread your little theory. I've never experienced being a female of your kind." He pulled a revolver, the metal dull in the bright light.

Fight or flight should have kicked in, should have made me bolt or shove the table—which I currently had a death grip on—at him. Instead I froze, unable to move, to think. Even the dagger's urging didn't penetrate my fear. The world slowed as he cocked the gun. Lifted it. But not at me.

He shoved the gun under his own chin.

Time finally caught up, and I jumped to my feet. "No!"

Too late. He pulled the trigger and the deafening bang of the gun boomed through the room. The thing inside Michael smiled at me before the body crumbled.

The room went utterly silent, still. Then the first scream sounded, followed by a chorus of screams and chairs screeching as people pushed to their feet. Chaos broke out as diners rushed for the exit. A chair toppled, sending one man sprawling. No one stopped to help him, they just kept running. Falin appeared at my side, grabbing my elbow as he tried to drag me away from the body with the ever-expanding pool of blood forming around it.

"No. It's not over," I said tugging away from him, because that thing, that awful, miasmic cloud that was both pure darkness and simultaneously every color, was pouring out of Michael's body.

"Go," I whispered, switching my grip on my dagger. Falin still tried to drag me away, but I jerked free. This close, I could feel the rider, feel the dark energy in it, taste the wind blowing through it. Wind I knew. The same never-ending tempest from the land of the dead. "Go, get away from here," I said, watching the thing lifting out of Michael's corpse growing larger, thicker.

"You think I'd leave you here alone?" Falin's daggers appeared in his hands. I doubted they'd touch this thing, but at least he hadn't drawn a gun.

"How are you going to fight what you can't see?" I asked, sparing a moment to look away from the growing form.

"Then make me see it."

I blinked. It was possible. It probably wouldn't be any harder to manifest the rider than a ghost, its energy didn't feel that different, just darker, so much darker. I shivered.

It was free of the body now. It had no face, but I could feel it studying me. Behind it, the gray man appeared. He glared at me, his expression a mix of anger and sorrow as he freed the stunned soul of a man who shouldn't have died. But I didn't have time to watch the collector. The rider was moving, fast.

I opened my shields, letting the planes of reality wash over me. The thing drew up short, the energy pulsing around it turning uncertain for a moment.

"A grave witch?" It wasn't so much that the thing spoke as that I felt the words crawl into my head. *"What a shining star you are. I'll enjoy you."*

Then it dove for me. In my grave-sight it had a more defined form, but it wasn't humanoid. There were no arms to grab, no blows to block. It came at me like a descending fog.

But I was a planeweaver, and like it or not, planes converged through me, making me real, solid, on every plane I touched. The rider slammed into me, no doubt intending to seep into my body, but the impact was physical, knocking me sideways.

I scrambled, trying to keep my footing. The rider drew back. I could feel the thing's confusion, but that bled to anger before I could get my feet under me.

The rider's rage poured over me, a psychic assault that rammed my shields and came closer to knocking me on my ass than his physical attack. My charm bracelet heated against my skin as the rider searched for cracks in my defenses. Then it found one.

The rider dove at me again, the attack both physical and psychic as it ripped into the still open wounds where a soul-sucking spell had snaked through me months ago. Disorientation and pain swept over me as it tore into my very soul.

And that was the downside of physically interacting with all planes.

I screamed, driving both the dagger and the fingers of my free hand into the center of the rider's mass. It was like trying to hold on to sludge, but I didn't have to grab hold, I just had to pull.

"Welcome to reality, asshole," I muttered as my power made the creature visible.

The silver gleam of Falin's blades flashed. He attacked with methodical precision, each movement of his body carving a runnel in the dark mass as the blades sliced through it.

The thing's scream was more tangible than audible as it roared in fury and pain. I pulled back my own dagger and jabbed the rider again. I didn't know if it could bleed, if it could die, but it could definitely be hurt.

It reared back, pulling away from me. I tried to hold on to it, to keep it solid, so Falin could see it too, but it slid through my grasp and zipped across the room.

"Where — ?" Falin started, his blades stilling.

"There." I pointed to where its retreating form darted toward the fleeing patrons. We couldn't let it reach them, to ride another body. It vanished around the corner of the dining room.

I started forward, and my knees locked, my legs collapsing under me. *Fuck.* The struggle with the rider had lasted less than a minute, but I felt like I'd been through a triathlon followed by a boxing match.

Falin was at my side in seconds, helping me to my feet. I

shook my head. "You have to go after it." The words came out slurred. I sucked down a deep breath. He *couldn't* go after it. He couldn't even see it.

But Rianna could, and her eyes were glowing like green ghost lights. She took one backward glance at me, but she didn't need to be told to follow it. She broke into a run, Desmond at her side.

I attempted to stumble after it, but would have collapsed again if Falin hadn't grabbed me. "We have to follow it," I said, the unspoken "help me" conveyed in my eyes.

He nodded, the daggers vanishing to wherever he kept them—I'd figure that out one day. Then he wrapped an arm around my waist, and we half ran, half hobbled into the hall. We didn't make it much farther. The stairs had transformed into a jumbled, chaotic traffic jam as people shoved and pushed, trying to get the hell out of the restaurant.

"I lost it," Rianna said, her eyes still glowing. "It was there, and then gone."

Damn it. That meant one of two things. If we were lucky, it had retreated farther into the land of the dead to lick its wounds—but I'd never had that kind of luck. Which left option two: it had jumped into a body. Rianna couldn't see souls while they were inside a body, so it stood to reason she wouldn't be able to see the rider either.

I scanned the crowd as they jostled for a spot on the stairs. With all the brilliant yellow souls, spotting the one coated in darkness wasn't hard. It was inside a woman clinging to her husband's arm. The yellow of her soul dimmed under the tarlike presence vying for control.

"That one," I said, pointing. "The woman with the red shirt and black hair."

"Ma'am, we need to speak to you a moment," Falin said, releasing me so he could hurry toward her. She didn't turn, didn't stop. Falin reached the couple and took hold of the woman's shoulder. "I'm with the authorities, and I need to speak with you." He flashed his badge too quickly for them to identify which "authority" he might be.

"We didn't see anything," the man said, which was a lie — they'd been in the dining room.

His wife clung tighter to her husband's arm. "I don't feel so good," she mumbled, swaying.

Her husband patted her arm. "It's going to be okay. We'll be home soon."

Not likely. The darkness was winning, only the thinnest shimmer of yellow human soul left.

"I can't let you leave," Falin said, keeping hold of the woman's shoulder.

"Please make him let go," she said, giving her husband a pleading look — a look coated with the oily darkness of the rider.

How had the rider taken over so quickly? Of course, we'd noticed he was gaining control quicker with every victim, but he took her in what, a minute? Two tops. This was bad, very bad.

"Can't this wait until we're outside?" the man asked.

I stepped forward. "No, it can't. Sir, I'd suggest you step back. That's not your wife."

The ridden woman turned, a hate-filled gaze aimed directly at me. "You're becoming a nuisance." The words emerged from the woman's throat, but they no longer sounded like her.

"Becky?"

The woman sneered at her husband, pulling away from him. In the same movement, she swung and landed a solid punch in Falin's stomach.

He grunted as the air was knocked from him, but it didn't slow him. His daggers reappeared.

"Don't hurt her. The rider will just jump to another host," I yelled as the woman ran, not toward the stair, but back toward the dining room we'd abandoned.

I could all but see Falin's teeth gritting as the daggers vanished and he gave chase. I stepped in front of the door, blocking it. The woman was a good eight inches shorter than me, but she charged me with the force of a linebacker, knocking me to my ass. A fresh wave of pain burst through me as air rushed out of my body. My dagger fell from my hand, skittering across the floor.

Desmond vaulted over me and tackled the woman. The rider might grant her extra strength, but she was still a small woman and Desmond was several hundred pounds of barghest. She went down.

But it's hard to pin someone who doesn't care how badly struggling might hurt or damage her body. She thrashed, beating at the large doglike fae. Falin was there before Desmond did something drastic, like bite off one of her arms.

Falin slapped cuffs on the woman and dragged her to her feet. She went absolutely still. I waited to see if the rider would pour out of her now that its host was captured. It didn't.

"The ABMU are on their way?" I asked Rianna as she ran her hands over Desmond's fur, searching for injuries.

"They should be here any minute."

Score one for the private detectives. Okay, and the FIB. I smiled, dusting myself off. I would hurt like hell in the morning, of that I was certain, but we'd closed our first case. Actually, first two cases.

I walked across the room to retrieve my dagger and the rider watched me, that oil-slicked darkness coating the woman's blue eyes. They held all the chill of the dead with none of the peace. It made my skin crawl.

"You couldn't leave it alone, could you?" it asked, the voice no longer sounding like the woman's. It was colder, harsher.

Her husband charged into the room. "What's going on? Why have you arrested my wife?"

I gave him a piteous look, but didn't answer. Instead I addressed the rider. "No, I couldn't let you continue your little spree, so don't bother jumping bodies. I'll follow you to anyone."

"Then it seems we have irreconcilable differences," it said and without warning, twisted hard. A snap cut through the air as something in the woman's shoulder ripped. The movement jerked her cuffed arms from Falin's grasp.

She dashed for the picture window. The second before she flung herself through it, the woman glanced back, the rider grinning at me through her face. Then the earth-shattering sound of smashing glass filled the room. A man screamed. And finally, almost imperceptible compared to the rest, a thud sounded as her body hit the ground.

For a stunned moment, everything slowed. Then my feet moved as if they'd made the decision before my brain had time to catch up. I ran to the window, the others at my heels.

Blood tipped the remaining jagged glass, and outside, below, a woman's broken body lay half on the sidewalk and half on the grass. The leap had been only one story, but her hands were cuffed behind her back, so there'd been no breaking the fall. Not that having her hands free would have saved her. Judging by the way blood sprayed from her, gushing less with each weakening beat of her heart, the glass had severed an artery.

From my vantage a floor above, I watched the rider pour out of her body. *Fuck.* But I could do nothing. I was too far away to physically attack the disembodied creature and as soon as it found a body . . . it had proven human lives meant little to it. And it had plenty of fresh bodies to choose from as it dashed into the crowd. I reached with my grave magic.

Too late.

It jumped into a new body. I cursed. My power couldn't touch the living. Within seconds a man broke away from the crowd, running the opposite direction as the other patrons. At this distance, and still gazing across planes, all I could make out was that he was male.

Damn.

I glanced at the broken body of the woman who, twenty minutes ago, had simply been a woman having lunch with her husband.

Death stood beside her body, he met my eyes for only a moment before looking away. I swallowed, fighting the burn that always preceded tears. He'd warned me. Told me not to stay, not to get involved. I'd thought he was trying to keep me out of danger. But maybe it was this . . . this utter waste and destruction of life he'd been trying to prevent.

And I pushed the rider to do it.

I glanced at the fleeing figure of the rider's new host. Watched him turn a corner and vanish. Not that it mattered. I'd tried the direct approach. Tried to stop a serial killer. Not only had I failed, but now it was my fault that two innocent people were dead.

Chapter 23

❦

The Anti–Black Magic Unit arrived four minutes later. Of course, by then they were too late to do anything but clean up the bodies. Falin vanished before they arrived. His last words to me? That I wasn't to mention the FIB involvement.

Great.

I knew most of the ABMU officers, either from dinners at John's or drinks after cases, but I hadn't officially worked a case with any of them, so they saw me as a civilian. Which meant, at a scene like this, I was either a witness or a suspect, possibly both. Considering I'd been with both victims directly before their deaths, one of whom wore cuffs that I'd refused to explain, I was lucky I wasn't arrested on the spot. Though that was still a possibility as I was asked—without the option of refusing—down to the station to answer more questions.

Which was why, two hours later, I found myself in John's office, shivering and partially blind. He'd rescued me from an interrogation room, but as red as his ever-expanding bald spot had turned, I thought I might be better off with the dispassionate woman who'd spent the last hour grilling me.

"What were you thinking, Alex?" John asked, not quite bellowing the question, but only just barely.

I ducked my head. "No one would believe that the deaths were homicides. I found the pattern, found the most likely next victim, and I made an attempt to detain him."

"Yes, and we all know how that turned out."

I sank lower in my chair, the heavy weight of physical and magical exhaustion mixing with the crush of guilt. "I fucked up, trust me, I'm aware."

"You're aware? Alex, your actions led to the deaths of two people."

I cringed, but a grain of anger competed with the guilt, so even to my own ears my voice sounded flippant when I said, "Technically, both were suicides, so as you told me, not a homicide case. Or are you finally ready to admit that something is wrong with the string of suicides in this city?"

John stared at me, his face so still, not even his mustache twitched. Then he pushed away from his desk, walked to his ajar office door, and shoved it closed. The resulting bang rang loud through the too quiet room.

Every step John took echoed between my ears as he walked back to his desk, leaned against it, and then stood there with his arms crossed. I shrank under his hard stare, wishing I had an invisibility charm on me. It wasn't the reprimanding posture that got to me, it was the disappointment in his eyes. I'd been seeing a lot of it recently, and that cut deep because I owed John. He'd set me up as a retainer for the police, and when I'd been floundering after Rianna's disappearance, he was the one to encourage me to get my PI license and open the business anyway. He wasn't just a coworker, he was a good friend, maybe even the closest thing I'd ever come to a father figure in my life. As he stared down at me now, I had the urge to pull my knees to my chest and hide my face.

"Tamara changed Kirkwood and Kingly's manner of death from suicide to undetermined yesterday," he said after what felt like an excruciatingly long time.

I frowned. Undetermined still wasn't homicide, and these people hadn't died by chance or simple misfortune — they'd been murdered by whatever had possessed them.

"Alex, do you really think no one but you sees the troubling connections in these cases?"

A queasy feeling crawled from my stomach to my throat. "You mean there's an active investigation? Why didn't you tell me?"

"Because the brass wants to keep this quiet. There's a good chance we won't be able to prosecute, so it was determined that keeping as much information from the press as possible would be best."

"But people are dying."

"Yes. From suicide." He threw out his hand to stop my protest as he continued. "Are there suspicious circumstances in the suicides? Yes. Did the strange anomalies contribute to the deceased's decision to take their own life? Possibly. But if that is the case, you're looking at charges of misuse of magic. Maybe, with the right judge and jury, you might prove manslaughter, but everyone knows magic can't force someone to kill themselves."

"Except you're not looking for a spell. You're looking for an . . . entity."

"Which is the conclusion the two ABMU agents working the case reached as well, and no, I won't tell you who they are," he said before I could ask.

"I could help."

"Like you're helping now? By kicking up dust on cases everyone was willing to accept were suicides? By making a public scene at a crowded restaurant?" He raked his hand over his bald spot. "This city is a powder keg. Too many unexplainable things have happened, too many magic-related deaths. People are scared. We've had multiple reports of hate crimes, Alex. Hate crimes—seventy years after the Magical Awakening. From property damage to actual violence against witches and fae. My parents told horror stories about the riots following the Awakening, and as close to boiling over as this city is, we may just see that kind of terror again. Is that what you want?"

I didn't justify the question with an answer. He continued as if he'd never expected me to.

"People are afraid of the unknown, of what they can't understand. With everything that has happened, with all the unexplained, hell, unexplainable, magic from ritual murders to surfacing body parts with no apparent means of being severed, to holes in freaking reality—strange things are happening. Things that break the rules of what we understand about magic. And now a magic that can overcome free will to the point the victim kills themselves? It's better if this stays quiet and doesn't stir up any more fear."

He had a point, and I sure as hell understood how terrifying it was when the rules changed—my entire understanding of the world was currently in flux. But I was one of the few people who could see the rider. It could walk by a dozen cops and they wouldn't notice, but if I looked, I could pick it out of a crowd. That argument wasn't anything John wanted to hear.

"Let's say that a creature that can take over a body exists—then you're talking about a nonhuman culprit. That makes it an FIB case—"

"Except it's not fae."

He continued without acknowledging me. "—and they obviously don't want a spotlight on the issue either. The sale of iron is at the highest it's ever been in Nekros, and the Ambassador for Fae and Human Affairs Office has been flooded with complaints from both sides. Then there are the political groups. Such as the group lobbying to make glamour illegal—"

As if they could enforce that.

"—and these people don't view witches much better than fae. You have heard about the bill being considered that mandates that all children take an RMC test before they reach school age."

I hadn't actually. As someone who may not test human, the idea of a mandatory Relative Magic Compatibility test terrified me. And I surely wasn't the only one. Besides, testing children was ridiculous. Unless they were wyrd, even people who peaked well above average on the RMC test had to choose to study and learn to use magic. And if people wanted to hate anyone with potential to use magic, only nulls were safe, and nulls were rarer than wyrd witches. The majority of the population could skim at least a little magic. Not much, and they couldn't do a lot with it, but as long as they didn't flatline on the RMC test, they had some small magical potential.

"So," he continued, "if you don't want to land in jail, you damn well better drop the case and leave well enough alone. Rebecca Cramer—that's the woman who went through the window, if you didn't know—her husband claims she was in police custody at the time of her death. He wants to press charges, except there were no NCPD officers on the scene when she went through that window. His description of the officer indicated that he was tall with long blond hair—does that sound like anyone you're known to associate with?"

I looked away.

"What do you think Cramer is going to do when he finds out an FIB agent was involved in the death of his wife? And your client, Nina Kingly, she's currently championing tighter restrictions on magic and its uses. Kelly Kirkwood has called the precinct a dozen times today. And an hour before your little lunch affair, I received a call from a reporter who was investigating the claims of a couple who said their son was murdered and the police dismissed the case. You're stirring up fear and creating a hell of a lot of bad press for everyone."

"I . . ." I had absolutely no idea what to say. He was right. I'd been careless. I'd been thinking about how to find the killer and giving the families peace of mind in the knowledge that their loved ones hadn't committed suicide. I'd never considered what they might do with that information. "So what should I do?"

"Stop playing detective. You're an exceptional grave witch, invaluable when it comes to questioning murder victims. But every time you get involved in a case, everything goes to hell. Leave the investigating to the police and stick to talking to the dead."

I stared at him, too stunned to speak.

I was saved the necessity by a sharp tapping on the door. John stalked across the room and jerked it open, looking every bit the part of a very pissed off bear. The uniformed rookie on the other side shrank back, his head ducking.

"Uh, sorry to interrupt," he said, "but Ms. Craft's brother is here. He said it was urgent. Something to do with their mother."

My breath caught, my heart forgetting it needed to beat. Could it be . . . ? I jumped to my feet, but made it no farther as John turned toward me, his bulky frame blocking the door.

"Since when have you had a brother?" The clinical skepticism in his voice brought reality back into focus. The hope that a moment before had crowded out room for doubt, withered and soured.

My legs weren't quite solid enough to hold me and I sank into my chair. John watched me, but if he noticed me deflating, he made no comment. He just waited. Which wasn't surprising, John had seen my background check when I'd been hired as a consultant. Officially, I had no listed relatives.

"My brother disappeared when I was eleven." And I'd never given up hope that I'd find him again one day. But today? At the police station? I didn't think so. "And my mother died when I was five. Whoever is in the lobby doesn't know me."

John grunted under his breath. "I'm starting to wonder if anyone does."

I cringed. How could I respond to that? Not that John waited for a response. His mustache stretched downward with his frown as he stepped around his desk, opened the top drawer, and pulled out his service weapon.

"What did you say the last guy possessed by this 'rider' looked like?" he asked as he holstered the gun.

"As of a couple hours ago? Male, probably average height. He might have had short hair, but I'm not sure the color."

"That describes half the population of Nekros."

I shrugged. It was the best I had. "I'll know with one look if it's the rider."

"No you won't. You're staying here."

"Like hell I am," I said, pushing out of the chair.

John shook his head. "Officer, arrest her."

I gaped at John. "For what?"

"Oh, I'm sure there's an entire list I can choose from after your little escapade earlier, but for now, let's go with endangering a civilian."

"What civilian?"

"At the moment, yourself," he said, heading for the door. He stopped long enough to shoot a hard glance at the rookie. "Officer, that wasn't a suggestion. Arrest her."

"Sir?" The man practically cowered in the doorway.

"You can't just arrest me," I said, trying to slip around John.

"I'll add resisting in a minute." He grabbed my arm. "Cuffs."

The rookie fumbled the cuffs from his belt, nearly dropping them before handing them to John, who slapped them around my wrists with the expertise of a veteran officer.

The iron content in the metal sent pain surging through my arms. I winced, cursing, but John had no idea I was anything other than human and that the iron hurt me. Ignoring my protests, he pushed me back into his office.

"Don't forget to read Craft her rights," he said, heading out the door.

"Yes, sir." The officer took my arm, and then after digging through his pockets and pulling out a small slip of paper, he Mirandized me.

Chapter 24

"This is ridiculous. You know that, right?" I said once the rookie finished literally reading me my rights.

"Just following orders, ma'am."

Yeah, I'd noticed that.

"Well, can't we do this without the cuffs?" A burning itch now accompanied the stinging pain, and I fought hard not to let it show in my voice, or worse, to whimper. Humans didn't have issues with iron and I was trying my best to pass as human.

The rookie not only didn't remove the cuffs; he didn't even bother answering the question. Grabbing my biceps, he pushed me toward the door.

"Uh, where are we going?"

"The cage, until you can make bail."

Oh, he had to be kidding. I was ninety percent sure John had me arrested to keep me out of the lobby—which I'd have to pass through to reach the precinct's cells. I was also sure he'd have thought of some other way to keep me out of the lobby if he weren't so pissed, but either way, if it was the rider out there, I didn't want my hands cuffed behind my back.

"Shouldn't we wait for John to get back?" I asked, edging away from the door.

"Don't make this difficult, ma'am." He shoved me forward.

Crap.

As soon as he pushed me through the doorway, I opened my shields, peering across the planes. He escorted me down a small hall of offices—very small, not many detectives got an office instead of a slot in the bullpen—and then we were in the lobby. I scanned the room, ignoring the decay and the magic, looking only for souls. John's cheery yellow soul was in the front, posture stiff and suspicious as he talked to a body filled with a soul coated in darkness.

The rider looked up as the rookie pushed me into the lobby. A smile stretched across his stolen face. "Sister."

Crap.

"That's him, John. That's the rider," I yelled.

Then all hell broke loose.

The rider lifted a gun, aiming it at me. Someone shouted for him to drop the weapon. He wouldn't. I knew he wouldn't. I threw myself down even before I heard the gunshot.

Pain sliced through my arm, hot and sharp. Then I hit the ground. I'd managed to twist enough to land on my shoulder, which kept my head from slamming into the linoleum, but the jarring impact sent another wave of pain through me. I didn't bother fighting the scream that burst from me— no one could hear it over the gunshots. Three of them, all in rapid succession.

The sudden silence following the loud shots sounded dull, empty, or maybe that was the ringing in my ears. Blood dripped down my arm as I tried to get my feet under me before—

Too late.

A large, shapeless darkness dashed through the station lobby, headed straight for me. No, not for me—we'd already danced that particular encounter—it attached itself to the rookie, pouring into him. I gulped, forgetting the hot pain surging through my body as I broke out in a frozen sweat.

Oh, crap, crap. "John, help."

My boots left black marks on the floor, accompanied by smudges of blood as I scrambled, pushing myself farther from the rookie. His soul continued to dim. Fast.

"Someone call a medic," John yelled as he headed for me. "How bad are you hurt?"

I shook my head, still trying to scoot away from the rider and his new host. "John, it's in the rookie."

The young officer smiled at me, his eyes glazing over with darkness. He drew his gun, leveling it at my chest. At this range, he couldn't miss.

"Good-bye, Alex Craft."

I wanted to close my eyes, but I couldn't. I stared at the gun and time slowed, narrowing to only his finger as it tensed, to the movement of the gun's action. I cringed, ready for the pain to blast into me. But his finger stopped, his face going slack.

I blinked. Death stood behind the rookie, the man's soul in his hand. A moment later a shot sounded. The rookie's body spun and collapsed in a heap.

I stared, my lungs burning from the breath I'd been holding too long. I let it out as the rider coalesced in the air above the rookie. No. This had to stop. It could keep jumping bodies until everyone in the room was dead.

But how the hell could I stop it? Would it follow if I ran, leaving the others alone? It was clearly after me. *And my big mouth.* I'd just had to tell it I could track it to any body it took, didn't I? I needed to get it somewhere with a hell of a lot fewer people. And guns.

But first I had to get out of the damn handcuffs.

As I doubted the rider intended to give me enough time to politely ask someone to release me, I had to be a little more creative. Or destructive. I was already touching multiple planes, how hard could it be to push the cuffs into the land of the dead?

Harder than anticipated. Especially since they were behind my back and I couldn't see them. I'd moved items to the land of the dead before, but typically by accident. Now I focused on what the metal would look like rusted and cor-

roded. I flexed my arms, trying to pull my wrists free. Agony
tore through my injured arm, but I didn't stop. I kept the
image of the cuffs degrading in my mind, and I felt the
metal give, a rung in the chain breaking. The bracelets dangled around my wrists, burning into my flesh, but I could
move my arms.

"Come on," Death said, pulling me to my feet. "We have
to get you out of here."

I couldn't agree more, but it had taken me too long to
break the cuffs and the rider had surely jumped bodies by
now. I needed to know where to expect the next attack to
come from.

"Where is it?" I whispered, searching for the rider as I
moved. Death didn't have time to answer before I spotted
the shadow. It was already squashing the soul of its next
victim, an officer I recognized from Kingly's crime scene.

Crap.

I pointed as I called out, "It's in Larid."

Some of the officers lifted guns; others kept their weapons pointed toward the ground. John's was halfway between
the two positions.

"You're sure?"

"Oh, she's sure," the rider said with Larid's voice as
Death pulled me back. "Will you kill this body too? I'll just
take another. Which one of you wants to be next? Or you
can let me kill Craft, and I'll walk out of here."

"Unacceptable options," a voice I didn't expect to come
to my defense said. Then Detective Jenson, John's partner
and a feykin in hiding who I was pretty sure hated me,
pulled the trigger on his Taser. Two probes attached to wires
shot out, hitting Larid in the chest.

Jenson sent thousands of volts of electricity into Larid,
and the rider dropped his gun, falling to his knees. But he
wasn't down. Reaching up, he pulled the probes from his
chest. They hit the linoleum with two soft clinks.

"Thanks for volunteering," the rider said to Jenson as he
reached for his gun.

He never made it. A blue foam dart hit Larid between

the eyes and magic exploded into the room. Larid collapsed, out cold under a combined knockout, immobilizer, and Aetheric blocker spell. I coughed, choking on the thickness of magic in the air, but I didn't dare take my eyes off Larid.

What are you going to do, rider? Can you leave a living but unconscious body?

Either the rider was as knocked out by the dart as its host, or the host had to die for the rider to jump to the next body. I had the growing suspicion it was the later. I could see it still coating Larid's soul, but it didn't pour out of him. The unconscious man had become a container.

But what would happen when he woke?

Of course, with that nasty combination of spells, it would be a while. A nasty combination I'd seen before. Which meant Briar was here. With everything else going on, I hadn't noticed her enter. I still didn't sense her or the armory she carried. My nerves were too frazzled to zero in on her magic through the lingering miasma of the spells from the dart. In fact, about the only thing I was up for right now was sitting down. But I forced myself to turn, to look for her.

The movement morphed into a sway and only Death's arms kept me upright.

"You're hurt," he said, his hand moving to hover over my wound.

There was a lot of blood, but the shot had only grazed me. "I'm a lot better than I would be if you hadn't . . ." I didn't finish because he'd ripped a soul out of a living body to save my life. Granted, the rookie had been shot seconds later, and those crucial seconds would have been too late for me, but collectors didn't take souls early.

Ever.

I'd known only one who had, but he'd been bad news. Very bad news. In the name of love, he and his lover had crossed line after line until they were willing to tear the world apart to be together. A month ago they'd almost succeeded. That night, the gray man had told me to remember what had happened in that ill-begotten clearing. That it was why Death and I could never be together. That was the night Death vanished from my life.

Now he'd just crossed a line to save me. A big line. And we both knew it.

People crowded around me, and Death leaned down, kissing my forehead lightly before releasing me to a pair of hands belonging to someone who had no idea I was already being steadied.

"We need to talk," I whispered to him.

But it was Briar Darque who stepped into view and said, "Yes we do. What the hell is going on?"

I suppressed a groan. Now that my adrenaline was dropping back to normal, my arm throbbed, as did my head, and my wrists, and the shoulder I'd landed on. And hell, pretty much all of me hurt. I'd been exhausted *before* this little adventure. Now I felt ready to collapse. I didn't want to talk to Briar Darque.

I twisted to see who had taken me from Death—and who would hopefully rescue me from Briar—and got another shock. Detective Jenson had a firm hold on my elbow, helping me keep my balance. With my shields open, I could see through the glamour he wore that hid the fact his lower jaw was elongated and two large tusks curved over his upper lip. He had troll blood somewhere in his history, but the only physical sign of it was that unfortunate jaw. He was the only feykin I'd seen who bore obvious traces of their fae ancestry—or who had enough glamour to cover it up. Of course, his soul was more silver than blue. My father had told me that there were humans with fae blood, and then there were fae with human blood. I wondered if Jenson was an example of the latter.

Jenson noticed me staring and that overlarge jaw clenched. He knew I could see through glamour. "Can you stand, Craft? Yes? Good." He released my arm, turned on his heel, and marched away.

I stared at his back. *So much for a rescue from Briar.*

"What are you doing here?" I asked her as I staggered to the closest desk to steal a wad of tissue. I was bleeding on the floor.

"I told you that I'd be keeping tabs on you. I heard you were involved in the deaths of two people, so I came to find out what happened. Now what the hell was that?" She pointed to the unconscious officer. Someone had put handcuffs and ankle shackles on him, which seemed like a good idea to me.

"He's possessed. The MCIB has protocols to deal with that, right?" Because I was so done with this case. I just wanted someone to take the rider and, I don't know, banish him? Bottle him? He obviously wasn't going to stand trial by a jury of his peers.

"Possessed?" Briar cocked a dark eyebrow. "That sounds more up your alley than mine."

"Isn't there someone in your division who deals with this sort of thing?" The MCIB had a ghoul hunter; surely they had someone who would know what to do with Larid and the rider.

She shook her head. "I'd execute the host. It sounds cruel, but just like victims infected by ghouls, it's better to put them down while they're human and not monsters."

"It jumps from host to host." I sank into a chair. I didn't know whose. It was just closest. "I think the previous host has to die before the rider can escape to a new body. Keeping him alive should contain it."

"Then you better try the hospital, because I don't have time to babysit."

So no help from the MCIB then. I sighed.

"Alex, let me see your arm," John said, stepping close enough that he crowded Briar away. Normally I'd have been uncomfortable, but I was glad for the break from the woman.

"It's just a graze." But I obediently pulled the wad of tissues away from the wound.

"You're right, but you should probably go to the hospital. You might need stitches."

I so couldn't afford a hospital bill. "If you have an OMIH first aid kit laying around, I'm sure that will be fine."

John's mustache gave an irritated twitch, but he called

for someone to fetch the kit and then offered to help me to his office. I started to refuse, but my legs felt like my bones had been replaced by cooked spaghetti, so I let him help me hobble to his office.

"What happened to those cuffs?" he asked, looking at the bracelets I still wore. I'd intended to turn the suckers into a shower of rust, but I'd barely corroded them. They looked weathered, not ruined, so I shrugged. Then I winced because the movement hurt.

John collapsed into his chair, his shoulders slumping as if a great weight pressed down on them. Then he unloaded his gun, preparing to turn it over when the inevitable internal affairs investigation started. "This is over now, right?"

I looked back toward the lobby. The idea of being blind after the attempt on my life terrified me, so I hadn't released my touch on other planes. Glancing out the door all I could see were crumbling walls and wisps of magic, but I knew that beyond that were two bodies who shouldn't be dead, and a third person spelled unconscious as a living container for a malevolent spirit.

"I hope so," I whispered, but as long as the rider still existed, I couldn't help feeling like the question wasn't *if* it would escape, but *when*.

Chapter 25

 ❦

"**A**lex, wake up."

I groaned, willing the voice away.

"Alex."

Grabbing my pillow, I pulled it over my head and rolled over. Which hurt like hell.

"Alex," Rianna said again.

"Go away." I didn't want to be awake. I felt like I'd been used as a giant's punching bag. I needed more sleep, and a pain charm. Or six.

"Alex, the equinox starts soon."

"Good for it."

"You promised you'd go to the revelry."

Why the hell would I do that? Waking up at o'dark thirty to go to Faerie was definitely a stupid idea. I pulled the pillow tighter around my head, but she was right, after weeks of Caleb and Rianna bugging me, I had promised.

But yesterday I'd spent hours at the police station, first answering to the ABMU and then to the OMIH, who were a hell of a lot more interested in Larid and the rider than Briar had implied. I'd also fended off a psychic attack, had my soul ripped at, been arrested, shot at, and saved by Death collecting a soul early. I seriously thought I deserved an out on that particular promise. Unfortunately it didn't work that way, and I felt the tug of magic below my sternum. I was fae enough that a promise was as binding as any magic-laced oath.

I spouted a few creative curses and pried open my eyes. I'd been blind when I finally closed my shields yesterday, and I wasn't surprised to discover that my vision was still dim, washed out. Rianna stood at the side of my bed looking like a grayscale image with a light wash of watercolors on top. Desmond, being black to start with, had no definition.

I glanced toward the windows but couldn't see any light. "Is it still dark?"

Rianna rolled her eyes. "Of course. The equinox starts at dawn."

And she couldn't be out of Faerie then. Right.

"She awake yet?" Caleb yelled from somewhere downstairs.

Rianna looked at me.

"I'm up, I'm up." And I needed coffee. Lots of coffee. "Remind me why I'm going to this equinox thing again?" I asked as I hit the BREW button. PC pressed against my legs, peering at Desmond from around my calves.

"You're going because revelries like this only occur four times a year."

"I'm really not up for a party," I said staring at my coffeepot and willing it to brew faster. It didn't work. I could screw with reality, but coffee still took forever to brew, or at least it seemed that way before my first cup.

Rianna pulled a mug out of the cupboard for me, which I accepted with all the grace of a hibernating bear woken far too early.

"It's not just a party. It's . . ." She paused, as if looking for the right words. Ones that would convince me—not that she needed to bother. I couldn't break my promise. "It's a neutral time, so it will be a safe time for you to experience more of Faerie. To interact with the fae and the courts. You're going to have to make your choice and pick a court soon." Quieter she added. "Or declare yourself independent and take their oaths."

Rianna might be spending an ever-increasing amount of time in the mortal realm, but she belonged and lived in Faerie. Me declaring myself independent would have potentially disastrous consequences for her. She wanted me to pick a court, any court. Caleb also wanted me to make my choice, if only to stop the Winter Queen's harassment, but he wanted me to declare independent so I didn't have to leave Nekros. I stared at the slowly dripping black gold filling my coffeepot. It was way too early for Faerie politics.

Forty-seven minutes later—and I'd felt every single one of them—I was begrudgingly awake, caffeinated, and walking toward the Eternal Bloom. Rianna had her arm hooked in mine, Holly doing the same on my other side. I'd like to say it was all cheerful camaraderie, but the truth was I couldn't see a thing in the predawn darkness and their scorching heat was better than falling on my face.

"So what will it be like?" Holly asked, practically skipping as we walked. She was way too much of a morning person.

"You'll have to wait and see," was Caleb's answer, and I could hear the smile in his voice. He always went to the revelries, disappearing for a day every few months, but this was the first time we'd accompanied him.

"And what is it I'm supposed to do?" I asked, and heard a petulant whine in my voice. I cleared my throat. I was *so* not that person. "You guys don't actually expect me to join a court today, do you?"

"Of course not." The smile wasn't in his voice this time. "You just need to enjoy yourself and stop seeing Faerie as terrifying. Go, interact with other fae, and have fun."

Yeah, I don't see that happening.

I took the Bloom's front steps carefully, and too slowly

for my friends, both of whom were far more eager than I. Which wasn't hard. All I wanted to do was go back to bed.

"Oh," Holly said, stopping short as we reached the top. "It says they're closed for the equinox. How are we—" She cut off abruptly. "Do you hear that?"

I listened, but all I heard was an old car chugging down a nearby road. "No."

"It's music." She dropped my arm, and took another step toward the door. "The sweetest music I've ever heard."

Her voice sounded dreamily far away, and I grabbed her, pulling her back. "Caleb, are you sure this is safe?"

"She's already addicted to Faerie food. There are few other dangers to mortals at revelries. I'll be with her the whole time." Something soft touched his voice as he said the last, but my thoughts were imagining endless dances, soul chains, slavers, beautiful things that liked to feast on mortal flesh, and somewhere in the back of my head, I heard the echo of words from when a fae had called Holly a lovely doll, saying that all changelings were dolls.

Of course, Holly wasn't a changeling yet, but she was a step away.

"Al, relax," Rianna whispered, her voice low enough that only I could hear. "I told you, the revelries are neutral. This is one of the safest times to enter Faerie."

Right. Then why was my gut twisting at the idea?

Because Faerie scares the hell out of me.

Caleb ignored the closed sign and ushered us into the small receiving room. Normally a bouncer sat in this room, making sure that humans went to the public side of the Bloom and fae were given access to the VIP room.

"Does someone want to sign us in?" I asked as I pulled my gloves out of my back pocket—I didn't want to see the blood on my hands as soon as I stepped through that door. Not that I could see much of anything. The overhead light was far too dim, or my eyes were just that bad right now.

"No need today," Caleb said marching up to the door to the VIP room. A door the bouncer normally kept hidden. "I need to use a couple glyphs to reveal the door. You'll have to give me a moment. My ability to weave the Aetheric makes my relationship with my fae magic . . . unusual." He sounded almost embarrassed, which was odd for Caleb—he always sounded so sure of everything.

I frowned at him. "We can't just walk through the door?"

"We could if we could see it." He stopped. "You can see it, can't you?"

I nodded. I could barely see the room around us, but I could see the damn door. It glimmered, as if a small sun blazed behind it, the light seeping out of every crevice.

Caleb stepped back and motioned to me with his hand. "Then by all means, after you."

The irritated note in his voice caught me off guard. It wasn't like I was *trying* to see the door. The queasy feeling in my stomach intensified, but I stepped forward and grabbed the door handle. It felt pleasantly warm under my gloved hands, as if it were alive, which was rather creepy. It had never been warm before.

Better get used to the unknown, Alex. The next few hours would be full of it.

Starting with the fact that what was on the other side of the door wasn't the VIP room, but a dense deciduous forest. I stood in the doorway, staring—and blocking everyone else. "Uh, where did the rest of the Bloom go?"

Caleb gave me a small shove in the base of my back, pushing me through the door. "It's the fall equinox. All doors lead to the fall court throughout the celebration."

"Guess that makes this their party then?" It wasn't really a question, just my mouth still moving as I stared at the scene around me. The trees in Nekros hadn't figured out fall was upon them and they should change colors, which wasn't their fault as it was still warm. Here a crispness in the air spoke of the changing seasons and leaves in shades of yellow, gold, orange, and red filled the trees. I held off blinking as long as I could, sure that when I opened my eyes again, the trees would be gone or draped in shadow. But no, I could see them. Could see the full glory of colors, bright and brilliant, despite no clear source of light. *I forgot that the damage to my eyes didn't affect me in Faerie.*

"We've talked about this before," Rianna said, sounding every bit as cross as one of our academy instructors when a student failed to retain a lesson. "On the equinox and the solstice, all doors to Faerie open to that season's court."

My mouth formed an "O" but I wasn't paying attention. I was soaking in the scene around me. Okay, so that scene was a bunch of trees, but I could see them. Really see them, in full vivid color. I hadn't seen this clearly since, well, since I visited Faerie a month ago. Maybe colors were just that much more vibrant in Faerie. I blinked back tears.

Crap, if I break down over a couple trees, what will happen when I reach the revelry?

It looked like I'd find out soon. A colorful trail of fallen leaves led between the canopy of trees and Caleb headed for it, Holly at his side, and Rianna and Desmond following. I hurried to catch up.

We emerged in a clearing filled with lively music and fae of every shape, size, and color. I'd never seen so many fae in one place before. Even when I'd unintentionally been the guest of honor in the Winter Queen's court, there hadn't been so many fae present. And more were arriving. As I stood, gaping at the sight from the opening of the tree line, a fae with flames for hair and eyes of ever-swirling smoke stepped around me. She took only a moment to look around before bounding toward a group of fae not far away, a smile on her face and a blaze of heat in her wake.

"Do all the independents come to the revelries?" I asked, looking at Caleb.

He was watching Holly's reaction to the scene. Her eyes were slightly glazed as they took in the clearing, but Caleb didn't seem worried. He also didn't look away as he shrugged and said, "Most. Not all." Maybe he wasn't quite as unconcerned as he appeared.

I wondered once again how safe it was for Holly to be here. Hell, for *me* to be here. "Maybe this has been enough for one visit and I should take Holly home?"

Her head snapped up at that. "No. I don't want to leave."

Okay, so not as entranced as I thought. At least, not magically induced entrancement.

"You can't leave, Al," Rianna said, then at my alarmed look, went on, "Well, you *can* leave, but you'll lose the entire equinox."

The unease clawing at my stomach reached deeper, hitting my spine as a wave of shock tore over me. "You mean, no matter what time I leave, I'll emerge tomorrow?"

She nodded.

Great. Just great. That sure as hell hadn't been mentioned—I'd have remembered that little nugget of information. I hated losing time to Faerie. And what about the twenty-four hours we were gone?

"Al, geez, you look like you're about to have an aneurism. It's going to be okay. I put a note on the door at Tongues for the Dead and Holly gave Tamara a key so she can walk and feed PC."

Was I the only one who hadn't realized stepping inside would cost me a day? *Apparently so.*

Several more fae had passed us while we dawdled in the clearing's opening. I didn't pay much attention, until a figure I recognized started past me.

"Jenson?"

The detective turned slowly, like if he took his time, maybe I wouldn't be there by the time he made it all the way around. "Craft," he said, and his frown made the calluses under his tusks stretch. "It's customary to drop your glamour for a revelry."

I blinked at him. What was he talking about? I didn't have any glamour.

Whatever Jenson saw in my expression made him growl—literally. It was a sound that shouldn't have come out of a human throat. He shook his head, collecting himself.

"Be merry, Craft," he said, the words oddly formal. Then he turned his back to me and scanned the clearing. A large conglomeration of trolls laughed and tussled in one area of the clearing. Jenson stared at the group but he didn't join them. After a few moments, he rolled his shoulders, straightened his back, and marched in the opposite direction.

I watched him go. *What's his story?* And what was his problem with me?

Desmond nudged Rianna's leg, and she knelt to his level, rubbing behind his ears. "You go on. I'll be fine."

Those eyes, too intelligent to belong in a dog-shaped body, studied her for a long moment. Then his huge head bobbed in a nod and he ran into the clearing, vanishing among the growing throng of revelers.

"We need to move," Caleb said as still more fae passed us.

Rianna nodded and wrapped her arm in mine when I would have stalled. I was already in Faerie, already committed to attending the revelry, but I felt safer among the trees than in a clearing full of fae. A clearing, I'd noticed, that grew to accommodate the ever-increasing number of fae. Rianna denied me any more time to linger, it was follow or be dragged, and as I still hurt all over—and she'd grabbed the arm with the bullet wound—I was disinclined to be dragged.

Caleb led our small group around several clumps of fae, some greeted him by name, others simply bid our group to "be merry."

"What's up with that?" I asked Rianna after a thorn fae pranced around us, the tangled briars of her hair rustling. She paused long enough to give me a brilliant smile, her barklike lips spreading wide to show her wooden teeth and then, like everyone else, she bid us to be merry before dancing off to mingle elsewhere. "Is it some sort of ritual greeting?"

Rianna shrugged. "It's just what it sounds like, a wish for us to have a good time. It's a revelry."

The farther we walked, the more aware I became of the hum of anticipation filling the air. It was like all the fae's combined emotions had become a tangible thing, or maybe it was Faerie itself that was anxiously waiting. But for what?

"Dawn," Rianna whispered, glancing at the sky. Far off

in the east, the slightest hint of light glowed over the tree line.

The near steady stream of fae trickling into the clearing had stopped, and every face turned upward, watching the brightening glow in the distance. Even the music, which had filled the clearing, stopped, the musicians' instruments silent as the fae playing them turned their attention upward.

"Get ready, Al," Rianna whispered, squeezing my hand.

The first ray of light sliced through the clearing, and a masculine, bellowing voice announced, "It begins."

Chapter 26

❯━━❯━≈❯ ❮≈━❮━━❮

"The equinox is upon us," that booming voice announced, and I whirled toward the sound.

The center of the clearing, where I could have sworn was a grassy patch before, now held a wide dais with three throne-sized chairs made of twisting branches. A Sleagh Maith stood in the center of the dais, his brown hair reflecting red and gold highlights as the light of dawn glimmered off it. On his head a circlet of fall leaves formed his crown.

I leaned close to Rianna. "So that's the Fall King?"

"He prefers Harvest King, but yes."

Behind the king, his queen wore a diadem of twisting red twigs decorated with mums in cool tones of cream and salmon. She held the hand of a boy who couldn't have been more than three. He lacked the brown hair and dark eyes of his parents—as well as the angular Sleagh Maith features. Instead he had a round, cherublike face with wide blue eyes and a mop of blond hair.

"The boy's human?" I asked in a hissing whisper.

"Leave it be, Alex. Now stay quiet," Rianna warned, recognizing the outrage in my face.

Folklore was full of stories in which beautiful children were kidnapped or switched for fae changelings. Treaties had been signed to prevent such behavior in modern society, but I knew it still occurred—Falin was proof of that. He'd told me how the queen had put him in the place of a human child so that he would grow up with an understanding of the mortal world and more resistance to its iron. The child he'd been switched with? He was in the winter court.

"Welcome, friends of the changing season," the king said. He wasn't yelling, but his booming voice reached every corner of the clearing. "Be one with us, make merry with us, and enjoy the bountiful harvest." He threw his arms over the top of his head in a wide "Y" shape, and a wash of magic flooded the clearing.

The magic wasn't overwhelming the way Briar's spells had been, but had a gentle, joyous feel to it, and where it passed, Faerie changed. The trees around the clearing filled with fruits and nuts, the bushes with berries. Banquet tables appeared, as did large casks.

A cheer rang out, and the music started again in earnest. Folk laughed, danced, and gathered around the buffet tables. The fall royalty sat on their thrones, watching. Someone brought the king a goblet and he toasted the fae as a whole—many of whom returned the gesture. Other fae approached the throne. All were greeted with boisterous joviality, but even though I was out of earshot, I could tell that some requests set before him were—however cheerfully— turned down and sent away.

"So this is it then?" I could feel the heady excitement in the air, but I wasn't exactly in a "merry" mood.

Rianna smiled, her lips curling at the edges as if she were holding back a secret. "Just wait."

A chime sounded, its crystal clear note ringing through the clearing, and the music changed, growing softer, more somber. The fae turned toward the hawthorn-ringed copse of trees we'd passed through to enter the large glen. Curious, I turned to look as well, but saw nothing under the arch of oak branches. Then as if a shroud of gloom had rolled away, a giant, pure white stag with arching antlers appeared. On its bare back sat a woman. I recognized her on sight.

The Winter Queen.

Frost kissed her dark curls and eyelashes despite the relative warmth of the glade. She wore a gown dripping with icicles that sparkled like diamonds, the long train falling over the stag's rump and blending with her white cloak that glistened like freshly fallen snow. No, not *like* snow, the cloak *was* snow. As the stag took each graceful step forward, the cloak blanketed the ground in their wake. But it was fall, not winter, and the snow melted immediately, revealing crisp, colorful fallen leaves once more.

An entourage followed the queen, some guards, based on their weapons and ice-scaled armor, but many were gentry Sleagh Maith, dressed in all their finery and moving with the haughty attitude of their station. A gaggle of nonroyal courtiers finished out her procession, many with their eyes as wide as their smiles as they looked around the glade.

Rianna and Caleb had said the revelry would give me a chance to interact with fae from all the courts, but I hadn't expected the Winter Queen to make an appearance.

"I have to get out of here," I whispered, backing toward the tree line. What if the queen saw me? This wasn't a bubble of Faerie like the Bloom. This was Faerie. Her domain and place of power.

Caleb grabbed my arm, stopping me. "Wait and watch."

The Winter Queen guided her stag to the dais where the Harvest King and Queen sat on their thrones of woven wood. She held out her hands, and two Sleagh Maith stepped forward. The first was Ryese, the second, Falin. My heart twisted in my chest as Falin took one of the queen's outstretched hands.

He's not mine. And he never would be, unless I was willing to bind myself to the frosty bitch he served. Probably not then either.

The Winter Queen dismounted with more grace than I ever would have thought possible, but it didn't surprise me. She was beautiful, elegant, and powerful—in other words, everything I wasn't. I'd have fallen on my face if I'd tried that move in a gown with a train that took three attendants to lift. Hell, I probably wouldn't have managed to mount the stag in the first place.

The knot tightening in my temples made me realize I was scowling and had been for some time. I forced the muscles in my face to loosen. I aimed for neutral, but clearly didn't succeed because when Caleb glanced at me he shook his head.

"You'll see," he whispered before turning his attention back to the center of the clearing.

Rianna locked her arm with mine again. "He's right. It'll be fine."

I wasn't convinced. Leaving without taking any chances sounded like a better plan, even if I lost a day. But I waited obediently, watching as the Winter Queen stepped forward.

"Hail majesties of the plentiful harvest," she said, and though she didn't yell or raise her voice, I could hear her crisp words as if she stood feet from me instead of more than a dozen yards away.

"Hail queen of the long slumber," the Harvest King said. It was a title I hadn't heard before, but winter was a time when nature appeared to sleep, so I guessed it was apropos. The king continued. "The oak is still ablaze with color and it is not yet time for your cold touch."

The Winter Queen inclined her head. "The time in which the oak's boughs are weighted with snow will come soon enough, but I am content to wait."

"Then for this day and night, join our revelry. Be welcome in our court and make merry with us as we celebrate the bountiful harvest of fall."

The words—actually, the entire exchange—had all the formality of a ritual. Which was confirmed when the Winter Queen curtsied and said, "The winter court joins the fall, debts and grudges forgotten for the span of this festive occasion when night and day are equal."

The gathered fae, of both courts as well as all the independents who had already joined the festival, cheered. Folk rushed forward, enticing the new revelers to join dances or lift overflowing flagons. But as the winter fae dispersed, attention turned to another group of newcomers.

"Did I understand that correctly," I whispered to Rianna as a couple crowned in woven flowers stepped into the clearing followed by their own entourage. "Did the winter court just join the fall court?"

Rianna nodded. "Only for the equinox." When I continued to stare at her, she went on, "Remember how Caleb said that all doors open to the fall court for the equinox? That means all the power from human belief is flowing into this court, making it the most powerful for the entirety of the festival."

And the rest are at their weakest, I suppose. I turned my attention back to the center of the clearing. A very similar ritualistic greeting was being exchanged, only this time the bit about the oak was something about budding and new life. *This must be the spring court.*

"Will all the courts attend?"

Rianna shrugged. "Maybe. The equinox and solstice revelries are unmatched, but debts and grudges truly must be forgotten for the revelry, and not every monarch can make such a promise."

That made sense.

As the sun continued to rise, the party around us grew livelier and more courts arrived to join the revelry. I watched as the summer monarchs and their court were greeted and invited to join, followed closely by my great-granduncle, the King of Shadows. His entourage was the smallest I'd seen, with only two Sleagh Maith attending him and a small group of nonroyals, most of whom were monstrous in appearance. Of course, until the High King decided to sever the Nightmare Realm from Faerie, my uncle had ruled that as well, so monstrous was to be expected.

I turned as yet another troupe of fae emerged from between the hawthorn bushes and my breath caught in my chest. I blinked, and then blinked again. All unglamoured Sleagh Maith had an ethereal glow, as if lit softly from within, but the woman making her way into the clearing went beyond an otherworldly shimmer to a radiance that brightened everything around her. An involuntary smile spread across my face as unbidden tears gathered in my eyes. She floated more than walked toward the dais, and had an ephemeral quality to her, as if she were a wisp of brilliance that a breeze would steal away.

"Who is that?" I asked, my voice coming out choked.

When I received no answer, I tore my gaze away from the apparition long enough to realize Rianna wasn't watching the procession of courts anymore, but staring at something—or someone—to our left. I had to repeat my question before she turned to me.

"Oh, the Queen of Light," she said, her attention wavering before she finished the short sentence.

Light? That fit her, and her court who shared that slightly out of reach ephemeral quality and radiance. From what I'd learned from Caleb and Rianna's crash course in all things Faerie, I knew that just as each season had an opposing season that balanced it, the court of light balanced the court of shadows. Or at least it once had. When the nightmare realm was severed, the shadow court lost the fear and night terrors that supplied most of its power. The counterbalance for the nightmare realm was supposed to be the realm of daydreams, which fed the light court through human creativity and imagination. Now my uncle had the smallest court, while the court of light was by far the largest I'd seen tonight. The darkness fading while the light thrived. *But isn't Faerie supposed to be about balance?*

Once the court of light was invited to join the revelry, I turned toward the entrance. All four seasons were now present, as well as light and shadow. "So all that's left is the high court," I said, waiting, watching. Out of all the courts, the high court was the one I was most curious about. Both Rianna and Caleb dodged my questions about the high court, so I knew the least about it. I was more than a little curious to see the High King, who ruled over all the other courts.

But no one appeared.

"The high court won't be here. They never attend," Rianna said, her voice more than a little distracted. She dropped my arm, taking a step away before stopping and saying, "Al, I have to go."

I started to protest, to stop her, or at least ask what was wrong. But when she turned to face me, the smile she wore was real, radiant. She grabbed my hands and beamed at me.

"Oh, Al, don't look like that. Today, tonight, Faerie is transformed and dedicated to making merry. Until dawn tomorrow many taboos are lifted and bonds broken." She tugged at the fingers of my right glove, pulling it up, almost off.

I jerked back, trying to stop her, but only ended up with a bare hand, my glove in Rianna's grip. Her smile widened and I stared in wonder at my pale, unbloodied palm. I opened my mouth. Closed it again. Pulled off my other glove. That hand was clean too.

"Make merry, Al," she said. Then, catching me off guard, she lifted onto her toes and kissed my cheek.

I gaped as she turned, and without another word, she wove through the throng of fae around us. My gaze moved past her, to where her beeline was headed, and her actions made more sense. Weaving toward her was Desmond, not in his familiar dog form, but in that of a man.

His smile matched hers as they met in the middle and he lifted her in his arms, kissing her. I looked away as that very deep kiss reached the point I was sure one of them would pass out if they didn't break for air. While their public display of desire might have made me uncomfortable, it didn't phase the revelers around them. In fact, I noticed more than a couple of fae pairing off.

"Please tell me a Faerie party isn't code for an orgy," I muttered, turning.

And found that I was alone.

Okay, I wasn't actually alone as I was in the middle of a crowd of fae who, now that all the courts had entered, were talking animatedly or passing around drinks in cups made

of trumpet flowers. But Caleb and Holly were gone. I
looked around, searching, which was harder to do than normal. Unlike in the mortal realm, I wasn't exactly tall in this
crowd as it boasted plenty of Sleagh Maith, not to mention
giants, trolls, and other larger-than-human fae. I turned
back to see where Rianna and Desmond had gone, but the
crowd had swallowed them, blocking them from sight.

Great. Abandoned. Now what was I supposed to do?

"What I wouldn't give for a Dummies Guide to Faerie."
I'd said the thought out loud, which earned me odd looks
from the revelers around me. I gave a fae with too few eyes
and too many heads a tight-lipped smile. Only one head
smiled back. Another fae, with legs like a goat but a very
female—and completely naked—torso held out a buttercup
filled with golden liquid. I waved a hand in refusal and
slipped past her. Weaving my way through the crowd, I tried
to look like I knew where I was going, but I was wandering
aimlessly, hoping to run into someone I knew.

I should have been more specific in my hopes.

"Lexi," a chimelike female voice said from behind me.

Crap. I turned, finding myself face-to-face with the delicate and perfect features of the Winter Queen.

"I have to go," I said, pointing in the direction I'd been
headed before she'd stopped me. I didn't know where it
would take me, but almost anywhere was better than here,
with her. "Some other time, maybe."

"Are you looking for someone? Should I guess who?"
She tilted her head slightly, giving me a coy smile. "Could
he be among my entourage?" She took a step back and
swept a hand, indicating the circle of Sleagh Maith behind
her.

I couldn't have stopped my gaze from searching for Falin
had I wanted to. But he wasn't there. Without a word, I
turned, intending to walk away.

"Dear Lexi, don't be that way," the queen said. "Perhaps
one of these gentlemen are who you're looking for."

I didn't want to turn. If she really was presenting Falin
this time there would be a price. There was always a price

and I didn't want to face the temptation. I might fail. And yet, I found myself turning, looking to where her hand gestured.

"Falin." The whisper escaped me before I was aware I'd spoken.

"Oh, poor Ryese," the queen said, her voice dramatically pouty. But amusement danced under that act.

I honestly hadn't noticed that Ryese was standing next to Falin. Ryese wasn't looking at me, his pretty features shut down, but I could see the muscle above his jaw bulging as if he gritted his teeth. Hard.

"What's the game?" I asked, turning away from the two men so I could face the queen.

"Game?" She batted long-lashed eyes at me. She really was too pretty. "Who said anything about a game? This is a revelry. They happen only four times a year. It is a moment of peace and merriment in Faerie. Tell me it wouldn't make you happy to spend it with a man you care about?"

I opened my mouth, but if I said it wouldn't thrill me, that would be a lie. She'd sidestepped my question though, which meant there was a catch. "The bonds you'd likely tie around me wouldn't be worth the 'moment' of merriment."

"You'll incur no debt or bonds from me, dear Lexi. I promise."

I cringed inwardly at both the endearment and the nickname, but I could feel the weight of that promise. It was genuine and she couldn't break it. So what was I missing?

"You've ordered Falin to have no contact with me," I said, because I was still trying to find the loophole she planned to exploit.

"I'll lift it for the revelry."

"Why?"

The skin around her eyes tightened, just slightly, but it betrayed her annoyance. "Must you ask so many questions? Perhaps I wish to engender goodwill from you. Perhaps I wish you to remember what you'd sacrifice if you decline my court. Perhaps I'm simply in a good mood as this is a joyful occasion—"

I seriously doubted the last.

"Now, pick your man before I change my mind," she said, her voice turning sharp.

It didn't escape me that she had yet again avoided my question. Something more was going on here.

I turned to the two fae. They were both Sleagh Maith, nobles of the winter court and currently both shimmering slightly without glamour to dampen their otherworldly qualities. And yet, the two men couldn't have been more different. Oh, they were both handsome, but Ryese was softer, his features more delicate, and his body, while as toned as most Sleagh Maith, was that of the pampered elite. Falin, on the other hand, was rougher around the edges. His muscles were earned from hard work, his handsome face almost always guarded, his lips slower to smile, but when he did, it softened his features.

He wasn't smiling now, but watching me with a predatory look. Ryese on the other hand, looked away as soon as I turned to him. I'd expected to see the same dark anger I had the other night in the Bloom—he didn't deal with rejection well—but in that split second, what I saw in those pale eyes was uncertainty. Which struck me as wrong. Very wrong.

She wouldn't have . . . ?

I opened my shields. I could tell from the way the woman beside me stilled that my eyes lit from the inside, but I didn't care if she noticed. She was playing a game, and I intended to See through it.

And I could.

Faerie had its own layers of reality, but the land of the dead and the Aetheric weren't among them, so while I could sense the realities around me, they weren't visible. That meant absolutely nothing obscured the fact both men were bound in glamour—a strong one, too. But while the glamour was thick, it didn't change the fact that with my shields open, the men switched places.

So that's her game. Now I knew why "Ryese" wouldn't meet my eyes—the queen had likely ordered Falin not to reveal the trick.

"I pick him," I said, pointing at the real Falin.

"Ryese?" the queen asked, those perfect eyebrows arching.

I almost said yes, as that was who Falin currently looked like, but stopped myself. She could drop the glamour at any moment. If I said yes to Ryese, she may do just that, and I'd be stuck with the real Ryese. "No."

"Then you mean him." She pointed to the fae glamoured to look like Falin.

"No," I said again and crossed the space to Falin. I opened my shields wider, until I couldn't see even a shadow of the glamoured shape hiding Falin's form.

Glamour is belief magic. I wasn't one hundred percent sure how it worked from the fae side, but the basic principle was that if you believed what you saw, it became real—at least temporarily. If enough people disbelieved what they saw, reality would reject the glamour. Not all glamour was equal, and Faerie accepted it easier than mortal reality—so much so that the first time I met the Winter Queen she'd transformed my outfit into a ball gown, which still hung in my closet, complete with ice embellishments that never melted. But even Faerie wouldn't accept that one man was another.

Normally it took a lot of like-minded people to disbelieve glamour, but reality and I had an interesting relationship. With my shields open, I could see the men as they truly were. I just hoped reality agreed.

"Him," I said again, and reached out and touched Falin's arm. As I did, I gave a push of power, willing reality to accept what I saw as true.

The queen's top lip quivered, as if she were fighting a scowl and close to losing the battle. Reality had clearly accepted my truth over hers.

"Very clever, Lexi," she said, the words clipped but even. The air tingled with her anger, but her face smoothed to controlled perfection. Then her lips curved into a cold smile. "Your prize then, I suppose. I promised you contact. I didn't promise you conversation. Knight, come here."

Falin didn't hesitate, striding to her without so much as a glance at me. She wrapped one pale hand around his neck, pulling him down so she could whisper in his ear. As she did so, she pressed her body against his. My jaw locked, a mix of anger and jealousy twisting in my guts. I turned away, not wanting to give her the satisfaction of seeing my reaction.

I glanced back in time to see Falin's eyes widen and then narrow, but whatever she told him, all he did was incline his head as she stepped back. She turned to me, that cruel smile still claiming her face.

"What ever will you do with my Knight for a day and a night? He's all yours, except his words, but you don't really need those." She tilted her head, but if she was aiming for innocence, she failed. "Be merry, dear Lexi." Then she glanced at her nephew. "Ryese, let's go."

While the Winter Queen might have control of her features, Ryese certainly didn't. His expression wavered between confusion and anger. I doubted the confusion had anything to do with me breaking the queen's glamour and a lot more with the very blatant thought of *How the hell did I lose?* When he stood there, staring, his expression darkening by the heartbeat, the queen called his name again. Ryese's head snapped up, and I wiggled my fingers in a mock wave good-bye. Ryese scowled, but turned on his heel, following his aunt.

"I have a bad feeling about this," I said once they disappeared into the crowd.

Falin didn't answer, of course. He just laced his fingers into my hair and leaned down. His lips claimed mine, and he kissed me as if in that one kiss, he could make up for a month of lost opportunities. My body responded, warming under his attention, returning his kiss.

Then my brain rebooted, screaming warnings at me. I flattened my palms against Falin's chest and pushed hard enough to get my point across.

He didn't release me, didn't let me step away from him, but he broke the kiss, giving me an inch or two as he stared at me like I could somehow save him. But I couldn't save him. Hell, I couldn't save myself. I'd won him from the Winter Queen, but for only a day and a night, and I had no idea what she'd told him. He'd spent the last month conducting raids on my home and being cold to the point of cruel because she'd commanded him to. I didn't know her new game, but I wasn't interested in playing.

Falin started to lean forward again, but I pressed my hands against his chest, feeling his heart beating fast and hard under my palms.

"Slow down, and let go of me."

He cocked his head to the side, but the look he gave me was more bemused than confused. I couldn't blame him. After all, we'd done a lot more than kiss several months ago. But now was different. The Winter Queen's plots aside, I needed distance now for the same reason I couldn't kiss Death yesterday.

Once I could have enjoyed the "right now." Could have lost myself in the moment and had no regrets. Could have relished the fact that for a day and a night, Falin was mine.

But Falin would walk away from me at dawn. That was inevitable. The only question was how many pieces of my broken heart he'd take with him. Between Falin's month long chill and Death's long absence, I didn't have many pieces left.

Chapter 27

Falin lowered me to my feet as the music stopped.

I was breathless, but smiling. I normally hated dancing. Not today. And not just because I had to figure out something to do with a man who couldn't speak. As the fiddler and the bagpipers started in on another lively tune, the music seeped into my blood, my bones, and combined with the heady merriment filling the toadstool-ringed circle. Falin led as we danced with a mix of fae. There was no choreography, just carefree movement, as if the spirit of the dance spurred us on. I laughed, losing myself in the excitement.

I wasn't the only one. The queen may have commanded Falin not to speak, but he could laugh, his face aglow. I didn't know if part of his compulsion was to stay by my side or if he simply wanted to be with me while he could—it wasn't like I could ask him— but he'd refused to leave despite my initial insistence. Now I was glad he'd stayed.

The setting sun coated the clearing in a golden-red glow, which added even more magic to the revelry. I finally understood why Rianna enjoyed Faerie. The day had been awkward, but fun. There were games, some familiar, some I hadn't known the rules but played anyway, Falin laughing as he tried to teach me through charades, which became a game within a game. There was music, and dancing, and everywhere the fae played, giggled, romped, and reveled in the gaiety. When the Harvest Queen and King had said to make merry, the fae had listened.

The song ended, and Falin led me out of the fray before the music started again. Walking arm and arm, I marveled at the beauty around me, at the way the last light of the day made the leaves look like they burned gold, red, and orange. At the fae, who even the most monstrous in appearance didn't look dangerous, not now, not here. Heads turned to the sky as the last ray of light faded and night descended on the revelry.

I waited for the night blindness to set in, but it didn't.

Hundreds of small lights in a dozen colors twinkled and then swirled and buzzed around the clearing like oversized fireflies. As a glowing blue figure passed in front of my nose, I realized they were pixies, the smallest I'd ever seen. Their light danced through the sky. But they weren't the only ones casting their own glow. All the Sleagh Maith in the clearing glimmered softly, pale light lifting from their skin as if each were a ray of moonlight. The court of light's members' glow was warmer, almost golden.

"It's so beautiful," I whispered.

Falin's hand tightened gently, as if in agreement, but he wasn't looking out across the clearing. He was staring at me.

I looked away. Once I'd realized I wasn't going to shake him this morning, and that I didn't really want to wander around the revelry alone, I'd told him we'd spend the time as friends—no more kissing and sure as hell nothing the Winter Queen had hinted at. He'd agreed with a disappointed nod. Despite that agreement, this day was the closest thing to a date I'd had in my adult life.

And it was nice.

Something constricted in my chest, warning me of the pain to come at dawn. I fought to suppress it—I still had a night left. Falin may have been having the same thoughts, because as the night progressed I caught traces of sorrow in his face when he thought I wasn't looking.

The Harvest moon rose, full, orange, and almost close enough to touch. Falin and I walked, going nowhere in particular. Now that night had fallen, more and more of the fae were pairing off, some disappearing into the outskirts of the forest, some not bothering with that much discretion. I found myself blushing more than once as my eyes tripped over bodies tangled in intimate positions.

Then I spotted a very familiar redhead lip-locked with a certain green-skinned fae. I stopped. "It's never a good thing when your housemates hook up, is it?"

Falin glanced to where Holly and Caleb were lost in their own little world and shrugged.

"I guess I should have seen this coming." Probably months ago. And they'd only gotten closer since Holly's first trip to Faerie. "But they better not start walking around the house naked or doing it on the dining room table," I muttered, making Falin laugh.

We moved on.

As we passed one of the large, endlessly overflowing banquet tables, Falin picked up a crystal flute and drained half of the amber liquid. Then he handed it to me.

I didn't think about it. Falin handed me the flute, and I was thirsty, so I drank. It wasn't until I'd taken a large gulp of the drink, which tasted of honey with a bite of alcohol, that I realized what I'd done.

I drank Faerie wine.

Falin snatched the flute from my hand, tossing it to the ground. Then he dragged me away from the table and into the tree line. I stumbled after him, my fingers pressed to my lips.

No. How could I be so stupid? Faerie wine?

No, no, no.

Once past the first few trees, Falin ground to a halt and flipped around. He grabbed my shoulders and backed me up against a tree. The bark scratched against my bare shoulders, but I hardly noticed. Something warm spread inside my chest. Something changing me. I could feel it.

"Alex. Alex, look at me."

I didn't. I was too focused on what I felt, or maybe imagined I felt, happening inside me. The fact he'd spoken didn't even register. My focus narrowed to the fact I'd drunk Faerie wine. Every human knew never to consume anything in Faerie. *And I drank Faerie wine.*

Falin kissed me, his hand cupping my face. I was too stunned to react.

He pulled back. Then he pressed his palms against the tree on either side of my head and leaned his forehead against the rough bark, his cheek pressed against mine.

"Alexis." My name, whispered so soft it barely made it past the buzz of shock in my ears.

I'd never heard my name said with so much heartbreak tangled in the simple syllables. I blinked.

"Alexis, I love you."

Now *that* got a reaction from me, and I startled at the barely whispered words. I'm not sure if I made a sound or if he felt me jerk, but he pushed away from the tree so he could meet my eyes.

"You can't trust me," he said, his hands falling from the tree to my shoulders.

I blinked at him, my brain muffled in shock so that all I said was, "You can talk now?"

Falin pressed his lips into a tight line. "*She* froze my voice only until I completed her task. Ryese told her that you don't eat at the Bloom. She wanted to see what would happen if you ate our food."

Too many shocks had struck me in the last few minutes, so this newest one took me a moment to get my still reeling mind to wrap around.

"Then she . . . You . . . ?" I hadn't had time to consider it, but I'd assumed he'd handed me the flute as thoughtlessly as I had drunk from it. But if the Winter Queen had wanted me to eat Faerie food. If she'd told him to make sure I did . . . "You did that on purpose."

He squeezed his eyes closed. When he opened them again, they were blue ice. Cold. Emotionless. His hands slid from my shoulders to my upper arms, and he gripped me tight. The bullet wound on my arm screamed in agony, making me wince.

"You can't trust me. Do you understand?"

"You're hurting me." My voice sounded a hell of a lot calmer than I felt. I'd have been proud of that fact, except it was from the shock, not any great inner strength on my part.

"Good," he said, but he frowned and his grip loosened. "As long as I belong to her, you can never trust me. I have to do whatever she commands. So don't call me, don't look for me, and if you see me, run away. Do you understand?"

I didn't say anything, and he squeezed my arms again, hard. It was meant to hurt. Even if I hadn't had the wound, it would have hurt. I yelped, I couldn't help it, and Falin shook me.

"Do you understand?"

"Yes," I said between pain-locked teeth.

"Then go." He released me. When I didn't move, his face contorted. "Go. Now."

Still I hesitated, and his blades appeared in his hands.

That got me moving. I darted around him, breaking into a run.

I glanced back only once, when I reached the tree line.

Falin had dropped to his knees in front of the tree, his head hanging low, and his daggers driven into the ground on either side of him. I almost stopped. Almost went back to him. But I didn't.

After all, I had no idea what other commands he'd received from the Queen Ice Bitch.

Chapter 28

❖

Returning to reality after a day in Faerie was like being pulled out of a dream by a splash of cold water. And then being smothered by the wet pillow.

The music cut off abruptly. The air, which in my previous breath held the earthy smell of the forest and heady laughter, was now too thin, too sharp. It smelled of car exhaust and metal, and it grated against my skin like steel wool. Grave essence, which hadn't existed in Faerie, crashed against my shields, reminding me that the world around me was dying. Darkness crawled over my vision and for a moment I thought I was blind, but no, it was night, dark, and my eyes were back to their normal, damaged state.

Burning hot tears welled in my eyes. Some were of self-pity. Some were because in returning to reality, to what should have been home, I felt like I'd lost a part of myself. But most were from anger at Falin's betrayal. I rubbed my arms where he'd squeezed me, intentionally causing pain, and a shiver ran through me as I remembered the glint of his blades in the moonlight.

A tear escaped and seared a line down my cheek. I blinked back the rest—they wouldn't help anything. Why waste energy on what I couldn't change?

But that betrayal hurt. Even though I knew it wasn't his

fault. That he was bound to the commands of his queen. It still made an agonizing ache twist under my sternum.

He's right. I can never trust him. Not while he was hers.

I lifted a hand to whisk away the single tear that had escaped and stopped, staring. My fingers shimmered in the darkness. My hands too, as well as my arms and what I could see of my shoulders and chest. I was glowing, pale light seeping from my skin like moonlight caught just below the surface.

Like a Sleagh Maith.

This can't be happening. But it was. Even my hair glowed, casting a halo of gold light. Damn the Winter Queen. She'd wanted to see what would happen if I ate Faerie food? Well, it apparently turned me into a glowworm.

And I had no idea how to stop.

How the hell was I supposed to pass for human if I could double as a reading lamp? *Maybe it isn't as noticeable as I think?* After all, just because I could see something, didn't mean other people saw it as well. Maybe I glowed on some other plane.

Only I wasn't actively touching any plane besides mortal reality.

I looked around. In the predawn the streets were quiet, empty. The early-morning hours, long after the bars had made last call and before business owners prepared for the day ahead, were one of the few times things were quiet in the Quarter. Which I was thankful for — except that there were no taxis and the buses weren't running yet for the day. I briefly considered calling Tamara, but dismissed the idea. One, I was glowing and I wasn't ready for the big "F" conversation. And two, if she was already awake she was getting ready for work, and if she wasn't, I didn't want to wake her. I'd been asking for far too many favors recently.

I glanced behind me at the door, waiting to see if Caleb and Holly were right behind me. I'd left hours before the end of the revelry, but the slowly brightening sky proved I'd lost the full twenty-four hours just as Rianna had warned.

Holly and Caleb would lose the same, but apparently not the exact same because the door remained shut.

What was I supposed to do now? I didn't have my purse as I'd known I wouldn't need it in Faerie. I only had my phone and my keys. I paused. My key ring did include the keys to the Tongues for the Dead office, and while it wasn't the most casual walk away, the Quarter had been designed for foot traffic. It was also considerably closer than Caleb's house and would get me off the street while I figured out what to do. Turning on my heel, I headed in the direction of the office.

I'd made it a block when a car turned the corner in front of me. The red glow of the brake lights flashing was the first indication something was wrong. I glanced up, hoping for a taxi. After all, who else would be stopping but a taxi that assumed I was a good chance at a fare?

But no, not a taxi. A silver coupe slowed to a crawl as it approached. I couldn't see how many people were inside, but I felt the stares. Even seventy years after the Magical Awakening, spotting an unglamoured fae on the street wasn't common—I'd once thought that was because they didn't like being gawked at, and in part that was true, but recently I'd learned that most used tightly woven glamours to insulate themselves from the iron in the mortal realm. I wasn't nine feet tall, blue skinned, winged, horned, or any number of the much more *other* aspects many of the fae displayed, but apparently glowing was enough.

I hunched forward, staring at my feet and letting my shimmering curls fall in front of my face like a shield. The car window opened, and something flew out, crashing into the facade of the building in front of me. The Styrofoam cup exploded on impact, showering me in soda and ice.

"Get out of our town, you faerie freak," a teenage voice yelled from the dark recess of the car. Then the vehicle sped off in a peel of tires and laughter.

I cursed at the car's taillights, and then stood in the center of the sidewalk, sticky soda dripping from my arms. *Okay, so the glowing is noticeable.*

I had to get off the street. I'd never make it to Tongues for the Dead before the Quarter began to fill with people, and I couldn't let more people see me glowing. If I were recognized . . . *Say good-bye to passing as human.*

I ducked into an alley. I'd lose my OMIH license if my fae heritage was discovered. I had to figure out how to stop glowing before more people saw me. *But how the hell am I going to do that?* Caleb hadn't left the revelry, and I definitely couldn't go to Falin—not that he was back from the revelry either. Hell, every fae I knew was in Faerie.

Well, not *every* fae. I knew of one person I definitely hadn't seen at the revelry. And not only could he help me; he damn near owed me the help.

I called my father.

Chapter 29

⊷═══⊷ ⊶═══⊶

A dark Porsche pulled to a stop and the window rolled down, showing my father's profile. Well, actually, showing his fae-mien's profile, but one couldn't expect the governor and prominent member of the Humans First Party to be seen in the Quarter picking up a glowing woman. I climbed to my feet slowly, using the crates I'd been hiding behind as leverage to pull myself up.

"This is becoming a habit, Alexis," my father said, and I cringed at his use of my name.

I'd become accustomed to hearing it on Falin's lips. Hearing it said in such a disapproving tone cut. *Of course, I may never hear Falin say my name again.*

My father glanced at me. When he wore his human glamour he was a respectably middle-aged man with dark brown hair and eyes. It always made me wonder where my sister and I got our coloring. Without his glamour it was obvious, his pale hair shimmered the same color blond as mine. I also had his green eyes. I looked away. I didn't like seeing the similarities.

"Alexis, you could have called a cab."

"Stop calling me that."

He frowned, a flicker of confusion crossing his brow. It

was the first real emotion he'd shown since I'd climbed into his car. "It is your name."

"Yeah, well, just don't use it, okay?"

"Shall I call you daughter dearest?"

I shot him my best death glare, which didn't faze him in the least.

"My, my, aren't we in a mood."

"Did you miss the fact I'm *glowing*?"

"Now you're just being dramatic." He shrugged as if glowing were no big deal. Of course, as he was unglamoured he also shimmered. "You're Sleagh Maith. This is our natural state. Though I must say, I'm quite surprised the glamour is failing so quickly. What have you been doing with yourself?"

Dancing in Faerie rings, playing their games, oh yeah, and eating their food. I cut off my sarcastic inner monologue as the implications of what he'd said sank in.

"Wait, what glamour?"

He didn't answer as he switched gears and headed over the bridge that separated what most people considered the "witchy" side of town from the rest of Nekros.

"What glamour," I asked again, "and how do I get it back?"

His fae face was as good at giving completely disinterested glances as his human one.

I ground my teeth but neither of us spoke for a long time, until I realized he was headed toward his mansion. The last time I'd called for help he'd dumped me in the mercy of an overly opinionated brownie at a ramshackle house in an old neighborhood.

"Going to risk being seen with me, huh?" I asked, and noticed that he once again wore his respectable gentleman glamour. If I had to guess, I'd also assume that the Porsche had changed colors and tags. My father's skill at glamour was second only to his ability to manipulate those around him.

"You called me for a reason, Alexis."

"Because I need not to be glowing?" I said as he pulled the car into the long drive.

When he stopped in front of the mansion he called a house, he turned, watching me expectantly. I knew what he wanted me to say, but the voice in the back of my head kept screaming that no, I wasn't a fae, I couldn't possibly . . .

I sighed. "I need to learn glamour."

He nodded as if satisfied. Then, leaving the keys in the car, he climbed out and headed for the front door. He didn't offer me a hand or wait, but he also didn't rush. I extracted myself from the car much slower, reluctant to enter the oversized house.

The gate guard had called ahead and a man rushed from the house, sprinting for the idling car. Another man, presumably the butler who'd replaced Rodger, opened the front door. My father nodded a greeting to the man before he led me into the enormous receiving room. Neither the disused chauffeur nor the butler stared as I passed, and while expensive help was trained not to pay too much attention, I was guessing if I glowed they wouldn't have been able to help themselves. Which meant my father must have extended his glamour to me when he changed the car and himself.

Good to know. As that immediate problem was solved, at least temporarily, one other rather pressing issue worried along the edge of my mind.

"Do you have any food?" I asked, and my father paused at the base of the marble staircase he'd been about to mount.

"Yes, Alexis, I have food." The look he gave me could only be described as calculated curiosity. "I take it you would like to break your fast?"

He had no idea. I'd had one potentially life changing sip of wine, and I needed to know if . . . if I could still consume human food. My father's studying gaze appeared to see straight through my skin, and I rescinded my earlier thought. Maybe he *did* know. I shifted uncomfortably, but when I nodded that I did indeed want breakfast, he turned to the butler who, in good invisible but always at hand mode, stepped forward.

"Would the young lady like to take her breakfast in the sunroom?" he asked, addressing my father, not me.

"That's fine, but something light and quick."

And that's my father. No consultation with me. I didn't care, as long as it was real food.

This house had never been my home. I spent parts of my summers here as a child, but that didn't create any warm fuzzy feelings in me, and my more recent memories of the place were far from happy. Which was a major understatement. Terrifying would be far more accurate. But I still remembered where the sunroom was. I didn't need a guide or a chaperone. I got one anyway, my father leading me to a beautifully decorated sitting room with a large bay window facing east so the morning sun filtered in, casting the room in a warm hue.

Casey, my sister, sat at a small dinette, a mostly untouched muffin sitting beside a half-filled glass of orange juice. A paper lay on the table in front of her, claiming more of her attention than the food.

"Morning, Daddy, did you see this article on—" She looked up and stopped abruptly, pushing to her feet. "Alexis, I didn't expect to see you here."

I bet she hadn't. It had been months since I'd seen my sister. She'd asked to see me when she'd been in the hospital recovering from the fallout of being the intended sacrifice in a megalomaniac's ritual. I'd gone to see her once or twice at the private—and very discreet—hospital my father had placed her in, but on my last visit she'd told me she wanted to forget what had happened. Her chilly demeanor made it clear that she considered *me* a reminder. It wasn't like we'd ever been close, so I'd made a polite good-bye and left. I hadn't seen her since.

"Hello, Casey. You look good," I told her, though I could feel the concealment charms she wore and I knew at least forty percent of her body, particularly her torso, was covered in scars. The glyphs that had been carved into her skin had a power of their own, so the doctors had to excise parts of them to make sure the glyphs remained inert.

Casey was everything I wasn't. Where I had the height and sharper lines of the Sleagh Maith, she was a good head shorter with abundant curves that she usually dressed to accent. Not today. Her clothes were loose fitting and covered everything but her hands and her face. The concealment charms could hide the physical scars, but I wondered if she'd ever again be comfortable in her own skin.

She blinked at me, not acknowledging my words. Then she turned away, as if she couldn't bear to look at me.

"Is there something you wanted to tell me, dear?" my father asked, his voice nothing if not the epitome of patience.

He never used that tone with me. I tried not to hold it against Casey.

"It can wait," she said, and then, leaving her barely touched food, she swept out of the room.

I listened to the retreating click of her heels. "She hates me."

"Does it matter?" His voice was once again empty, dispassionate.

I shook my head at him. "Sometimes I wonder how I ever believed you were human."

"An unkind thing to say."

Yeah, to the other fae I know.

I was saved any further awkward conversation by the older gentleman entering the room with a large blueberry muffin and a tray with coffee. The man glanced at Casey's hastily abandoned food. "Should I take the remainder of Miss Casey's food to her suite?"

At my father's nod, the man gathered the food and silently excused himself from the room.

I sank into the seat opposite from where Casey had been and poured my coffee into the too dainty cup. Then I hesitated. *What if I can't eat mortal food anymore?* I broke a section of the sugar-encrusted muffin top free, but I didn't eat it. I was starving, but as soon as I tried it, that was it. If I'd become addicted to Faerie food, there would no longer be the hope I wasn't.

"For goodness sake, Alexis, just eat the food. It doesn't matter what you did at the revelry. You blooded true as Sleagh Maith. You are fae."

I blinked at him, the break of muffin nearly falling from my fingers. He shook his head.

"Do you think I don't know what the date is? Now eat. I don't have all morning to waste on you."

Nice to know I'm important. I popped the piece of muffin in my mouth. Not only did it not turn to ash, but it was absolutely delicious, the relief making it one of the best things I'd ever tasted. I polished off the rest of my breakfast quickly, and then followed my father out of the sunroom and upstairs.

I expected him to lead me to his office or a sitting room. Hell, maybe even my old suite. Instead he stopped in front of the last door I expected—or wanted to walk through. He pulled out a ring of keys, and unlocked the deadbolt securing the suite that until three months ago had belonged to my sister. That was before a dark ritual had been performed in her bedroom and I'd unintentionally torn reality apart.

"Um, why are we going in there?" I asked, hearing the slightly too high pitch in my voice. Casey and I both had nearly died in that room. I still had nightmares about bodies decaying under my touch as a swollen red moon hung overhead.

"Because what you need to learn will be easier taught inside." His eyes cut sideways, as if ensuring the hall was empty. Then he traced a glyph into the door, just above the lock. The unfamiliar glyph glowed green for a moment, but though I'd recently become more sensitive to fae magic, I felt nothing from the glowing symbol, even when it faded and the door popped open.

I held my breath as I followed my father inside. The sitting room wasn't bad. Nothing had happened there—it was the bedroom where everything had gone down. And that was exactly where he led me. My steps grew heavier the closer we walked to the bedroom door, so by the time I reached the threshold, I could no longer lift my feet, and I stood frozen outside the door.

Casey's furniture had been removed from the room, but the division where Coleman's circle had been drawn was obvious. On the outside of that line, the room was a normal room with plush carpeting and tasteful wallpaper. Inside, now that was a different story. Inside that circle reality looked like a child's finger painting—if the child were insane. The Aetheric broke into reality in large, color-filled blotches. In other places, the decaying stain of the land of the dead leaked into our world. Emotional imprints, old ones ranging the gambit of emotions from Casey's many years in the suite, to the raw pain and horror from that night, stained the room.

"Don't dawdle."

Easy for him to say.

But if following him into the backdrop of half my nightmares was what it took to stop glowing, I could do it. After all, I'd survived what happened here. And I'd faced real nightmares—the creatures, not just the dreams. I could face an empty room.

I stepped over the edge of the circle, ready to be assaulted by my own memories. Instead a gentle warmth slid over my skin. The air seemed thicker, more real. Somewhere in the distance I heard laughter, music. It felt like . . . Faerie?

I looked up, sure enough a sky filled with early-morning sunlight replaced what from outside the circle had been a ceiling. And not only that, but the shadows in the room disappeared. I turned a small circle, trying to see everything at once.

"It feels like home, doesn't it?" my father said.

I froze. He was watching me, a bemused expression on his face—his fae face. He'd dropped his glamour again.

"I don't understand. Faerie and mortal reality don't overlap."

"Coleman's spell created a tenuous, unstable pocket of Faerie. I believe your magic cemented it in reality." He walked a weaving path across the room to a small stone bench surrounded by containers of flowers I'd never seen the likes of before and could only guess were native to Faerie.

"You come here a lot, don't you?"

He ignored the question, instead motioning to the spot beside him. "I don't have a lot of free time, so let's not dally, but do mind the dead zones. The clothes will rot off your body if you touch them."

I was aware of that fact, but that he knew confirmed he visited this chaotic pocket more than occasionally. I knew he was in deep hiding, and that he hadn't attended the revelry, so the fact he came here and described it as *home* somehow made him seem more like a person with actual emotions and stuff.

"Why here?" I asked as I wove my way to the bench. The heady embrace of Faerie held back the threatening panic attack, but I could almost feel the tightening of a remembered soul chain around my throat, the sting of a knife biting into my torso.

"Because Faerie will accept glamour more readily than mortal reality. Think of this space as your training wheels."

Right.

My father then spent the next twenty minutes explaining the basic principles of glamour to me followed by an hour of trying to teach me how to feel Faerie's magic. I was sensitive to Aetheric magic, and I was growing sensitive to fae magic as well, but reaching out and actually touching that very foreign energy? That was something different altogether.

Unlike Aetheric magic, which took ritual to reach and then had to be used or stored, Faerie magic was readily available but it was like water flowing through a grate. It couldn't be stored. It was drawn as needed and passed through the user, bending to their will, and left nothing behind. In the mortal realm, iron blocked the magic and it was thinnest at dawn and sunset. Too much disbelief in a concentrated area could not only break glamour—it could thin Faerie's influence.

The sun was high in the sky by the time I managed to pull the thinnest sliver of Faerie magic. It felt as soft as silk but had a strange weight as it entered my body, which wasn't exactly unpleasant, just odd.

"Good, now imagine your skin a normal, human tone," my father said.

My teeth were gritted from the hours spent attempting to reach the magic, so the fact his instructions made me laugh was more from tension than amusement. "Trust me, imagining myself not glowing isn't hard. I shouldn't *be* glowing in the first place."

Except as I tried to direct that thin sliver of hard-won magic, it floated away from me without any noticeable change.

My father shook his head. "No, that's disbelief, not belief. You can't disbelieve the truth away. You can cover the truth, you can create something new, but either way you have to believe what you are creating."

"So what you're saying is that all faeries are delusional. Great. No wonder it's the crazy ones that are in charge."

He frowned at me, and then letting his hands fall to his thighs, stood. "I think that's enough for today."

"What? But I'm still glowing."

"Did you expect to learn glamour in a few hours?"

I opened my mouth to reply, but stopped. The truth was, I'd hoped he'd tell me what the hell was going on and make me stop glowing. "Can't you just . . .," I waved my shimmering fingers.

"If I glamoured you, it would only last until sunset. But why bother, or take the risk someone could trace my glamour back to me? I can't hide you from the courts anymore—you've spoiled that completely."

Why bother? *Why bother?* I glared at him. "Because I'm running a business under an OMIH certification. The 'H' in that stands for human, and humans don't glow."

His expression of detached disinterest persisted. Not that I expected anything more from him. Unless he was talking to lobbyists or potential voters, it was his most common expression. That thought made me pause, and I could feel just how devious the slow smile that crawled over my face must look.

Judging by the sudden spark of interest in my father's eyes, I wasn't wrong. When I just sat there, that smile still claiming my face, he broke the silence first.

"Yes?"

"You should bother," I said, the words as slow and meticulous as my smile, "because if you don't make me stop glowing, I'm going to call Lusa Duncan at *Witch Watch* and give her an exclusive about being your daughter." I cocked my head to the side, gazing up at him. "I heard you're planning to run as the presidential candidate for the Humans First Party. Just imagine the scandal when the story goes national, which I imagine would be, oh, dinner time-ish."

He stared at me. I stared back. Making threats against the person I needed help from could backfire, but whatever his "long game" plans, as he called it, his political career somehow played into the scheme. I gambled it was one of the few things he cared about.

I wasn't sure what response I expected from him, but it certainly wasn't for him to smile. And not the false friendly controlled smile that the politician wore, but a smile that spoke of mischief and made his eyes light with amusement.

"An admirable attempt, Alexis. Flawed and doomed to fail, but quick and targeted." He almost sounded proud. I was never going to understand the man. He pursed his lips, staring at me, and then said, "Stay here a moment."

He left me sitting in the chaotic mess. I'd been in the room so long, the panic had been forced to either ebb or send me into a breakdown. Since I'd been busy trying to draw magic I'd never used before, I'd been too focused to panic, but now that I was alone, I couldn't help noticing my location again.

Think about something else, Alex.

I stood, no longer able to sit still. It wasn't until I'd paced a full circle around the bench, my arms wrapped tight around myself, that I realized I was touching the edge of the bullet wound in my arm. It didn't hurt. In fact, I realized that aside from when Falin had gripped me with the intention of causing pain, I'd barely noticed it since before the revelry. I peeled the gauze away and marveled at the pink and white edges of the wound. It looked weeks old, not a day. Even the OMIH-approved healing spell in the dressing couldn't cause it to heal that fast.

"You'll heal faster inside Faerie," my father said from the doorway, and I jumped. I hadn't heard him enter. I clumsily pressed the gauze back in place as he wove his way through the maze of Aetheric and dead-zone holes. "You probably heal faster than human normal in the mortal realm, but not by much. Faerie's magic isn't strong enough to combat the iron and the human belief in how long it takes to heal."

"So if Faerie is so great, why are you here?" I wasn't expecting an answer, so I wasn't surprised when I didn't receive so much as an eye twitch from him.

"Here." He held out a hand. In his palm was a necklace that glittered like silver but the small rectangular charm was inscribed with fae glyphs so I guessed it was the same metal as my dagger.

It was also very familiar. I reached out and touched the edge of the charm. It was warm. Not like it had absorbed my father's heat but like it pulsed with its own energy.

"That was Mother's, wasn't it?"

My father frowned. "She wore it for a while."

A dodgy response.

He touched something on the charm, and what had seemed a solid piece opened to reveal a small compartment. "It needs your blood and hair."

I cringed. "And what does it do exactly?" I hated magic that involved blood. Yes, it personalized charms and made them stronger, but the pain and ick factor aside, that same ability to create a powerful link with a good charm made blood a dangerous connection if used for less virtuous spells.

"It will help conceal what you are. Which includes dampening your glow so you appear human."

I regarded the charm. "Mother needed it?"

"In the end, it turned out not to be enough." No sorrow or loss touched his voice. "Until you can use glamour properly, it should be sufficient. It won't protect you from iron though. Now that you are fully awakened and the last layer of the spell has been stripped away, you'll be more susceptible."

More? Being around it already made me uncomfortable to the point of feeling ill. But more important, what spell? He'd alluded to the fact I'd been glamoured before, and now layers of a spell?

When I asked he gave me one of his meaningless smiles but no answer. *Great.* I reached for the charm, but he pulled it out of reach, and looked at me expectantly. I sighed. He hadn't offered me anything to prick my finger, so I leaned down, pulling my dagger from my boot. To my surprise, he looked pleased when he saw it.

"Has it bonded to you yet?"

I froze, willing my expression blank. The dagger had been a gift from Rianna when I'd graduated from academy. I'd never shown it to my father and he surely hadn't seen enough of it to identify it. So what did he know about it. *And how?*

He watched me, that neutral look on his face as if he didn't care if I answered him or not. I made a mental note to question Rianna about where the daggers had come from. I knew that mine was part of a matching set that she'd been gifted, but I was now extremely curious by *whom*.

Without answering my father's question, I focused on cutting the tip of one curl and then pricking my finger without allowing the dagger to bite too deep. For once, the dagger behaved. I placed the small lock of hair in the charm and squeezed out a single drop of blood. He held up a hand before my blood could drip into the small compartment.

"That is for something else," he said, snapping the charm closed. He flipped it over. The faint outline of glyph was carved into the back. "Trace this with your blood."

I hesitated, staring at the unfamiliar glyph. This wasn't just personalizing a charm. This was blood magic.

"What does it mean?"

The name of the glyph rolled off his tongue like a musical note, which didn't tell me anything about what it was or did. When I didn't make any move to do as told, he sighed.

"A rough translation would be 'chameleon.' Now you've stopped bleeding so you'll need to open the wound again."

I glanced at my finger. He was right: the drop of blood had dried, turning flaky. *Damn.* I didn't trust the dagger to behave as well a second time. Of course, I wasn't sold on the charm yet either. Blood magic combined with glyphs I didn't understand? A dangerous combination.

"What's the worst possible outcome from the glyph and charm?"

He thought for a moment. "The charm isn't a controlled glamour. You aren't choosing how you appear to people—they are seeing what they expect. As long as they assume you are human, you will appear as such. If they believe you are not human . . ." He shrugged.

"Will I be able to tell what they see?"

"Only by their reaction."

Great. Perception charms were something I understood, even if this one was a little different from a witch's charm. I drew the dagger again. I still wasn't thrilled with the idea, but as I couldn't use glamour, this was the best option. After pricking my finger, I reached for the charm.

"Do I need to channel Faerie's magic to activate the glyph or will Aetheric energy work?" I hoped the latter would be sufficient—I might have to bleed myself several more times before I managed to draw on Faerie's magic again.

"Neither. You are Sleagh Maith. The magic of Faerie runs through your veins. Your blood will be enough to activate the glyph."

Right. My finger felt large and clumsy as I traced the intricate glyph, smearing blood more than drawing anything recognizable, but as I added the last line, Faerie's magic moved through me, pouring into the charm. The metal warmed, not exactly an uncomfortable heat, but noticeable. I slid the necklace over my head and the light in my skin faded. I let out a sigh of relief before tucking the charm under my shirt.

I looked back up at my father. "Shouldn't you warn Casey about all this? Because let me tell you, being blindsided by 'awakening' to a fae nature is hell. She's been through enough already. A responsible parent would warn their child about something like this." Okay, so maybe the last comment was as much about me as about my sister.

"Casey?" He gave me a bemused look. "She is none of mine. She and Bradley are simply backups of your mother's genetic line."

I blinked. "Hold on. *What?*"

His glamour flowed over him, turning him back into the respectable middle-aged man. "I suppose you need a ride somewhere?"

I stared at his retreating back. Sometimes my father scared the hell out of me.

Chapter 30

My father dropped me off at the Tongues for the Dead office. The drive was tense, for me at least. He'd refused to answer any more questions. In fact, all he'd said during the drive was that I should call him later in the week to schedule another lesson. As much as I needed to learn glamour, I doubted I'd take him up on the offer. Caleb could help me from this point out. I'd lose the opportunity to work in a private pocket of Faerie, but I hated feeling like a pawn and the more I talked with my father, the scarier his living chessboard became.

After he drove away, I gave a weary glance at my office. It was Saturday, and we weren't open, but I needed to update my clients and I wasn't up for long phone calls and extended explanations. E-mail sounded a lot easier, but both Nina Kingly and Kelly Kirkwood's contact information was at the office. So, first stop office, and then I was going home, burying my head under my pillow, and starting the day over. Or was it that I had to start yesterday over? I'd lost most of the night, so my internal clock was off, but the last few hours would have exhausted me even if I'd had a good night's sleep.

I dug out my keys but before I could lift them, the lock clicked open. I froze. *Who . . . ?*

Roy's head popped through the closed door. "About time you got here. Where the hell have you been? We have a client."

I blinked at him. *A client?* Maybe I'd fallen asleep and this was a dream because ghosts didn't bring in clients.

"Hurry up, Alex," Roy said, stepping farther through the door. "He's been waiting for hours now and he's jumpy."

Could this day get any weirder? Roy had already unlocked the door for me, so I pushed it open and stepped into the sunlit room beyond. Roy had the client waiting in the dark? And how would a customer get in—the door had been locked. Of course, Roy had proven he was more than capable of overcoming that particular hurdle.

I turned on the lights and headed for my office—which I could already tell was also dark. *Where . . . ?*

"My office," Roy said, striding toward his door.

"You put a client in the broom closet?"

That earned a frown from the ghost, but he ignored me as he floated through his "office" door. I, on the other hand, had to actually open the door.

I don't know what I was expecting, but a ghost huddling in the back corner of the closet wasn't on the list. The ghost, who was faded to the point that even in my eyes all his color had washed away, cringed as he caught sight of Roy. He backed farther into the corner until his shoulders passed into the unpainted sheetrock of the walls.

"It's okay," Roy said, but he kept his distance. I don't know if it was because he was trying to put the other ghost at ease or because he didn't want to take the chance of getting too close. Once he'd crossed the threshold, he'd moved no farther into the small room. "This is Alex, the friend I told you about."

"But she's alive." The ghost's voice was like a whisper carried on the wind. I was surprised he'd managed to cling to his identity. Most ghosts as far gone as him were merely haunts.

"Yes, I'm alive," I said, and turned to Roy. "I thought you said ghosts didn't do the social thing? What's going on?"

Roy shrugged. "Special circumstance. I found him trying to coax his body out of a graveyard."

Why was it the more he explained the more lost I became? "I think you better start at the beginning."

Roy looked over at the other ghost. "Steven?"

"My body, it's stuck in Sleepy Knoll Cemetery—not that it's listening to me anyway." The ghost wasn't whispering, but he might as well have been. It was hard to listen to.

"Give me your hand," I told the ghost.

Steven backed farther into the wall. "Why?"

"So your voice doesn't sound like wind rustling through dry reeds," I said, taking a step forward and lifting my palm toward him.

The ghost stared at my outstretched hand. "But, you're alive."

"Yeah, we covered that part already. Trust me, okay?"

Steven reached out a tentative hand so transparent that for a moment, I was afraid he was so far gone we may not be solid to each other. But as his trembling fingers touched the tips of mine, I could feel the resistance, the weight, of the other being.

His nearly clear eyes flew wide, staring at where the tips of our fingers touched. I stepped forward and wrapped my hand around his. Those eyes, wide with both fear and amazement, stared and I felt him preparing to jerk his hand away, but after the initial flicker of panic that made his entire body jolt, he went still.

Opening my shields a crack, I channeled the slightest bit of power through my body and into the ghost. Chill bumps lifted on my skin, the lightest breeze crossing over from the land of the dead. The ghost's shape filled in, becoming more solid. I'd raised a lot of shades over the last few days, plus the crash course in glamour, so I didn't give him much energy, not even enough to bring about more than a hint of color, but the trickle I channeled into him carried him closer to the land of the living.

"Wow," he whispered, his voice stronger, clearer. Which was what I wanted. I closed my shields and dropped his hand.

"I think I'm jealous." Roy made the comment light, like a joke, but he shoved his hands into his pockets with more force than normal and his shoulder slouched so far forward that he looked like he had a humped back.

Nothing sexual existed between Roy and me, which meant if he was jealous it was all about power. "You start treating me like a food source and I'm cutting you off," I warned him and the ghost gave me a big-eyed "who me?" look before shoving his glasses farther up his nose and looking away. I shook my head with a sigh—sometimes I really didn't know about that ghost.

I turned back to Steven.

"You said something about your body being stuck in a cemetery—that's where your body is supposed to be. You're lucky you were smart enough not to follow it or you'd be stuck there too."

"No, you don't get it, my body, it's *walking* around the cemetery. Well, really, more like scuttling. And what it's doing . . ." He shuddered. "It ate a woman. I mean, she was already dead, but my body *ate* her."

I went still, my pulse crashing in my ears. "Your body is a ghoul? When were you attacked and where?"

The ghost frowned, and Roy stepped closer, elbowing me lightly. "This is the really good part. Tell her, Steven."

"I, I don't remember being attacked. I remember fixing myself a bowl of bran cereal—my wife has been on a real health kick lately—and the next thing I knew it was night and I was squished under a park bench and something dark and frightening was sliding into my body, pushing me out."

That doesn't sound like a collector.

"Then this guy showed up and told me it was time to go, but my body was all wrong and it was shambling away. So I fought with the guy, because I couldn't just let my body walk away like that. And the man let me go, telling me he'd be there when I was ready."

Now *that* sounded like a collector. In fact, it sounded like Death—he'd told me the exact same thing once, only it hadn't been my soul in question. Choice. It was the hardest damn lesson I ever learned, and I was only five.

Steven continued his story without notice of my momentary distraction. "I followed my body, trying to figure out how to make it stop. I mean, if I was dead, I should be properly dead, right? It headed straight for the closest cemetery, and I almost followed it inside, but the gate felt wrong, so I waited. That's when I noticed the moon. I'm a bit of a star freak, and I'd been using my telescope the night before— only it wasn't the night before. Somehow between breakfast and waking up under the park bench, I lost three whole days."

Oh crap. That sounded awfully familiar. The rider's victims always lost three days, at least before he killed them. But they weren't ghouls—they were just corpses.

"Steven, I need you to think hard. When you were following your body, did it look hurt? I mean, claw marks, or signs that you might have killed yourself and not remember?"

The ghost shook his head. "No. I mean, I didn't look like myself. I was thin, my skin drawn back tight, and I had scary-ass teeth and talons, but I didn't look hurt."

The blood drained from my face and a shiver shook me. I'd never seen a ghoul, never thought about what they looked like. Briar had mentioned something about a transition, but I hadn't considered the physical changes. Like the sharp teeth that allowed them to rip through flesh—teeth like I'd seen in Kirkwood's burnt body. And then there was the rapid burning of all fat and desiccation of the body, which every one of the rider's victims displayed to some extent or another.

The rider wasn't committing suicide just to jump to a new host—he was killing his host before his presence turned the body into a ghoul.

Chapter 31

❦

"L arid," I said again to the bored-looking secretary at the front desk of the local branch of the OMIH. "L-A-R—oh for goodness sake, I'm sure he's the only possessed guy that came in here two days ago. I'm not trying to see Larid, I just need to talk to the official in charge of his case, or study, or whatever you guys call it."

"And you are again?"

I sighed and passed her my identification, for the second time. "Alex Craft. I'm the person the thing inside Larid was trying to kill."

She touched a charm on her desk and a privacy bubble enveloped her as she picked up her phone and made a call. One day I was going to have to learn to read lips. The conversation was a short one, which hopefully meant I got a pass, not a quick "no."

"Well, Ms. Craft," she said after she deactivated the privacy charm. "You'll be relieved to know he won't be a problem to you anymore."

A cold jolt of warning shot up my spine. "Why's that?"

"He died an hour ago."

"He died?" I repeated, my voice lifting high enough to be just this side of panic. "Was it suicide?" *Please, please have been suicide.* If I fully understood the implications of

what Steven had told me and the physical evidence I'd seen,
the rider remaining in a body caused eventual death and
ghoulification. It had only been two days. The rider never
discarded a body until it started to turn ghoul—which apparently took about three days—unless cornered. So Larid
couldn't have turned yet, could he? *It had to be suicide.*

The secretary gave me a look that questioned my intelligence. Of course Larid hadn't died from suicide—the
OMIH would have kept him secured and possibly sedated.

"Where is the body now?"

"I've told you all I can, Ms. Craft." She looked down at
her computer, dismissing me.

Damn it. If he'd drained the body, I had no idea how long
it took between being deemed medically dead and becoming a ghoul. Surely he was circled at the time of his death,
but did they contain the rider before breaking the circle to
check the body?

"I need to talk to the official in this case. I have information."

"He isn't in the office."

"Then where is he? This is urgent."

She gave me an unimpressed glare.

"You have a problem and your official needs to know," I
said, trying to keep my voice polite and avoid imagining
hitting the woman with one of Briar's triple-threat darts.
"That body might have been dead an hour ago, but chances
are good that it will be up, walking around, and hungry very
soon. If it's not in a circle anymore, it needs to be. So pass
that along to the official or let me know who I can talk to
with the authority to contain that body."

Her expression shifted toward unsure, but not actually
convinced.

I trudged on. "There is a high probability Larid will become a ghoul, so someone needs to take a couple of preven-
tative measures to ensure that doesn't happen." I wasn't
sure exactly what those measures were, but I figured cutting
off his head would work—cockroaches were the only thing
I knew that could survive a beheading, otherwise it was a

pretty equal opportunity killing method. Briar would know for sure, but I had no idea how to contact her.

As if my thoughts summoned the woman, a black leather–clad figure walked into the lobby. "Craft, I've been looking for you. I don't like it when my suspects close shop and disappear."

The secretary's eyes widened at the word "suspect" and I lost any ground I'd gained with her. She was never going to give me any information now.

I whirled around to face Briar and had to unclench my jaw before I could speak, but I figured if anyone would know what to do about the rider/ghoul situation, it would be her. She listened, her lips thinning as I spoke. Once I finished, Briar marched over to the secretary and flashed her badge.

"Where's the body?"

The woman didn't hesitate. "The two officials on the case are currently escorting the corpse to the city morgue for an autopsy."

I turned on my heels, running for the front door as soon as the word "morgue" crossed her lips. I dug my phone out of my purse as I ran. "Call Tamara," I yelled into the mouthpiece, holding the VOICE COMMAND button.

Tamara's name flashed across the display before the phone announced it was calling. It rang once, twice. I reached the street. No taxis.

Crap, I had the worst taxi karma recently.

"You need a ride, Craft?" Briar said, two steps behind me.

The offer shocked me, but I guess the enemy of my enemy and all that, though I wouldn't come close to saying friends. Still, she didn't have to ask me twice. As I followed her to her vehicle, Tamara's line rang a fifth time and then went to voice mail. I hit REDIAL.

Come on. Pick up your cell.

It rang twice this time before her recorded message started. She'd sent me to voice mail.

Damn it.

I didn't have the morgue's direct line on my voice command list, so I had to scroll for it. We reached Briar's car as

I found the number, and I paused. She drove the biggest SUV I'd ever seen and it might as well have been an armored tank with the amount of metal I felt coming off the thing. Just standing outside it made me nauseous. I couldn't imagine climbing inside.

I did anyway.

"Craft, you look like you're going to retch."

"I'll make it. Can I open this window?" I didn't wait for her answer but hit the window button as soon as she cranked the vehicle.

It helped only a little.

I can do this. Then another thought hit me. Iron blocked faerie's magic, was my perception charm working? I glanced at Briar, but she wasn't aiming any weapons at me, so I guessed I wasn't glowing.

I hit the CALL button and my phone dialed the morgue's main line.

Tamara picked up on the first ring.

"Alex, this isn't a good time. I have a cop's body coming in. People are going to want answers."

"I know. Larid, escorted by two OMIH officials. Listen, you've got to stay away from the body. Keep it contained if you can. If you can't, then lock yourself in your office."

"What are you talking about?" she asked, and in the background I heard voices. A vehicle idling. A door slamming.

"I think it will turn ghoul. Don't go near the body."

"It what? You've got to be kidding," she muttered then yelled, "Reggie don't—"

A masculine scream boomed in the background, then another and I heard a crashing crack. Static filled the connection.

"Tamara?"

No answer.

"Tam?"

Another scream, this one higher pitched, cut through the static.

I whirled to face Briar. "Drive faster."

*   *   *

Briar managed the half-hour drive from the Quarter to
Central Precinct in eighteen minutes. Every single one of
which made the sick feeling in my stomach worse—and I
wasn't sure if that was because of the iron or the fact that
Tamara's phone had gone dead after her scream. The SUV
hadn't come to a complete stop when I jumped out of the
passenger side and ran for the morgue. Briar called my
name, commanding me to wait, but I didn't stop. Visitors
were required to go through one of the main entrances and
a security check as well as sign in and get a pass. I didn't
have time for that. I jogged around the side of the building
heading for the entrance funeral homes used when picking
up bodies.

   I wasn't the only one.

   A flock of police officers were at the scene. Of course,
considering most had been in the building during the attack, it wasn't surprising they were here. Between the press
of uniformed and plainclothes cops, I couldn't see much as
I approached, but near the open doors of the body mover's
van I could just make out a white sheet with deep crimson
stains. Another bloodstained sheet covered a body a few
feet away. I ground to a halt, still a good distance away. I
didn't want to know, but I *needed* to know who was under
those sheets.

   Heat burned my eyes as tears threatened. I blinked them
back and opened my senses. If I'd have moved closer, I
wouldn't have needed to let my awareness drift, but then, if
I started crying, all the cops would see. So I reached toward
the bodies.

   Male. Both of them.

   I let out a relieved sigh, which immediately made me feel
guilty because that had to be Reggie and at least one of the
OMIH officials. But I'd never met them, didn't know them,
and if it had been Tamara . . . I didn't finish that thought.

   A hot hand landed on my shoulder. "Craft, I told you to
wait."

I didn't turn. "Two dead. Both males, one in his late twenties and the other late thirties to early forties."

"Can that grave witch sense of yours tell their pants size and marital status too?"

I shot a frown at Briar, but she was already moving, hurrying the rest of the way down the steep drive. I jogged to catch up, but drew up short as we reached the back line of cops.

How the hell am I going to get through that? Only a handful of cops were actively working the scene, the rest were stuck between transfixed terror—after all, they'd known the officer-turned-ghoul—and trying to appear helpful so they weren't sent away.

Two police dogs were present and one officer had a law enforcement grade tracking charm, but they seemed to be having trouble finding a sample for the dogs or charm.

Briar pulled her badge and muscled her way through the crowd, flashing her credentials to anyone who gave her trouble. I followed in her wake, spotting more familiar than unfamiliar faces as I moved through the throng of officers. Some nodded grim greetings with tight lips and burdened eyes; others didn't seem to notice me at all. Only a few officers' features hardened as they spotted me, but no one stopped me as I followed Briar.

"I'm not your ticket onto a crime scene," she told me when we reached the front of the blockade of officers.

"Didn't expect you to be." I turned on my heel, walking toward the morgue's back entrance. I almost made it too. Then a large hand landed on my shoulder, the bear-sized palm burning against the skin my top didn't cover.

"You shouldn't be here," John said, and his mustache tugged down toward his chin with his frown.

"I'm not here to interfere. I just want to check on Tamara."

He stared at me for a long moment, the deep lines around his eyes sharper today, the crease between his brows tight. "This thing was responsible for the suicides, but what the hell happened here?"

"Ghoul," I said and his mustache managed to pull down another notch. "I think the rider was killing the victims to prevent them from turning into ghouls."

"How humane." He made a sound between a snort and a grunt.

Then we both stood there, not looking at each other. What else was there to say? That I'd told him the suicides were homicides and if they were treated as such this might not have happened? That he'd told me to stay out of it, and if I had, the rider would have never decided I was a threat and a lot of good cops would still be alive?

The silence hung heavy and thick, a tension that had been building one secret and small hurt at a time so that now a wall towered between us. "I'm going to check on Tamara," I finally said.

He gave a weary nod, but I think he was relieved the conversation ended. I hurried inside before anyone else could stop me.

While cops packed the back entrance, the morgue was as cool and quiet as ever. I found Tamara in her office, one of her new interns stitching four nasty-looking lacerations. The skin around Tamara's eyes tightened in something not quite drastic enough to be called a wince every time the needle pierced her skin.

"Are you sure you don't want me to drive you to the hospital?" the intern asked as I walked through the door.

Tamara shook her head. "You're doing fine and you're half done."

"But the hospital would have local anesthetics for the—"

"You're the one cringing, not me," Tamara said, her voice sharp, which made the other woman flinch worse. It was true, the woman acted like she was the one being sewn up without painkillers, instead of the reverse. Tamara noticed me in the doorway and nodded in greeting.

"Guess I won't be buying a short-sleeved wedding dress, huh?" The words came out tense despite her attempt at humor, and her brown eyes had the glassy shimmer of shock.

"Best charm witch I know not able to cover a couple of

scrapes? As if," I said in reply, forcing a smile, but my stomach was in my throat, or at least the taste of bile and the fact I couldn't swallow or breathe suggested it had lodged there.

My gaze stuck to the four jagged claw marks. Ghoul claw marks. I didn't hear what the intern said because inside my head, I was screaming. Which is probably why I didn't hear Briar behind me. Or maybe she really was that quiet.

"Craft, I told you not to run off."

I whirled around. I almost corrected her and told her she'd actually said she wasn't my free pass onto the crime scene. But I remembered what she'd told me two days ago, that killing a ghoul victim was more humane than letting them turn into monsters. I couldn't let her know Tamara was hurt.

Unfortunately, someone had already told her. "The dead are the body mover and one OMIH official. The other official survived and was rushed to the hospital. I'm told the ME was injured as well. Is that her?"

Crap.

She shoved past me, not waiting for an answer. She walked over to Tamara and examined the half-stitched wounds. The intern's hands shook under the scrutiny and Tamara finally winced.

Without a word, Briar turned on her heel and walked back out of the room. I followed her.

"Is she going to be okay?"

"She a friend of yours?"

I nodded.

"Then you might want to clear any bad air and say all the things you've always wanted to say. One scratch is enough to infect. If I don't find this ghoul, she's got forty-eight hours, maybe seventy-two since it's such a small wound."

My throat closed.

Two days.

If the ghoul wasn't destroyed in two, maybe three, days, Tamara would die and turn ghoul. Or Briar would terminate her first.

Chapter 32

"Let me help you hunt the ghoul," I said after Briar finished telling the officer in charge that Reggie and the OMIH official's bodies should be cremated in the next twenty-four hours to prevent any chance of them rising. I still needed to find out what had happened to the rider after Larid's body had died. Had the OMIH contained it or had it jumped hosts? But right now I couldn't worry about the possibility a stranger was being ridden—all my thoughts were on Tamara and preventing her from changing.

Briar gave me a skeptical look as she headed toward her SUV. "You want to hunt the ghoul that hurt your friend? What do you know about hunting ghouls?"

Not a whole hell of a lot. Most of what I'd learned in academy were warnings, not practical information on how to destroy a ghoul if a grave witch did screw up and end up with a nest of corpse-eating creatures. I'd actually learned more in my short conversations—or should I say, interrogations—with Briar than I ever had in school. But I had one hell of a motivation to find and destroy that ghoul. One of my best friends was infected. *And her baby.* Yeah, motivation wasn't an issue.

That must have been obvious in my face because Briar's dark eyes turned sympathetic. "I know you want to help your friend, but you'd just be in the way."

"Ghouls are dead. I can sense the dead." I could also accelerate the decay of a dead body and I'd ripped souls out of the dead before, though I didn't have a clue if I could rip a ghoul out of a body. I couldn't touch the rider, but he inhabited live bodies. The dead were a different story.

"A human divining rod for ghouls, huh?" She crossed her arms over her chest. The movement made the vials in her bandolier rattle. "Normally I have to wait until night when the ghouls are active, but if you can find them . . ." She opened the hatchback of the SUV and grabbed a map. Then she unfolded it on top of a crate. "Ghouls don't like the sun. It doesn't hurt them or anything, so don't think they're easier to kill in the light. They just avoid it. As the police haven't received any reports about people being mauled on the street, the ghoul must have found a sheltered place to spend the rest of the day, or it found the sewer system. Either way, it will be drawn to the nearest graveyard." She scoured the map. "Damn. Rosemount Cemetery and Oak View are nearly equal distances from here."

"You're sure it will head to a cemetery? If the goal is dead bodies, why not stick around the morgue?"

Briar considered this. "It's possible, but ghouls are hive minded. If even one other ghoul dwells in one of these cemeteries, the new ghoul will be drawn to it. Besides, ghouls don't eat the freshly dead."

But we couldn't be sure Larid wouldn't stick around. I glanced back down the hill where the crowd of cops had begun dispersing. The bodies had been moved into the morgue and half the force had volunteered to start a grid search of the area, looking for the ghoul.

Briar shook her head. "We'll have more bodies on our hands if one of those cops finds it first."

"Bullets won't work?"

"They work if your goal is to piss it off. The only way to stop a ghoul is to destroy the body."

Which explains the incendiary rounds. It also might explain why the rider killed the victims in such extreme fashions—he wanted to make sure they didn't get back up.

Briar looked from her map to the sky and then back. It was slightly past noon and a good six hours until dark. "You're sure you'll be able to sense ghouls?"

"I've never tried before but I'd say it's likely."

"Then we'll start with Rosemount—it's the older of the two. If we don't find anything we'll head to Oak View." She folded her map. Then she opened the huge crate and pulled out a vial of something that my senses told me was particularly nasty. And flammable. "If we find anything, I want you to get the hell out of the cemetery, I don't have time to babysit. You run into trouble reaching the gate, toss that at a ghoul and it will be too busy burning to follow you."

"Right," I said, holding the vial carefully, I didn't need to break the thing and end up like Kirkwood.

The drive to Rosemount was agonizing. I all but stumbled out of the SUV when it stopped. Briar gave me a strange look but didn't comment. I hoped she assumed I got carsick easily.

"So?" she asked within two seconds of stepping through the cemetery gates.

I frowned at her and without answering, reached out with my senses. Grave essence battered at my mental shields. It's hard to open yourself and barricade your mind at the same time, but I didn't dare let the grave essence in—I needed my eyes.

I let my mind skim over bodies as I walked a spiral pattern through the graves. Briar stalked in my wake at first, but as I worked my way inward, her impatience got the better of her. She sat down on a bench and pulled out her crossbow. The way she handled it was almost loving, as if it were her closest friend—which would be very sad indeed. I assumed she was cleaning or adjusting it, I didn't pay much attention.

By the time my spiral led me to the center of the graveyard, I had a pounding headache, but I was confident I'd checked every grave or area a ghoul could hide. My search had turned up half a dozen haunts and one grave with two bodies, but nothing else of note.

"Well, that took long enough," Briar said, tucking a knife into her sleeve.

"I wanted to be thorough."

She made a noise that was either a choked laugh or a snort—I was leaning toward the latter. Then we headed for Oak View Cemetery.

As soon as I stepped through the gate, I realized I hadn't needed to be quite so diligent at Rosemount. I hadn't even opened my senses yet and I could feel the hungry darkness lurking in the shadows.

"We have ghouls."

"Where?"

"I haven't gotten that far yet." Though it wasn't hard to feel where we should start looking. The closer I got to the ghouls, the more every instinct in my body told me to run away. The ghouls didn't feel evil the way the rider did, they just felt . . . primal. Their drives were simple—feed and replicate.

"Here," I said, stopping. They were directly in front of me, in a small crypt. I could feel them sensing me back and I shivered. "There are six, maybe seven. How the hell did there get to be so many?"

"They see anything living as a threat. Enter their territory at night or on a cloudy day and they'll attack to kill. A couple of days later you have a new ghoul."

I thought about all the missing person reports I'd sifted through and wondered how many were desiccated corpses inhabited by creatures from the land of the dead.

"Seven, huh? Damn. I don't like those odds." Briar circled the crypt. When she reached where I was standing again she looked me over and cocked a dark eyebrow. "You ever shot a crossbow before?"

I shook my head and she cursed.

"Remember when I told you to get the hell out once you located the ghouls? Well, now is your chance. Or, if you really want to help your friend, I'll give you a couple more potions, but if you die, it's not on my hands. Got it?"

Did I want to die? No. Did I want to help Tamara? Hell yes. One outweighed the other. "Give me the potions."

Briar nodded and unhooked three more vials. I accepted them gingerly, wishing I had some safe way to carry them. I considered tucking half in my pocket, but I didn't want to accidentally incinerate myself. So, I gripped three in one hand, and prepared to toss the fourth at anything that moved out of that crypt.

"You ready?" Briar asked, slinging her crossbow in front of her. At my nod she grabbed two more vials and marched toward the crypt. "If we're lucky, this will take care of at least one before we start."

She stopped in front of the door to the crypt and took a deep breath. Then, almost in one movement, she kicked down the door, hurled the two vials into the crypt, and threw herself backward. She rolled over her shoulder and came up on her feet, her crossbow already aimed. A *twang* sounded and her bolt took the thing emerging from the crypt in the chest. Flames burst over it.

The entire sequence happened so fast I hadn't even had time to consider throwing my vial.

The ghoul let out an inhuman howl as the flames consumed it, and it threw itself to the ground and rolled—which didn't help with the magical fire. Two more ghouls barreled out of the crypt, they charged forward, talons flashing like rusty spikes. Briar's crossbow twanged again and one burst into flames. I hurled my vial at the other.

It landed a good two feet shy of the ghoul, creating an explosion and singe mark in the grass, which attracted the ghoul's attention. It turned toward me, running full tilt. The thing barely looked human anymore, with its leathery skin pulled tight over its bones and eyes blue in death. I fumbled for another vial and hurled it at the ghoul.

This one hit its mark, flames bursting to life everywhere the liquid touched. It didn't go down, at least not before I hurled the third vial. Then with flames consuming it, the ghoul fell.

Another followed right behind it.

I stumbled back in surprise, throwing the vial at the same time.

I missed.

The ghoul was three yards away and closing fast. It was as leathery and deformed as the previous, rows of sharp teeth flashing in its gaping mouth, but I recognized something of Larid in the features. This was the ghoul that had attacked Tamara. Destroy it and the chain of infection broke, sparing Tam. Larid had to die—again.

And I had no vials left.

I threw open my shields as it lunged. Grave essence plowed into me as the planes of reality splashed together in my vision. The ghoul didn't change. It was already connected to the land of the dead. I had a moment of shock. Then the ghoul slammed into me.

Pain stabbed through my chest and tore into my stomach as the ghoul's talons sank into my skin, ripped at me. The ground jumped up to hit me as the ghoul's weight knocked me back. It rode me down, the impact making its claws dig deeper.

I didn't have enough air to scream.

Those teeth were inches from my face when the ghoul burst into flames, a silver bolt sticking out of its side. A black motorcycle boot smashed into the thing, knocking it off me. Its claws ripped free. Now I screamed.

Briar stood over me, her crossbow twanging once more. Then, nothing.

Everything was silent except for the sound of sizzling, dead flesh and my thudding heart, which seemed too slow for the situation. That suddenly became very important to me, and I tried to count the seconds between beats, but blackness took me before I reached two.

"Hey, you alive?"

I blinked, opening my eyes. It was hard to focus on Briar, but I tried.

"Damn, you're conscious," she said. "Listen, your wounds are bad. I can sit here and put pressure on them and you might live five extra minutes. Otherwise, you'll either drown or bleed out in the next couple of minutes. Or I can save you the misery and end it quick. Preference?"

I blinked again. I was dying? I couldn't die. Not here. I opened my mouth but instead of words, I coughed. It hurt like hell and tasted of blood. Fuck. She was right. The ghoul had hit a lung.

I tried again and this time managed to croak the words "out of graveyard."

The blurry Briar gave me a confused look.

"Can't die"—cough—"in graveyard."—cough—"Get me out."

She looked around, but the shock was peeling away under my panic. "Get me out."

"Okay, okay." She leaned down and wrapped my arm around her neck. Then she half carried, half dragged me toward the entrance.

I tried to help, but I couldn't get my feet to cooperate. The gate looked a million miles away. *I'm not going to make it. I'll be stuck here forever.* Somewhere I knew that my spirit wouldn't just pop out of my body once I died, that when they removed me from the cemetery, the collectors would come, but all I could think of was that I'd end up a haunt.

"Hurry." The word was broken and slurred, but Briar understood enough to curse about the demand.

The gate was closer now. I was going to make it.

And Death was on the other side. Waiting.

Briar dragged me just beyond the gate and then lowered me to the ground. "Happy now?"

I was. But I didn't waste the strength to tell her. All my attention was on Death.

"I'm glad it's you," I said, or at least, I tried to say. Everything was darkening now.

"Why can't you at least try to stay alive?" Death asked, dropping to his knees by my shoulders. "For me?"

I was out of words. Which was okay, because Death's hand slipped under my head, and his mouth covered mine, negating the need to speak. His lips were warm and soft, but his mouth pressed hard against mine.

Well, if I was going to die, it might as well be kissing a very sexy soul collector.

The kiss sent a wave of heat starting at my mouth and spreading outward, but that was chased by a cold so biting I flinched. Death's hand behind my head ensured I couldn't pull back as the chill poured into me.

"What the hell?" I heard Briar say, but now I was actively struggling against the cold Death shoved into me.

And I had the strength to struggle, which was odd as I'd barely had the strength to keep my heart beating the moment before. *What's happening?*

Finally, once I felt like all my organs had frozen, the chill stopped and Death's lips on mine were once again warm. He pulled back, not far, but far enough that I could focus on his eyes.

"You okay?" The question was a whisper.

And oddly, the answer was yes. I hurt like hell, but the darkness had pulled back, and I could feel all my limbs again.

"What did you do?"

At my question, he smiled, his eyes closing in an extended blink. I could feel the relief vibrate off him. Then he went still.

"Who and what are you?" Briar said, and I wiggled so I could see around Death.

Briar had her crossbow pressed against the back of Death's head. *Oh, this is bad.* I was suddenly not dying and Briar could see Death—and I wasn't forcing him to manifest. I could think of only one explanation. Death had switched life essences with me. It saved me, but it made him mortal.

Which meant if Briar shot him, Death would be very dead.

Chapter 33

"Don't shoot him."

"Craft? You sound pretty alive down there," Briar said without moving her crossbow. "This thing heal you?"

"He's not a thing. He is . . ." I hesitated. Explaining soul collectors to someone who couldn't see them—at least under normal circumstances—wasn't always easy. It probably also wouldn't help convince her not to shoot him.

"He's what, Craft?"

"Well, I'm starting to think he's my guardian angel." Though angel of death was what most people would call him.

Despite the crossbow pressed to his head, Death smirked.

"Do you shoot anything that catches you off guard?" Death asked without moving. I flared my eyes at him. Didn't he have any sense of self-preservation? You don't poke bears—or a witch armed for war.

"It's worked for me so far," she said, but she lowered the crossbow. She didn't put it away, but at least it wasn't pointed at his head anymore.

He straightened, helping me up as he climbed to his feet. I moved slower, wincing. The stabbing pain was still in my chest and abdomen. I glanced down at myself, and then wished I hadn't. There was a good reason the pain was still there—I'd been gored and though I wasn't dying, I also hadn't been healed. Shiny strips of flesh showed in my abdomen. I wrapped my arms around my stomach, trying to hide the wound from Briar.

Not that she was paying attention. Her eyes were devouring Death. "Do I have to sell my soul to get a hot guy to show up and bring me back when I'm fatally injured? Even if the answer is yes, just tell me where to sign."

I frowned. I wasn't used to anyone else being able to see Death, and an oddly possessive streak urged me to step between them and tell Briar that if there was going to be any ogling, it would be by me. I didn't do either, but I did move closer to Death. And my shoulder might have been slightly in front of him.

Though he didn't make a sound, I could feel the amusement radiating off him and knew he was aware of exactly what I was doing. Then he stepped behind me and wrapped his arms around my shoulders, the hard planes of his chest against my back and his warmth engulfing me.

"Damn, Craft, I never thought I'd be jealous of a girl who just got her guts ripped open."

Yeah, about that . . . I forced a smile. How the hell was I going to hide the fact I was walking around with large holes in my abdomen? Redirection.

"It was a good day," I said. "We got the ghoul, saved Tamara and the OMIH officer, and no one else died." Much. "But I think we should probably leave."

She glanced back into the cemetery. "You sticking around for clean up?"

Crap. Yeah, I guess we couldn't leave smoldering ghoul around for visitors to find.

"I actually need to steal Alex," Death said, releasing my shoulders.

Briar's dark eyes darted to the parking lot, where only her SUV was parked. She gave Death a sideways glance, but shrugged. "I'm used to working alone anyway." She started to turn, and then stopped. "Craft, aside from the almost dying part, you did okay in there. I've seen grown men wet themselves when facing ghouls."

Crap, compliments. I nodded in acknowledgment. "It would have been better without the ghoul ripping me apart."

"The MCIB wouldn't pay me so much if more people survived my job." She shrugged before reaching into her jacket and pulling out a small card. "Taking out a nest in the middle of the day is a good way to do things. Call me if you're up to searching more graveyards for me." She held out the card. I was still hiding my stomach wound so Death was the one who reached out and accepted the card. She stared at him a little too long before turning back to me. "But, Craft, don't think this means I'm not still watching you. Don't leave the city."

I smiled, hoping she'd take it as agreement and get the hell out of there. The look she gave me wasn't quite as suspicious as any previous time she'd studied me, but even if the woman had complimented me, it was clear I hadn't won her trust.

Finally she headed into the cemetery to deal with the corpses, and I turned to Death.

"I take it you swapped our life essences?" I asked and at his nod, I opened my arms to reveal my destroyed torso. "So now what? Will I heal?"

"Not exactly. Alex, I'm going to need an oath from you that you won't reveal the secrets you learn in the next few hours."

"You don't need my oath for that." I rarely discussed the collectors and I never revealed anything that wasn't common knowledge, at least among grave witches.

"I do, and not just a promise because even a fae can be forsworn."

Damn. I hated oaths, but I tapped the magic in my ring and forced it to coat my words as I let him swear me to secrecy. Once I finished, he nodded his approval.

"Now close your eyes and hold your breath," he whispered.

I did, and his warm arms wrapped around me.

Then the world vanished into a sea of magic as cold as the grave.

We reemerged a second later. As the warm air wrapped around me, I opened my eyes, gasping.

"What was—" I stopped. We were in my apartment.

PC jumped to his feet in the center of my bed, his tail tucked and ears quivering. Then he realized it was me and yipped in greeting before lunging from the bed.

"Hey, buddy," I said, but as I moved to pick him up, I felt things inside my gut shift and squish in ways that seemed more than a little not good. Nothing was falling out at the moment—I wanted to keep it that way.

PC danced around me, but when I didn't pick him up, he gave up and moved to Death. The dog was *so* not loyal. Death leaned down and petted the small dog, a strange look on his face.

"What?"

"He feels different from what I expected."

I had no response for that. Until the last month, he had been in my apartment all the time. It never occurred to me that I'd never introduced my dog. He'd been able to interact only with objects that I touched while touching him, my planeweaving forming a bridge long before I even knew about the ability. But now Death was mortal and could interact with anything he wanted. He couldn't stay mortal. That had to unbalance the world or something, didn't it?

"So, uh, what now?"

"We have to get you mended," he said, picking up PC.

"Excuse me?"

He pressed those full lips together, as if he wasn't sure he should say what he was thinking, but he already had my oath so after a short hesitation he said, "Soul collectors aren't exactly immortal, but we are unchanging."

"Like the fae."

He shook his head. "The fae like to think themselves

unchanging but they are simply unaging." PC licked Death's chin and he jerked back in surprise before smiling and scratching behind the dog's ear.

"Okay, so soul collectors don't change. I kind of knew that. You've looked exactly the same since I was five."

"It's more than the way we look. We can have that altered if we desire. But we don't change at all, which means if we are hurt, we don't heal. We have to be mended."

I absorbed all this. The last time Death had exchanged essences with me a cop had shot him—that's sort of a hazard when you do major magic in the middle of an active crime scene. He'd seemed fine as soon as I gave him back his essence, and I'd assumed he'd healed. Of course, I had holes in my lungs and rearranged innards and they weren't slowing me down.

"So then, I need to see this . . . mender? Where is he?" And would he fix me? I wasn't a soul collector.

Death frowned and set PC back on the bed. "I can't take you. This mortal body has certain limitations."

"If you took my essence, your body should be fae."

"Still mortal." He smiled and walked over to me. "Just much longer lived." He put his hands on my hips, careful not to touch any of the wounds. "Now we need to get you cleaned up so that the others can take you to get mended."

Others? "Not the gray man."

His brow pinched. "Gray man?"

Crap, I always forgot that the collectors didn't know what I called each of them. But they wouldn't give me their names, what was I supposed to do?

After a moment, Death nodded. "Appropriate description," he said. "Fine, not him."

Which left the raver. I didn't offer her nickname, but retreated to the bathroom. I grimaced when I glanced in the mirror. With my tattered clothes—and stomach—covered in drying blood, I looked like an extra in a horror flick. And all the drying blood? It made getting my top off hell.

I ended up wearing the shirt into the shower until the water loosened the blood enough that pulling the fabric free didn't threaten to skin me. Once I scrubbed clean, I dried off, trying to avoid my mirror. But I couldn't seem to help myself.

Four ugly—and fatal—puncture marks pierced the right side of my rib cage. Ribbons of flesh hung from around the wound in my stomach and I could see darker things beyond the torn flesh. My stomach clenched at the sight, but at the same time, even though I could feel the wounds, they didn't seem quite real. Maybe it was the lack of blood.

Just to be safe, I wrapped gauze around the stomach wound. I didn't bother with charmed OMIH-certified bandages—they were expensive and if I couldn't heal, an accelerated healing charm wasn't going to do me any good.

Death looked up as I emerged from the bathroom in just the gauze and a towel. His gaze trailed over me, not in a searching-for-wounds way but with eyes that were all male interest and heat. A flush burned across my cheeks, but what was under that towel wasn't anything I wanted to show off, that was for sure.

"I made you coffee," he said, holding up a mug.

"Now that's a change."

He smiled. "Want me to hold it for you?"

I giggled, a girlish peal of a sound. The movement hurt, but I couldn't seem to stop. It was the stress. I'd been betrayed and then warned off by Falin, feared I'd been addicted to Faerie food, started glowing, spent too long with my father, one of my best friends had been attacked by a ghoul, whom I then almost—should have—died from, and now I'd exchanged life essences with Death. It was too much for one day and I was either going to laugh or cry, though at some point, it became both.

"Hey," Death whispered, wrapping his arms around me. "Hey, what is it?" He stroked his fingers through my wet curls. "I'll leave the coffee making to you from now on, okay?"

I buried my face against his hard chest, but I had to smile. "It's not that. It's just, everything." And I poured out every action, every fear, because he was Death. He stood there, holding me, making comforting sounds at times, offering a word or two of understanding, but mostly listening, his fingers twisting in my drying curls. "And what if the mender won't fix me?"

"Then you'll be a planeweaver in an unchanging body and I'll be a collector in an unaging one."

I shook my head. "You can't remain mortal. But if your mender does fix me, and we switch back . . ." The last time I'd taken back my mortality I'd had a seizure. And we'd only switched for maybe fifteen minutes. What would happen this time?

"We'll figure it out," he said, and stepped back. The friendly comfort in his eyes took on a glint of a much different kind. "But for now, your coffee is getting cold."

This time I accepted the mug when he handed it to me. It wasn't cold yet. In fact, it was perfect. For his first time making coffee, I was more than impressed. Of course, he'd spent years watching me.

"It's good," I told him, and he flashed me that dazzling smile of perfect teeth and smooth lips.

I swallowed. It was a good thing the ghoul didn't get my heart, because it was suddenly working double time. I glanced into my coffee mug. "I should get dressed."

"For now." That same heart-melting smile.

Oh, I'm in so much trouble. But I couldn't understand how he could look at me with so much heat. I had to look terrible. I'd been crying and my curls were half air-dried, and then there was what hid under the towel. I cringed and set down my mug. "So if taking my life essence gave you a mortal body, how come I don't have your incorporeal one?"

"You do. You just haven't stopped touching mortal reality yet."

Right. Planeweaver. Well, I had no intention of letting go of the mortal realm. But one more issue nudged at the edge of my brain.

"You have a fae body, so why aren't you . . . glowing?" After all, my Sleagh Maith body glowed.

"We switched life essences. It gave you my immortality

and me your mortality, but magic is part of the soul, not the body."

"Oh." I didn't know what else to say. I'd never considered that the Sleagh Maith glow might be part of their—*our*—magic.

After I was fully dress and I'd walked and fed PC, Death held his hand out to me.

"Ready?"

I accepted his warm hand, and this time, when I closed my eyes, I was prepared for the cold.

"A night club?" I asked, eyeing the exterior, which wasn't impressive with the bass thumping through the brick walls.

"Trust me, this is the most likely place." Death started for the door. Only to be stopped by the bouncer, who wanted IDs and money.

I balked at the cover charge, but dug in my purse. Death put a hand on my arm, stopping me.

"Never mind," he told the bouncer. Then he turned and walked back the direction we'd come. I had little choice but to follow.

"I thought you said this was our best bet?"

"It is. Hold your breath." Then his arms were around me, a warm anchor in the sudden cold.

A moment later the chill abated. I looked around at the ugly green tiled walls with rust-stained urinals. "The men's restroom?"

Death shrugged. "Normally if I pop into the mortal realm and a person occupies the same space, they get a chill. But with this body, I'm not sure what would happen."

The fact it probably wouldn't be pretty didn't need to be said.

"Come on." He pulled open the door and then led me into a madness of lights and bodies.

While I liked barhopping, I'd never been a clubber. Dim rooms with flashing strobes equaled one blind grave witch not having a lot of fun, so I avoided dance clubs like a particularly vicious curse of pox. This club was worse than most with fog machines pumping onto the floor and the dancers using glow sticks and charms to create elaborate trails of light following their movements. I might have Death's unchanging and hard to kill essence, but that clearly didn't fix my eyes.

I squeezed them closed and opened them again. All I could see were random flashes of light. Except, out in the center of the floor, I could clearly make out one solitary figure in a bright orange top with matching dreads that glowed in the black light. Her movements were fast, her body moving in time with the pounding bass. At least, until she spotted us. Then she stopped dead, her scowl exaggerated by the black light–sensitive makeup. As she stalked across the dance floor, she swept straight through several of the other dancers, making them pause and shiver. Of course, as hard as they where moving, the chill might have felt good.

"What have you done?" she asked, ignoring me completely as she whirled on Death.

"It was a necessity."

"Well, I suggest you switch back before anyone else finds out."

I frowned from one to the other of them. Apparently I wasn't invited into this particular conversation. Not that I wasn't going to join. "I need to see the mender."

The raver glanced at me, blinking long eyelashes that glowed brilliant blue in the light.

"She means she needs mending," Death said, wrapping his arm around my shoulder and pulling me close to him. I didn't know if it was worry or amusement.

"You must be out of your mind if you think I'm taking her." She threw her hands in the air, waving her nails in front of his face. "Actually, I know you are. Only a mad collector would do what you've done. Do you know what he'll say about—"

"Will you take her or won't you?" Death asked.

She cocked an orange eyebrow. "What kind of damage are we talking about?"

She doesn't seriously want me to show her the wounds here?
But she only looked on expectantly and Death nodded for me
to show her. Great. I glanced around, but no one was paying
attention. I lifted the bottom of my shirt, the white gauze
glowing in the black light. Still the raver waited, her long nails
tapping her elbows where her arms crossed her chest.

Fine.

I unwrapped the gauze. She studied the wound with
more of a detached analytical expression than anything that
could be considered sympathetic. "Wrestling tigers?"

"Ghouls actually."

She nodded, and then turned, dismissing me as she addressed Death. "Well, I see why you decided this was the
only option. I don't approve, and you know he won't either."

He? Was she talking about the gray man or the mender?
Or someone else? I had no idea how the soul collector hierarchy worked.

"I'm assuming if I disagree you'll either find someone
else or you'll stay in that decaying body."

"One day, you might understand," he said.

The raver shook her head. "I sure as hell hope not." She
glanced at me. "Fine. I'll take her, but if she's too mortal to
make the trip or he won't mend her, it is not my fault."

Death smiled and inclined his head graciously. The raver
only scowled in return. Then she turned to me.

"Give me your hand and drop your shields. All of them."

I blinked at her. Was she crazy? I glanced at Death, but
the raver clicked her nails.

"Now would be good."

Death nodded, stepping back. Then he either vanished
or the darkness of the club devoured him. I shivered at the
thought and turned away.

I took off my charm bracelet before taking the raver's
outstretched hand and lowering my outer shields. Realities
swam over my vision and grave essence reached for me,
making the wind from the land of the dead tear through me.

"Look at the people—what do you see?"

"Their souls. They glow softly under their skin."

"Good," she said, her hand tightening around mine. The wind was still swirling around me and several brightly colored souls were beginning to stare.

"Do you have any of your shields still locked?"

I didn't answer.

"Take them down. Now."

"I—"

Her hand around mine tightened so hard her nails bit into my skin. "Now."

Dropping my innermost walls wasn't so simple as opening them like my main shields; I had to deconstruct them. By the time I finished I could barely make sense of the scene in front of me. I had to be looking at a dozen different realities, all blurring into a jumble far more chaotic than the manic light show on the dance floor.

I swayed, and the raver kept her hand locked around mine. "Can you still see the souls?"

I blinked, trying to focus. It was like looking at one of those 3-D images that you had to stare at until it suddenly jumped into focus.

"Yes, I see them."

"Good, keep your attention on the souls, just the souls." She took a step forward, or maybe a step up, dragging me with her.

We didn't move in space, we moved in realities. Bright light filled the previously dark room, several of the other realities falling away. The wind from the land of the dead cut off.

"Can you still see the souls?"

I could. They looked different now, somehow more like crystal than light. I nodded and she stepped again.

"You can close your shields now," she said.

I did and blinked into the brilliant light surrounding us. I could still see aspects of the techno club we'd been in, but now the people were colorful jewel-like beings and the walls crystal.

"Is this what you always see?"

She frowned like she wouldn't answer the question; then

she cursed under her breath. "I guess it doesn't matter now, does it? No. I prefer to stay as close to mortal reality as I can. This place is too sterile for my tastes. Come on. Now that you've finally let go of the mortal form you were holding, we'll be able to move faster."

"I what?" Was that squeaking sound my voice? Still, I *needed* my mortal body, and as pretty as this place might be, I didn't want to hang out here forever.

I looked around. Even with my shields up, I could feel that there were other realities around me, some I could tell instinctively shouldn't touch this place but were trying to move through me.

"Stop thinking about it or you'll spoil everything we've done so far. Now face me and give me your other hand as well."

Well, I've come this far. And if this was what it would take to reach the mender, so be it.

The crystal plane swirled around us and I couldn't tell if we were moving or if it was, but without warning a large structure appeared in front of me. The building glowed with life as if it were made from living rock. A man stood outside on the stoop, as if he'd been waiting.

"This is the girl?" he asked, looking me over.

The raver dropped my hands. "Unfortunately."

Gee, thanks. I turned my back on her and faced the man. He had an ageless quality to him. Actually that wasn't quite accurate. It wasn't that he was ageless so much as his age seemed in flux. When I first saw him I would have sworn he was in his late sixties but as he studied me, he appeared younger, much younger. Surely no older than thirty.

"Hello," I said, stepping toward him. "I'm Alex."

He huffed, and walked inside the softly shimmering building.

Well, things were going just smashing, weren't they? I looked at the raver. She shrugged and followed him. I fell in step behind her.

"I suppose he sent you to be mended," the man said once I'd stepped through the door.

I assumed "he" referred to Death. "Yes."

From the outside I'd thought the structure was a building, but the walls contained a garden filled with the most perfect flowers I'd ever seen. Every rose and lily glowed with its own light and I realized I was seeing the plant's life force, not quite a soul, but definitely a life.

"Your garden is beautiful," I said, turning a full circle to admire the clematis and ivy climbing along the inner walls, the carefully laid out plots of perennials, and the waterfall trickling into a pond of colorful koi.

The man squinted at me, looking old once more. "What do you see, girl?"

"Life," I said without even thinking about it. From the birds to the stones everything glowed with its own form of life.

The man nodded. "Let's see your wounds."

I tore my gaze from the beauty around me and looked at the ageless man. *What would he have done if I'd just said "pretty flowers"?*

I didn't dare ask. Lifting my shirt, I unwrapped the gauze around my stomach. He studied the wounds in silence. "That's not all of them?"

"Uh, no." The rest were higher. Much higher.

"Off with the shirt," he said and when I didn't immediately comply he frowned at me. "You're not the first female to require mending. Do you want to be fixed or not?"

Right. The top was fitted and tight enough that I hadn't worn a bra underneath—poor planning on my part. Hindsight and all that. I unzipped it reluctantly and shrugged it off. I felt more than a little exposed as the mender examined the punctures in my upper rib cage, but he studied me the same way Tamara examined bodies during autopsies. Not as a person, but as a puzzle to be solved.

Finally he nodded and his callused hand pressed against my skin. I cringed back and received a disapproving glance. Then the mending began. I don't know what I expected. Healing magic is usually warm. I've even felt my skin stitch back together under powerful enough magic.

This was nothing like that.

The man put his hand on me, and my flesh turned to something liquid, rippling under his touch. I would have gasped, but I couldn't seem to draw air, as if for a moment, I had no lungs.

"Does he realize how foolish his actions are?" the mender said as he worked. If he was talking to me, I had no breath to answer. "The essence and soul are not meant to be separated. You are both divided in half and vulnerable. Beyond foolish."

Yeah, but I'm alive. For now. I was still worried about switching back.

My skin settled and his hand moved to my stomach. Again the rippling sensation, but this time I could see my skin flowing under his touch. It smoothed as if he were re-shaping plastic. Finally he moved his hand to the nearly healed bullet wound on my arm.

"Oh that's not—"

He cut me off. "I never do half a job."

I shivered as the skin on my arm crawled and solidified, whole and unharmed.

I looked down at myself. Not only had he repaired the damage, but the scar where I'd once had a dagger driven into my abdomen was also gone. It was like I'd been re-formed from the original plan. *I wonder if he can fix my eyes?*

I didn't ask the question aloud but the mender frowned at me. "That is from your own magic. I can do nothing for it."

"I—" What, exactly? How was I supposed to know he was telepathic? It wasn't like I'd actually asked.

"You can dress now," the mender said, nodding to the shirt clenched in my hand. I'd forgotten about it. Shrugging into it, I zipped it closed and then looked between the mender and the raver. Neither said a word, but the raver nodded.

"I have a message for you to pass to him," the mender said, walking up to me again.

"I'm all ears."

The mender's face crinkled in confusion. Then, as if he realized it was an expression, or perhaps he read the meaning from my mind, he shook his head. "I'll give you the message, not tell you. Hold out your hand."

I did as told and he pressed two fingers into my palm. A surge of cold shot into my skin, making my fingers curl.

"Pass that to him in the same way," the mender said, taking a step back. He nodded to the raver and she motioned for me to take her hands once again.

The plane was sliding out of focus when the mender's voice broke into my thoughts. *"Remember child, the essence and the soul are not meant to be divided during life."*

Then the blinding light blinked out and we were back in the club.

Chapter 34

"So, what did it say?" I asked, sitting cross-legged on my bed, PC in my lap. The little dog's head swiveled back and forth, following Death's pacing.

"I've been given a choice."

"Choices are good?" Unless they were choices between two bad options.

He stopped midstride and turned toward me. "Alex—" He paused, his expression going distant. This time I was sure the colors in his eyes swirled, just a little. "I have a . . . job." He frowned. "Would you like to come?"

I assumed by "job" he meant a soul needed collecting. "A death scene? You offer to take me to the sweetest places."

He shrugged.

"Wait." I threw out a hand in a stopping motion before he could disappear. "I didn't say no."

Setting PC on the bed, I slid to my feet and accepted Death's hand. After all, how often did I get to learn more about the collectors? Besides, I was already oath bound, so I might as well learn as much as I could. The cold sea of darkness washed over me and in the next moment we were somewhere else.

The scent of antiseptic and bleach hit my senses as a

loudspeaker crackled and paged a doctor. Everywhere I looked there were beds divided by flimsy curtains. Monitors beeped, breathing machines whooshed, and nurses checked patients' vitals, noting results on small clipboards kept at the foot of the beds. The room reminded me of one I'd spent far too much time in as a child.

"An ICU ward?" I asked, clinging tighter to Death's arm.

"I can take you back," he offered. He knew how I felt about hospitals.

I shook my head as a nurse hurried past us without so much as a glance. "They can't see us?"

"No, but don't let go of me."

Right. Why a race who couldn't be seen by most humans needed extra magic to be unseen was interesting, but more than once I'd suspected he was around. I just couldn't see him. This pretty much confirmed it.

I scanned the occupied beds. "Which one?"

Death pointed to the still figure of an older woman. Her skin was pale and waxy and a breathing tube disappeared into her mouth, but her brown eyes were open, aware of her surroundings. They were the only part of her that moved.

I swallowed. *I probably should have stayed behind.*

"When will it happen?"

"If she dies, it will be within the next two minutes."

I looked at him. "If?"

"See that doctor?" He pointed across the room to a man in blue scrubs and a white coat. "He's trying to quit smoking, but right now he is seriously considering a cigarette. If he gives in, he won't be here when she codes, and she will die."

"And if he's here he'll save her?"

Death nodded.

"Then shouldn't we—"

His hand jerked back, pulling me closer to him.

I frowned. "But you said she could live if he stays."

Death's nod was slow, his hooded eyes watching my response.

The doctor glanced at the elevator, and I could only imagine his thoughts. His need for just one cigarette.

"What if he makes the wrong choice?"

"It is his to make. That's why I'm here."

"And you don't know which way it will go?" I asked. Death shook his head. I frowned. So he could see possibilities of the future? I hadn't known that. Clearly it was different from a premonition witch's visions. Those were always the final outcome, no matter what anyone did to try to change the future.

I turned to stare at the doctor, willing his resolve to stay strong, for him to fight whatever craving ate at him. "Aren't you tempted to tell him. Or to stall him? It could save that woman's life."

Death's arms slid around my shoulders, drawing me against his chest. "I think we're both aware I've been more than tempted in the past."

For me. He'd saved my life more than once.

"Well, I for one think you made the right choice."

"I wish that were a more popular opinion." His embrace tightened, until I was engulfed by his heat, his scent. It helped block out the room of people barely clinging to life and the sounds counting down their heartbeats, waiting for the last. "From the moment I pushed you out of the path of that bullet several months ago, I changed the pattern of time."

"That sounds awfully drastic. You said you see possible outcomes. How could you change what isn't settled? You made a choice, just like he" — I nodded to the doctor, who pressed the button for the elevator — "is making a choice."

"Mortals have choices. Collectors are forbidden to interfere."

I didn't know what to say to that, so I said nothing. I watched the floor numbers light up above the elevator as it approached, overly aware of the woman who was about to die. I looked at her, at the lines snaking off her that were supposed to save her, or at least preserve her, and I shuddered. For a moment I was in another hospital room, listening to a different set of machines as I huddled in a too large chair beside my mother's bed.

"You okay?" Death asked, pulling me out of the memory.

I nodded, but my eyes burned. The door to the elevator slid open. *Don't go.* Two nurses stepped out, chatting animatedly about something. The doctor in his scrubs and coat stared at the open door. Then he watched it slide closed again and turned away.

I sighed and Death gave me a gentle squeeze.

"We can go now," he whispered.

I took one last glance at the woman, whose machines were making erratic noises, nurses and the doctor rushing toward her. But I knew she'd live.

This time.

We popped into existence in my apartment, startling my poor dog once again.

"So this teleporting thing," I said, shivering from the lingering chill of Death's magic. "You've never taken me with you before. Is this something you can do because we switched essences, or . . . ?"

He pointedly didn't look at me.

"Seriously? So, for example, when I'd been kidnapped by the skimmers, and you and the two other collectors were with me, you could have teleported me out at any point."

"We're not supposed to interfere."

Right. "Tell me you saw that I wasn't going to die."

He frowned. "I can only see the possibility threads of those souls assigned to me at their birth."

"You're not my collector?"

He shrugged. "I adopted you."

"Cute. Why haven't I ever seen another collector come for me?"

"You don't have one. You must have been born in Faerie."

I froze. The strange little brownie I'd met when my father had stashed me at his secret house had mentioned taking care of me when I was a child. And my great-granduncle on my mother's side, who happened to be the king of the shadow court, had welcomed me *home* when I'd encountered him a month ago. But I had no memories of Faerie as a child. Not one.

"You've known I was fae from the beginning, haven't you?"

"I've known you were special from the moment you hit me with that medical chart, but in many ways you are and always have been a mystery."

"Is that a good thing, or a bad thing?"

"Recently, it's been terrifying." He stepped closer to me, moving his hands to my hips, as if he needed the reassurance that I was there, whole. "I can only tell you're in danger if the possibilities affect one of my souls."

He'd never told me any of this. After a lifetime of his secrets it was strange for him to share. Almost unbalancing. And I was off balance enough.

I stepped away from his hands, wrapping my arms around myself. "It's probably time for us to—"

"Have you lost your senses?" an angry voice that hadn't been in the room a moment before said.

I whirled around as the gray man stormed across my small apartment. Death turned as well, frowning at the other collector.

"It is my choice to make."

"And you're a fool for considering it." The gray man's cane swung wildly, punctuating his agitation.

In contrast, Death was still, to all appearances calm, his posture relaxed. But it was like a calm before a storm, and the hooded eyes that watched the gray man held a warning.

A warning the gray man ignored as he turned to me. "Do you understand the danger you're allowing him to put himself in?"

"Leave her out of this," Death said at the same time I asked, "What is he talking about?"

Death didn't answer me, but the gray man did. "A mortal body isn't made for what we do. The risk you're allowing him to take is immense." He pressed the silver skull on his cane against my shoulder. "If you care about him, you'll return his essence."

The blood drained from my face. I'd already intended to do that. I turned to Death but he held up a hand before I could say anything.

"Alex, we'll talk about this later," he said, before turning toward the gray man. "This doesn't concern you."

They stared at each other. The gray man displaying his agitation through jerky movements, Death still, like a tightly coiled trap.

"Does she really mean so much, my friend?"

Death didn't answer, he moved. Fast. One moment he stood with his thumbs hooked in the loops of his jeans, the next he was in front of the gray man. He grabbed the other collector by the shoulders and both vanished.

I stared at the spot where they had been. Gone. Like so many times before. Only this time I could feel the distance as my essence left with Death. It was an odd sensation. I sat down on my bed, picking up PC absently and cradling the small dog as I continued to stare at the last spot Death had been.

"He has to come back, right?" I asked PC, whose only answer was a tail wag, happy for the attention. I rubbed his head.

Death would come back. He had to. I still had his essence.

Chapter 35

❧❧❧

I paced across my kitchen, PC following in my wake as I listened to the woman on the other end of the phone.

"So you don't know if they managed to contain the rider before they released Larid's body?" I asked.

Briar's voice was sharp, annoyed. "With one of the officials on the case dead, the other in ICU, and the OMIH office closed, finding the answer to that question isn't exactly easy."

"But if it is out there . . ." I trailed off. If the OMIH had failed to contain it, someone else was slated to die. Either by suicide, or, if the rider hung out in the body until he drained it, by turning into a ghoul.

"Yeah, and chances are good that it's contained. Either way, what are you planning to do at this hour? It's late, Craft, and I have more cemeteries to clear. Now, are you going to join me to do your little ghoul-divining trick or not?"

The air chilled as Death's magic filled my apartment. "Briar, I have to go."

"Craft—"

I hit the END button before she had a chance to say anything else. She was right. There was nothing more I could do to search for the rider—if I even needed to—tonight.

I studied Death. "Well, you don't look like you've been in a fistfight. That or you won with no contest."

He gave me a startled look and then glanced over his shoulder. I wasn't sure if he was checking to see if I was talking to someone else or he was thinking about what had happened in the ten or so minutes he was gone. Then he shrugged. "There was no violence. We simply disagreed."

Right. "Should we expect any more surprise visits?"

"No." The word was flat, emotionless, and when he didn't offer to expand on the answer, I didn't press him.

"So . . ." I shoved my hands in my back pockets to keep from fidgeting and studied my boots. I was not looking forward to what was bound to come next—namely pain and possibly a seizure. But it had to be done. "I guess we should get this whole essence switching thing over with."

"What if we didn't switch back?"

My head jerked up. "What?"

"What if I remained mortal?" He moved closer, filling my space. "No more vanishing."

My chest tightened at the idea, part fear, part excitement. The prospect of him not up and vanishing on me—it had appeal. But the gray man was right. Death wasn't meant to be mortal.

I shook my head, backing up until my back hit the counter. "It's too dangerous."

He followed me. "I'll be careful."

"No, it's my mortality. You be safe and I'll be careful."

"You haven't done a good job of that so far."

Okay, he had a point. I should have died more than once this week, but that didn't mean I agreed. "What if you have to collect the soul of someone in a burning building? Or your soul is the victim of a drive-by and a bullet hits you? I bet you can't see possible time branches for yourself. What if something happened to you?"

He brushed a curl behind my ear. Then his hand lingered, his finger trailing down my chin. My skin tingled with the light touch and I swallowed as he traced the curve of my neck.

"If you're trying to distract me, it's not going to work." My whisper didn't hide the fact my voice shook.

The smile that curved Death's lips was full of the knowledge of exactly what reaction his touch woke in me. It was an intimate smile, full of promise and want, but there were emotions other than heat in his hazel eyes. Something was off. Something I couldn't quite read but the twist in my gut hinted I wouldn't like.

"What aren't you telling me?"

"The mender, as you call him, gave me a choice," Death said, and his finger reached the dip above my collarbone. I shivered and he paused long enough to watch my reaction. Then his fingers fanned out, and he placed his palm over my racing heart.

I grabbed his hand. "I can't think when you're doing that." I intertwined my fingers with his. "Now what choice?"

"As long as you are not mortal, there's no taboo against us being together."

I was glad I'd moved his hand because my heart knocked hard against my rib cage, though I couldn't tell if from excitement or my heart was making a run for it. Neither of us said anything as I let the implications of that statement sink in. If he remained mortal, there was nothing standing between us. But he'd be vulnerable.

There was still something he wasn't telling me. Something important.

"A choice implies options. What happens if you choose not to remain mortal?"

Death's hand closed tight around mine. "Then he will take away my ability to exchange my essence. I'll never be able to become mortal, or make you immortal, again."

Which meant no more mending for me. Well, I'd cheated dying more than my fair share already. If I understood everything Death had told me, that meant time had changed in ways it wasn't meant to. There had to be consequences for that.

"Alex, if we switch back, the shock as mortality takes hold could kill you." He released my hand and drew me into a tight embrace. "I can't lose you," he whispered into my hair.

I leaned into him. So I could let him take the risk of being mortal or gamble whether or not switching back would kill me?

"It's not safe for you to stay like this," I said, but my voice sounded dull, hollow. It wasn't exactly fear, not yet. I hadn't enjoyed my return to mortality the first time we'd done this. I certainly wasn't looking forward to it now, but I also didn't want Death in danger to keep me safe.

I pulled away from his arms, but the counter was behind me, so I had nowhere to go. His hands moved to my waist and he lifted me effortlessly, placing me on the countertop. That put our heights closer, forcing me to meet his gaze.

I needed to think. To be logical about this. "If you remain mortal, how will you live? I'm guessing soul collecting doesn't pay the bills."

A slow grin spread over his face. "Is Tongues for the Dead hiring?"

Did I have room for one more in my unproven firm? I already had a changeling, a ghost, and a brownie. Why not a mortal soul collector?

But my mind kept circling back to what the gray man said. The intensity of his eyes when he'd told me that if I cared about Death I'd return his essence.

My thoughts must have been transparent because Death reached out a hand to cup the side of my face.

"Hey," he whispered. "Nothing is going to happen to me."

"Well, what if you don't like being mortal?"

He laughed, the sound deep and masculine. "Alex, I've been mortal before. Admittedly a long time ago, but I remember parts of it."

I blinked at him.

"Why do you think I can exchange essences in the first place? If a collector ever grows tired of our unchanging life, we have the option of imbuing a soul with our essence, making them the collector and freeing our soul to move on.

Of course, the new collector isn't really a collector until the mender gives him his powers, but you get the point." He shrugged. "The fact you touch my reality is the only reason we could exchange essences, but it was never meant to be used like this."

"So if the mender takes away that ability, you're forever stuck a soul collector? You never get to move on?"

All the humor bled from his face. He shrugged but the movement was stiff.

So if he remained mortal he was in danger but if I returned his immortality, it would condemn his soul.

I scooted forward, my knees moving to either side of his hips so that I could wrap my arms around him and rest my cheek on his shoulder. "Those options suck."

His arms dragged me closer, and I felt the rumble in his chest as he laughed again, softer this time. "Yes, well, being around you more often will certainly be a trial, but I'm guessing a slightly better option than eternal servitude."

"Hey." I straightened, pushing back from him, but I was smiling.

So was he.

We were close, almost too close for me to focus on his entire face. I was suddenly very aware of his hands on my waist, of the heat of his hips pressing into my thighs, of his familiar scent filling the air between us. I swallowed, my breath turning ragged. *This is really happening.* He was going to remain mortal. Remain with *me.* It was crazy. Reckless.

It matched the rest of my day.

My arms were still around his shoulders. It was easy to lean in, to press my lips against his. He startled at the kiss, but when I ran the tip of my tongue along the crease of his lips, his mouth opened to me and he returned the kiss in earnest. His hand moved to cup the back of my head, his lips firm and smooth against mine as his tongue dipped into my mouth, bringing with it the sweet, clean taste of morning dew.

I'd fantasized about kissing Death since I was a teenager,

but I was always afraid it would change everything. Now everything had already changed. The desire from months of ghost kisses and years of flirting poured into that kiss, sweeping us both along with it. Tomorrow I'd worry about the rider, about Faerie, about mortality. Right now I abandoned myself to the feel of Death's lips against mine.

He dragged me to the edge of the countertop, but left that last inch of space between our bodies. I closed it, my legs locking around his hips. The feel of him, hot and hard straining against his jeans, brought a moan from me, a sound he matched. Then he broke the kiss, pulling back.

"Alex, love." His voice was strained, his mouth still close enough that I felt his quick breaths featherlight against my lips.

"Mmm?" My hand moved to his hair and I ran my fingers through the dark strands.

Death's eyes fluttered closed, his fingers tightening on my hips as if I'd touched something much more intimate. I smiled and kissed him again.

There was no hesitation this time. He kissed me like I held his life in my body—actually, I guess I did, but that was one of the things I wasn't thinking about right now. I focused on the softness of his T-shirt under my fingers and how it contrasted with the hard muscles underneath. I'd never seen him out of it, and I suddenly needed to more than anything else. My hands crawled down his waist as his moved up mine, as if mirroring my movements in reverse.

The shirt was tight, stretched over his muscles, and I hooked my hands under it, letting my fingers trail over flesh as I pushed it up his chest. He broke away from me long enough to pull the T-shirt over his head. A light feathering of dark hair covered his chest, coming to a point that drew a line down the center of his stomach and disappeared into the top of his jeans.

He watched me study him, that knowing smile on his lips again, but when I reached out, he caught my hand. He lifted it to his lips, pressing a kiss on my knuckles—an oddly restrained and formal gesture.

I frowned. "What's wrong?" The question was more a pant than words.

"I'm just seeing if you're really here, with me."

Now I was confused. "Where else would I be?"

"Turning off your mind and focusing on your body. I know you, Alex. And I don't want you to start thinking later and pull away from me."

Heat burned in my cheeks. *Way to make a fool of yourself, Alex.* I unlocked my legs, scooting back on the counter. Death caught my hips, stilling me. One of his hands moved to my face, guiding my chin up, but I didn't lift my eyes to meet his.

"Don't do that," he whispered, his lips finding mine.

I resisted the kiss at first, expecting him to return to those teasing, brush-of-the-lips kisses, but he deepened the kiss, and my body responded. I lifted my hands to his strong shoulders, now deliciously bare. Death's thumbs brushed over my nipples through my shirt, and I gasped, things low in my body tightening. He drank down the sound and then broke off the kiss and stepped back again.

I was left breathless and cold without his body pressed against mine. "I'm not sure I like this game."

"No game. I want all of you, Alex. Body." His hands moved to my waist. "Mind." He kissed my forehead. "And soul." His hand moved and my back arched as a pleasure so thick it verged on pain spread through me.

When I could think—and breathe—again, I met his eyes. "Did you seriously just touch my soul?"

"Just a little."

"Do it again?" I panted the request.

He stepped forward and kissed me, but there was more than just lips in this kiss. He touched something deeper. Something that made heat spiral in my core. I ground my hips against him, resenting the amount of clothing we both still wore.

Death made a noise deep in his throat and his lips moved from my mouth to my neck, trailing kisses down my throat, over my collarbone, to my chest. His hands moved to the zipper on my shirt, releasing me as he leaned me back against the counter. His lips never left my body as he stripped off my top. His hand moved to the thin silver chain holding the fae perception charm and started to lift it over my head.

"Not that," I said, gasping.

He looked up. "I can See you, Alex. It won't change anything."

But it did for me. As soon as he removed the charm and set it on the counter, my skin turned luminescent. My pale glow was a strong contrast to his tanned flesh. He smiled at me.

"Just as beautiful," he whispered, running a finger down the length of my torso. Then his mouth was on my body again, making me forget all about my strange glow.

His tongue circled one nipple, making it pebble under his attention. Small sounds escaped me. His mouth caressed me on more than a skin level and the tightness building low in my body, in places he hadn't even touched yet, increased. He pulled back slightly and blew gently on the skin his tongue had moistened. I shivered in pleasure at the contrasting sensation, and squirmed, pressing myself against the hardness I could feel through his jeans.

We needed less clothing. Now.

I started to push myself up, but Death caught me, kept me from moving. His gazed up the length of my body to watch me as his lips moved over my breasts. I was lost in pleasure and the kaleidoscope of his eyes. I writhed under him. When he straightened he was panting almost as hard as I was.

This time when I struggled back up to a sitting position, he let me. I ran my hand through that downlike hair on his chest, feeling his muscles quiver under my touch. I used the slightest bit of nail, and his skin broke out in gooseflesh. I smiled. My hands traveled downward, toward the button of his jeans.

He grabbed my wrists, halting me. "Are you sure?"

Oh, I was more than sure.

I let him see my desire, my need. But that wasn't all he wanted. I could read it in his face. He knew me, perhaps too well. We'd both danced around this attraction for a long time. It never occurred to me he was as afraid as I was that if things changed we'd risk the relationship we shared.

"I won't run tomorrow, my word on it."

He watched me with those multicolored eyes for several seconds. Then he released my wrists and his hands moved to cup my face, his lips taking mine, a wave of pleasure cascading from my lips to much deeper places as his soul touched mine. His hands slid over my shoulders, along my torso, pausing briefly to torment me with need as his thumb circled my nipples. Then he moved to the button of my hip-huggers.

"Hey, that was my idea." I said the words directly into his lips and felt him smile.

"I got to it first."

Which led to a race to see who could get the other's clothes off faster. I should have won—gravity was on my side. But he was stronger, lifting me easily, which not only helped him with my hip-huggers, but pulled me away from his jeans.

I resorted to cheating. Sliding from the counter, I went down on my knees, dragging his jeans to his ankles. All that was left were a pair of black boxer briefs his body strained against. I happily freed him.

I took him in my hand, and ran my fingers down the velvety softness covering all that hard heat. Above me, Death shuddered. I smiled. Then I ran my tongue in a circle over the tip of him, tasting his saltiness.

"Alex."

I looked up, meeting his gaze as I took as much of him into my mouth as I comfortably could. His eyelids fluttered, his chest hitching as his breath caught, but he didn't look away as I slid down him. My hands moved to his thighs and then trailed up to his ass. Every part of him was toned, perfect. And there wasn't a tan line in sight. I let my mouth move tortuously slow, swirling my tongue around the head of him as I reached the end. Then in that same smooth glide, I slid down his length again.

"Alex," he said again, his voice hoarse, as he grabbed my shoulders. He pulled me up. "Not the first time. I want to be buried in your body."

He lifted me back on the edge of the counter.

"I own a bed."

"We'll use the bed next time," he said, and slid two fingers inside me. "So wet but still so tight," he murmured.

I forgot all about the bed.

He moved agonizingly slow. Teasing, sweet torture. I gripped his shoulders as the warmth built in my center. My breathing turned erratic. Sounds escaped my throat.

The orgasm hit hard. Fast. My head fell back as every nerve ending flooded with sensation. Exploded in pleasure.

Death's mouth covered mine and claimed my scream. He scooped me into his arms. The cool wall met my back, Death supporting my weight as the head of him pressed against me, into me. Even as ready as I was, it was a tight fit.

He slid in slow. Each inch sending ripples through me that mixed a bit of pain with exquisite pleasure. I writhed in his arms. He slid in the last inch, our bodies meeting.

I locked my legs around his waist as he began to move. He was gentle until his body could glide in mine; then his rhythm changed, sped up and he thrust harder. Every movement made things inside me tighten. My body clenched hard. His pace changed again.

I came screaming, my hands moving to the wall so I didn't claw Death's back. His rhythm faltered and he drove himself into me one last time, hard. The feel of his orgasm threatened to bring me again.

He leaned into me. We both breathed heavy, riding the aftershocks. I was caught between him and the wall, my legs curled around his waist, and I could feel his pulse pounding, matching mine. His fast breaths tickled my neck and I reached up, moving damp locks from his face. Death pulled back enough to smile at me, and the amount of emotion in his eyes was enough to scare me. He didn't give me time to dwell on it, but kissed the last of my breath away. Then without letting go of me, he moved away from the wall, carrying me.

He didn't lie. We moved to the bed next.

Later we lay with our legs in a tangle, happily exhausted. Death ran his hand along my hip, touching just because he could.

"Alex?"

"Mmm?" I was close to sleep. I'd skipped most of the hours of the night before, but it had still been at least twenty-four hours since I'd last slept and they'd been long, busy hours.

"Remember what you promised me?"

"No running," I murmured as a yawn made my jaw crack.

I felt more than saw him nod. "No running." He wrapped an arm around me, moving us closer together. "I love you." He whispered the words as if he wasn't sure he wanted me to hear them.

I stopped breathing. From the tension in his arm, I knew he felt the change. I wished I could have hidden the reaction; if I'd had warning, I might have been able to. It wasn't even the confession that made me react — I'd heard him say as much when I was dying under the Blood Moon months ago. I'd known. I'd pretended I didn't. But I'd known.

No, what made me react was the fact I'd heard those very same words from another man in the last twenty-four hours. At least Death didn't pull daggers on me after saying them.

As if he knew where my thoughts had traveled, Death pulled me even closer, and in a low, quiet voice said, "And I think you should toss that *other* toothbrush."

Chapter 36

A loud banging woke me, pulling me out of my first nightmare-less sleep in months. I felt Death's warm chest under my cheek and, remembering the night before, a blush burned up my throat and into my face.

"Morning," he said, his voice rough with sleep. Clearly he'd been as rudely awakened as I had.

"Hi." The heat still burned my cheeks, and I wanted to look away, but I couldn't tear my eyes off Death. I'd never seen him look anything but perfect, so seeing him in my bed, his hair mussed from sleep, those deep eyes only half open, he looked so . . . real. It was cute.

With a move almost too fast to follow, Death rolled us so that he pinned me down with his body. I gasped, and his mouth suddenly covered mine. The knock sounded again and Death broke off the kiss to glance over his shoulder.

"Think they'll go away?"

"Probably not. Let me up."

He twisted his head, cocking an eyebrow over one handsome eye. "You're a little pink there, Alex. Not going to risk forswearing yourself, are you?"

"I'm not running," I said, not sure if I should be insulted or not. But he was smiling and I found myself responding with the same expression. *Damn, it's hard to be mad at the man.*

"Well, in that case . . ." He rolled again, taking me with him so I ended up straddling his hips. "This is a rather nice view."

He reached up, running his thumbs along the undersides of my breasts and my skin tightened in response. I was sore from last night, but it was a good kind of sore, and I could feel he was not in the least bit displeased to be where he was.

Another bang sounded on the door.

I twisted, sending my door a glare that should have melted it on the spot. PC whined at the foot of the bed, as if complaining about me not answering the door. I sighed and extricated myself from Death's arms. Which took a hell of a lot of willpower and yet another banging knock at the door.

"Geez, I'm coming," I muttered as I stalked across the room looking for something to wear. I spotted my robe and shrugged into it.

"Your charm, Alex," Death called from where he'd propped himself up on one arm on the bed.

Right, I'd actually gotten used to the pale glow, especially since it was barely noticeable in the light streaming in through the windows. But barely wasn't "unnoticeable" so I slipped the perception charm over my head.

I jerked open the door, ready to give whoever was on the other side an earful—until I saw the gaunt figure with long brown hair and deep sunken eyes.

"Tamara?"

She gripped a coat closed around her despite the warm morning air. I'd seen her wear it in the morgue only a few days earlier and it had fit fine. Now the coat swallowed her frame.

"Something's wrong," she said, her voice raw, as if she'd been crying, but her eyes were dry. She lumbered through the doorway, her movements strained and jerky, like a badly controlled marionette. "You said you got the—" She cut off as her eyes landed on the man in my bed.

"Oh, you have company." Her voice was completely flat. She turned to Death. "Sorry to break up your morning, but I need Alex now. She won't call, she doesn't do second dates, and she won't remember your name next month, so you don't really need a long good-bye."

My eyes bulged. "Tamara."

She turned. "What? It's true."

"He's not random," I hissed under my breath, and her pale lips formed a small "O" before she turned and gave him an appraising glance.

"He's also not you-know-who," she whispered, shielding her mouth with her hand.

"I can hear you," Death said as he sat up and stretched. "I assume you're not coming back to bed?"

Damn, I wish I were. I shook my head. He sighed and climbed out of the bed, gathering the sheets around him as he moved. He kissed the top of my head as he passed me on the way to the bathroom. My eyes followed him, taking a more than appreciatively long study of his broad shoulders and muscled back that tapered down to a very nicely defined ass that the sheet did little to disguise.

I wasn't the only one staring.

"Remind me I have a fiancé."

"Stop ogling my—" I cut myself off and Tamara whirled around.

"Were you about to say boyfriend?" She grinned, which with her gaunt cheeks was a rather ghastly expression. "I want details. Dish."

I'd actually been about to say my Death, but I wasn't going to tell her that. Or talk about him. Besides, there was a far more pressing issue.

"What happened? I know we destroyed Larid. Trust me, I got a good look at him." Way too close of a look.

"Well, something went wrong." Tamara let the coat fall open. Her clothes hung off her emaciated body. "I know every bride wants to lose a little weight before the wedding, but this isn't exactly what I planned."

I chewed at my bottom lip, staring at the way the skin sank into the hollows between her sternum and ribs. It was like she'd burned off all the fat in her body in a single day. It would start eating her muscles next—if it wasn't already. *And what about the baby?* I was too afraid to ask, but I saw the haunted look in her eyes that was for more than herself.

We'd killed the ghoul. I'd been under Larid when the creature went up in flames. Why was she still turning?

"And then, well, see for yourself." She opened her mouth, peeling back her lips. Her teeth were slightly pointed. Not yet full-on ghoul-like, but definitely changing.

"Damn. Wait here, okay?" I hurried around her and tapped twice on the bathroom door before bursting through it.

Steam rolled out of the shower as Death stuck his head around the curtain, water streaming from his hair and over his broad shoulders. "Here to offer to wash my back?" he asked, dark eyes twinkling.

"This is serious. Can you see Tamara's timeline?"

Death frowned, the flirtatious glow leaving his face. "She's not one of my souls."

"Well, can you find her collector? I need to know how much time she has before she turns ghoul."

"Alex, you're not even supposed to know about the fact we can see time fluxes."

I wasn't above indebting myself over this one, but before I could shape more than the *pl* in "please," Death held up a hand.

"I've watched several of these things form. Based on how fast she's progressing, she has less than a day left. In a couple of hours, the changes will be irreversible."

Hours?

"How do I stop it? We killed the ghoul. I—"

"Love, if we're going to continue this conversation, either join me in here, pass me a towel, or let me finish and I'll be out in a minute."

I left him to his shower. When I stepped back into the main room of my apartment, I found Tamara collapsed in the only chair I owned, her head buried in her arms on the short bar. She looked up when she heard me, and her pale lips tugged downward.

"By your grim look I take it that wasn't a quickie in the shower."

I tried to smile, to make my face more reassuring but the word "hours" echoed in my head. "Let me see your arm?"

She nodded, sliding out of the coat. She'd covered the stitches with a gauze infused with a healing charm. And not an over the counter OMIH issued bandage either, but one of her own creation that was probably a hell of a lot more potent. Unfortunately, it wasn't working on this particular wound.

"Damn," I whispered, looking at the blackness that crept like rot around the edges of the sutures.

Tamara glanced at her arm, a puzzled look crossing her face. "Of all things going wrong, the wounds not healing as fast as expected is the least of my concerns."

"Not—" A thought occurred to me. "They don't look black to you?"

"Uh, no. Alex, you just went pale. What?"

I didn't answer but cracked my shields. I'd seen the patch of darkness bleeding over into reality, but once I opened my shields I saw thinner black lines snaking completely through Tamara's body, her very soul, as if the rot had entered her blood and now filled every vein. I thought I caught sight of a twisting cord leading up, out of the wound, but there were too many different layers of reality to keep one thread in sight. I opened my shields wider. Before the raver had moved us through the collector's plane, she'd forced me to narrow my focus on one reality. I'd done that by watching only the souls. Well, I could see the yellow glow of Tamara's soul just fine; what I needed to see more clearly was the darkness.

I focused all my attention on that darkness and the room around me decayed as wind whipped through my apartment, blowing the mail off the counter and ripping free cards usually held to the fridge with magnets. PC yipped, a high-pitched, nervous sound, and vanished under the bed.

But the other realities dimmed and the thread jumped into stark relief. From everything I knew about ghouls, they were connected in single chains. The prime was on top, and then like family lines, those infected by a ghoul were tied to that ghoul—or ghouls as was sometimes the case when a person was attacked by more than one. Kill the ghoul directly above on the chain and everything under them broke. Ghouls died and those infected were no longer in danger of turning.

Except Larid was dead and Tamara was still tied to the land of the dead by a thread.

Actually, it wasn't a single thread. There were three dark lines. One had a jagged, twisted end, clearly severed. *Larid.* That had to have been the link to him. The next was thin and spindled off, deeper into the land of the dead. *The bridge to the ghoul waiting to take her body.* Which left the final cord. It was thick, glutted with Tamara's draining vitality, but it didn't fade into the depths of the land of the dead like the other. Instead it snaked out of the room, leading . . . somewhere. To the rider? *It's feeding off the bodies its ghouls create?*

If each ghoul had a second link back to the prime, that could explain why Briar was having so much trouble clearing the cemeteries. The chains didn't break. It also explained why cutting the link with Larid didn't stop Tamara from turning.

"Alex?" Tamara's voice trembled and she stumbled back as I stepped forward.

"I can see it," I said. "If I can sever it . . ." I retrieved my dagger from where it sat in its sheath on the dresser. The dagger had cut through a soul chain once, hopefully it could cut these threads as well.

Tamara's tired eyes widened as I approached, but she didn't move. I reached out, grabbing for the threads, but my hands passed through the darkness as if it were a shadow and not a feeding tube draining my friend. *I need to be deeper.*

I let my mind cross farther over the chasm. My apartment crumbled around me, but the threads solidified. I tried again, both with my bare hand and with the dagger. I nicked the tube, making it ooze gaseous drops of darkness. *How much deeper into the land of the dead can I reach?* I was close, I just needed to push a little farther. I let myself drift in the tempest.

Barely tangible arms wrapped around my waist in a ghostlike embrace.

"Come back," a distant but familiar voice whispered. *Death.* "Alex, I need you to come back."

I looked at the threads I was so close to reaching, but the desperation in his voice tugged at me. I drew back, pulling my psyche out of the spreading wasteland until I could see the ruins of my apartment, and then the apartment whole once more as I crossed the chasm.

Death's arms around my waist solidified as reality settled around me again, but they were cold, a slight tremor running through them. I twisted in his arms. He was pale under his tan, his breathing labored; water streamed from his hair, dripping onto my shoulder as if he'd rushed out of the bathroom—though at least he had on a pair of jeans.

"Are you okay?" I asked.

His arms around me tightened, the tremors already passing, and he nodded. "I will be. Alex, please don't take my essence to planes where my soul can't reach it." The last was a whisper for my ears only.

Take?

"Alex?" Tamara's voice was thin, high, and tainted with fear. "What was that? You were less substantial than the shades you raise."

Crap. I forgot I wasn't actually a corporeal being. My psyche kept me grounded in reality, but when I'd reached into the land of the dead, I'd sent my psyche there.

And I'd nearly killed Death in the process.

Chapter 37

Death looked a little better after food and coffee. Tamara not so much.

I needed to learn what had happened to the rider. Briar Darque hadn't known last night, but I hoped she would have learned something by now.

"Good timing, Craft," she said. The sound of a radio and wind contending with her voice betrayed the fact she was driving. "I was headed your way. Have you seen your friend?"

An icy warning slid down my spine, chilling me. "Which friend?"

"The medical examiner, Tamara Greene. She's not at work or at home."

I glanced at where Tamara was fidgeting more than eating her toast—I didn't have a lot in the house in the way of food, big surprise. Then I pointedly turned around so I couldn't *see* her. Just in case.

I shrugged and in as an off-handed tone as possible said, "She's probably having breakfast somewhere."

"Her husband thought she might have gone to see you."

Thanks, Ethan. "He's her fiancé, actually."

"Yeah, whatever. If you see her, let me know."

"What's going on?"

"The OMIH agent who went to the hospital yesterday? The nurse called me this morning. He'd dropped sixty pounds and grown talons. I had to ensure he didn't turn ghoul in the middle of the surgical ward."

The toast soured in my stomach. *As in she killed him.* I forced myself not to turn and look at Tamara's drained figure.

Briar was still talking, though my brain didn't want to accept her words. "Your friend wasn't as badly hurt, but I've got to find her before she turns. Damn, I really thought we got the ghoul."

"We did. I recognized Larid."

"We couldn't have. Ghouls are linked."

Yeah, that was the standing assumption. The problem was that it didn't apply in this case. Not that I could tell her how I knew that fact. "Have you ever hunted ghouls created by something from the wastes in the land of the dead?"

Briar was silent as she considered the possibility.

"Did you find out if they contained the rider before they released the body from the circle?"

"They didn't. Fuck. So that thing is out there. I've never seen anyone ghoul out as fast as that official. If it's because of that rider thing, we could be in a hell of a lot of trouble."

Understatement.

"I'm pretty sure it can't get far outside of a body. Do you know if anyone who came in contact with Larid was acting strange yesterday?"

"Why would I know that?"

"Well, if we're going to find the rider, you're going to have to ask around because the people at the OMIH won't talk to me. You're looking for someone who most likely didn't respond to their own name and would have made some excuse to leave early. They wouldn't have gone home last night and won't be at work today."

"That's pretty specific, Craft."

"I've been tracking the rider. It's predictable," I said, and hoped that the rider was holding true to pattern. Of course, it was a Sunday, so the possessed victim might not be missed yet. "Once you talk to the folks over at the OMIH, will you call and let me know what you learn?"

"Why?" The suspicion was so thick in her voice I could feel it through the phone.

"Well, for starters, if it is hurting my friend, I have a vested interest. I also have two clients who I already told we'd captured their husbands' murderer and I'd rather not have to inform them it escaped."

"Fine. If I find out anything and I have time, I'll call, but you need to let me know if your friend shows up."

"Right." As Tamara was already here, "showing up" wasn't an issue.

Briar hung up without saying good-bye.

"Do I want to know?" Tamara asked as I turned around.

"Probably not," I said and tried to convince myself some of her grayish pallor was just my eyes recovering from my stepping into the land of the dead. But the color had returned to everything except Tamara. I could practically see her fading in front of me. *The change can't happen that fast.*

I glanced at Death. He shook his head but I didn't know if he was telling me there was nothing he could do to help or just confirming that Tamara wasn't holding up well. He'd told me we had only hours. We'd lost what, thirty minutes of that?

I shoved the phone in my back pocket and paced across my kitchenette. I'd dressed while the coffee was brewing so my boots made dull thudding noises that accented the helpless feeling vibrating through me. There had to be something more I could do besides wait for Briar to call.

I might be able to trace that feeding tube of a thread back to the rider, but I'd have to be halfway across the chasm while tracing it who-knew-where in the city. Even if I could manage the mobility and not get beaten to a pulp by grave essence while leaving my psyche that open outside wards or a circle, I had no idea if Death could survive me taking his essence halfway across the chasm for who-knew-how-long. *Well, I guess I won't be going to Faerie anytime soon.* Or possibly ever. Death's plane didn't exist there, which meant it was a no go.

My head snapped up and I stopped pacing, one foot hanging in the air before falling hard, the step forgotten. The land of the dead didn't exist in Faerie either. If Death couldn't reach his essence through a plane where he didn't exist then it stood to reason the rider's threads wouldn't pass into a place where the land of the dead didn't touch.

It was a stall tactic, but it would give us time. I looked at Tamara. "We have to take you to Faerie."

Four eyes, two hazel and two dark brown, looked at me with equal amounts of confusion. Yeah, I guess that comment came from nowhere if you weren't inside my head. I explained my logic. Death gave a begrudging nod as I spelled out my thoughts, but Tamara's sunken eyes rounded until they dominated her face.

"I know you stumbled into a pocket of Faerie once, but even if we could get back there, would I be any better off or just in a different kind of danger?" Tamara asked, pushing her uneaten toast aside.

Crap. We were going to have to have the Faerie discussion. I really didn't want to have that conversation, but the more I thought about it, the more convinced I was that she'd stop transforming as soon as she was in Faerie. Slivers of the land of the dead slipped into the Bloom, so she'd have to go to Faerie proper.

Pulling out my phone, I tried Rianna's cell. She had no reason to leave Faerie today, so I wasn't surprised when an operator announced that the customer I was trying to reach was out of range. Faerie didn't have cell towers.

"We need to talk to Caleb," I said, heading to the door that connected my apartment with the main portion of the house. I also effectively avoided having to discuss the "F" issue for a couple more minutes.

Tamara stood slowly, as if she were trying to haul six hundred pounds instead of her skeletally thin form. I chewed at my bottom lip as I watched her dragging steps.

Faerie will work. We just had to get her there. An added bonus? No way would Briar find Tamara in Faerie.

Death moved to follow.

I stopped him with a hand on his arm. "Would you wait for me here?"

"Embarrassed to be seen with me?"

"It's not that. We need to get Tamara to Faerie pronto, which means getting everyone moving with as little explanation as possible." And explaining who Death was—especially since I didn't have a name to introduce him with—would slow everything down. Tamara was so ill she'd accepted my explanation that he was an old friend without further prying, but Holly would press me.

He studied me, and I had the feeling he saw more than I liked. I squirmed. He knew me too well, and I could feel his gaze peeling back layers. Then he leaned forward and kissed the top of my head. "Just make sure you're being honest with yourself in your reasoning."

I watched him walk back into my apartment. I really was just in a hurry, wasn't I? I was fine with my friends meeting him. Just not right now. Right?

I didn't have time to think about it as I hurried to catch up with Tamara. We reached the bottom of the stairs and I pushed open the door. "Caleb?"

It was still fairly early, but he usually started working in his studio earlier than I preferred waking—which was one reason the studio ceiling had a soundproofing charm. But the garage-turned-studio was dark. Today apparently wasn't an early day.

"Hello? Caleb? Holly? Anyone home?"

I glanced out the front window. Both of their cars were here. I headed for the back of the house. I hated waking Caleb, but as I couldn't enter Faerie without cutting Death off from his life essence, Caleb was the only person who could take Tamara.

As Tamara and I turned the corner into the back hall, Caleb's door opened, but it wasn't Caleb who stepped out.

Holly, wearing one of Caleb's shirts and nothing else, froze.

For a moment no one said anything. And then Tamara shook her head and muttered, "It's like walking into a den of bunnies around here."

That effectively broke the shocked silence.

"Uh, good morning?" Holly said, holding the button-up shirt closed with one hand, her other smoothing her tousled hair. She smiled, but the expression was a cringing flash of teeth as her eyes darted toward the elusive safety of her own bedroom door farther down the hall.

Oh yeah, it wasn't the air of the revelry; my housemates were definitely sleeping together. This could get awkward. *Unless I ignore the entire situation.*

"I'm going to be in the living room. Can you see if Caleb's awake?"

Holly glanced back at the room she'd been trying to sneak out of. "I'm sure he'll be there in a minute."

It was more like five minutes, but both he and Holly were fully dressed when they joined us. Holly may have been too shocked or embarrassed to notice Tamara's condition a few minutes earlier, but she didn't miss it now.

I gave as quick and condensed a version of events and my plans as possible. When I finished, no one looked terribly convinced.

"Where am I supposed to take her in Faerie?" Caleb asked.

I had an answer to that, I just didn't like it. "I own some . . . property, in Faerie." And by property I meant a castle, but that was beside the point.

The admission earned an eyebrow lift from Caleb and a "You what?" from Holly.

Tamara shook her head, "What is going on? Why would you own property in Faerie? Hell, how would you own property?"

Cards on the table time. I pulled the charm free of my shirt and lifted the chain over my head. "I, uh, well, you see," I said as my skin gave off its own light.

Tamara blinked. "You're fae?" She leaned back against the couch. "And I thought I was the one keeping secrets." She placed a hand over her too thin stomach. Then she turned to Holly. "Alex figured it out already, but I'm pregnant. Or I was. Do you think . . . ?" Her eyes shimmered with tears ready to spill over.

I bit my lips. Tamara was the one with the medical degree; if anyone knew, it would be her. Holly pushed out of her chair and joined Tamara on the couch. She wrapped her arms around the other woman.

"It's going to work out," she said, hugging Tamara. "We'll find this rider thing on this side, and you'll be safe in Faerie."

"How could I possibly be safe in Faerie?" A tear slipped down her cheek. "No offense," she said, nodding to Caleb and then as if an afterthought, to me. "How can you be fae?"

"It's a long story that we don't have time for."

Holly gave Tamara a squeeze. "As we're all confessing our secrets, the reason I've been a little weird lately? I kind of got addicted to Faerie food."

Tamara gave a start, and fear pooled in her sunken eyes, dragged at her lips so that they twitched.

Holly just held her. "Don't worry. Faerie is actually really very nice. Just don't eat the food. It looks good, but it's made out of toadstools." She stuck out her tongue, making it sound like a joke.

Caleb pushed out of his chair. "Okay, the share-fest you girls have going on is great, but I think we need an actual plan. Al, if you own the property, why don't you take Tamara? I don't know where your property is."

"I can't go to Faerie without potentially deadly consequences. I can't even enter the Bloom right now."

Anyone human would have questioned me, but Caleb was fae and there had been no wiggle room in my statement. "Okay. I'm assuming you inherited something that is currently in Limbo?"

I nodded. "Get a message to Rianna. She can take Tamara the rest of the way." Once he was in the Bloom, the bartender would be able to pass along the message. I still wasn't sure how it worked, but Rianna usually appeared about five minutes after I let the bartender know I was looking for her.

Caleb nodded and looked down at Tamara's miserable form where she leaned against Holly, silent tears streaming down her cheeks.

"Ready?"

Tamara looked up. "This is really the only way?"

"It's the best I can come up with," I said. "But it's only a stall tactic. It won't cure you but it should stop the transformation. It will give you a little time to rest as well. There's a brownie named Ms. B who runs my property, let her know you're my friend, and that you're human so can't eat Faerie food."

"I'll pack you a care package," Holly said, pushing off the couch. She disappeared into the kitchen and the sound of drawers and cabinets opening followed. With Holly eating all her meals at the Bloom and Caleb eating at least half of his there, I wondered how much food they actually had around the house.

I slid my necklace back over my head, letting the charm fall under my shirt and between my breasts. The glow cut off abruptly, at least to me. Tamara just stared.

"Why are you still all shimmery?"

Great. "It's a fae perception charm. People see what they believe they'll see." Which meant she now saw me as fae. *Will that change our friendship?* I cringed inwardly, but before I started worrying about what might happen, I needed to find the rider or she'd either be a ghoul or stuck in Faerie. I turned to Caleb. "Can you ask Rianna to meet me at the Tongues for the Dead office once she gets Tamara situated?"

He nodded, and we both looked at Tamara, who had curled in on herself. She looked so small and deflated that she barely resembled the strong, take-charge woman I knew.

"We're going to stop the rider," I said, wishing I had

something more reassuring to say. "You just take care of yourself." I almost added *and the baby* but I was afraid she'd break down again.

"What do I tell Ethan? We promised never to lie to each other or to keep secrets. But I'm thinking saying 'Sweetie, I'm turning into a monster, so I'm going to hide at Alex's place in Faerie until the bad guy is caught' won't go over well."

I was so not the person to ask about relationship issues. "Tell him what you have to?"

She sighed, fumbling with her phone but not making the call.

"I'd wait until you're almost to the Bloom though— Briar is looking for you, and you don't want her to find you."

"Right." She shoved the phone in her pocket without hesitation. That clearly wasn't a call she wanted to make. I didn't blame her.

"This should do it," Holly said as she reentered the room with two reusable grocery sacks filled with boxes and cans. "I threw in a couple of paperbacks and my supersecret stash of chocolate, so you should be set until we can get this straightened out."

Despite Holly's perky optimism, Tamara didn't look the least bit cheered. Caleb helped her to her feet and we made quick good-byes. The door had barely clicked closed when Holly whirled around, all the softness gone from her face.

"What can I do to help?"

"I don't know yet. I'm sure someone from the OMIH headquarters was infected, so unless the rider has already killed that host and moved on, we need to figure out who on the staff is missing or has been acting erratically. Or we need to figure out where the rider is most likely to go next." Assuming it wasn't planning to come after me again, but after everything that had happened, I guessed it would be trying to keep a low profile. Which would make it harder to find.

If the rider had killed off its latest victim, one of the collectors would know. Maybe they'd know who it had taken next. Of course, convincing the gray man or the raver to help would be quite a trick. *Death may be able to persuade them.* Thinking about Death, I glanced toward the stairs. Tamara was safely on her way to Faerie now, which meant no more excuses. I took a deep breath.

"Uh, Holly," I said, and then had to stop because my tongue was paralyzed, stuck to the roof of my mouth. She gave me a questioning head tilt. I swallowed and straightened. "There's someone I'd like you to meet."

Chapter 38

◆━━◆ ◉ ◆━━◆

Several hours later, Rianna, Holly, Caleb, and I were in the Tongues for the Dead office, searching for any clue to where and in whom the rider may be. Holly had used her contacts in the DA's office to get access to the missing persons database, but no one had been reported missing in the last twenty-four hours. I'd left at least four messages on Briar's voice mail, but she hadn't returned my calls, so I had no idea if she'd learned anything. Death had left to see what he could find through his own networks, which, when he eventually returned, he may or may not be able to share.

Introducing him to Holly and then Caleb had been interesting to say the least, especially when we got to the part of *no, sorry, you can't ask his name* and *no, you can't ask what he does either*. Awkward was an understatement. Though, watching Rianna's reaction was rather entertaining as she'd seen Death before and knew exactly what he was. Roy was far less amused that I had a soul collector with me, but when I sent him to the OMIH office to eavesdrop and snoop, he was so happy to have what he called a *real* assignment that he let it slide.

"No, that's okay. Have a nice day," I said, and hit the END button on my phone. I scratched through the name and then stretched. "That was the last one on my list."

Holly looked up. "You want some of mine?"

Yeah, no, not really. We'd spent the last hour and a half cold calling the OMIH employees listed on the local Web site. We were look looking for someone who hadn't come home last night, but there were several problems with this plan, primarily that half the calls weren't answered so had to be noted as question marks.

"Hey, girls," Caleb called from where he worked at Ms. B's desk. "I have good news and bad news. You might want to come here."

Holly and I exchanged a glance, but as I stood, Roy popped into the room.

"I found him," he said, vibrating with excitement. "His name is Martin Tanner and he's a magical technician. He helped scan the room after Larid died, and soon after became *ill.*" Roy used finger quotes around the last word. "That's got to be him, right?"

I'd bet on the chance.

I walked out into the lobby. "Roy might have found our guy. His name is—"

"Martin Tanner," Caleb finished for me.

The ghost's shoulders dropped. "Wow, way to steal my glory."

I was more curious how Caleb had found out. He turned the screen of the laptop toward me and bumped the volume.

"Police say Tanner is considered armed and dangerous, so if you spot him, do not try to approach him. Instead, call the tip line at the bottom of the screen," the news anchor said as a phone number flashed below him. The superimposed image of a middle-aged man with a cheap hair regrowth charm and thick framed glasses floated behind the anchor.

"Of all the idiotic, stupid things to do." I pulled out my phone, and dialed the fourth number on my speed dial.

A gruff voice answered with, "If you're calling to bitch, I was against it." John sighed and I heard something hit the mouthpiece of the phone as if his knuckles brushed it as he rubbed his mustache. "No one in the squad room three nights ago would have okayed that press release."

"Then who did?"

"The chief of police and that MCIB investigator thought it would chase the rider out of hiding."

Briar Darque. Great. She sure kept me in the loop.

"Yeah, he'll come out of hiding." I stalked across the office. "By walking into traffic or in some other horrific way murdering his host so he can have a new body." I knew John already realized that as well, but the anger bubbling in my blood refused to shut up. A warm arm wrapped around my waist, stopping me from stomping into my office. Death. "John, I've got to go," I said, making a hasty good-bye.

"Anything?" I asked, looking at Death expectantly.

"It sounds like you know more than me."

Damn. "It looks like our current victim, who is being smeared on the news as armed and dangerous, is a magic tech named Martin Tanner. Caleb, do they have a picture of him posted on their site?"

Caleb clicked a button and what was either a driver's license or work ID photo—both tended to be equally bad—popped up of the mild-looking tech. Death frowned at the image but I thought I saw something akin to recognition pass through his eyes.

I dragged him into my office, shutting the door behind us. "You know him?"

"Alex, I have a lot of souls, most of whom don't come close enough to dying that I'm called to them more than a couple of times during their life." He leaned against the edge of my desk, crossing his arms over his broad chest.

"But you think you recognize him."

He lifted one shoulder in a half shrug that could have meant anything. "Even if he is one of mine, it's not like I'm omnipresent. I can't find him out of thousands any easier than you can, not until I'm called."

"You always find me."

That earned me a grin, and he reached out, pulling me closer. "I keep an eye on you." His hands ran down my waist until his thumbs rubbed over the ridges of my hip bones. "Besides, you are easy to find." The words were low, his mouth temptingly close to mine.

I sucked in a breath, my body becoming hyperaware so that the heat from his hands spread through me. But this wasn't the time or the place. I had one friend waiting in Faerie, almost everyone else I cared about outside the door, and a gluttonous creature from the land of the dead out there who was likely to kill as soon as he realized he was wearing a wanted man. *Definitely not the time.* I stepped back, out of Death's hands.

He started to follow me, a teasing glint in those hazel eyes. Then he froze. I saw the colors dance in his iris and knew he was seeing threads of possibility in someone's life. His brow creased in something that mixed sorrow with anger.

"I found him."

"Tell me I'm allowed to interfere. The rider is definitely not part of the normal mortal world."

"I only see one possible end for this soul."

Yeah, well I have to try. I darted across the room and threw open the door. I ran passed a shocked-looking Caleb and Holly to Rianna's office. She sat in the center of a circle drawn in the corner of her room. Desmond, in his doglike form once more, sat in front of the circle as if guarding her. Even through my shields, with the amount of magic Rianna was actively wielding, she glowed a slight purple from Aetheric energy.

"Is it ready?"

She looked up. "Almost."

I doubted almost was soon enough. We hadn't figured out how we were going to stop the rider yet, but if we could trap it in a body again, it would give us time to figure something out. Not much time. The rider had drained Larid in only two days. But a day or two was better than nothing. Unfortunately, Rianna and Holly both specialized in active casting, so creating a weaponized knockout potion was taking time.

Time we didn't have.

Death stepped into the room. "Alex, you're not going to be able to save this one. If you're coming, it has to be now."

Damn.

I knew he was right. I had no way to stop it from killing its current victim, but maybe I could stop it while it was between victims. *Or I could make it worse. Like I did at the restaurant.* But Death wasn't warning me off this time, he was taking me with him. I accepted his hand, and his cold magic washed over me.

The next moment we were on a street somewhere downtown.

"Where—?" I didn't finish the question, as Death dragged me flat against a building.

A body hit the pavement where we'd been standing the moment before. *There had never been a chance.* Maybe if we'd left when Death had first felt the call. My anger made hot tears lift to my eyes. I ignored them. It was too late for Martin. But maybe I could stop the rider from taking another victim.

The darkness rose from the body as people stopped, turning. There were screams, and I saw several cell phones appear. People drew nearer, even as they averted their eyes.

"Don't let go of my hand," Death said, drawing me far closer to the body than I wanted to be, but I could see the soul, knew it needed freeing.

I watched the miasma pouring out of the broken form. I'd tangled with the rider at its full strength before. I didn't want a rematch, not a fair one at least.

Unfair, well, I wasn't above that.

Reaching out with my ability to touch the dead, my senses brushed against the darkness and tried to shy away. I pushed, psychically reaching into the miasma. Roy had said that everything in the land of the dead was energy. Manipulating the energy from the grave was something I was very familiar with. Reaching into that forming mass, I tugged with my magic. The effect was the exact opposite of how I channeled energy into Roy. I drew energy from the rider, pulling that thick ugliness into my body. I'd done this once before, months ago—it was no better a second time around.

The rider poured out of the body, fast, definitely faster than I could drain it. Desperation vibrated along the energy I pulled. *Good.* I wanted it off balance. I forgot that desperate creatures were twice as dangerous. To escape me, it dove for the closest mortal.

Death.

No.

I pulled with everything I had, drawing hard with my magic. But it seeped into his body too fast, disappearing behind living skin that my magic couldn't penetrate.

Death went ridged, the soul of Martin Tanner still in his hand. Gritting his teeth, Death flicked his hand, sending the soul on. But the rider was inside him now, spreading.

"Alex, get out of here." Death fell to his knees, sweat breaking across his forehead as he struggled with the foreign invader. "I can feel this thing's hate for you. It will kill you."

"I won't let it have you." Though how the hell was I going to stop it? Inside a body it was beyond my reach.

Usually, at least. But I had a direct link to Death. He carried my life.

I dropped to my knees beside Death, my hand still in his, giving me an extra link to him as I opened my mind, sensing the connection between us.

"No," he said in a strained whisper. "Run. I can't fight it."

I didn't care. The rider was not going to use and discard Death.

I felt the darkness filling his body, but it was my life force it attached itself to. I tried to reach for that darkness.

I wasn't fast enough.

Death's head shot up, his hazel eyes turning oily black. The thing inside him smiled, the expression a defilement to Death's features.

"Hello, Craft. Look at us holding hands. Was this body important to you?" it asked as I jerked away.

A wave of dread and sickness washed over me, my blood turning thick with it. This couldn't be happening. It couldn't. "Why are you doing this?"

"Why? You're a grave witch, so you've seen my world. That desolate place where thirst is never quenched, where everything is dry dust. Dead. Decayed. So unlike your living world. This realm of decadence is marvelous." He spread Death's arms, as if embracing the world.

My disgust with the creature redoubled. It had killed how many people, had created how many ghouls, because it wanted to indulge in the living world? Well, Death wouldn't be the next victim to its hedonism. I wouldn't let it have him.

I was still trying to figure out how to reach the rider, to draw it out of Death. Which meant I had to keep it talking. "That's a crappy reason to kill people."

The thing snapped Death's gaze toward me, eyes dark. "Mortals die, but if you are so distressed, let me free you from your pain."

Death's hand shot out, crashing into my chest. Literally. His hand broke flesh and snapped bones. It wasn't fear that tightened around my heart, but Death's fingers.

The rider in Death's body jerked his hand, and my heart, free of my chest. Pain radiated through me, too much for my body and brain to process. I collapsed.

"Good-bye, Craft." The rider made Death's harmonic voice sound rough, hard. He dropped my heart in the grass beside me.

I stared at him. Not breathing. Not blinking. Waiting to die. Except I didn't. My body didn't even have the decency to lose consciousness.

Not that the rider noticed.

"This body," he said, stepping over me and holding up his hands, letting my blood drip down his arm. "How very different. I shall enjoy it."

The rider in Death's body walked away. I watched, unable to stop him. As I lost sight of Death in the growing crowd, my anger warred with crippling despair.

Anger won. The fury consuming me left no room for physical pain. I had to do something. Death was vulnerable only because he'd become mortal to save me. I couldn't let the rider have him.

With effort, I pushed away from the grass. People stared. Too many people. Too many witnesses. Not that I could do anything about them. But I had to get out of the area before the first responders arrived.

Moving was slow at first. Even with a nearly impervious body, it took time to figure out how to function without a heart. Precious time because every second Death's body traveled farther away. I couldn't see him, but I felt the growing distance from my life force.

I had no idea how long I'd lain near the dead man. It felt like hours but couldn't have been more than minutes. I did know one thing: the rider was gone, taking Death's body with him, and I had to find them. I had to eject the rider from Death. I even had an idea how—return Death's essence. No body left nothing for the rider to inhabit.

But first I needed to see a man about a heart and a soul.

Chapter 39

I felt like the tin man, off to see the wizard. Except I already had a heart. It was in my purse. The saddest thing about the whole situation? I had my heart in a Ziploc bag and that wasn't the worst part of my day.

I'll find him. But despite the fact I didn't currently have a heart, I ached as if I did.

It was early afternoon, so I wasn't sure the club where Death and I had found the raver would be open yet, but I lucked out. I had to pay the cover this time to get inside—no convenient teleporting for me—but it was open. The club was quieter this early in the day, so it wasn't hard to find the raver in the thin crowd. Or for her to spot me.

"Oh, I'm clearly going to have to find a new place to party," she said, shaking her head and making her dreads quiver.

"I'm pretty sure this is the only techno club in the city."

"So how about we say it's off limits to you," she said, her long fingernails making dull thud sounds as she tapped her bright PVC pants. Then she looked at me, really looked at me. "You don't look so hot, chick. What did you get into now?" She paused. "And why are you alone?"

"I got my heart ripped out."

"And he left you with his essence in you. Why—" She stopped. "Fuck, you're being literal."

"I'm guessing the mender will need it to fix me?" I held up the bag with the aforementioned organ.

The raver glanced at the plastic bag, her eyes rounding. "You are one weird chick. Well, come on, then."

A reassuring *thump* knocked in my chest as my flesh stopped rippling. The mender dropped his hand.

"You get into even worse trouble than I'd been warned," he said as my heart pounded out another beat and fell into a regular rhythm.

"I assure you, this was a first for me."

"Good to know. I have collectors who've been with me for decades and haven't received as much mending as you have in two days." He made a motion as if dusting off his hands. "I expect you not to make this a habit."

That wasn't going to be a problem. *I doubt I'll be returning.*

"Really, and why is that?"

Crap, I forgot he was telepathic. Well, now or never. "The last time I was here you gave me a message for"—I hesitated before referring to Death the way he and the raver did—"him."

The mender nodded again, waiting for me to continue.

"Well, he's not in a position to make a choice. I'm going to be forced to return his essence to save him."

"That is good. I value him as a collector. He has compassion for his souls but aside from recent transgressions, still does his job efficiently. That is not always the case."

I shook my head. "That's not where I'm going with this. The options you gave him, I need your word they are negated since he cannot make a choice."

"Child, he already made his decision. He could have exchanged your life essences the moment he got my message. By not doing so, he made the choice that left him vulnerable to his current predicament."

I shook my head again, and the look the mender gave me was one an elder might give a young child: sympathetic, but unwavering in resolve.

"No, I refuse to accept that to save his life I condemn his soul. I want another option."

"He knew the dangers when he made his choice."

My fists clenched at my sides. The mender's glance flickered to them, and I forced my fingers straight. "No. I can't accept that."

"Which is also a choice."

He said it so calmly, so assured in his position—I'd never wanted to hit someone so bad in my life. I was pretty sure this guy could give my father a run for his money.

"I can't make the decision to trap his soul for all eternity."

"Then you decide to let him die, and when he does, you likely will as well."

"Are you trying to frighten me?" Even as I asked I knew he was only stating the facts as he saw them. "Fine. You said you value him as a collector. Wouldn't you rather have him back than dead?"

His eyes softened as his face turned to that of an elder's again, his features full of sympathy. "Child, in all likelihood, you will not survive the trial ahead of you and he will choose to follow you before I have an opportunity to stop him. It is why they dislike you, you know. It isn't due to our laws—or because of the secrets he's revealed to you—that they resent you. No, don't think to deny it. I know what he has done and said." He took my hand and patted it gently. "They dislike you because they fear losing him when your time comes, as others who have loved mortals have done before. There used to be four in their little group, you know."

I guessed by "they" he meant the gray man and the raver. I glanced over my shoulder at the latter, who stood by herself on the other side of the garden, scowling at me.

I shook my head. We were getting sidetracked.

"You said likelihood, which means even if you see the

possibilities, you don't know the definite outcome. I may not die. Or if I do, he may not follow."

"You seem very calm about the possibility of your own death. That is rare in a mortal."

What was I supposed to say to that? It wasn't like I wanted to die. The idea scared the hell out of me. But I'd learned a long time ago that *everything* dies.

The mender nodded as if I'd said the thought aloud. Then we both stood there in silence for a moment, until he asked, "What is it you want from me? In the event either or both of you survive, I cannot allow you to continue to switch life essences."

"I understand that. All I'm asking for is your oath that when he's ready to move on, you free his soul."

"*All* you want is my oath?" The way he said it made it clear I'd insulted him.

"I meant no offense."

He laughed, catching me off guard. "You became very fae rather quickly."

Because I didn't apologize?

"There is that. And, yes, eventually you'll remember I'm telepathic but it won't help you not to think." He smiled, any insult either forgiven or forgotten. "But you also see the world differently now, don't you? As a fae your word is your oath, but a human's words are as fickle as a breeze without a sworn oath. You have no idea what I am or the value of my words."

I didn't deny it because he was right. I wanted a guarantee that I wasn't making a choice between Death's life and his soul.

"And if you had to, which would you choose?"

I didn't have to think about it. I already knew. "I'll fight to save his life, but in the end I'll choose to save his soul."

"Even though you know your own death is inevitable with that path, but you might survive the other? That both of you might survive?"

I'd answered that question already. There was nothing more I could say. I wanted to think I wouldn't damn Death's soul to save myself, but nothing I said now would prove that I'd sacrifice myself.

Even if there is a chance we could still be together if I returned his essence?

I wrapped my arms across my chest, hugging myself. It was a deceitful thought, and a selfish one. I was going to lose Death, one way or another. If I convinced the mender to release him from his ultimatum, then once I returned Death's essence, he would be a soul collector again—our relationship forbidden. And if the mender didn't agree ... then I'd fight the rider, but I wouldn't condemn Death to eternity as a soul collector.

The mender watched me for several moments before nodding. "You may deny the names of your emotions, but nothing is wrong with that heart I put back in your chest. I will offer my oath on the condition that you promise me a boon. He has broken many of our covenants. Do you feel the weight of debt you will incur if I grant your request that I reverse my decision?"

The possibility of debt opened between us. The enormity of it crushed the air out of my lungs, threatening to smother my newly repaired heart—and the debt hadn't even solidified yet. I gasped, trying to catch my breath. What could I possibly do for a being as powerful as the mender to pay off such a level of debt?

He took my hand, patting kindly. "Actions have consequences, and you've asked to take the cost of his consequences on yourself."

And by actions, the mender meant Death saving my life. If he'd been willing to pay such a price for me, I could do the same for him.

I nodded, rolling my shoulders back as I accepted the weight of that debt. "I promise a boon in exchange for the freedom of his soul."

"My oath then. If you both survive, he will be stripped of his ability to switch life essence but only until the time he is ready for his own soul to move on."

I measured his words. "And if only one of us survives?"

"Then one way or another, it will no longer be an issue, will it?"

No, I guess not.

I was still adjusting to the debt weighing down on me when he lifted a hand and the raver joined us.

"Good luck, child. You'll need it," he said. Then the appearance of an elder was gone, and with a younger, much less comforting face, he said, "I'll see you again."

Chapter 40

An hour later I was whole and back at Tongues for the Dead. And at a complete loss of how to proceed. I could feel Death, could close my eyes and point in the direction he was because my soul craved its essence, which he carried in his body.

But even though I could find Death, I'd never get close enough to him to return his essence without the rider either making another attempt at killing me, or worse, harming Death's body. We might be able to get close enough to douse him in the sleep tonic Rianna had created, but again, that took someone getting close.

The rider definitely knew me on sight. Rianna too. He hadn't seen Holly or Caleb, but they'd still have to get close to splash the potion on him. We needed a delivery method like Briar's foam bolts. *Or Briar herself.*

But asking her for help didn't seem like my best option. After all, she'd cut me out completely with Martin, and her decision to go public had caused the rider to dump the body. I couldn't let that happen with Death.

We also had to figure out what to do with the rider after I ejected it from Death. If I could get the rider into a circle it wouldn't be able to jump into any more bodies, but could I go one-on-one with the thing? It had ripped into my soul the first time we fought. The second time I'd managed to siphon some of its energy, but I doubted I could drain it faster than it could tear me to pieces.

"I might be able to help drain it," Rianna said from one of the armchairs in the lobby.

Holly and Caleb sat in the love seat, which left one chair for me, but I couldn't stay still. The rider wasn't only feeding on Death, he was sucking on my life essence, and I could feel the drain.

I shook my head at Rianna. "You can't make Roy manifest, so you probably can't drain the rider. Besides, if you were in the circle with me, you'd be a mortal body for it to jump into and I don't know how we'd get it back out."

Rianna frowned and Holly sat forward.

"Alex, that artifact the witch used when she was trying to merge the planes, do you still have it?"

"What's she talking about?" Rianna asked.

Rianna knew about Edana and her reaper, but I didn't talk about the artifact. It had been a set of panpipes when Edana had it, but once I'd picked it up, it had turned into a ring. As it was an artifact tied to the soul collectors and planeweaving, I hadn't turned it over to the police but slipped it on my finger until we left the scene.

"It's at the house, in my magic dampening box," I said once I explained what the artifact did.

Rianna's eyes brightened. "If it let the witch interact with collectors, it might let me interact with ghosts."

"She was fueling it with *souls*. The artifact is bad news."

"No, she was fueling her mega ritual with souls," Rianna said. "She was clearly interacting at least partially with other planes with the artifact alone. I could at least try it, see if I can figure it out."

I frowned. Working with magic you didn't understand was always bad. Working with relics you didn't understand? Worse.

"Just let me try."

"It's dangerous."

Rianna huffed. "And walking into a fight you have no chance of winning isn't?"

I had *some* chance, slim though it might be.

"It's a shame you can't shove the rider in a magic damp-ening box like you can an artifact," Holly said, leaning for-ward to balance her elbows on her knees so she could prop her head in her hands.

"Yeah." I stopped. "Wait. Can we?" I looked at Caleb. "You can build wards that can block grave essence and spir-its. Could you put a ward like that on something as small as a box? A ward that would activate as soon as the lid closed and trap the rider inside?"

Caleb's fingers twitched, as if he were working out the spells in his head. Slowly he nodded. "I think I know what would work, but how would you get the creature into the box?"

That was a problem.

We'd need some sort of spirit trap. Or a spell that could suck it inside. My hand moved to the shoulder where I'd once been infected with a soul sucking spell, and my thumb caught the thin chain of my necklace. I glanced at it and the thin glyph on the back that still showed specks of my blood.

Glyphs had been used in the soul sucking spell. And when I'd had them translated, one had been for a trap . . .

I looked at Rianna. "Do you know the glyphs Coleman used to trap souls in the body of his victims so his spell could consume them? Could some of those glyphs be mod-ified to trap something from the land of the dead?"

She buried her hand in Desmond's coat, which broadcast how uncomfortable the idea made her, but after a moment, she nodded. "I know a combination, but Al, I can't activate the glyphs."

I gripped my father's charm. "I can."

Or, at least, I hoped I could. It would take blood magic, but if my fae blood could save Death and stop the rider, it would be worth it.

"Okay, so Rianna, will you work with Caleb and carve the glyphs into the box so all I have to do is trace them?" I asked and they looked at each other before nodding.

"The box will have to be something sturdy," Caleb said. "Something that once closed can be locked."

Definitely.

"I still want to check out that artifact." Rianna held up a hand. "You're planning on walking in with an untested spelled box and glyphs you don't understand. Don't lecture me on using unknown magics. If I can't interact with your pet ghost, I'll give up on the idea."

"Hey, I heard that," Roy said, sticking his head through his office door. Not that Rianna could hear him—she wasn't in touch with the grave.

Rianna and I stared at each other, neither blinking. Desmond looked between us and then walked across the room to sit beside my legs, clearly falling on the side against Rianna doing anything stupid. Holly and Caleb sat in silence, waiting for us to work it out ourselves.

"At least you'd have an ally in there," Rianna said without looking away.

"It's too risky."

"You take risks for your friends. Let someone else take a risk for you."

My eyes burned from not blinking. Finally I looked away. "Fine. But if it doesn't work the way you think, you'll stay outside the circle, right?"

She gave me a curt nod and Desmond growled his dissatisfaction.

"What about me?" Holly asked. "What can I do?"

"For now, will you give me a ride to the house to retrieve the ring. But when we go after this thing, will you maintain a circle?" Because if I went down or it infected Rianna, we needed a strong witch to hold the circle.

"And me?" Roy asked, sticking his head through his office door again.

The trap box was the best idea we'd hit on, but using it required me being alive. Which meant I had to survive regaining my mortality first. If I didn't, a plan B, one that was actually planned for once, was a good idea.

"Those insatiable ghosts, would they be able to feed on the rider?"

Roy frowned. "It would consume any one of us."

"But if there were several?"

"I'll see what I can do, but no one is going to agree to be encircled with a collector."

I guess I couldn't blame them. "Could you get them to stand by in the land of the dead? In case the rider attempts to escape that way?" Though I had the feeling if it crossed completely into the land of the dead, it wouldn't be able to make it back on its own. Still, better safe than sorry.

It said something about my friends that when I turned around no one was looking at me like I was crazy for speaking to thin air. Rianna had tapped into the grave to listen, but Holly and Caleb didn't even bat an eye.

I had good friends.

"Okay, so everyone clear on what to do next?" Everyone, even the ghost, nodded.

"I'm not," a new voice said as the front door of the office opened. "I see you're alive, Craft. I heard a rumor you got your heart ripped out."

We all turned to stare at Briar.

"Same rumor says it was torn out by that handsome guardian angel of yours and that you then stood up, picked up your heart, and fled the scene."

Okay, now everyone was staring at *me*.

"You shouldn't believe everything you hear," I said, but my recently repaired heart felt like it might explode if it pounded any faster.

To my relief, Briar shrugged. "So you're hunting the rider. Fill me in."

"He's in there," I said, pointing to the community theater building.

"And how did you suddenly gain the ability to track the rider?" Briar asked, as she checked the bolt in her crossbow.

"Not the rider, the man he's riding," I said through gritted teeth. I was exhausted. I'd spent most of the day away from my life essence while the rider sucked on it, which definitely didn't help. At the same time I'd had to work with Rianna, first learning the order in which the runes needed to be activated and then puzzling out the artifact—which had turned into a spear as soon as she touched it.

The plan was moving forward, the trap half set. I had the spirit box, which was small enough to carry one-handed but Caleb assured me could hold whatever size spirit or any amount of energy I needed to shove in it. Holly and Rianna had a double ring of circles ready to be erected behind the theater. Now I just needed Briar to stop asking questions and do her part.

"Well, I guess when you hear the screaming, you'll know it's done," she said, stepping around the corner and striding toward the small theater.

"Just drop him. Don't hurt him," I called after her, but if she heard, she made no indication.

She was right about one thing. People screamed.

Caleb and I exchanged a glance, and then we both ran for the theater. We were headed against the flow as we pushed our way into the building that people were trying to escape as fast as possible.

Briar stood in the center of the theater, her badge over head, yelling her credentials and commanding everyone to remain calm. Clearly that failed, but her aim had been dead-on. Death sat slumped in a seat in the front row.

"You get his feet," Caleb told me, and I nodded.

Caleb took Death by the shoulders and in that way we carried him toward the emergency exit. Briar opened the door for us, the alarm going off as she did, but the patrons had already evacuated, so it couldn't make anything worse.

We carried Death's unconscious body past the edge of the first inactive circle and into the center of the second. Then Caleb retreated, and Rianna walked into the circle, the enormous relic-turned-spear in her hand. When she channeled the grave through the spear, she could physically touch Roy. I only hoped it would be enough to protect her from the rider.

"Everyone ready?" I asked and got a chorus of nods. *But am I ready?* I had to be. "Remember, don't drop the circles until the rider is trapped or destroyed, no matter what happens."

This time the nods were more hesitant.

"Be careful, Al," Caleb said.

"I will. Just keep the circles up." I took a deep breath and then nodded to Rianna and Holly. "I'm ready. Let's do it."

Rianna's circle was the inner one, and it sprang to life first, followed closely by Holly's. I didn't bother erecting a third circle—my Aetheric magic was the weakest in the group. The two different colors of their magic barriers obscured the world beyond the circles but I smiled at Holly, Caleb, and Briar's silhouettes. Then there was no more prep work.

"Moment of truth," I muttered. I pulled my dagger from my boot. Then I knelt beside Death's prone form and opened the spirit box before setting it beside my knees. Using the dagger, I opened a deep cut in my finger—I didn't want it closing before I finished tracing the runes.

"Al?" Rianna sounded uncertain.

I hadn't told her I planned to use blood magic.

"Just be ready, and don't let go of the grave."

She nodded, her knuckles turning white around the shaft of her spear.

I looked down at the man who held half my life, who'd become mortal to save me.

"No matter what happens, I want you to live," I whispered to him despite the fact I knew he couldn't hear. Then I placed my hand on his cheek, opened myself and gave his essence a push. It didn't want to be in me anyway, it belonged with its soul. As Death's cold immortality fled my body, my own living essence flooded back into my body.

Death's eyes flew open, Briar's spells no longer affecting him. He separated from the rider as well. For a moment they occupied the same space, but no longer the same body or even the same plane.

I gave myself one single heartbeat to smile at him. "Live," I said, and then grabbed the box at my side.

The rider rose like a black tide, but I didn't stand—that would just be farther to fall. I touched the first glyph on the box, saying the name Rianna had taught me and letting my blood fill the thin groove as I traced the intricate shape. Magic rushed through me and the rune glowed blue.

The rider descended on me, ripping at the wounds in my soul, trying to draw my living energy out of me. I couldn't fight back. Couldn't defend myself. I just had to endure as I activated the glyph.

The rider reared back, the head of Rianna's spear emerging through its dark form. It bought me time as she pulled the spear back and drove it into the rider again. The creature descended on her, and Rianna screamed.

I looked up, still in the middle of the third glyph. Then the first seizure hit. The box fell from my hands.

Fuck.

I did the only thing left to me. As my body began to convulse, I threw open my shields and lunged at where the rider ripped at Rianna's soul. Sinking my hands into the creature, I fell into the land of the dead, taking the rider with me.

Chapter 41

The buildings crumbled. Turned to dust. Then even the dust vanished.

I stopped falling. The *waste*.

The rider bellowed in rage. I thought its earlier attacks had been vicious, now they turned into an onslaught. I was too weak to fight back.

Then a shimmery form flickered somewhere in my peripheral and a ghost dove through the rider, taking a piece of the creature with it.

The rider howled. He grabbed for the offending ghost. Two more dive-bombed him. Then another ghost appeared. The rider lashed out at random, but the ghosts were quick, flitting away while another hit the rider from a different direction.

"Up you go," Roy said, as arms lifted me by the armpits. "You got the ghosts."

"Hey, it was my job, right boss?" He smiled and shoved his thick glasses farther up his nose. "You don't look so good."

I looked down at myself. Neither the soul nor the psyche can bleed, but it could show tears. He was right. I looked bad.

"Well, you going to join the buffet?" he asked. Then he darted forward, taking his own chunk of the rider.

It had shrunk in size, its darkness thinning. I couldn't quite see through it, but at the rate the ghosts were stealing away chunks of it, I'd be able to soon. I hated the idea of that thing's sludgelike energy in me, but I reached out anyway, drawing hard. A thick funnel of energy shot from it to me and the rider screamed. He shrank. I, on the other hand, felt more steady on my feet, if a little greasy from the energy's source. Reaching out, I drew more energy.

"Alex."

I paused. I knew that voice. I couldn't remember why. But I knew it.

"Alex, are you out there?"

It was a female voice. Somewhere far away a woman with red curls and blazing green eyes stood, straddling an enormous chasm.

Rianna.

I looked around. I was in the waste. No grave witch was supposed to reach the waste, and I couldn't feel the land of the living.

"Alex, if you can hear me, you need to get back to your body. Now. Your collector caught a part of your soul and is holding it in your body, but you need to come back."

My body. Where was it?

"Roy? How do I get out of here?"

The ghost looked over at me, stopping midattack. "You go up."

Up?

I looked around. There, right behind me, was a thin silver thread that shimmered like a soul. My soul.

It led up, and up.

Arms grabbed mine. "Come on, Alex," Roy said, pulling me. "Time for you to get out of here."

He pulled again and the wastes changed. He wasn't the only ghost with me either. A dozen hands grabbed at me, pushing and pulling me toward the surface. The farther I traveled the more the world around me rematerialized. Dust turned to crumbled ruins, and then to dilapidated buildings. But the farther I got, the thinner the thread became.

I'm running out of time.

The ghosts pulled harder and the landscape smeared past me as I sped along, following the thinning thread. Then I hit the chasm. A chasm I was on the wrong side of.

"This is the end of the line for us," James Kingly's ghost said.

I looked out across the impossibly large chasm. How was I supposed to cross that abyss? In my hand, the thread tethering my soul to my body thinned.

I was a grave witch. I'd bridged this gap hundreds of times. I could do it. Normally I opened myself to the grave. But I was already immersed in the grave and the land of the dead. Instead I opened myself to life.

Warmth rushed into me, color flooding the world.

"No you don't," the rider screamed in my mind. Something with claws grabbed hold of me as I crossed.

I gasped, lungs burning as if I hadn't taken a breath in a long time. I opened my eyes, my real eyes, to Death's concerned face, his hand planted firmly in my chest.

"I thought I'd lost you," he whispered.

"It's not over." My voice broke in my too dry throat. I swallowed and looked around. Something was missing.

Crap. "Get the circles up." The yell was more of a croak than words, but circles in purple and red popped up around me.

Just in time.

I arched my back as the rider moved *through* me. It had ridden me across, but it couldn't take my body. It hurt, not in a physical way—it was too drained for that, but it ripped at my psyche to get through.

I tried to scramble to my feet, failed, and Death pulled me up. Held me there when I would have fallen.

"The box? Where is the box?" My gaze shot around the circle and I spotted it several yards away. I scrambled for it

and nearly collapsed. Again it was Death who kept me upright. He reached for it and horror appeared on his face as
his fingers slid through it.

I collapsed beside it because standing was too hard. The
first two glyphs still glowed faintly blue. My throat didn't
want to cooperate, but I got out the name of the third and
pressed my still bloody finger against the box, tracing the
faint glyph. Magic ripped through my raw psyche.

The rider stalked along the opposite edge of the circle,
looking for a weakness or a hole it could exploit. I aimed
the opening of the box at it and named the final glyph, tracing its form.

I felt more than saw my skin heat and glow as Faerie's
magic filled me. A whirlwind caught the rider, dragging it
toward the box. It struggled, its dark form twisting and
fighting the pull.

It lost.

The whirlwind sucked it into the box and the lid snapped
shut. I flipped the lock. Relief washed over me, mixed hard
with exhaustion and I leaned against Death. "It's over
now."

The circles dropped, my friends running forward.

Caleb hauled me to my feet, clearly unaware I was already in good hands. Holly threw her arms around me.

"I thought you were dead," she whispered, hugging me
tight.

I handed off the box to Rianna. "Somewhere in that
castle is a secure place to store this, right?"

She smiled, her eyes full of relief. She tucked the spear
in the crook of her arm so she could hold the box with both
hands. "I'm sure we can find somewhere."

Death stepped back as my friends crowded around me.
I twisted, reaching for him.

"Don't go. I need you."

He stared at me for a long moment, and I was sure at any
second he'd vanish and I wouldn't see him again. Then he
stepped forward, swept me into his arms, and kissed me.

"Uh, is it just me," Briar said somewhere behind me. "Or is she floating and glowing? Humans don't glow."

She'll definitely put this in her report. I didn't know if it would negate my OMIH license, and in that moment, I didn't care. We were all alive, the rider was trapped, Tamara would be safe, and Death didn't forfeit his soul.

We won.

Chapter 42

"**C**an he hold him?" Nina Kingly asked, looking from me to her husband's ghost. She looked exhausted but she glowed with her new motherhood. She'd also taken meeting her husband's ghost a lot better than I thought she would. A whole lot better.

She handed the baby to her husband and I kept a firm grip on the ghost, making sure he remained corporeal enough to hold his son. Iridescent tears streamed down his cheeks.

"He's perfect," he said, staring in the same wonder any new father would have. Then he handed the baby back to his wife. "I guess it's time then?" he asked, looking toward Death, who stood in the doorway of the hospital room.

The soul collector gave him a small nod.

"I love you, Nina." Kingly leaned down and kissed his wife's forehead and then turned to me. "I wish I knew how to thank you, Alex."

Considering he'd been one of the ghosts who'd led the assault on the rider and got me out of the land of the dead, I figured we were even.

With one last look at his wife and son, Kingly turned and walked to Death. The collector reached out, taking the ghost by the shoulder and the shimmery iridescence of the ghost turned to the bright yellow of a soul again before Death flicked his hand and Kingly disappeared.

"Thank you, Ms. Craft," Nina Kingly said and the balance shifted.

I left soon after.

Death waited for me in the hall. "The mender told me what you did. He's a dangerous being to owe that kind of debt."

"It was the best option." I shrugged. "So considering it's been nearly a week, I guess you're going to start vanishing on me again?"

His wince was slight, but I saw it. "There will be certain . . . restrictions. I may be away for some time."

He didn't give me a chance to ask how long or what restrictions, but leaned down and kissed me. Not a teasing kiss either. He stole my breath with a kiss full of promise.

Then he vanished.

I leaned my head against the wall and laughed, though it wasn't a happy sound. When a nurse stopped in the hall to make sure I was all right, I decided it was time to head home.

Maybe I should have waited longer.

"What the hell?" I asked as I opened the door and found not only PC to greet me, but several boxes, a suitcase, and a certain blond fae.

Falin looked up from where he was unloading groceries into my fridge. He reached into his suit jacket, and walking across the room, wordlessly handed me a folded document.

The single page of text was signed with the Winter Queen's official seal. I reread it three times.

"You can't be serious. She's making you move in with me?"